# THE RECKONING

## OF

# GODS

BOOK TWO OF THE ASTRELLIAN HEIRS

## MORGAN KIELISCH

SECOND CHILD PRESS

# The Continent of Astrellia

To those who are chronically underestimated.
I hope you find your strength and show it off to the world.

# The Awakening of Gods Recap

Elana Sable, the youngest princess of Adrithia, has spent her entire life in her sister Aislinn's shadow. It's a position she doesn't mind, since she has trained to be a healer for years. Aislinn, one of the strongest warriors Adrithia has ever seen, is set to be officially crowned as the next heir at the Crowning Ceremony, when the Gods choose Elana as heir instead.

It's a move that has consequences across the kingdoms. Elana has to quickly learn politics, combat, and basic survival skills, because she's about to travel to the Gods' Territory, where she will compete in trials alongside the heirs from the other four kingdoms to earn an elemental power from one of the five Gods.

Elana's best friend and guard, Aric, tries to convince her to run away with him, insisting that the dangers of the trials are too much for her. She rebukes him and stays true to her duty.

While in the Gods' Territory, she encounters the heir of Ocarin, Aidan, two strange felines, and mysterious servants of the Gods, known as The Maiden and The Messenger. They're siblings, and two of the last shifters on the continent of Astrellia. The heirs meet Elana for the first time, and they begin their ascent up the Gods' Peaks.

Calder, the heir from Hotharia, takes an immediate disliking to Elana, and tries to convince her to leave the mountain. When she refuses, he tries to kill her, but is stopped by the two mysterious cats. Rayna, heir of Melinor, says she will look out for Elana, having received a letter from Aislinn, begging her to help Elana.

A dragon attacks the group, marking the first trial. Aidan saves Elana from the flames and is able to defeat it when the goddess of fire, Enya, appears to him and grants him her power.

While climbing the second peak, the group finds they can't pass a raging river, so they try to find another path through a cave. They take advantage of a pool inside the cavern and go for a swim. The second trial turns the water into a whirlpool. Elana pushes Rian, Aaranor's heir, to safety, causing her to get sucked under the water and nearly drown. Calder meets Kai, the water god, and stops the whirlpool. Rian insists he owes Elana a life debt.

The third trial comes in the form of a mudslide. Rayna's perseverance in the face of the disaster earns her the ability to move earth after meeting the goddess Avani.

Having mostly run out of provisions, the heirs are eager to find any source of sustenance in the wilderness. Unfortunately, the fruit that Calder finds is highly poisonous, and he ignores Elana when she tries to warn him. He eats the fruit, and nearly dies, but Elana is able to save him with an antidote. While this is happening, large vultures appear and snatch up their supplies. While Calder lies unconscious, Aidan and Rian chase after the birds. They return with news that Rian met the air god Sepher and earned the air element.

Elana starts to doubt herself, since there's only one element left, and she feels no affinity for metal.

They continue to climb for days, until they reach the final peak. There, Calder tries to kill Elana once more because he believes ending her life is the final challenge, but Aidan steps in, stopping him. Their attention is drawn away when shadow creatures appear and attack. No matter how hard the heirs fight, they don't gain any ground with the creatures, until Elana figures out the true challenge is not defeating them with force, but by refusing to fight at all. She tries to convince the others, but the only one who believes her is Aidan. He and Calder break into an argument once more and Elana jumps between them.

Two goddesses appear before her, Nura and Nisha, the forgotten twin goddesses of light and darkness. They grant Elana their powers, and she uses them to stop Aidan and Calder's fight.

The trials are completed. The shifters arrive to bring the heirs back down, where they part ways.

On their journey back to their kingdoms, Elana has trouble controlling her shadows, and Aidan helps her. They meet Aislinn and Queen Amira of Ocarin on the road back, and say their goodbyes.

Once home, Elana shows her powers to the people of Adrithia, and her mother plans a celebration ball. At the masquerade ball, Elana is approached by a masked man, who reveals himself to be Aidan. He tells her and Aislinn that Adrithia is in danger, and that he's been at war for several weeks with an unknown enemy. He produces a black dagger, which is imbued with an incurable poison. Elana feels drawn to the blade, and when she touches it, the metal purifies.

Aidan and Elana share a dance before telling her parents of the danger. Aidan reveals that his mother is a seer, and receives visions of the future. In these visions, she saw the enemies attacking Adrithia's coast.

The Adrithians march to war. Aric once again tries to stop Elana from going, insisting she will be in danger. Elana shuts him down.

Their army arrives at the coast in time to see ships approaching the shore. Several of them are flying Hotharian banners, meaning the Astrellian Peace has been broken.

Elana discovers her light powers can heal injuries, so she becomes invaluable in the healer's tents while the battle rages along the coast. Hours into the fight, and the planned reinforcements from a nearby city never arrive. Elana starts to worry for her father, sister, and Aidan. She receives a message from Queen Amira, encouraging her to use her power to end the battle.

She rushes into the fray, making her way to the center of the battle, where she finds Aislinn and Aidan. They protect her while she uses her light to nullify the poisoned weapons of the enemy. They retreat to the coast, and the Adrithians believe they've won. Until they spot more ships approaching the beach.

Elana's father makes the ultimate sacrifice, splitting the coast with Avani's power, but falling to his death in the process.

After the battle, Elana and Aislinn determine that their reinforcements never arrived because they were betrayed by Aric.

# CHAPTER ONE

## ELANA

My leather boots clack against the ground as I stride through the dimly-lit, dank halls of the dungeon to the one person I never thought would betray me. I casually sidestep a puddle of gods-knows-what on the pockmarked stone floor. My sister is an angry shadow at my side, but the only sound between us is our footsteps echoing off the walls. She has barely left me alone since...well for almost two weeks now.

Two guards in navy uniforms with broadswords at their hips stand at a cell halfway down the row. Torches illuminate the walls, casting dancing shadows across their faces. They bow low to us when we come into view.

"We need a few moments with the prisoner," I demand.

They clasp their fists over their hearts and one of them answers, "yes, Your Majesty."

He produces a large silver key and places it into the lock, turning until the mechanism clicks. The door swings open and the guards step back, giving Aislinn and I a semblance of privacy with my former guard.

The dim light inside the cell does little to disguise Aric's disheveled appearance as he shakily stands from the cot against the far wall. His blonde hair is matted and dirty, there's days' worth of stubble on his face, and dark bags under his wide eyes. He scans me from my boots up, his gaze lingers on my twin daggers for a moment, which I wear strapped to the side of my leather training pants.

"Your Highness," Aric's gaze at last meets mine, and he drops to his knees, bowing low.

"Actually, it's 'Your Majesty' now," I say, my voice dripping with venom. "Since you killed my father."

Aric flinches and I want to scoff. The nerve he has to show remorse after everything he's done. I never thought I would hate him. Besides my sister, he's the closest thing I've ever had to a real friend. But after it was discovered that he failed to deliver a vital message that could have saved my father's life, I haven't been able to think about his treachery without my blood boiling. Even now, my shadows leak out of me as my control slips in my anger. I clench my jaw and reel them back into me slowly, tightening the lid on that well of power that churns within me.

"Elana, please. I'm so, so sorry. Please let me explain," he pleads, tears pooling in his deep blue eyes.

"Why should we listen to you?" Ash snarls from next to me. "Our family gave you everything; an honorable position, a generous salary, and a family when you claimed you hated yours."

I glance at my sister. Her knuckles are white around the hilt of her heirloom sword, the one our ancestor, Hale Sable, gave his life to forge.

"I love my family, though I haven't seen or heard from them in years. I doubt any of them would still recognize me," Aric's whisper is barely audible as he drops his head to stare at the ground. "I have three brothers and a sister. My parents passed away when we were young. There was no one to protect us from my uncle, King Skade. He's holding my sister, Ingrid, hostage to make sure my brothers and I stay compliant. My real name is Aric Vernier."

Is he finally telling the truth? I catch Ash's gaze and she gives a nearly imperceptible nod. Once we discovered Aric was spying for Hotharia, I tasked her with uncovering as much about him as she could, by whatever means necessary. Somehow, she managed to track down Aric's false family in Adrithia and got them to talk. I don't need an imagination to know how she accomplished the feat.

Months ago this thought would have abhorred me, but now I'm not sure there are lines I won't cross to protect this kingdom.

"Tell us," I demand quietly, putting as much authority into my tone as I can.

Aric's shoulders droop, his gaze on the floor. "After my parents passed, my uncle brought my siblings and I to the palace and told us he would provide a better life, that we were family and should be treated as such. For a few years we attended lessons with our cousins Calder and Leif, and trained for combat. One day my brothers and I were brought before my uncle in the throne room. Ingrid was on the floor, crying, in chains. She was covered in blood and bruises. My uncle whipped her into unconsciousness in front of us while the royal guards held my brothers and me back."

My stomach twists.

"He told us we were being sent to spy on the rival kingdoms. If we failed our tasks in any way, Ingrid would be punished again. We were guaranteed her safety if we cooperated."

I bite my lip at the kingdoms being called rivals. The Astrellian Peace ensured that the kingdoms remained aligned for centuries. When did Hotharia start to think of us, or any of the other three kingdoms, as adversaries?

"Of course my brothers and I agreed. My uncle ensured us Ingrid would be treated fairly as his ward as long as we followed his orders. A few weeks later I left with two other trained spies posing as my parents. We traveled to Sandral under the guise of seeking a better life as a family, and the rest you know."

I do know. I remember the first time I saw him in the sparring ring, shortly after he'd been spotted by our weapons master and chosen to train amongst the other household guards. Even as a young man he was an accomplished fighter.

"What kinds of information did you pass to your true king, Aric?" Aislinn asks.

Aric stays silent, head bowed, refusing to look at either of us. I seethe. After nearly a decade of friendship he's still loyal to Hotharia. Was our friendship even real?

Aric's head snaps up. Determination darkens his features. I realize I must've spoken the question out loud, because his answer comes immediately. "Yes. Yes, of course Elana. You have to know that. I wasn't supposed to enjoy my time here, to get this close to you, but I did. I've loved you for years, and I wanted to keep you safe. It was always my plan to take you with me when I went back to Hotharia."

A wave of hot rage rushes to my cheeks. I feel my face burning with it, and the flickering shadows across the cell spring to life, coiling around my feet, running between my fingers.

"You can't expect me to believe that. Our father is dead because of the letter you refused to send to our army. How do you expect me to believe you love me after you did nothing but betray us?"

A whip of darkness shoots out from my hand and wraps itself around Aric's neck. It holds him steady, but does not squeeze. His eyes bulge and flash with fear as he looks at me. A part of me relishes this. Knowing I possess the ability to cause him the same pain he caused me. It would be so easy to take his life right here.

A cool hand on my arm, and then my sister is there, standing between me and Aric.

"El, not like this. Trust me." Her blue eyes bore into mine. The disappointment written on her face is a slap to mine. I reel back, inhaling a shaky breath. Gods, she's right. What was I about to do? I'm furious beyond words at Aric, but if I'd actually hurt him I don't know if I could forgive myself. I give Aislinn a grateful nod. With another breath, I snap my fingers into a fist, recalling the darkness with gritted teeth. My nails bite into my palms as I shake with frustration, but I slowly release Aric and return the shadows to the far corners of the cell.

"Do you have any useful information for us, Aric? Anything you can give us that will lessen your sentence?" Aislinn turns back to him, taking over the interrogation while I compose myself.

Aric drops his head again, shaking it slowly. "There's nothing I can say that won't endanger Ingrid. I've already told you more than I should."

"Can you at least tell us who is allied with Hotharia? Who attacked our borders and what sort of powers they possess?"

Aric lifts his gaze, his brows pulled together. "What do you mean, 'what powers they possess'?"

Ash presses, "the cursed weapons we told you about before we went to battle. Do you know anything about them?"

"No. Most of the contact I've had with Hotharia involved me sending information, not receiving any. I wasn't even aware that anyone allied with Hotharia," he stops, as if carefully debating his next words. "I was told to stall the forces and impede the arrival of any reinforcements. My uncle said that if I did this, my sister would finally be free. I swear, Your Majesty, I had no idea what their plan was."

"What did you think would happen, after hearing Prince Aidan speak about the attacks in Ocarin?" Aislinn snaps, hand white-knuckling her sword hilt again.

"I-I don't know. I thought it would just be a raid. Our warriors are well-trained and should have easily beaten them back," he stammers, his shoulders heaving as he runs a hand through his messy blonde hair.

"Not 'our' warriors," I say, my voice quiet but filled with the churning rage I've been trying so hard to keep tamped down. "Adrithia's warriors. Warriors you betrayed on the battlefield. If Tierth's reinforcements had come, our father, our King, would still be alive. You left us there to die!"

Aric recoils again, the final shrieked word hitting him like a blow. For the thousandth time this week, I feel like I'm about to break down in violent sobs.

"Elana, I'm so sorry. You have no idea how much I wish I could take it back."

Rather than respond or act with my shadows, I exchange a look with Aislinn, wanting out of here, now. Recognition flares in her eyes, and she sighs dramatically, rocking back on her heels.

"If you think of anything else that could be helpful for us, *or for yourself*, tell one of your guards. Otherwise, Aric, enjoy your cell," Ash says, storming towards the door. There's nothing more we can get from him, and we both know it.

I spin on my heels and move to follow her out, but a hand grips my wrist and stops me.

"Aric, release me," I say with barely restrained fury.

"Please, Elana. I don't care what happens to me, but please promise me you'll look after my sister. She doesn't deserve torture by my uncle's hand. Please get her out of Hotharia and look after her," he begs, still on his knees, with tears pooling in his eyes.

My father's face flashes in my mind. The last hug he gave me, right before he rode off to the battlefield, and his death. This time I let the shadows free, just enough to wrap around his wrist and squeeze hard, grinding together the delicate bones.

His breath wheezes out of him as a cry of pain escapes his lips. His fingers loosen and he finally releases me, holding his arm to his chest with a look of betrayal on his face. Oh, the irony. "Elana, please."

"No," I say to him as he sidles away from me, fear and pain further distorting his features. "You destroyed my family. Yours doesn't deserve to be saved."

I turn my back on him and stalk out of the cell.

Outside, Aislinn faces the guards. "There will be no special treatment for him. If he decides to loosen his tongue, send word to us immediately."

The two guards place their fists over their chests and bow low. "Yes, Your Highness," the two say in tandem.

Ash and I walk away as they lock the cell door. We start to climb the stairs when she asks, "do you want to talk about it?"

I sigh, releasing a long breath. It feels like the first time I've been able to breathe freely since we stepped into that cell. "No."

She doesn't say anything while we climb, but I can tell she wants to. She keeps opening her mouth, sucking in air as if readying for a speech, before closing it again.

"Do *you* want to talk about it?" I finally ask, a little belatedly. It's only fair. After all, he was her friend, too.

"I do, actually," Ash says, flipping her long, golden hair back behind her shoulder. I don't respond, waiting for whatever she's got brewing in her mind. "It's been almost two weeks since the battle on the coast, and you still refuse to talk about it."

*This again*? Gods spare me.

Since we've returned from our so-called victory, that's all anyone has been trying to talk to me about. 'Whose forces attacked us? What does the enemy want? Are we going to be at war?'

The same questions keep me from sleep at night. The questions I do not have answers to, even after replaying every second of the battle in my mind, turning over detail after detail in hopes I'll realize what we missed. Whenever these questions come up, I give a practiced nod and tell practiced lies, saying they don't need to worry, the threat is defeated and we are safe.

The truth is terrifying. We don't know who attacked us or why. We don't know if another war is upon us. And as difficult as it is to lie to people asking these questions, they're not the ones I dread the most. No, those inquiries come in the form of concerned looks, heavy sighs, and backward glances when they think I don't notice. It's the questions like, 'How are you holding up? Are you getting enough to eat? Are you getting enough sleep?' which bother me most. And it's what I fear Aislinn is about to bring up for the hundredth time.

"Elana, I know you don't want to talk about what happened to Father, but you need to understand it's not your fault," Aislinn says, her voice barely a whisper.

"I'm not talking about this," I brush past her, ascending the winding staircase as quickly as my short legs allow. Ash, being nearly a head taller, catches up without any trouble.

"Why not? El, I hear you awake at night, I know you can't stomach food. If you don't talk about it, this shit is going to fester. Being a healer, you should know you need to deal with it before infection sets in."

She doesn't realize she's twisting the knife by mentioning healing. I don't blame her, as I've told no one about my *other* power. I'm silent for the rest of the climb, my only reply is the hollow clack of our footsteps. Right before we reach the corridor that leads to the library, where Sir Rigel

Brand, Father's, I mean my courtier, is no doubt waiting to ambush me with pressing matters, Ash grabs my hand, twining her fingers through mine.

"Whatever it is you're feeling, we can get through it together. It's selfish of me, but I miss my sister. And I need her to get through this, too." Her palms are warm in mine as she stares at our hands.

I use the moment to take her in. Dark circles frame her lower lid, and her hair lacks its natural shine. Her skin, usually tan and flush with life, appears sallow. My heart beats a heavy rhythm in my chest. She's been suffering, too, and I've been too wrapped up in my own grief to recognize hers. Gods, I'm a terrible sister.

I cover her hand with my own, squeezing it between mine. "I'm sorry, Ash. I'm not ready, yet, to talk about...what happened. But I want to be there for you. I'll try harder, I promise."

She lets out a long exhale. "You know I'm here for you, too, right? Always."

"I know," I say, dropping one of my hands but keeping hold of hers with the other.

We walk together to the informal sitting room where, sure enough, Rigel stands waiting. We should call him "Sir" Rigel, but years ago he insisted that we drop the honorific, claiming it made him sound too pretentious. He bows low to me and Ash, clearing his throat before launching into a tirade.

"Your Majesty, some of the noble families have requested, rather adamantly, that we hold court. I'm afraid the traditional royal mourning period has been extended about as far as possible. They're growing restless; the Lyons family in particular is working the other nobles into a tizzy. I've received several grievances already this morning."

I groan, pulling my hand from Ash's to rub my already aching temple. Having restless nobles never leads to anything good. It's true that I've pushed back holding my first court, as it's typically customary for court to be held a few days after the reigning monarch's death, but no monarchs have been killed in such a brutal way since the founding of our kingdom. I figured that would elicit some sympathy, and I could avoid the event for a few weeks.

The fact that it's the Lyons family stirring up ill-will does not escape my notice. I rejected the marriage proposal of their eldest son, Percival, several weeks ago. I wonder if they're still bitter over it.

"Fine, we'll hold a formal court tomorrow. Please ensure preparations are made," I say, already regretting my decision. Best to get it over with quickly. Many of the noble families are residing at their estates in the capital city of Sandral, due to the masquerade ball that we hosted weeks ago, the upcoming resting ceremony, and my looming coronation.

Rigel bows again, turning to leave, when a thought occurs to me.

"Oh, one more thing, Rigel," I start and he turns back around, brown eyebrows raised over his spectacles, "inform the attendees that there will be no discussion on my or my sister's betrothal. We have no interest in pursuing courtships at this time, so they can leave their unwed children, siblings, cousins, and kin at home."

He nods his head. "Of course, Your Majesty, I will see to it."

I give him a slight smile in thanks, and then he's gone, rushing through the halls to no doubt enlist the assistance of all able bodied staff in the castle.

Ash bumps into me, wearing a bemused smile. "You know that's not going to stop the noble peacocks from shoving their eligible relatives at us, right?"

I flash her a brief grin. "I'm aware, but it might spare us from a few matchmaking mothers. Not everyone is bold enough to go against a monarch's word."

"One can only hope that no one feels that bold tomorrow," she mutters.

I move to sit on the cushioned sofa, but Aislinn clicks her tongue, waggling her finger at me. "No, no, no, get up. It's time to train. I've let you relax for far too long."

I let out a dramatic sigh and consider running towards my rooms. But, that would be about as useful as a sitting room without furniture. She's been trying to get me back into the training field ever since we returned from the coast. When I again refused, 'It's your responsibility to become untouchable, to make the other kingdoms respect and fear you,' was her argument. And honestly, I agree with her, I really do, but the thought of holding a weapon again, wielding one against another person, makes me sick to my stomach. It's bad enough I see that bloodied killing field every time I close my eyes at night. I don't want my nightmares chasing me in my waking hours.

"I can't, Ash. I have to prepare for court tomorrow," I say, holding up my hands. It's true, I do need time to figure out how to lead the discussion. I also need a refresher on the noble families and their relationships to the crown.

My sister gives me an assessing stare, and I look anywhere but her eyes. At last her posture relaxes, and I know I've won. "All right, no training today. But after court tomorrow, I'll expect you in the field."

I nod my head, though I swear we both know I'll have another excuse tomorrow.

"Come on then, let's go study in your chambers. I'll grab some recent correspondence from Fath- I mean, *the* study and meet you there," Ash says, quickly recovering and heading off in that direction.

I'm grateful she's going to retrieve them without me. I don't think I could bear to be surrounded by so many of my father's possessions.

The walk to my chambers is quick, although when I see who's waiting for me there, I wish I'd gone with Ash to the study and braved the ghost of my father instead.

I have successfully avoided Prince Aidan for the last week, until now, it seems. He leans against the wall beside my rooms. I nearly stop short when his molten gold eyes, framed by ridiculously long lashes, meet mine.

"Magpie, I hope I've finally caught you at a good time," his low voice rumbles.

I consider breezing past him, maybe casting a wall of shadow to give myself time to escape, but no. If I am to be queen, I will have to learn how to handle difficult conversations. I straighten my shoulders and meet his gaze with my own narrowed eyes.

"Aidan, if I wished to speak to you, I would have already," my reply is cold, cruel, almost. I need to make this as quick and painless as possible. I'm done dancing around him. I've been wearing a mask of apathy since the battle, since Father...and now all I want to do is rip it off and start screaming at everyone.

A flicker of hurt and confusion darkens his features for a brief moment. "Perhaps you could tell me what I did to incur this ire of yours?" Aidan asks, leaning closer, crossing his muscled biceps over his chest. His expression is carefully neutral, and a pang of guilt spears through me. But I can't shake the accusations that ring in my mind. It was actually my mother who put the idea in my head. When we came home, victorious but defeated, from the battle, she was distraught. She blamed everyone for her husband's death, and in her rage she made several valid points about Aidan that I wasn't ready to confront.

I take a breath and blurt out before I lose my nerve, "did your mother know that my father would die? Did you know?"

Aidan's prolonged silence is all but confirmation. "Magpie, I-,"

"Don't use that name. Not now," I snap.

He sucks in air and lets out a long sigh. "My mother's visions don't always come to pass."

"That's not an answer," I say, and he lets out a frustrated noise, running a hand through his wavy dark brown hair. When he doesn't say anything, I take a different tactic. "Why did you really come here? Was it because it was the right thing to do, or to make sure my father died?"

He turns to me sharply. "I came here for you, Elana! I could have sent a simple letter warning you, or left for home after delivering my news, but I stayed for you. I fought on the front lines against those monsters again for you."

"And you watched my father die, for me? You wouldn't let me help him. You held me back when I could have saved him."

"There was nothing you could have done. Your power was spent. You would have risked your own life for nothing."

"You don't know that!"

"I know I didn't want to leave it to chance. Your father made the decision to stay and fight and hold back the enemy. He knew what he was doing."

"I could have saved him." I repeat.

"No, Elana, you couldn't have. And Aislinn and I would have watched you die, too."

I draw in a shuddering breath, my hands shake at my sides as the shadows beg me to release them, to make him pay for his words, for letting my father die. "I want you out of this castle, Prince Aidan. Be gone by tomorrow morning, or else I'll have what remains of my army remove you."

He reaches a hand towards me, but pauses midway, seemingly thinking better of it. "I know things are a mess right now, but you need allies. Let me stay and help you."

"You've done enough," I turn towards my door, resting my hand on the knob, but shoot him one final glare. "And tell your mother the next time I see her, she will face a reckoning for her choices."

His eyes darken as he gives me a curt nod, his jaw clenching. He turns and walks down the hallway, not sparing me a second glance. It feels like a piece of my heart is leaving with him. A looming quiet presses in behind me as I open my door and shut it behind me.

# CHAPTER TWO

## AISLINN

The Crown Prince of Ocarin stalks towards me, his hands glowing with the power of his flames. Not that I blame him, I overheard everything my sister said. And while I don't agree with her pushing him away, I do understand it.

"Aidan," I say to halt him, trying to think of the right words to say to him. I'm grateful for his help in protecting my sister both in the battle, and on the Gods Peaks. Plus, a strong alliance with Ocarin will be helpful in the uncertain times ahead of us. "Don't give up on her."

He leans back, crossing his arms in front of his chest. "Not to worry, Aislinn, I'm not the giving up type. However, she made it pretty clear she doesn't want me as a guest in the castle anymore. So, it's probably best I take my leave."

I silently curse the Sable stubbornness. "Stay in Sandral temporarily. There's a little over a fortnight until my father's resting ceremony. You'd barely make it back to Luxoria before having to turn around."

Aidan lets out a long breath. "I'll consider it." He gives me his signature smirk and a slightly sarcastic bow before turning towards his guest quarters.

In a final effort, I call after him, "these next few weeks are going to be hard. Elana's going to need friends."

He turns enough for me to see the profile of his face, and the ghost of a smile that brightens his features, if only for a second. He walks away as he says, "Elana doesn't need anyone, and once she figures that out, she'll be a force to be reckoned with."

I stare at his back, turning over his words. Could he be the only other person who sees, truly sees, my sister for who she is? Elana has always been the chronically underestimated member of the family. While it's true that I inherited the fighting prowess and passion for political maneuvering, she fostered compassion and an inner strength that could only come from being continuously told you're not important. Once she learns the nuances of ruling, I have no doubt she'll be one of the greatest monarchs Adrithia has ever seen.

The thought makes me smile as I knock on Elana's door three times in quick succession, then once more before opening it and slipping inside. It's been our secret knock since we were children.

I find Elana lying on the settee with one arm draped over her face, blocking out the midday light streaming in through her windows.

I close the door behind me, glancing at my chamber door across the hall. After Father's death, we returned home to discover half of Elana's belongings out of her rooms, and our parents' personal effects scattered in the hall outside the Royal Chambers, which take up practically the entire west wing of the castle. Rigel explained it's customary that the new monarch be placed in the Royal Chambers as quickly as possible. Elana, exhausted both mentally and physically from the week-long trip back to Sandral, somehow mustered enough energy to throw the most impressive fit I've ever seen. She demanded that her possessions be moved back immediately, and that our mother would maintain her residence in the Royal Chambers. It wasn't customary or proper, but none of that mattered to her. She slept in my bed that night while the situation was remedied, and we haven't broached the subject since. It became yet another thing we don't speak of.

Placing the small stack of correspondence from Father's study on her desk, I plop myself down on the settee next to her.

"Do you want to talk about Aidan?" I ask. "Because for the record, I think he's right."

She lets out a noise of disgust. "Ash, don't even start."

Of course, I do start. "At risk of you throwing me out of the castle too, there was nothing you could have done. Even if Father knew his fate, he would have met it anyway."

She doesn't look at me, but I can hear the anger, and something else, in her tone as she responds, "you don't know that. There was time. I could have *done* something."

"You would've gotten yourself killed, Elana," I press.

Elana lets out a huff as she sits up. "Didn't I just say I wasn't ready to talk about this?"

I hold up my hands and stand, giving her the space she seems to need; and picking up the handful of letters, fan myself with them. "Fine, then let's go through these messages then."

We spend the entire afternoon going through the letters and sending replies to those that require it. We prioritize nobles and landowners from remote parts of Adrithia, who won't be in attendance tomorrow. Many of their concerns stem from apprehension over whether taxes are still due, and what will happen to their farms and estates now that there is a new monarch. I push Elana to provide her solutions first, and then I give her suggestions and, occasionally, steer her in a better direction. Most of these citizens are looking for validation, and to know that their voices are being heard, so we make sure we respond to them all, no matter the size of land they own.

Senara, Elana's lady's maid, brings us refreshments while we work. Rigel pops in twice to inquire if we need his assistance, and to bring updated lists of those who will be attending tomorrow. We study their family histories, their relationships with the crown and other nobles, as well as recent requests of Father, both fulfilled and unfulfilled.

My head is swimming by the time we head to the informal dining hall. El and I have taken to eating in this space since we returned home as a way to avoid painful memories of our family happily sharing meals, but also as a way to escape our mother, who lingers like a dark cloud lately.

Queen Maris did not take the news of her husband's death well. She grieved openly for days and lashed out when given any opportunity. I don't blame her, but a part of me wishes she could pull herself together and help us. Elana and I have had to plan Father's entire Resting Ceremony on our own. Since his body was never recovered we've had to answer difficult questions like what we should bury instead, and where we should memorialize him. We chose a spot in the expansive bluffs surrounding Sandral's crystal clear lake. Several of our Sable ancestors were also laid to rest there, so it seemed like an appropriate spot. As for the *what* to bury, we commissioned a stonemason to carve his likeness onto a stone casket.

Across Astrellia, each of the five kingdoms and their rulers practice different funerary ceremonies based on which God or Goddess is their current patron. For monarchs blessed by the Earth Goddess, Avani, the ritual is burial in the ground. Those blessed by the Fire Goddess, Enya, have their bodies cremated. Rulers blessed with water by the God Kai have a burial at sea. The Air God Sepher demands a sky burial, and those blessed by Tolliver, the Metal God are cremated and then their ashes are forged into a metal monument of their choosing. Citizens of the kingdoms are welcome to practice whatever funerary right they wish.

Elana and I walk through the understated archway to the informal dining room, and both of us nearly stop short. Our mother is sitting, back ramrod straight, at the head of the table, facing us.

"Daughters," she says, the most composed she's sounded in the last week.

I dip my head and Elana mutters, "Mother."

We take our usual seats in the middle of the table across from each other. I spare a quick glance at Maris. She's dressed well, in a simple long dark gown with a black veil over her unbound blonde hair.

"Mother," Elana says tentatively, clearing her throat. "You look well."

"Thank you, Elana," she replies, picking up her soup spoon and delicately scooping a bite. "What is this I hear about you holding your first formal court tomorrow?"

El and I exchange glances. Rigel, or one of the other castle staff no doubt already requested her presence.

"Yes, Mother. It's time. Some of the nobles are growing restless and demanding," I say.

She turns to me, her eyes so similar to mine it's almost like looking into a mirror. A cold, lifeless mirror. "They're nobles, not the royal family. Let them stir. They do not get to dictate when a monarch decides to hold court." Her assessing stare turns to Elana. "Are you sure you're ready for them?"

El shifts in her chair, but keeps her back straight as she nods. "Yes, we've waited long enough. We need to prepare for whatever is coming next. The enemy may have been deterred from attacking our southeastern coastline, but they could try landing in the Cerulean Bay, or go back to Ocarin or another kingdom. We still don't even know *who* we're facing. We only know that they've allied with Hotharia."

Mother nods contemplatively. "Do you still trust Prince Aidan and Ocarin? Even after your father's death could have been avoided?"

"Ocarin is no friend of Hotharia. That much I know for sure. No matter the poor choices they made during this battle, I know without a doubt that they wouldn't betray us," El says.

"Hmm," Mother hums, taking another spoonful of soup. "I heard that the prince was packing his belongings this afternoon, and made haste to leave the castle. You say you trust him, and yet you banish him from your home?"

Gods, this woman knows the right place to poke. I glance at El as I, too, dig into the truly exquisite roasted duck soup.

"Just because I trust him doesn't mean I agree with his actions. Now, if you don't mind, Mother, I'd rather not talk about him," Elana rips her small loaf of bread into chunks and viciously dunks it into the bowl in front of her, perhaps filling her mouth so she no longer has to speak.

Mother sighs. "Very well. How about we discuss your plans for court tomorrow?"

El swallows the bite she's been chewing. "First we're going to acknowledge the loss of Father, and reaffirm our commitment to the people of Adrithia. Then I'm going to announce the trial of my former guard, and Aislinn's appointment to my advisor. Then we'll open the floor for any grievances, as is customary."

It's quiet for a moment while our mother sets her spoon down. "You're appointing your sister as your advisor?"

"Yes," Elana answers immediately.

Mother temples her fingers together, leaning forward and glancing between us. "I'm not sure that's wise."

We both bristle.

"Why not?" Elana demands. "She's the best person for the role."

"Yes, she is, but the nobles are particular about this appointment. They will see it as a snub if you don't select one of them."

I roll my eyes. "So this appointment is to serve egos, and not about the years I spent shadowing Father?"

Mother nods, her face grim. "Exactly. You should know this, Aislinn, since you spent so long learning from Devon. The nobles care about power and their standing within society. If you threaten that standing, or boost up someone they feel unworthy, they will make your lives incredibly difficult."

"They would actively go against the Queen?" I ask, gesturing to Elana.

"Yes, perhaps not outright, but it would be easy for them to delay requests for aid, misplace taxes, and spread discord. And we've seen enough of that since the Crowning Ceremony."

I sit back in my chair, swirling around chunks of carrot and celery in the soup. Mother's right. We have to be careful about this.

"So we present it in a way that doesn't offend them. We could say it was Father's wish," I suggest.

Mother nods. "You could, but it may not matter. Elana is young, and they'll likely be vying for a position to control her, and thus, control Adrithia. Duke Lyon may prove an especially difficult challenge. He's been trying to gain more power for years. And now he's been given an opportunity, in the form of an unwed monarch."

"You're saying he's going to push for a betrothal to his son?" Elana asks. "Even though he has the personality of a mucus toad."

At that, Mother lets out a trilling chuckle. It's the first joyful noise I've heard from her since the ball we hosted weeks ago. "Oh dear, most men do.

You're going to have to learn how to look past that. And yes, that's exactly what I'm saying."

"Rigel has already informed the nobles that any conversation about marriage matches will not be tolerated," I say, hopeful.

"If you think that will stop him, then I clearly haven't taught you well enough," Mother says, shaking her head slightly.

"Well there has to be something we can do to avoid the topic? Or keep the Duke off my back?"

Mother turns back to El and asks, "do you have a different engagement you wish to announce? From Adrithia or abroad?"

At that, El's face turns beet red, and she sinks into her seat, shaking her head. I glower at our mother. "Of course she doesn't, but that doesn't mean that she should pick the first eligible bachelor that brags about his the size of his-,"

"Aislinn!" Mother chastises as I finish, "-coinpurse."

It's Mother's turn to flush, and I sit back with a satisfied smirk.

"Regardless, Elana, without a sanctioned engagement in place, there's no way to prevent that conversation."

The main course of our meal arrives, and we eat in relative silence, each of us in our minds. When dessert is brought to us, Mother excuses herself, so Elana and I split her slice of cake.

We retire early. Tomorrow's going to be a long day.

I dress for court like I'm preparing for battle. My lady's maid, Kalena, helps secure the silver corset, while leaving room for me to move, something she's been doing for me since I was a teenager. I've chosen a navy dress with tight sleeves that don't impede my range of motion and a high slit up the leg, so I've got easy access to a hidden dagger strapped to my thigh. The heirloom sword forged by my ancestor Hale Sable sits securely at my waist, and though I hope I won't have to use it, I'm prepared for anything. My hair is tied up in a formal style, and I wear one of my simple silver crowns.

I keep my makeup minimal today, only using some powder to conceal the dark circles under my eyes and a dark pink lip rouge. Strange dreams chased me from deep sleep again last night. It's been happening ever since the battle. I haven't paid them much mind, since I forget what transpired the moment I awaken. There's no use worrying over dreams I have no ability to recall.

Elana meets me outside of her door, looking resplendent in an elaborate navy ball gown, her auburn hair styled similarly to mine, and her stunning gold crown on top of her head.

Her dress is accented with gold instead of silver, and her lips are painted a subtle red. Dark kohl on the top of her eyelids accentuates her gray eyes. She wears no weapons that I can see, not even her twin daggers from the Hale trove, but she doesn't need weapons to exude power and invoke fear. Especially not since she inherited two incredible powers from the long-forgotten twin goddesses.

"I see I'm not the only one who's ready to go to war with the nobles," I remark.

"Do you think it's too much?" She asks self-consciously.

I hold her gaze and give my head a firm shake. "No, I think it's perfect. You're going to do great."

We walk to the great hall together. Rigel opens the double doors as he announces our presence, and all eyes turn to us. Elana walks one pace in front of me, keeping her eyes straight ahead and head high, while I scan the gathered crowd for threats.

Elana gets to the dais and climbs the three steps to her throne. I follow and stand to her right. She turns around to face the assembled nobles, who bow low. I drop to my knees as well, showing fealty to my sister, my family.

She sits on her stiff-backed throne and addresses the crowd, "Rise."

All attention is on us, mostly on Elana, but some faces, either curious or sneering, turn in my direction. I refuse to shift under the scrutiny. I'm used to it. Ever since the Crowning Ceremony, when my sister was chosen instead of me, I've been the subject of suspicion.

I don't know why I wasn't chosen. As proud as I am of Elana, a part of me will always wonder why. Did I do something to offend the Gods?

What bothers me most are the whispers. The hushed insults, the accusations strangers throw my way when they think I can't hear. *Bastard*, they call me, even though only a true-blooded Sable could wield Hale's sword. But people will always harshly judge what they don't understand. Only the Gods know their reasoning.

I glance at my sister, noticing the subtle differences between us. As children, we looked more alike. Elana's hair was lighter, and slowly warmed to a reddish brown in her teenage years. My face thinned out during that time, while hers retained some of its youthful roundness. My body lengthened, and I grew taller, while her curves matured.

Looking at her now, she commands the room with a quiet sort of strength. "Thank you all for your attendance on such short notice. I'm honored by your presence for my first formal court. I wanted to start off by acknowledging our terrible loss."

Elana rehearsed this speech in front of me at least a dozen times. About half of those times she stumbled over the next words as her emotions overwhelmed her. I hold my breath, sending her strength.

"King Devon was a worthy ruler and leader of Adrithia. He spent years keeping the Astrellian Peace, negotiating advantageous trade agreements with the other kingdoms, and building the new temple in Sandral. His life accomplishments are too many to list, such was his greatness. I will never be able to replace him, but I swear to you all that I will put Adrithia's best interests ahead of my own. I will protect its citizens from the new looming threat. And I will help secure a new era of peace across Astrellia."

She pauses, and I relax. She got through the most difficult part. I scan the room, taking note of the few nobles with watery eyes.

"Now we must move on and look ahead. My former guard's trial will be held in two days. He is accused of treason, resulting in my father's death. Are there any here who oppose these accusations?"

The hall is silent. We expected this.

"Next, on the appointment of a new chief advisor. As we know, it's not customary to have a chief advisor, but my father wished for me to learn the intricacies of court from someone he taught himself. This person is someone he trusted wholly, and someone who has shadowed him for more than a decade," she takes a deep breath, and I watch her throat bob as she swallows before continuing, "it's my honor to appoint Aislinn Sable as my chief advisor."

Several whispers hum and grow louder as people murmur and shoot me looks of distrust or anger. I give Elana a nod encouraging her to continue, but one man steps forward, breaking free from the crowd.

Duke Lyons clears his throat loudly. "Excuse me, Your Highness," he starts off, not earning any favors by addressing her as less than a monarch. "I want to extend my deepest condolences for your father's passing. We all express our deep sadness at his loss."

He pauses, with his hand over his heart, a show of respect and sincerity. Elana is forced to acknowledge his condolences with a curt nod. He continues, "on the matter of chief advisor, I would like to assure you that there are more experienced persons who would make a fine advisor in your court.

No one is doubting the skills of Princess Aislinn with a blade, but wouldn't you agree that someone with more exposure to court proceedings would be a better fit for Adrithia?"

I resist the urge to snarl at him. He's seen me attending court for more than a decade. He has no right to insinuate that I am not experienced enough. I glance over at my sister, and can see she is having a difficult time keeping the scowl from her expression.

The Duke must not see the ire in her eyes, however, because he charges forward. "As a well-respected Princess of the Sable line, your sister could provide us with an advantageous match, perhaps securing us an alliance with another kingdom. I believe Prince Aidan of Ocarin is available, or perhaps we could avoid war altogether with Hotharia if Princess Aislinn would marry Prince Cald-,"

Before he has a chance to finish his sentence, the room is drenched in pitch black. All the candles are snuffed out and the windows blanketed in shadow as my sister's temper snaps. No one breathes too loudly, and I smirk with satisfaction as everyone freezes in uncomfortable silence while Elana commands the room. Five heartbeats turn into ten, turn into thirty until she's satisfied.

I expect pure golden light to burst from her, to bring the great hall back to its glory, but instead the shadows slowly recede, letting light pour back in through the windows.

All eyes are on Elana, where she sits glaring down at Duke Lyons.

"My sister is not for sale. We are not here to discuss marriage, and we're certainly not here to discuss any kind of alliance with Hotharia. We're here to discuss how we move forward, and protect our kingdom," Elana snaps. Gods, I'm so proud of her. Some of the nobles drop their heads, backing up, but a few, those closest to the Duke, stand their ground.

"Princess Elana," Duke Lyon starts, and I can see that his hand shakes ever so slightly. "I'm sure you're aware that the nobility provides ample resources and soldiers to Adrithia's army. In uncertain times, such as these, there are instances throughout our history in which the noble families withdraw such support in order to ensure their lands are protected and prosperous. Especially if it seems like the ruler is too young or unfit for the position."

Elana visibly bristles, and I take the moment to step in front of her, deciding enough is enough. "A thinly veiled threat is still a threat, Duke. Be careful how you speak to your Queen."

Duke Lyons backs up, dramatically putting a hand over his chest and sucking in a deep breath. "Of course it wasn't a threat, Your Highness. My family is as loyal as ever to the great Sable family. However, my loyalty is also to the people of Adrithia, and it is for them that I believe we should reinstate the Ascension Rite for your coronation, Princess Elana."

This fucking asshole. I grip the hilt of Hale's sword as a few of the nobles gasp. Whispers break out across the hall. Elana catches my eyes briefly, eyebrows pinched together in confusion. Of course this snake would find a way to bring up the most outdated practice in our kingdom's history.

"There hasn't been an Ascension Rite for over 500 years," I say. "It's nothing more than a formality anyway."

So this is his ploy to circumvent Elana's right to rule. He's trying to ensure it never happens.

"It's typically a formality, yes, but it would allow the nobles a voice in deciding whether young Elana is ready to rule. Should the majority of noble families think she should wait until she's wed, then a regent will be appointed to rule in her stead, for the protection of our kingdom and the Sable line, of course."

I grind my teeth together to keep from cursing him for his thinly veiled manipulation. Gods, what a bastard. One look at my sister shows me how close she is to lashing out as well, and I move to argue as loud, confident footsteps clack down the center of the great hall.

# CHAPTER THREE

## ELANA

The sea of nobles parts for my mother, draped in formal mourning clothes with a sheer black veil draped over her head. I don't think I've ever been happier to see her. She strides toward the dais with absolute authority. Lords and Ladies bow their heads as she passes. She curtsies to me, a gesture that would make me uncomfortable in any other setting, and moves to stand on the left of my throne. A show of solidarity.

I glance over at my sister and see a smirk on her lips. I'm tempted to lean back on my uncomfortable seat and watch the drama unfold.

"Your Majesty," Duke Lyons says. "We are so sorry for your loss. King Devon was one of the finest rulers in Adrithian history."

"Thank you for your kind words, Duke Lyons. And apologies for my tardiness. I'm afraid my husband's brutal death is wearing on me," Mother says, eying him with barely disguised distaste. "Which is why I was surprised that a formal court would be held so swiftly after his passing. I'm sure everyone here also wished for more time to grieve such a loss."

The Duke's face reddens, and he nods his head vigorously. "Of course, it's truly a tragedy for our entire kingdom."

Mother gives him a soft smile, one that I know from experience cuts deeper than steel. "Now, Duke, I am just as surprised to hear this suggestion of an Ascension Rite. I'm sure it wouldn't be necessary, considering the precedent for it predates this castle. In times like these, we must focus on moving forward rather than returning to archaic ways. I have every confidence that with the wisdom of the noble families and the powers the twin Goddesses have bestowed, Adrithia can assuredly meet these trying times."

She doesn't give anyone time to object as she continues, "now I believe there are a few pressing matters to discuss before we adjourn for the day. A coronation date must be set. We have to give the people of Adrithia a sense of security. We must also allow time for the royal families of Ocarin, Aaranor, and Melinor to arrive. I believe we should plan the coronation three days following King Devon's Resting Ceremony, in accordance with Astrellian tradition."

Mother turns to me. "Would that be agreeable, Your Majesty?"

An unsettling feeling winds its way up my back, making me sit straighter. "Yes, that is agreeable to me."

She flashes me a genuine smile, and it quickly fades as she turns to address the gathered Lords and Ladies. "Are there any objections to Queen Elana's coronation in 20 days?"

The hall is once again silent. Even Duke Lyons seems to be subdued. I may be blessed with the power of two Gods, but with words alone, my mother was the one to humble the duke. That's the power of my mother. She commands respect and doesn't take offenses lightly. She managed to turn a roomful of hostile nobles into reluctant allies with nothing more than a dramatic entrance and a few sentences. I clearly have much to learn from her.

"Very well," Mother says, moving down the steps. "We thank you all for your attendance today. We wish we had more time to spare, but coronations don't prepare themselves. If you have matters you'd like to discuss at our next court, please see Sir Rigel."

It's official. My mother is brilliant. She excused us from accepting grievances without making us look bad. I really should be writing all of this down. Aislinn steps closer to my side, nodding her head to encourage me forward. I stand up and follow Mother, keeping my focus ahead instead of on the nobles bowing as I pass them.

A set of guards opens the doors that lead to our sitting room while the nobles are ushered through the hand carved doors.

I let out the breath I've been holding and allow my shoulders to slump. The first thing I'm going to do is take off this damned crown. As I take it from my head, a flash of movement reflects in the polished gold. In the same instant I hear someone shout behind me, "death to the monarchs! The Empress will rise!"

I barely have the time to think, *who the fuck is the Empress,* then I'm crashing to the ground, a heavy weight on my back. My breath leaves me in a whoosh as I hit plush wool carpet. The weight leaves me upon impact and I flip around, stunned to see Aislinn with her sword out, rushing towards a man in the retreating, screaming crowd. He's dressed in formal garb, and holds a small dagger. A small, black dagger.

A body falls to the floor next to me. One of the hall's guards lies there, groaning, a second black dagger sticking out of his chest. I scramble over to him, laying my hand on his shoulder. The wound is black as the dagger, his exposed skin darkening as the blackness spreads from the gash. The corruption from the cursed blade spreads quickly. Oh Gods, oh Gods, oh Gods. I have to help him.

I'm dimly aware of Aislinn and the other guards disarming the intruder as I reach inward, searching for that second well of power, seeking the light. I feel the overwhelming pool of darkness, always there, always ready to burst. I need the light. Instead of feeling that glowing warmth, there's an empty chasm. Panic and desperation fuel me as I tear into that abyss in my mind, searching for anything, even a droplet of the light. But there's nothing to be found. My gift from the Goddess Nura, has vanished.

I grip the man's hand, careful to avoid the dagger. Gods, he looks so young. Possibly even Aislinn's age, 23, or a year younger like me. His breaths are ragged, his eyes are open, but glassy, as they dart around, looking at the ceiling, then at me, then to the dagger's hilt. There's so much pain and fear cut into the twisted expression on his face.

"It's going to be alright," I whisper to him, even though it's a lie. "You're all right."

I don't know why I say it. Perhaps to calm him. Perhaps to calm myself. The guard sputters, his breathing raspy and shallow. He won't last much longer. Black lines crawl up his neck. If only I could access my light, I could heal him. This is yet another failure on my shoulders. Nura must have taken her power back when I proved unworthy.

"Elana, we need to get you out of here," Aislinn is suddenly at my side, looking from the man to me. "Can you help him?"

I refuse to voice my answer, instead shaking my head as tears form in my eyes.

"Okay, then we need to go. It's not safe here," Aislinn grips my arm, hauling me to my feet and deeper into the castle. Half a dozen royal guards surround us and our mother, while nobles still shove each other to get outside the walls. Two guards drag the attempted assassin towards the dungeon, his body limp, possibly unconscious. And, in a growing pool of blood, the guard bleeds out alone.

"Wait, Ash, we can't leave him," I struggle against her hold, turning back to face the man on the ground, gasping for breath.

She pauses for a brief moment, then shakes her head. "There's nothing we can do for him, and we can't spare guards to bring him with us even if we could help."

She tugs on my arm, but I stand rooted to the spot.

"Let me rephrase that. I'm not leaving him here," I say.

Ash's hard gaze meets mine, and it's a momentary battle of wills before she sighs heavily and motions to two of the guards, commanding, "bring him."

My shoulders sag with relief as she ushers them along. We arrive at the study, and Rigel is there, opening the door, waving our group inside.

"Lock down the castle and check everyone for cursed weapons. Take the attacker to the dungeon and make sure he stays alive for questioning. Check every room, every alcove, and every closet. Make sure it's secure. Assign two guards to this door, and the rest to the search," Ash demands as the pair of guards lay their injured companion down on the chaise. The lead guard, who I now recognize asCaptain Matteo, bows quickly to us, then makes a hasty exit. Aislinn shuts and locks the study door behind him.

I rush to the sofa and kneel, grabbing the injured man's hand, careful to avoid touching the cursed blade. Without my light powers, I'm not sure I'm immune to the curse's effects. As I tear my eyes from the guard's ghastly wound to scan his face, his eyelids flutter open, gaze flitting around the room before landing on me. He lets out a pained moan, and the sound is a dagger to my heart. A bead of sweat rolls down his forehead into his already damp dark hair.

"Do you know his name?" I ask Aislinn. She's on friendlier terms with the guards than I am, since she spends much of her free time training with them.

She shakes her head, a deep frown pulling at the corners of her mouth. "He's one of the newer recruits."

The black lines inch past his chin, and his raspy breathing quickens. Pained whimpers leave him. I want to comfort him, but there's nothing I can do. I'm helpless again. As helpless as I was months ago, before the Gods chose me, before I left for the mountain.

Fingers brush my shoulder, and I turn, expecting to see Ash, but it's my mother who kneels next to me.

She takes the man's head between her hands and brushes his wet hair back. "Shhh, child. It's all right. The Gods are waiting for you."

Then she starts to sing. Her voice is soft and melodic as she sings an old lullaby, one that she used to sing to Ash and I when we were too wound up to sleep at night. The man stares at my mother, completely enraptured by her voice, just like we were as children.

*When the elements are one*
*And the song has been sung*
*The Gods will decree*
*That magic flies free*

*Careful not to invoke*
*The wrath of the soul*
*Hold on to the hope*
*That the mind breaks control*

*When the elements are one*

*And the song has been sung*
*The Gods will decree*
*That magic flies free*

*The flames shall cleanse*
*The winds change anew*
*The ground will transcend*
*The waves shall pursue*

*When the elements are one*
*And the song has been sung*
*The Gods will decree*
*That power flies free*

*When the old Gods wake*
*Destruction on their heels*
*A new world we will make*
*By shattering our old ideals*

The man's eyes are open, staring up at Mother without seeing. He lies unmoving, chest still, but his face shows no pinched signs of pain. Slowly and with gentleness only a mother can possess, she closes his eyes.

"May the Gods lead you with honor into the afterlife," she whispers to his forehead.

My vision blurs as I abruptly stand up, sniffling and rubbing away the trails of tears on my cheeks. I pace in front of the desk, trying and failing to steady my rapid heartbeat. "How long do we have to stay locked in here?"

Ash raises an eyebrow at me. "As long as it takes for the guards to make sure the castle is clear."

"I need to get out of here, I need to do *something*," I say, looking between the man and my sister.

"Elana, you just survived an assassination attempt. The best thing you can do now is stay put while those guards do what they've trained for years to do. If you leave this room, they'll worry about protecting you rather than checking the castle," Ash says, placing her hands on my shoulders. "I know it's difficult to wait, but we need to do this."

"Your sister's right," Mother stands up, removing the mourning veil from her head and draping it over the face and torso of the guard. "The best thing we can do right now is stay here. There's more at stake than your life alone. We have to think about the entire kingdom. If something were to happen to you, there is no heir. Adrithia would be lost."

I let out a noise of disgust, gearing up for an argument. "Mother, please don't turn this into a discussion of my marriage. I don't have the energy to argue right now."

Mother sighs. "I'm not trying to have that conversation now, either. But you need to understand how precarious our situation is."

Ash places a hand on my shoulder, locking eyes with Mother. "Nothing is going to happen to Elana while I'm here, I swear it. The kingdom is secure."

Hours and a few strained words later, the light streaming through the windows of the study takes on a golden hue. Aislinn sits behind Father's desk, flipping through papers. Mother is seated by the window, looking out over the gardens. I pace back and forth in front of the desk, trying to avoid anything that reminds me of my father.

The large round stone on a pedestal next to the desk, which used to spin and twirl with Father's power, is stuck in its perpetual unmoving state. On the desk, underneath the pile of papers, is the rock map he once brought to life to illustrate places and people. It's now as smooth as glass.

Even the desk makes me think of him, and how Ash and I used to hide under it as children, waiting sometimes hours for Father to appear, so we could jump out and scare him.

Tears prick my eyes, and I furiously blink them away. Surrounded by all of these mementos of his, I find myself reliving his final moments. How he went off to split the coast and stop the second wave of soldiers from overwhelming us, the lone surviving enemy plunging his sword into Father's back. Then, his last look at us, when he knew he was going to die. Aidan, holding me back from helping him, Ash and I looking over the edge of the chasm Father had just created. The frothy waves at the bottom, from which no living thing could have emerged.

My hands shake as I release a shuddering breath, trying to clear the picture from my mind. I've turned the events over hundreds of times since our return, trying to examine what I could have done differently, knowing I should have stepped in earlier to save him. I could have watched his back, I could have healed him.

"Did anyone else hear the assassin say something about an Empress?" Ash's words break through my self-deprecating spiral. Right before my sister knocked me to the ground, I remember hearing something about an Empress rising.

"Yes. He said, 'death to Adrithia. The Empress will rise'," Mother says.

I worry at my bottom lip. "There are no Empresses on Astrellia, are there?"

Mother shakes her head. "No, and there haven't been, as far back as our history goes."

"What about outside of Astrellia?" Ash wonders aloud, staring down at a large piece of parchment she unrolled on Father's desk.

I walk closer and see she's staring at a map. It shows all five kingdoms of Astrellia and the Gods' Territory. The sea surrounds our continent, and extends to the map's edges.

"There are no other lands out there," I say tentatively. "There is nothing beyond the sea, which is why the Astrellian Peace is so important."

"I know that is what we've always been taught," Ash says, staring at the boundless stretch of water past Ocarin and Hotharia. "But what if we've been taught a lie. No one has ever really explored, because we've been led to believe we are alone. I wonder if we've been intentionally misled."

The idea is ludicrous. Surely, if there were other lands beyond our own, someone would have sailed there, right?

"We can't just commission ships to sail out into the unknown. Especially if they might encounter hostile lands. That would be asking the sailors to risk their lives," I complain, not wanting to give more Adrithian lives needlessly.

"Many sailors would relish the chance to discover new islands. It would be their honor," Ash argues.

"We'd be sending them to their death," I fire back. There must be another way for us to get information. Perhaps the extensive library in Aaranor would hold the answers. "Maybe there are more complete maps in Numai's archives," I tell her. "I'll write to Rian and request he research the matter."

Aislinn scoffs. "El, the answers aren't going to be in any books. They're going to be out there, in the world."

I'm about to launch into a well-rounded defense of books, when Mother clears her throat. "I think we're overlooking a wealth of knowledge. One that's easier to access than crossing the ocean, and is possibly more knowledgeable than thousand-year-old tomes."

Ash waves her hand at her. "The assassin will never talk. We tried to get more than a dozen prisoners to talk after the battle, to no avail."

"I'm not talking about the soldier taking up space in the dungeon."

Ash and I stare at her, waiting.

She sighs, as if she finds it a chore to give us the answer. "I'm talking about Hotharia."

Oh, right.

"Mother, if they're allied with the enemy, don't you think it's in their best interest to keep us in the dark?"

"Of course it is, but that doesn't mean we won't be able to get them to talk. Have they accepted our invitation to attend Devon's resting ceremony yet?"

I shake my head. "No, they haven't sent a response."

Mother hums to herself, looking down at the map. "What of their merchants? Are they still actively trading with us?"

I'm not sure, so I look to Aislinn, who responds, "I believe there are one or two trading vessels docked in Tierth. We've locked down the bay. No ships are allowed in or out right now. The crew is probably still in Tierth."

Mother nods. "Good, then give the orders to have the crew brought here. We must question them. All of them."

We all agree it's the best course of action. Aislinn writes up three copies of the orders, just in case, and I sign them. We emphasize that the merchant crew are not to be harmed in any way, but they're to be escorted here by a unit of Tierth's soldiers.

Several knocks on the door finally release us from the study. The royal guards have finished their search of the castle and grounds and have found no additional attackers.

Two men come in and carry away the body of their fallen companion. I give orders to inform his family that he died with the highest honors, and a resting ceremony will be provided at our expense. It's the least we can do, considering his family never had the chance to say goodbye.

# Chapter Four

## Elana

The next morning, I'm shoving a warm scone into my mouth, completely oblivious to the flavor. The guard's face keeps flashing in my mind, scared. I could have saved him if only I had access to my healing power.

Across the table, Aislinn says something, but I merely stare at the half-eaten pastry in my hand. On the battlefield, I helped people with injuries worse than his. My light was the only thing that could purify the corruption left by those cursed weapons. If I'm unable to use it, what will happen if we're attacked again? How many more of our warriors will we lose?

The last time I felt the light was the morning after the battle. I'd healed countless injured during the early hours of dawn. I worked mindlessly, keeping my thoughts off my father. When I used the last dregs of my light to heal the final soldier, reality had set in. Father was gone. He was really gone. I haven't felt the light return since.

A raspberry smacks me square in the forehead, startling me from my introspection. My eyes snap to my sister, who stares right back, a serious expression on her face.

She slowly asks me, punctuating every word, making me think she may have asked several times before, "can you pass the jam?"

I blink a few times, unsure if I heard right. She points at the jar of strawberry preserves next to me and motions for me to hand it over. I slide the jar across the table and she catches it with ease.

"Great, now that I have your attention, we're training today," she says, slathering the jam on a piece of warm bread.

"What? No, I'm not ready yet, and besides, we have a prisoner to question," I say, dropping the scone onto my plate.

Ash levels her knife at me. "Yes, you are. If I have to drag you to the training field, I will. Besides, I already questioned the assassin."

"You questioned him without me?" I demand, immediately frustrated.

She nods, her gaze on her bread as she rips a bite off. She chews quickly and swallows. "You didn't want to be there for that. Trust me. I still have blood under my fingernails." She waggles her darkened fingernails at me for emphasis. My stomach churns. I don't know what she did to the man, and I don't want to know. She doesn't exactly have a reputation for being the gentle sister.

"Gross, Ash," I scowl. "What did you learn?"

"Absolutely nothing. The only thing he would say is what we heard yesterday. 'Death to the monarchs. The Empress will rise'."

Ash viciously rips off another chunk of the bread, glaring at a scratch on the ancient table. She's not used to failure.

"Maybe he'll talk more after a few days," I say.

"Perhaps," she grunts, then nods to my plate. "Get eating. We've got training to do."

The sun is still low in the sky when we circle each other with practice swords. I'm dressed in my training clothes, soft leather pants, boots, and a loose-fitting top. I spent weeks in these clothes on the mountain, and I'm surprised by how much I missed their comfort . No tight corsets and useless slippers to be found out here.

I exhale an uneven breath, mimicking the footwork Ash drilled into me before I left for the Gods' Territory. I'm sloppy, and I notice my sister clocking my missteps with narrowed eyes. Giving me little warning she lunges at me, disarming my blunted shortsword in two precise movements.

"Again," she says, nodding at my weapon in the grass.

I grab the hilt and sink into the stance Aislinn taught me. This time when she charges, I see the black armor and cursed sword of a soldier on the battlefield. I backpedal, but there's carnage all around me. Bodies litter the ground, blood splatters my face when a soldier next to me is stabbed through the abdomen with a spear. Ahead of me, the captain of the unit pushes forward. "Keep moving!" He yells, and there's no time to pause.

I pant, wide-eyed, staring at the slaughter on the slopes of the shore. I drop to my knees in the blood soaked grass, covering my ears against the screams of the dying. Oh Gods, oh Gods, oh Gods, not again.

Two hands grip my shoulders, and the shapes around me brighten, until it's only my sister's face I see. Eyebrows pinching together in concern, my name shouting from her lips. "El, you're all right. You're home."

I suck in gasping breaths. My cheeks are warmed by the tears streaming down my face. "Aislinn?" I manage between gulps of air.

"Yes, I'm here. Everything's okay," she says, rubbing her hands up and down my shoulders, as if she's trying to warm me up. I realize I'm shivering, my teeth chattering uncontrollably. "I'm so sorry, I shouldn't have pushed you. We can stop."

I grab a fistful of the thick grass at my side. It's bright green, not drenched in blood. The thought centers me, calms me as much as my sister's presence.

"No, I'm okay. Just give me a moment," I barely whisper out, taking a few deep breaths.

"You saw the battle, didn't you?" Ash asks, and I nod in response. "It's okay to not be ready for training. We can pick it up another time."

I shake my head, knowing if I give in to the trauma now, it'll be harder to pull myself out of it. "We should keep going. I need to work through this."

"Are you sure?"

My only reply is gripping my sparring sword and standing up, getting back into my defensive stance. Ash gets back on her own feet, squares off with me, and lunges. This time, I see nothing but her, and I meet the blow. The force of it sends me stumbling back, and she's on me quicker than I can blink, disarming me and sticking the blunt point into my chest.

"We don't have to keep going," she says, lowering the blade.

I pick up my sword and face her. "Again." This time it's a demand.

Ash responds by rushing me like lightning, sword raised. There's blood on the grass, screaming in my ears. I shut it out as I focus on my sister. I parry once, twice, three times, before she knocks my blade from my grasp.

I'm already breathing hard, but this time I don't give Aislinn the chance to charge me as I attack her, blade poised for a quick strike. She whirls around, deflecting my strike and using the opening to land a blow on my bicep that has me wincing in pain. I drop my sword and hold my arm, my skin already turning bright red. That'll be a nasty bruise later.

"Heal it," Ash commands, nodding to my arm, giving me a suspicious stare. Shit.

"It's fine," I lie. "Not worth the energy to heal it."

She narrows her eyes. Double shit. She knows, or at least suspects. "El, just heal it. It's going to be painful for weeks, and you can't afford the disadvantage."

I grit my teeth together. I was hoping to keep this a secret for much longer. "I can't."

"What?" She asks, going preternaturally still. "What do you mean you can't?"

"Ever since the morning after the battle, since I used up all my energy healing the wounded, I haven't been able to sense the light. The power is just...gone," I study the hilt of my training sword.

She lets out a sigh. "I thought so, and yesterday all but confirmed it. Why didn't you tell me?"

"Because I was embarrassed. No monarch has ever lost their power before," I fidget under her judgment.

"No monarch has ever had two powers before," Ash says. "You're the first to do a lot of things, El."

A reluctant smile tugs at my lips before reality draws them down again. It still doesn't solve anything. The light was our one saving grace during the battle. If it's gone, how can we win if the enemy strikes again?

"There has to be a way to fix this. Maybe you should commune with the twin Goddesses at the temple," she says. My sister, always the problem-solver of the two of us. She thrives under the pressure of intense situations, whereas I often stumble my way through.

"You don't even believe in temples," I remind her, returning my practice sword to its stand on the edge of the field. "You called praying a waste of time."

"Well, it can't hurt to try. If visiting the temple helps, I'll fall to my knees and admit I was wrong."

Under the heat of the early afternoon sun, we exit the carriage outside of the temple Father erected near Sandral's city center. I hike up my simple navy dress as we ascend the steps inside. The temple is an expansive stone structure constructed of speckled white marble. It has five sides, and the roof is punctuated by five towering spires.

Aislinn and I step through the temple's massive arched entrance into a lush courtyard. We're greeted by a garden veiled with a domed glass ceiling. A gnarled yew tree stands alone in the center, surrounded by ferns and flowers of all colors. Large doors and hallways branch from the courtyard and lead into the interior of the temple. Glass stairs lead up on the right, and a descending stone staircase lined with torches is on the left.

Priestesses and visitors hustle about, mostly ignoring us. No one here cares about status or power. They're here in service to the Gods, or seeking guidance from them. Several priestesses pass us wearing gold chains across their chest, attached to gilded plates atop their shoulders. From the chains hang medallions. Most of the priestesses wear one or two of the discs, though I spot one tall woman with three medallions. She speaks in hushed tones to several young priestesses following her. Those young girls wear no chains, and are likely in training.

I've only been here a handful of times, and I've always followed my mother straight to Goddess Avani's chamber, since she was Father's patron goddess.

Now, I find myself unsure where to go.

Luckily, we don't have to wander for long. A middle-aged priestess glides towards us. She wears the same creamy white robes of her peers, adorned with gold jewelry. Her raven hair reflects the light of the courtyard around us. She has a warm smile and rich brown eyes framed by delicate wrinkles.

Across her chest is a chain with five gold medallions. Upon closer inspection, I now see that each has a symbol of the God it represents. A single flame for Goddess Enya, a wave for the God Kai, a stone for Goddess Avani, two intersecting blades for the God Tolliver, and swirls in a cyclone pattern for Sepher.

"Welcome, Your Majesty," she says quietly, curtsying low to me, then to Aislinn. "And welcome, Your Highness. I am Head Priestess Rosalind. What brings you to the temple today?"

It never occurred to me before this moment that there might not be a place to commune with the twin goddesses. They were forgotten. No one knew they existed until they appeared to me on the mountain.

"I'm here to, uh, try to commune with the goddesses Nura and Nisha," I start and immediately feel foolish. "But, I just realized there might not be a place here dedicated to them, so we'll just go." I snap my mouth shut and spin on my heels, intent on heading back to the archway.

Ash's firm hand stops my retreat. I glance back over my shoulder at the priestess, who's doing her best to rein in a gleeful expression.

"Your Majesty, all the Gods have space here for those who seek them out." She gestures with her hand towards the ascending stairs. I share a look with Aislinn and she shrugs.

I give Priestess Rosalind a nod, and she leads us up the steps. The staircase leads to a second level, then a third, until I'm sure we're near the top of the temple.

The priestess beckons us down a short hall and into a round chamber lined with white stone columns. Half of the rotunda is drenched in shafts of light pouring from large windows, while the other half is bathed in shadow. Benches line the exterior of the room, and in the center is an altar with two stones the size of my palms resting on its polished surface. One glimmering crystal, and one onyx, so dark it seems to devour the light around it.

"We had this chamber commissioned the day you revealed the twin goddesses to us. While none of our priestesses have successfully communed with them, we hope the space is suited to your needs."

The expansive chamber is bare of decoration and finery, but the elegant design of the columns seems purposeful. It makes me wonder. "Priestess, what was this space used for before?"

"We never had much use for this room. We would occasionally conduct parts of our ceremonies here, but it never had a specific purpose. We aren't sure why your father built it. The rest of the chambers were created for a reason, with our needs in mind, but this one has always perplexed us."

My eyes are transfixed on the altar. "And what about the stones?"

The priestess follows my gaze. "The Messenger of the Gods gifted them to us after your return to Adrithia."

My breath catches. So The Steward was here. One of the two remaining shifters in the employ of the Gods. He's widely known as the Messenger, which is only partially correct. He and his sister are so much more, and only the rulers of the kingdoms know it. It's too bad we can't speak of it to anyone.

I glance around the room, marveling at how well suited it is for the twin goddesses. Did Father somehow know I'd need this chamber in the temple? He was just as surprised as anyone when I showed up with the powers of two goddesses. Was that an act? I catch Ash's eyes, and see the same confusion I feel reflected back at me.

"Hopefully this space will allow you to commune with your goddesses. I'll leave you to it. If you need anything, ask any of the priestesses here," she says, and with another dip of her head, she walks back down the hall towards the steps.

"Should I stay here with you?" Ash asks, taking in the space around us.

I look to the center of the room, where the two stones seem to vibrate, calling out to me. "No, I need to do this alone."

"Good luck, El," she says, following the priestess back to the staircase.

My feet move without conscious thought. The closer I move to the stones, the more they pulsate, one glowing white and the other leaking darkness. "Goddesses, are you there?"

I blink, and the altar is directly in front of me. A high pitched sound rings in my ears as I instinctively reach out and grasp one stone in each of my hands.

The ringing crescendos and I'm suddenly back in the cave from my dreams. There's a storm raging outside. Inside, a single torch casts my shadow on the wall, and a cacophony of whispers scream at me.

I fall to my knees, covering my ears, the stone still clenched in my hands. "Nura, Nisha, please, I'm here to listen."

I try to open myself up to them, as I had during the trials on the mountain. Slowly, the whispers quiet. I don't know why, but I start to think of my father, and an enormous sense of guilt overwhelms me. I choke on a ragged sob, trying to shut the images and feelings out to listen to the goddesses, but before I can discern any words, the cave trembles and a chunk of rock separates from the ceiling, crashing down. I throw my hands up to protect my head. The rock doesn't stop.

My body spasms, and I wrench my eyes open to find myself back on my knees in the chamber at the temple. The stones in my hand, which seconds ago were buzzing with life, are now cold and silent. They no longer glow or pulsate with power. I stand, unsteady, set them back on the altar and put my head in my hands, trying to parse through the whispers from the cave.

After several agonizing moments, I give up. There's nothing to decipher. I couldn't make out a single word.

Tears prick my eyes, and I brush them away viciously. I don't want to cry here. Why can't the goddesses give me a straight answer for once? They're supposed to be all-powerful, so why is it so hard for them to speak to me?

I suck in a shaky breath and move to sit on one of the benches in the sunlit part of the room. I stare down at my hands, willing a drop of light to appear. A glimmer, a shimmer, I'll take anything to know I'm still in Nura's good graces.

Nothing happens. If I still have the power, it's far away from my grasp. Honestly, it wouldn't surprise me if the goddess decided to rescind her gift as a punishment for my failure. I couldn't even protect my own father when he needed me.

"Goddesses, I'm so sorry," I whisper, not knowing if my words will reach the Gods on their plane of existence. Once I start, the words keep flowing, "I'm too weak to have these powers. I couldn't save Father, and I can't protect the people of Adrithia. Maybe it's best if you take these gifts and give them to someone worthy. Like my sister. Aislinn was supposed to be the one to rule, anyway. I never wanted this."

More tears threaten to fall, and I slam my eyes shut, squeezing my hands into fists so hard my nails indent my palms.

Here I sit, quietly cursing the Gods, and cursing my life until the pain from my hands dulls. Only then do I relax my fingers, staring down at the deep red crescent-shaped marks on my palms. I take several deep breaths before standing up and leaving the chamber behind.

# Chapter Five

## Aislinn

I sit on a bench near the old yew tree, leaning back and absentmindedly using one of my daggers to clean under my nails. As children, Mother would drag my sister and I to this temple before special occasions. When we got older we decided we had better things to do than give up hours praying and offering paltry gifts to the Gods. At least, that's how I felt, and when I insisted on staying behind one day, it seemed to give Elana the encouragement to dig, literally dig, her heels in too.

The memory brings a smile to my face. Mother was so mad. Luckily, our father never spent much time in the temple, and he argued that we were old enough to make our own choices. He insisted he honored the Goddess Avani every day by using his power to keep the people of Adrithia safe and as prosperous as possible.

Footsteps sound behind me, and I grip the dagger tighter on instinct before turning to meet the warm gaze of the head priestess. I stand, sheathing my dagger and hoping I didn't cross some line by having a weapon out in this place.

"Princess Aislinn, there is something you wish to ask of the Gods," Priestess Rosalind says in a tone that suggests she's telling me, not asking.

I blink and shake my head. "Oh, no, I'm only here for my sister."

The priestess smiles warmly. "No, you're not. Please follow me."

For a split second I consider making a dash for the door, but a phantom force stops me. I stand, not entirely of my own volition, and walk after the priestess. It's as if there's a hand on my back, leading me forward. I don't fight it.

She leads me down several sets of stone stairs, each darker than the last, until the only light available is from the torches lining the walls. "You're not leading me to the gates of the Hells, are you?" I joke.

A light chuckle from in front of me. "No, we're going the wrong way for that."

I scrunch my face in confusion, which quickly turns to wariness as I gaze upon the room she leads me to. Lit by dozens of flickering torches and hundreds of candles, there's a single wooden bench in the center of a square room.

Priestess Rosalind motions me forward. "No one will disturb you here. You may speak freely to the Gods."

With that, she gives a quick bow and glides from the room.

"Okay...," I say to the empty space, and take a seat on the bench. The flickering of the candles at the front of the room draws my gaze. After a few moments of nothing happening I'm tempted to get up. This is pointless. I don't have anything to say to any of the Gods. They're the ones who scorned me, after all.

I let out a heavy sigh and stand, brushing out invisible wrinkles from the front of my navy tunic.

"Aislinn Sable, sit down," a deep male voice booms from every corner around me. I grit my teeth against the sharpness of it, the commanding tone.

"I'd rather stand, thank you," I say, crossing my arms over my chest. Standing is better. Standing means I can rush out of here quicker if necessary. Three strides to the door, and then fifteen steps up until the landing, then a sharp turn and another fifteen steps-

"Ask your question, daughter of Sable," the voice says, and I swear it reverberates through my entire body. Echoes reach in through my chest and rattle my spine.

I inhale a breath, trying to steady my rapidly pumping heart. I'm not sure what question this god thinks I have, but I'd better make something up quickly. He called me a daughter of Sable. Good to know I'm not a bastard. I tuck away that bit of knowledge for later. "I wish to know how my father fares in the afterworld."

This god manifests no physical form, but I feel his presence looming over me all the same. "I did not come here to speak of those beyond my reach. I have come to speak of you."

"I don't know what you mean," My eyebrows pull together.

A deep noise that sounds a lot like a scoff rings out. "I don't have the energy to stay here long. You must seek me out. If you fail to do so, Adrithia will fall. All of Astrellia will fall."

I shake my head. "I can't leave my sister. She needs me."

"The entire world needs you, Aislinn. And you need something from me."

"What do I need from you?" I challenge, looking around me with arms spread wide. "I have everything I could ever want."

"Seek me out, and you'll discover what you need," he says, his voice fading slightly.

"No," I say firmly, clenching my fingers into fists at my sides. "I won't abandon Elana."

The god sighs, and it's a deep rumbling sound. "You have always forged your own path, and for that you have my respect. But heed my warning: If you do not come to me, all will be lost." His voice is quiet at the end, so quiet I have to focus on listening.

"Who are you?" I shout, trying to grasp this last bit of information from him before he leaves.

He responds, his voice a whisper no louder than leaves blowing gently in a summer breeze, "I am your past. I am your future, Aislinn Sable. I hope we will meet again."

A heavy feeling lifts from my chest, and I know the god is gone. My breaths come easier, and I turn to the door, pinching the bridge of my nose. "I suppose it would kill you to give me a straight answer. You Gods just love to confuse the Hells out of us mortals."

I practically run up the steps back to the courtyard, trying to shake my frustration. Elana stands near the yew tree, her eyebrows shooting sky high over her gray eyes when she sees me crest the top of the stairs.

"Taking in the sights?" She asks, her questioning eyes looking down the steps.

I scoff. "Something like that. Shall we go?" I'm eager to get out of this place.

She nods, leading the way to the carriage outside. Her shoulders seem to sag, her walk noticeably slower than her usual pace. Sadness practically pours off of her, and I'm surprised no shadows loom at her heels.

"Everything okay?" I wonder, keeping my tone neutral.

We climb into the carriage and settle in for the ride back to the castle on the other side of the capital. She gazes out the window, eyes unfocused. I watch her, trying to gauge whether I should push for a response. I don't want to pressure her, but she can't keep holding emotions in. Just as I'm about to open my mouth, words tumble from her lips like a confession, "the goddesses tried to speak to me, but I couldn't understand what they were trying to say. It was the same as the dreams I was having before the trials. I tried to open myself up to them, but I still couldn't hear."

"Maybe the Gods enjoy watching us squirm," I say nonchalantly, thinking back to the one who spouted nonsense to me.

"Maybe," El says, her voice sounding dull and faraway. "Hopefully you found the temple more enlightening than I did. Did you find what you were looking for?"

I have to bite my tongue to stop myself from telling her about the god I met. She has enough going on right now that she doesn't need anything else to worry about. "Not exactly, I was just wandering."

The lie tastes like ash on my tongue, but El nods, then continues looking out her window. We sit in silence until the carriage bumps to a stop in front of the castle's grand main entrance. The door swings open, and Rigel Brand stands there with two of our household guards.

"Your Majesty," he says, bowing quickly, then he turns to me, giving me a respectful dip of his head. "Princess, the prisoner has asked to speak with you."

"Aric?" Elana asks, almost hopeful, as she steps down from the carriage.

Rigel shifts on his feet, then clears his throat. "No, Your Majesty, the attempted assassin."

Elana's shoulders droop slightly, but she covers her reaction with a shrug, turning to me. I give a quick nod to Rigel. "Very well, I'll head to the dungeons now."

We start to move toward the main doors, when the two guards move to flank us, keeping at a distance, but still close enough to make the hairs on the back of my neck stand up. Elana must feel similarly, because she turns raised brows on them, then whips around to ask Rigel, "what are they doing?"

I look between the two, standing rigidly, with their hands on their swords. Now that I'm paying attention, I recognize them both as long-time staff here at the castle. Matteo, who stands at Elana's right, is a captain who used to train with me. He's several years older than I, at nearly 30, but looks young for his age, with a clean-shaven face and mousey brown hair, which is often kept tied into a knot at the back of his head. He's one of our best warriors, and I genuinely enjoy his company. He never utters a single curse when I put him on his ass in the field. He just gets back up and works harder, which is more than I can say for the pompous man standing to his left, Donne. He grew up in an aristocratic family who bought his way onto our staff by bribing our weapons master. I never figured out what leverage he used, but I know he didn't earn his current rank as the second to the captain. He struts around like a peacock, but can't even hold a sword correctly. The few instances I've had the displeasure of seeing him train, he resembled a quaking newborn foal standing on wobbly hooves for the first time. The man possesses no combat skills or instincts whatsoever.

"They're to follow you from now on. They're your personal guards," Rigel says.

"On whose authority?" Elana demands, glaring daggers at him. A tendril of shadow catches my eye as it slowly inches towards her feet. It's not enough to be threatening, but a reminder that she carries a god's power within her.

"Your mother. She insists."

I almost scoff. Of course Mother would do something so ludicrous. As if I'm not enough to protect her. Elana looks equally irate, crossing her hands in front of her chest. "Did she forget that I can control shadows?"

I huff my agreement. I've seen what she can do with those shadows when prompted. Although it's still my responsibility to protect her.

"We'll speak with her tonight," I promise. We head inside to one of the sitting rooms, where Rigel mentions some correspondence about minor land disputes and gives an update on preparations for Aric's trial. When it's clear Elana can handle things, I give my excuses and make my way to the dungeon, stopping by my suite to grab a few extra weapons. A woman can never carry too many blades.

I make my way down the damp stone stairs leading to the dungeon. The torches along the walls flicker as I stride past. I tie my hair back into a simple knot as I pass the two guards outside of Aric's cell. I despise washing dried blood out of my hair.

There are now four guards stationed in the dungeon, and I greet the pair outside the attacker's cell while I wait for them to open the door. I palm one of my daggers, flipping the handle and catching it as I step into the dim, damp cell.

A man, the attempted-assassin, sits in the center of the small room, facing the door. When I *questioned* him earlier, he hardly moved a muscle. Similarly to the soldiers we faced on the battlefield, he seemed to feel no pain. I left him with a blackened eye, bruised ribs, and a deep cut on his forearm. If I thought torture was the way to get him to talk, I'd have kept going. The entire time, he didn't speak a word, cry out in pain, or beg me to stop. It was unnerving to say the least.

I bite my lower lip, wondering why he asked to see me. I crouch down in front of him, snapping my fingers in front of his face. "You asked to speak with me?"

Nothing. He doesn't blink or acknowledge my presence. I sigh, rocking back on my heels, inspecting him. I'd guess he's in his mid-thirties; his brown hair is streaked with gray and a few days' worth of stubble framing his plain face. He possesses no distinguishable features, which is probably why he was chosen for his task, so he could blend in. Even the man's clothing reveals no secrets. The dark brown outfit is a simple design, average quality, and bears no insignia.

"What's your name?"

No reply.

"Where do you come from?" I repeat my questions from earlier. My knuckles are still sore from the last inquiry, but that just comes with the territory. It's a burden I'll happily bear in place of my sister. If I have my way, which I will, she'll never have to sully her hands with this kind of task. She's not like me. The guilt would eat her alive.

It's not that I don't feel remorse, it's all about compartmentalizing. I can push my dangerous thoughts away, lock them up and work them out in training. My sister allows her emotions to run rampant. I see her guilt whenever someone mentions Father, or the battle. I wish she would open up to me about what she's feeling, but she insists on holding it all in.

Apart from our different natures, I've been wielding weapons for far longer than my sister. I understand how to hurt people, and that means I'm the best woman for this particular duty. I will do what is necessary to protect my sister and my kingdom.

"Who is the Empress?" I ask, rising from my crouch and staring the man down. He says nothing. I swallow my disappointment at how little I've managed to learn about the enemy.

A shadow behind me blocks out the torchlight momentarily, then Elana's voice says from the cell door, "How's it going?"

With a speed I swear is inhuman, the man suddenly lunges forward with his bare hands outstretched like claws. "Death to the monarchs!" He shrieks, trying to skirt around me. I angle my body and plant a quick, hard kick to the man's stomach, sending him sprawling back into the stone wall. His skull makes a sickening *crack* but the blow doesn't deter him. He scrambles to his feet and tries to lunge again.

This time, I draw my sword and dig the tip into the man's chest to prevent his advance. Hale's sword thrums, comforting in my hands. But it turns out my efforts are unnecessary. Tendrils of shadow wrap firmly around the man's limbs. His arms, legs, and torso are all secured with unbreakable ropes of darkness. He writhes against the hold, and his wild, black eyes are trained on my sister as he thrashes and sputters.

I raise my eyebrows at her, smirking. "Nice job, El."

She flashes me a quick grin before turning her attention back to the man. "You can lower your sword, Ash, I've got him."

Every instinct in me rebels against the order, but I do as she asks and relax out of my attack stance, moving to the front of the cell again to stand slightly in front of her. I'll be damned if I let this monster anywhere near her.

"The Empress will rise. Adrithia will fall. All of Astrellia will fall! Your pathetic Gods can't save you." The man says through bared teeth, flecks of spittle flying from his mouth.

"Well, that's new," I remark, leaning closer to him, staring at his eyes as if I expect to glimpse a puppet master hiding behind the black irises. "He's never said anything about our Gods or Astrellia before."

Elana stays quiet, staring at the man with a pinched expression. This is the most reactive he has been since he tried to kill her. I knocked him unconscious before he had the chance to say much in the great hall yesterday. I thought his refusal to say anything to me or the other guards was purely because he lacked the intelligence to do so. His outburst now, however, proves that he still has some mental clarity.

"Try to talk to him, El," I say to her, and plant myself firmly between them. "He was mindless before you showed up. This is the first time he's said anything."

She gives me a shallow nod, then turns her focus to the assassin. Much to my relief, she stays behind me. "What's your name?"

The man tugs at the shadows, thrashing his head back and forth. "I am one of many."

Wonderful, so that means there could be more assassins out there targeting Elana.

"Who is the Empress?"

His mouth curls up, up, up, until his lips are stretched so wide over his exposed teeth I spot his rotting gums. "She is all-powerful, she is eternal."

"What is her name?" Elana presses.

"She is the Empress. Gods and men alike tremble in her wake," he says, utter reverence in his tone as he lifts his head to the stone ceiling.

Elana shifts on her feet, and we exchange a disturbed glance. I give her an incline of my head, prompting her to press on.

"Where do you come from?"

The man hums, then chuckles a wet, raspy sound. "Far away, across the vast blue sea. But not for long, not far away. The Empress is coming. She is coming, she is coming, she is coming to bring you all to your knees."

I take a half step forward. "When is she coming?" I demand.

His head whips toward me, and he spits a glob of saliva at my feet and stays silent.

Elana, from behind me, makes a sound of disgust. "Answer her."

The man's gaze returns to my sister. "Soon."

Fuck. My hand clenches around the hilt of Hale's sword even harder, seeking the comforting assurance of the weapon. During the last battle, we lost a decent amount of our forces, and if Elana can't use her healing powers, it means she can't dispel the cursed weapons. We're ill-prepared for another attack.

"What about Hotharia? Are you allied with them?" Elana asks, the shadows in the cell darkening.

"That pompous, arrogant king jumped at the chance-," his eyes suddenly widen and he lets out an animalistic shriek.

He takes one quick breath, and then, with more force than humanly possible, his neck viciously twists a half turn. The sound of his spine breaking is unmistakable.

Elana lets out a startled noise and backs out of the cell, covering her mouth. The shadows drop the man's lifeless, distorted body on the ground.

I stare at him, slack-jawed. He broke his own neck. Right when it seemed like he was about to give up valuable information.

I'm out of the cell in two long strides. "Burn his body immediately. His clothes and effects, too. Make sure nothing of his remains. Then scatter the ashes to the wind."

The two guards look taken aback by my order, but nod anyway, moving into the cell without another thought.

I see Elana moving towards Aric's cell. She stops suddenly, wobbles, bends over, and vomits onto the stone floor. I rush to her, grabbing her long auburn hair before she gets her sick on it, holding it away from her face.

"What," she starts, wiping her mouth with the back of her sleeve as she rights herself and I let her hair fall back down her shoulders. "What the Hells was that?"

I let out a long exhale. "I don't know. It's asinine to even suggest, but it seems like he wasn't in control of his actions."

"That's what I thought, but that's just not possible, is it?"

My first instinct is to shake my head and deny it. But something stops me. The way he and the other soldiers couldn't feel pain, their black eyes, the cursed weapons, I feel like we're missing something. I decide it's best not to offer empty comfort, so I say again, "I don't know."

Elana groans and covers her face with her hands. "I can't do this. I can't lead our kingdom into war."

Determination tightens my features. I grab her hands and tug them away from her face. "Listen to me, Elana. You can do this. The Gods chose you, and they chose well. We'll get through this together. If you ever need a helping hand, reach out and I'll be there. It's you and me against the world, now and always."

No matter what happens, no matter what armies come for us, I'll stand by my sister's side. Together, we'll forge the world we want to live in.

She grips my hands, taking a few steadying breaths. Then she nods, and I swear I see a determined ember of light sparking in her eyes.

# Chapter Six

## Elana

Gods, would it have killed the throne maker to craft a comfortable chair? This seat is the most unyielding piece of furniture I've ever sat on. A rock would be more comfortable. I shift on the thin cushion for the seventh time since Aric's trial began and resist the urge to rip the heavy crown from my head while Rigel reads out the extensive list of treasonous accusations.

My former friend, the one responsible for my father's death, kneels on the floor with chains binding his wrists and feet. His blonde hair, matted and oily, hangs over his downturned face. The coward hasn't had the courage to meet my eyes since he was hauled in here.

Noble men and women give him a wide berth. Either they don't want the taint of treason to infect them by association, or his ripe smell offends their noses. In the crowd I recognize Duchess Lyons and her son, Percival. Duke Aldrich Lyons is noticeably absent.

"And finally, for refusing to send a vital parchment to our warriors in Tierth. A parchment which would have provided ample reinforcements to the battle along the coast that cost King Devon his life," Rigel finishes in a heavy voice, thick with emotion and I notice Aric's flinch. Rigel rolls up the long parchment and looks at me.

I swallow thickly, recalling last night when Aric broke down and called for me. Ash and I joined Rigel in the cell and listened while he tearfully confessed every treasonous act and every message he remembered passing along. As Rigel recorded Aric's testimony, he had to summon a servant to bring him a second ink pot. I've never seen anyone write as ferociously. It was one of the most impressive things I recall him doing.

Ash asked him if he expected leniency in exchange for his confession, which he declined, saying he deserved everything that was coming to him. I wholeheartedly agreed, while my sister, for the first time, seemed to soften. The two of us argued in my chambers long into the night about the proper punishment. She mentioned he was doing everything to protect his younger sister, and showing him some mercy could go a long way to improve relations with Hotharia. In an effort to compromise, I suggested a quick death rather than the long, torturous one I preferred for him. However, she eventually talked me out of that, too, and we settled on his banishment to the Gods' Territory. A sentence used across Astrellia that typically ends in death for the exiled. The Gods aren't known for their mercy, and there are countless hungry beasts that roam the sacred land. Occasionally someone survives the ordeal and makes it into another kingdom where they disappear or claim sanctuary, but that's rare.

I stand up slowly, concealing my wince at my sore muscles and making sure not to tilt my neck too much and risk the crown falling. Every head in the hall whips to me as I raise my voice, staring at Aric. "Do you wish to dispute any of the charges?"

He finally lifts his gaze, and I take in the dark purple marks under his blue eyes. I guess sleep isn't easy to catch in a cold, damp cell underground.

A pang of something that feels an awful lot like regret hits me, but I shove it back under the intense anger of his betrayal. He lied to me for years. His actions killed my father. There is no forgiving him.

"No, Your Majesty, I do not," his voice is low, and deep lines appear etched into his face, where mere weeks ago there was healthy, unmarred skin.

"And is there nothing else you wish to say to me or my family?" I wait with bated breath.

Aric's eyes bore into mine, but his posture remains loose, as if he's already given up. "No, Your Majesty. Everything I needed to say, I've already said. I've made my peace with the Gods."

Cries of "Guilty!" ring out from around the room erupting into an echoing chant.

There's nothing else to say or do. I draw in a long breath as my stomach twists with nerves. I take a few steps off the dais towards Aric. I feel Aislinn at my back, her hand no doubt poised on her sword. I pause directly in front of him, wanting to look him in the eyes as I announce his sentence. I raise my hand for silence. A hush promptly falls over the room, the last shouts dying away.

"Aric Vernier," I start, hating the way that name feels in my mouth, hating that I never knew his true name until mere weeks ago. "I hereby sentence you to-,"

"Your Highness! Stop!" a booming voice calls from the back of the chamber.

Ash jumps in front of me, her sword halfway out of its sheath, until she recognizes Duke Lyons, a rolled parchment in his raised hand. I exchange a quick glance with Aislinn, who steps back to my side, but doesn't release her hold on the sword. Mutters break out among the nobles, craning their necks to get a better look at our reactions and to gawk at the duke.

"What's the meaning of this?" My mother calls from her place on the dais, draped in mourning garb.

"Your Highness," he gives a perfunctory bow to me, then my sister before sweeping low in my mother's direction. "I have an urgent letter from the King of Hotharia. I believe it would benefit you greatly to read it before continuing with the sentencing."

He extends the letter to me, but ever the faithful courtier, Rigel steps forward and snatches it from Duke Lyon's hand first. He breaks the seal and reads quickly. His eyes bulge as they snag halfway down the paper and he swallows hard before handing it to me with a nod.

It's with his approval that I grab the parchment and begin to read. I scan the words and my hands clench around the paper, wrinkling it. The fucking audacity of King Skade. My teeth grind together as I try to rein in the shadows that have slithered out from the corners of the room.

"What is it?" Mother asks, now standing at my side next to Aislinn. She promised that she would let me handle this matter, and she was supportive of the decision Ash and I came to when we told her at breakfast.

"Hotharia is demanding," I say under my breath, through clenched teeth.. I finally manage to unlock my jaw, which takes more willpower than I'd like to admit, "that Aric be returned to them."

Aric's head whips up, his confused gaze landing on the parchment. Mother holds out her hand and I drop the letter into it. She scans it, narrowing her hazel eyes at Duke Lyons as she passes it to my sister. Ash's tan skin pales as her eyes track down the letter.

"We have no choice; we have to release him," Aislinn hisses between her teeth, barely loud enough for Mother and I to hear.

"We can't," I whisper back. "He must be punished for his actions."

Aislinn and I wait for Mother's input. "Your sister is right, Elana," she breathes. I let out a frustrated breath, careful to keep my reaction within.

King Skade has grown bold in his allegiances. This letter will be invaluable in convincing the rulers of Melinor and Aaranor that the threat he poses is real, and to join forces in putting an end to whatever is going on in Hotharia.

Mother's eagle eyes narrow on the duke. "How is it that you have obtained this correspondence from the King of Hotharia?" She snaps at him, every bit the queen.

He clutches his chest, indignant. "Your Majesty, I was on my way here when this arrived via royal messenger hawk. It was a happy coincidence that your messenger was on his way to deliver this when he ran into me. I promised to personally deliver it to Princess Elana."

I scowl at his unbelievable story. What's his game? Is he also in league with Hotharia, or does he stand to gain something by getting Aric to trust him? I have no doubt that he chose this exact moment to make his possession of the letter known, for greater impact, or attention, I'm not sure.

"What a coincidence indeed," Mother says, her tone sarcastic and revealing how little, she too, trusts him.

"What does it say?" Duke Lyons asks in a loud voice, for the benefit of the crowd.

I resist the urge to unleash my shadows on him, instead fisting my hands at my sides while I recount the letter to those in attendance.

"King Skade of Hotharia has requested the return of his spy unharmed," my eyes flick down to Aric, who has resumed his vigil staring at the floor. And other than the weariness and layer of dirt coating him, he looks pretty unharmed to me.

As for the rest of the letter, I'm not sure if it's beneficial to share. I quickly look at my sister and she glances at the letter before giving me a nearly imperceptible nod. Message received.

My focus is drawn back to the great hall, where dozens of Adrithia's nobility scrutinize my every breath.

I fold my arms in front of me. "In addition, if we refuse to send Aric, the king implies there will be steep consequences for the Astrellian alliance."

The nobility stirs with gasps and whispers. I'm fully aware that I need to put an end to this trial before their unease becomes unrest.

Following Mother and Aislinn's advice, we have to honor this demand, even though the thought of doing so makes me break out in a cold sweat. I won't risk more Adrithian lives because of one spy. There's only one thing to do. As voices raise around me, I turn slowly and head back towards the dais. Aislinn stays by my side.

I take my time, allowing the din in the room to reach its crescendo before I ascend the steps and pivot to face the court. I stand there, in front of my throne, watching and waiting as one by one, the nobles notice my attention and fall silent. When their silence lasts three sweet seconds, I speak, "Aric Vernier, you have been found guilty of treason against Adrithia. However, it appears your loyalties have never been to our kingdom, but to another."

Aric finally lifts his head, and his sad eyes, reminiscent of a dog's, bore into mine. What a fitting analogy for him now. Someone else's dog.

"I want his life," I say loudly, clearly. I take a deep breath, savoring this next part, watching him squirm. For my father. For all those deaths that are on his hands. "But I will accept his banishment. He will be returned to Hotharia, and will never again be allowed to set foot in Adrithia."

The nobles seem to agree with the sentence, since several start clapping. Aric's tense muscles relax with what I can only imagine is relief. I hope he realizes how lucky he is. He gets to have his cake and eat it, too.

I turn to my sister, who gives me a questioning glance, and address her with a raised voice for all to hear. "Aislinn, I charge you with delivering Aric Vernier to the Hotharian border. There is no one I trust more with this task. Take as many guards as you see fit, and return before Father's resting ceremony."

Aislinn's brows pinch together, but she quickly masters herself and bows low, putting on an act for the benefit of those around us. But later I'm sure I'll hear all about this. "Yes, Your Majesty."

With everything settled, I motion guards forward to take Aric back to the dungeon. He goes in silence, with only a few jeers following him. It used to be customary to bombard guilty persons with rotten fruit, but Mother put a stop to it shortly after she married Father. She claimed it attracted ants. And no one wants ants.

Once Aric is out of sight, I dismiss the court, watching as they filter out. A few nobles give me respectful nods as they go, but most ignore me, exiting the hall and talking amongst themselves. Mother gives a quick nod and exits through the back of the hall. I'm about to follow her when one of the nobles breaks away from the retreating pack, a woman in her mid-thirties who I don't recognize. Her long, light brown hair is bound in a knot at the back of her head and she approaches with a tentative smile. Aislinn subtly moves closer to me, gripping the hilt of her sword.

"That's far enough, Lady Grimhart," she says, warning sharpening her tone.

Lady Grimhart startles, but seems to remember herself and drops into a low, clumsy curtsy, her posture far from perfect. "Your Majesty."

"Rise, please," I gesture to her and she stands.

She straightens and folds her hands in front of her, wringing her fingers together. "I apologize for approaching you this way, but I've been hoping for a chance to speak with you since the battle at the coast."

I stiffen somewhat, but give her a nod to continue.

"I wanted to thank you," she says, and I don't miss the tears welling up in her amber eyes. "You saved my son."

"I...what?" I ask, dumbfounded.

She gives me a wobbly smile. "My son is a captain who marched south with you. He was injured near the end of the battle, pierced through the side with a cursed arrow, and you healed him. Because of you, he came home to me. I am forever in your debt."

Her words are like an anchor, dragging me down into the seas of my memory. There were so many injured that day, so many I healed, that I can't say I remember him. For every person I saved, it felt like five more perished before I had the chance to intervene. My hands begin to tremble at my sides as I remember blood soaking the grass, the screams of dying men and women, the vicious waves as Father collapsed the earth into the sea, and as he fell into the frothy-

"Is your son well?" I ask, and even to my ears, my voice sounds a bit too loud, too disjointed.

"Oh, yes, he is. He's back in Sandral with the rest of our main forces, healthy as he was before he left, and it's all thanks to you. We're so lucky to have you as our queen. Of course, it's terrible what happened to your father. King Devon was a great man. But I think Adrithia is in good hands."

I try to reciprocate her warmth, her kindness, but all I can manage is a stiff nod and a wobbly upturn of my lips.

"I appreciate the confidence, Lady Grimhart," I manage to say before my throat closes with the emotions raging through me. Wispy shadows twirl around my feet and I force myself to grab the tendrils in my mind and wrench them back into their natural places.

"Please, Your Majesty, call me Tessa. I hope you know I mean it about being in your debt. If there's anything I can do for you at court, if you need an ally, I'm here."

She gives me one last kind smile before nodding her head and leaving.

I exhale the long breath I didn't realize I'd been holding. The coil of darkness unwinds when I allow my shoulders to droop.

Ash gives me a gentle bump with her shoulder, as if to reassure me that she's still here. "I didn't realize Lady Grimhart's son was in the battle with us. She's not the most influential person at court, but she holds some sway within her circle, mostly the young widows. Her husband died a few years ago from some illness, I believe."

"She's lucky I was able to help her son. There were so many I couldn't save," I bite out, thinking back to the healing tents, and the cots with dirty sheets covering the still bodies underneath.

My sister studies me through her long eyelashes. "Your power meant everything to some of them. No, you couldn't save everyone, but you saved a lot of them. I'm so proud of you for that."

I scoff. "Proud of me? What is there to be proud of, Aislinn?" I don't even realize I've raised my voice until I see some of the guards take a few wary steps back, giving us a semblance of privacy. I shake my head, barely containing my rage and the darkness that once again springs to life, fueled by my emotions. I shove the lid on my power closed, sealing it with sheer will. Gods, I can feel it fighting back, like it senses my anger and wants to hurt the person who put it there. But what if that person is my sister? No, I won't even entertain that thought.

My feet move, backing up a few steps, putting much-needed distance between us. I need to get a hold of myself before something happens that I can't take back.

"El, please talk to me," Ash pleads, closing the distance between us again. "Of course I'm proud of you. You handled today so well, and you've been doing great-,"

A bitter laugh escapes me. "Oh yeah, I'm doing so great. I've somehow managed to make an enemy of the entire kingdom of Hotharia and one of the most powerful families within our own court. Really doing well. On top of that, I let Father die, and wasn't strong enough to save many of our soldiers. I'm really living up to the dismal expectations everyone's set upon me since the damned Gods chose me instead of you. I don't think anyone believed I'd make it off the mountain alive, so I suppose the expectations for my rule were on the ground to begin with. As long as I don't get everyone in Adrithia murdered by the end of my reign, I guess I'll be doing all right."

Aislinn flinches like I've just hit her. "Elana, what happened to Father wasn't your fault. You didn't let him die. And our warriors didn't die because you weren't strong enough. They died to keep our Kingdom safe. You can't keep harboring this guilt. It's going to eat you alive."

My fragile control nearly snaps as I whirl to face her, snakes of darkness surrounding my legs, ready to strike. I force them back down, into a puddle at my feet. I grit my teeth against the effort, sure I'm going to slip. I need to get her away from me in case something happens. Words fly from my mouth before I have the chance to stop them. "Easy for you to say. I don't see you wracked with guilt over this. Even though you stood there, too, on that cliff. Ash you're the best among us, and you just stood there with me and watched as our Father was murdered."

The blow hits home, and Aislinn stumbles back, mouth agape. She looks at me like she's seeing me for the first time. She turns away and shuts her eyes. White hot regret closes my throat at the sight of her tears trailing down her cheeks. I reach forward, trying to close the distance between us, to apologize, because Gods how could I say something like that, but this time she takes several steps back.

"Father made a decision. He did what he thought was right to keep us and Adrithia safe. We have to find it within ourselves to live with his actions." She wipes her eyes with the back of her hand and turns away.

"Now if you'll excuse me, Your Majesty, I need to prepare for my trip to Hotharia with the traitor."

She storms from the great hall without another word or a glance behind her.

# CHAPTER SEVEN

## AISLINN

'*You stood there and watched'*, Elana's words ring through my mind as I run laps around the castle. I sweat out my frustration, my anger, my hurt. I'm on my fifth lap when the afternoon rain rolls in, cooling my heated body and sending me inside to seek a bath. I drip water up the elaborate stone staircase and down the hall to my suite. If Mother could see me now, she'd be red-faced and shrieking at the mess I'm making. Thankfully, though, I see no one as I trudge through the castle, purposely picking a route that allows me to avoid my sister.

Inside my rooms I immediately strip off my drenched clothes and throw them in a heaping pile on the floor. I spend the next hour in the bath, turning my fingers to prunes and doing my utmost to wash away the grime and my sister's words. She didn't mean what she said, she's lashing out because she's hurting. At least, that's what I tell myself. There's no use trying to speak with her about it before I leave. If there's one inherited trait among the women of the Sable family, it's that we're all stubborn as hells.

I hold my breath and sink to the bottom of the large copper tub. I think of the journey I'll be taking tomorrow, and who I'll bring with me, cataloging the royal guards. Matteo is a great warrior, and a trustworthy captain, perhaps one of the few people I can still say that about, therefore he should guard El. I'll take three guards with me, including Donne. That man can't be trusted to guard my sister, therefore I'll bring him along where I can keep an eye on him.

Standing up out of the cooling water, I wrap myself in my favorite dressing robe, sparing little time to dry off, and head to my desk to write assignments for the guards while I'm gone.

I stare at a messy stack of letters on my dark wood desk. A dried up ink pot sits on the edge of the worn wood and I spy the hawk's feather quill poking out of the parchment. I pick up the letter on top, taking in the familiar polished script.

*"Dear Aislinn,*

*Words cannot express how deeply sorry I am for your loss. Your father was a kind ruler, and I know you looked up to him. He will be missed dearly. I know my words won't ease your suffering, but know that I'm thinking of you often. May the Gods offer your family peace during this difficult time. If there's anything I can do to ease your sorrow, just say the word.*

*Yours,*

*Rayna"*

I trace her name, the elegant but strong curvature to her signature. Setting that letter aside with a tight chest, I shuffle through the pile, until I at last free the quill and the letter it has been resting on. A dried drop of ink stains the words I wanted desperately to reply to.

*"Dear Aislinn,*

*I don't know what to think anymore. You haven't responded to me in weeks. Rumors are abundant regarding your father's passing. I've heard it was murder by a senior member of your staff, I've heard it was demons from the Hells themselves, I've heard it was Hotharia. Did they really betray the alliance? My father is up in arms about it, locking down our border and preparing our army, but for what, we don't know.*

*Aislinn, I don't know why you've stopped responding, but if I've done something wrong please tell me. Whatever is going on, we can fix this together.*

*Yours,*

*Rayna"*


I wanted to reach out. I wanted nothing more than to throw good sense aside for once and allow myself to be weak, to be comforted by someone else. But even now I can't show weakness. I'm once again second in line for the throne. I need to be the strong one, since it's clear Elana is struggling. I have to be the solid foundation for our family. As much as I want Rayna to come here, or to go to her, I can't. So her letters have gone unanswered. Because I don't know how to lie to her and tell her everything's fine.

When I see her at Father's Resting Ceremony, I'll tell her what I haven't been able to put into writing.

With careful fingers, I roll up her letters and stuff them in the drawer. After too much time spent searching for usable ink, I give up the hunt and decide to verbally assign duties for the guards. I tie my wet hair into a braid and dress in my leathers before making my way to the yard where the guards should be performing their late afternoon training. They operate on a strict schedule, rotating positions around the grounds, guarding the dungeon, and now protecting my sister.

Captain Matteo runs the men and women through coordinated hand-to-hand drills, and as I approach, he gives me a swift, low bow. "Your Highness."

I wave him off with a grin. "Captain, how many times do I have to tell you to call me Aislinn?"

He gestures to the guards around him. "If I started calling you Aislinn in front of this lot, they'd think they could do the same. And I'd have to rattle more heads than I already do."

I give him a smirk. "I trust you to keep your charges in line, Matteo."

"An honor I'm happy to live up to," he jokes, his voice light with an accent that hints at his time along our western border. "Will you be training with us today ahead of your departure?"

He knows me too well. During long days of meetings and political maneuvering, there's nothing I love more than seeking out our top fighters for an intensive sparring session. There's something about the dance between two people, or more in some cases, that soothes me. Even better is the reverberating shockwave of steel striking steel. It's a grounding feeling, and one I desperately wish I had time for.

With much regret, I shake my head. "No, I've actually come to speak with you about the guard assignments while I'm gone."

"Of course," he says, waiting.

"I'll take Donne, Tallisa, and Gregory with me," I say. Tallisa and Gregory were both recently appointed to the guard by my mother and I want the chance to get to know them. "I want four guards assigned to my sister at all times until I return. Station them outside of her door at night. Only my mother, Rigel, and her lady's maid are allowed inside of her chambers. She's going to hate it, but it's for her safety. She might also order you to stand down or try to release you from your duty. You will not obey. You will not adhere to any of her requests to remove yourself or any of the guards from her side."

Knowing her, she'll try to connive her way out of having a guard. Seeing her command of the shadows, I have no doubt she can protect herself from known threats. But without her healing abilities, I worry she is vulnerable if caught off guard.

"Understood, Your Highness," Matteo says, and I have to roll my eyes at his formality. "When should l tell the three to be ready to travel?"

"We leave before dawn," I say, and he nods. "If any of them are late, they'll be mucking out the stables for a fortnight upon our return."

"I'll make sure they're ready."

"Thank you, Matteo," I turn to leave, but shouting has me turning around.

A man in fresh, stiff fighting leathers adorned excessively with silver yells at a much younger boy. My eyebrows narrow as I recognize a still-shouting Donne. "I told you not to hit my face, you absolute imbecile!"

"Perhaps you should have blocked better," the younger boy says. The urge to laugh halts when Donne growls a derogatory slur referencing the boy's red hair, and shoves him hard into the dirt. I make my way over to them, Matteo a shadow behind me. Donne pulls back his leg, and I lunge, putting myself between him and the boy, catching his swinging leg. His eyes go wide as I yank his booted foot to the side, causing him to lose his balance and tumble to the ground.

"Haven't you ever heard not to kick people while they're down, Donne?" I snarl, jamming my heel into the fleshy part of his throat and putting some of my weight behind it.

He sputters and turns red, smacking at my leg, then at the ground in surrender. I release him and take a step back, hands on my hips as he gets to his feet, breathing hard.

"You-," he huffs out, "you could have killed me."

"Could have, but didn't," I shrug. It would have been easy, but I refrain from telling him that. As I reminded him, there's no need to kick a man already down.

Donne's face goes redder, resembling a tomato. He jabs a finger in my direction. "I challenge you to a duel."

A slow smile spreads across my face at the prospect of a duel. To see what he's made of and work off some of the frustration I'm feeling. I have a lot to accomplish before leaving tomorrow, but I don't anticipate the duel will last long.

"Donne!" Matteo snaps. "You can't challenge Princess Aislinn. She's not part of the guard."

I hold up my hand in his direction. "Captain, it's all right. I accept the challenge."

I've known Matteo long enough to know his skeptical look isn't out of concern for me. After a moment of silently pleading with me to reconsider, likely so he won't have to clean up the mess afterwards, he sighs. "Very well. Weapons?"

I jerk my head in Donne's direction, giving him the right to choose if he'd like to be beaten by my fists or my sword.

"No weapons," Donne says with a smirk. "Let's see how good you are without your famous sword."

It's an effort to hold back my smile. If he thinks I'm any less dangerous unarmed, he's in for a nasty surprise.

We move into the nearest pitch. The training guards make room for us, each stopping their respective matches to stare between us.

I roll my neck, wringing free a few pops as I face down my opponent. He's taller than me by at least a head, but moves awkwardly, like a bull unaware of its own size. As the son of wealthy aristocrats, with private guards of their own, he shouldn't have had any problems securing extensive private training, but I know from years of watching his fights with our castle guards that money doesn't equate to talent.

"Ready?" Matteo asks us. I nod. Donne grunts.

"Princess, I promise to leave your face untouched so you can still secure an advantageous betrothal for the kingdom."

His words slide off me and I pay them no mind. He starts to circle me in the pitch, kicking up dust with his heavy steps. I watch for signs of weakness or previous injury. He bends his knees slightly and he launches himself at me. At least, that's probably what it feels like he's doing. His advance is so slow that I almost sigh before moving to counter it.

He opens his arms as if to grab me, but I spin with ease under his meaty limbs, jabbing my elbow hard into his lower back. I pivot and face him quicker than he can turn and kick out his knee, sending him to the dirt. He yells out in frustration and recovers quickly, but not fast enough to catch me off guard. He throws out several enraged punches, which I easily avoid. He's coming at me with everything he has, but I dance around him on light feet, letting him wear himself out while testing his defenses with superficial punches and kicks. As I feared, they're severely lacking.

By the time he's panting, I've barely warmed up. He moves in for another attack, but stumbles as the knee I kicked earlier gives out under his weight. I decide to put him out of his misery with several sharp blows to his stomach, and a jab to his jaw. Donne lets out a wheeze and collapses to the ground, breathing heavily.

I stand over him, staring down with disappointment. From someone who has been training for most of his life, I was expecting more. His eyelids flutter open, and he has the sense to look embarrassed. I lean over and offer him my hand. He may be a narcissistic asshole, but he's still a member of the guard, and a citizen of Adrithia.

His eyes flit back and forth between my hand and my face. He reaches out his own and I grasp it, bending my knees to help pull him to his feet.

"Now that's been settled, as a senior, high-ranking guard, you should be setting a positive example for the new recruits, not instigating petty squabbles," I say, dropping his hand when he comes to his feet, looking thoroughly flummoxed. "Now, clean yourself up and prepare for a week-long journey. We leave for the Hotharian border before daybreak."

The rest of the evening passes quickly. I take my dinner in my chambers as I reorganize my pack about a dozen times, folding and refolding essential clothes and making sure extra daggers are within reach.

I pace back and forth in front of the door to the hallway, a thousand thoughts running through my head. I should try to talk to my sister before I leave, but what if she won't see me? What if she really does blame me for our father's death? I'm not sure I'm ready to hear that again.

After hours of aimless pacing and picking at my fingernails, I finally collapse in bed.

#####

"Aric, time to face your consequences," I say, rattling several heavy lengths of chains in my hands. I'm flanked by Tallisa and Gregory, but they hang back slightly as requested. I have no reason to think Aric will make this more unpleasant than it has to be.

As expected, he stands from his dirty, musty cot and holds his hands out. I snap the manacles around his wrists. I shackle his ankles next, leaving him just enough chain to walk.

"Let's go," I say, grabbing his elbow and leading him from the cell that's been his home for the past few weeks.

He moves slowly up the stairs, his muscles slightly atrophied from the lack of exercise in the space he's been confined to. We head out a back exit that leads to the yard and stables. Five horses are saddled and ready for our journey. By the light of many torches, Donne helps the stablehands attach two large black horses to a prison cart. I'm taking no chances with this transport. If he doesn't make it to Hotharia, it could have deadly ramifications for us all.

We'll travel swiftly but safely. Aric will be in chains the entire time. We'll use main roads and only stop when necessary. I'm not sure what awaits us at the Hotharian border, but I will see this order through. Aric will be returned to his homeland, relatively unharmed.

I lead the traitor up the few rickety steps and through the door of the prison cart. He sits sullenly on the wood bench and stares at the castle beyond the door.

"If you're looking for my sister, you won't be seeing her," I say cooly. "She doesn't know we're leaving this early."

Aric's blue eyes meet mine, and I'm struck by how similar they are to Prince Calder's. The same icy hues and long blonde lashes. How none of us realized their relation before astounds me. For years, we only saw what he wanted us to see. A stableboy turned guard turned close friend. "I don't deserve a goodbye."

At least we agree on that.

I lock the door of the cart and stash the key inside the inner pocket of my leather armor. I chose the black leather for its comfort on a long journey. The metal armor I wore on the battlefield is no doubt sturdier and safer, but it's also heavier and cumbersome. We need to travel light to make it back in time for my father's Resting Ceremony.

My horse snorts when I pat his neck. "Ready for another trek across kingdoms, Hector?"

He nudges his big head into my shoulder and I laugh, taking that as a confirmation.

Without further pomp and circumstance we mount up, Donne at the reins of the prison cart, and make our way east.

# CHAPTER EIGHT

## ELANA

"What do you mean my sister's gone?" I demand, whirling to face Senara.

She visibly pales in the morning light that streams through one of my sitting room windows. "I'm sorry, Your Majesty, but Princess Aislinn left before dawn."

My heart plummets to my feet. How could she leave without saying goodbye?

Tears prick at my eyes, and I lower myself to my settee, folding my hands together, staring at them as if they possess the power to whisk me away to wherever Aislinn is. Of course she left without giving me the chance to apologize. The words I spoke to her left a leaden pit in my stomach. I don't blame her for Father's death, so why did I say that? Gods, I feel horrible. I must be the worst sister.

A heavy weight sits on me, making it nearly impossible to want to move.

Senara brings me breakfast when I make no moves to eat at the table I shared with Aislinn, and Rigel brings a stack of parchment, a quill, and an ink pot to me mid-morning. I take care of simple state matters and leave the rest for when I can discuss them with my mother, who has also apparently left the castle grounds, visiting the temple for the first time since Father's death.

With nothing else to do, and no motivation to train, I head back to bed, where I spend the rest of the day.

The next morning, Mother is gone again, and I have little to do besides stare at the walls of my chamber. I lie on my bed and practice a few moves with my shadows, turning them corporeal and incorporeal at the blink of an eye. I'm getting better at wielding them. The shadows respond with the same dexterity as my hands. They feel more like an extension of myself than a separate entity. They're strongest at night, and weaker during the day, but no less dangerous.

I spend the third day after Aislinn's departure in my rooms as well. Senara has to coax me into a bath, but there's no reason to leave my chambers for anything else.

On the fourth day, I'm still in bed at midday when the doors to my suite slam open. I sit up, immediately draping my hands in shadow, only to recognize my mother's furious form silhouetted in the doorway.

"Excuse me? No daughter of mine, nonetheless the future Queen of this Kingdom is allowed to wallow in her own self-pity on my watch," she storms in like a tempest, ripping the blankets from my bed. "Get your lazy ass out of bed this instant, or so help me I will order a dozen buckets of cold water dumped over your head."

Well, that does it. I learned at a young age that my mother means what she says, and always follows through on her threats.

I'm up and half-clothed by the time Senara sheepishly shuffles in to help me wrap my chest. I've chosen my comfortable training clothes again today, not sure I could handle a corset right now. My mother hovers in the sitting room while Senara ties my hair in two braids.

"Would you care to visit the temple with me today, Elana?" Mother asks when I emerge from my bedroom. Her eyes roam over my form, and whatever she sees hardens her gaze.

"No," I reply. I don't wish for a repeat of the last time I visited.

Mother sighs but doesn't argue. Instead, she produces a rolled-up parchment from her billowy sleeve. I wonder how long it's been hiding there.

"Duke Lyons is requesting our company for tea at his estate. It's my belief that he will attempt to bring up a potential marriage between you and his son once again," she says.

Biting back the urge to groan, I opt for the silent eye roll instead. "I thought I made myself clear in court, but it seems I'll have to say this again. I decline. Both the offer for tea and the proposal. I want nothing to do with Percival or his father."

"Elana, be reasonable," Mother argues, "you're about to be an unwed queen. We have to be serious about your marriage prospects. These are uncertain times, and you must have an heir. If you refuse to even consider it, you put the entire kingdom at risk. Our people are looking to the crown for strength and stability. We must give them that."

I grind my teeth together, holding back the curse words so they don't accidentally slip out. "If the people only wanted a broodmare they should have crowned a horse. I refuse to be a ruler in title alone, someone who does nothing but pass on a title."

The parchment my mother holds crinkles in her hand as she squeezes it. "Did you think ruling would be easy, my naive daughter? What do you think will happen if you die during the next battle, a very real possibility at this point considering we still don't know who allied with Hotharia. If you die and there's no one to pass on the power to, the other kingdoms would destroy us. They would claim our land for their own and our people would be an afterthought."

"Aidan, Rian, and Rayna would never let that happen," I say, waving my hand dismissively at the thought that any of my friends would betray Adrithia.

Mother scoffs. "Oh please, Elana. You've known the heirs for a few months, and they're not even the ones sitting on the thrones. You don't know the monarchs like I do. Hotharia, especially, wouldn't hesitate to take advantage of our misfortune should it arise."

"Hotharia, sure, but the rest of the kingdoms? You're saying they'd all abandon the Astrellian Peace that quickly? They'd so easily scorn the treaty that has kept this continent unified and prosperous for nearly a thousand years."

"The Astrellian Peace is built upon a foundation that all kingdoms are equally powerful. There's balance in knowing this. A land without an elemental power, or with two," she gives me a pointed look, "throws everything into chaos. To correct this imbalance, the other kingdoms could try to bring our land under their rule and we'd be helpless to stop it."

"That's not going to happen, Mother," I say with a firm shake of my head.

She grips my hand hard in hers. "That's what your father said to me right before he went galloping off to war. 'That's not going to happen, Maris,' and yet, he never returned. And now we don't even have a corpse to bury to commend him to Goddess Avani."

Tears fill her eyes, but her hands remain tight, almost painfully so, on mine. I try to pull back, but her grip is like iron. This is the most emotion I've ever seen my mother reveal. Her usual mask of indifference seems abandoned.

"Elana, I refuse to lose you and watch this kingdom fall to ruin. The fate of every person in Adrithia is our family's responsibility. We must do everything we can to secure the Sable lineage."

"Now," she continues, barreling forward like she's reading from a parchment, unaware or unconcerned that I feel the walls closing in around me, a keening noise ringing in my ears that sounds an awful lot like screaming. The shadows at my feet spring to life at my discomfort, swirling out from my impractical slippers like ripples on a pond. "I know you were never fond of the duke's son, but you were all set to marry him before the trials. What changed?

Aidan's smirking face pops into my head at that exact moment, completely unbidden, and my face starts to heat. "I changed," I whisper, "my position changed, and I thought I finally gained some control of my life."

Mother blinks. "I agree that your recently elevated position certainly means you deserve better than a duke's son. There are several princes of the other kingdoms who look promising, perhaps from Melinor, or Ocarin, just not the crown prince, obviously. You two seemed to be on...friendly terms before the battle at the coast, but then you sent him away. A smart move, as a match between you two would never work. I shall compile a list of eligible princes and when they're here for your coronation we'll make introductions."

The room darkens as my shadows begin to grow. I'm not sure whether it's her blatant disregard of Aidan or the way she discusses throwing me at other princes, but it's an effort to bring the darkness back to heel. "Mother, you're not listening to me," I take a long deep breath, using the moment to calm my racing heart. Then I exhale and stare into her hazel eyes. "I appreciate all you've taught me. Your tenacity knows no bounds, but right now I need you to understand that I will never, ever marry someone against my will. I won't have children against my will. I won't be furthering the

Sable line against my will. And right now, the only way you could get me wed is against my will. When or if it happens, it'll be on my own timeline and for my own reasons."

I clear my throat and finally pull my hands from hers, stepping back. My chest heaves as I catch my breath, shocked that I stood my ground against my mother. Immediately the shadows lighten, sinking back into the corners and overlooked places of the room. I turn towards the window and peer out at the grounds, taking a few moments to ground myself and allow my rapid heartbeats to slow.

After several moments of silence, Mother takes a step to stand at my side. "You've never spoken to me like that before," she pauses, as if waiting for my response. When I give her none, she continues, "I've always thought you were weaker than your sister, but you've exceeded my expectations at every turn. From the time you were just an infant, tiny and fighting for every breath, until now, a grown woman, fighting for your future."

I shift uncomfortably on my feet, still gazing at the sunny gardens. The late season chrysanthemums are just starting to bloom.

"I don't agree with your choices, but I respect your resolve, and I will help you in whatever way I can for as long as I can. Elana," she says my name and I finally turn to her. She looks tired. Raw. Like she's wearing her emotions for the first time, and she doesn't quite know how to shoulder the burden. "I haven't been the most loving mother to you and Aislinn. My mother died when I was young and my childhood died with her. I didn't know how to be that doting parent I've seen others be, the way your father was when he had time. I'll try harder to fight for your well-being. Not what I think it should be, but what you want it to be. I don't say this enough, but I love you, daughter."

My breath hitches, and I barely repress a sob. I'd never realized it before, but these are the words I've been waiting to hear for years. "I love you, too, mother."

Her answering polished smile looks so much like Aislinn's it sends a pang of sadness through my heart. Gods, I miss her.

A knock at my door saves me from having to continue to make conversation, and Rigel enters, holding the day's stack of parchment.

His eyebrows raise when he spots my mother, but quickly recovers, giving her a swift bow after me. "Your Majesty, please forgive the intrusion. I have the day's correspondences."

I wave off his politeness. "Please, sit, Rigel. Let's go through them together."

Mother shifts and angles herself towards the door, moving a half step. "If you need me, I shall be in the-,"

"Of course I need you, Mother. Sit down," I gesture her to her spot on the settee. Rigel, who now that I think of it, I've never actually seen sitting, hovers by the edge of the armchair. He thumbs through the stack of parchment, reading off the first item of business. It's a land dispute between two minor lords. One of them accuses the other of stealing ten sheep, while another correspondence accuses the first lord of stealing the other's daughter. I fight back a groan. It's going to be a long day.

I shovel a large bite of steaming shepherd's pie into my mouth, nearly moaning at the taste. It's the first time I've had an appetite since Aislinn left. Mother convinced me to eat our evening meal together, so she's sitting to my right, at the head of the table, eating demurely and sighing in disapproval whenever I do something to offend her delicate manners.

"You could try not to sound like a giant while eating," she says curtly.

This bite I let out a long moan as I chew, chuckling as she scowls at me. "We're the only ones here, there's no reason to be perfectly proper right now. And besides, you've never seen a giant. They were wiped out centuries ago, so how would you know what they sound like?"

She flashes me an uncharacteristically mischievous grin. "Were they?"

My mouth drops open. "Weren't they?" I demand. To my knowledge, the elusive race of giants was killed centuries ago, along with the last of the shifters. But now that I know shifters are still alive, I suppose it's a possibility that the giants are, too. They were a peaceful race of farmers and gatherers that occupied shared stretches of land with dragons. The two species coexisted peacefully for generations, giants and the great winged serpents. According to our history, the giants experienced a plague which nearly decimated their entire species. To worsen matters, humans also played a part in their demise by pushing them to the boundaries of where they could eke out an existence. Fighting wasn't in their nature, so instead of forcibly taking the lands that could sustain them and saving their race, they died out over time. The last colony was said to have existed west of the great Taishan mountain range in Aaranor.

Mother lifts her eyebrows at me, a playful smile on her painted lips.

"Are you saying that the giants still exist?" I stare open mouthed at her.

Amusement shines in her eyes as she takes a long, drawn-out breath to answer, "-"

The double doors to the informal dining room burst open, splintering part of the frame. I jump to my feet, a whip of shadow already within my grasp. I hear a utensil clatter to a plate as Mother also stands. It takes me a moment to recognize Matteo, the captain of our castle guard.

"Your Majesty," Matteo huffs, bending over his knees to catch his breath for a few sharp intakes. "There's a fire at our armory."

# Chapter Nine

## Elana

I sprint through the castle on pure adrenaline. Matteo is by my side, and a host of guards follow behind. When I first realized they were assigned to watch me like a hawk days ago I was furious. Even more furious when I found out it was on Aislinn's orders and they wouldn't listen to me. But, as I race to the stables and my horse, I'm almost grateful. A few guards stayed behind to protect my mother, but ten are now at my heels. More hands to haul buckets of water if my shadows fail to contain the flames.

Mother tried to stop me from going, saying it was the city guard's job to put out the fire, but there's a chance I can do something to help, so I refuse to sit back and do nothing.

We burst through the castle's side door and race across the yard to the stables. A dozen horses are already saddled outside the stables, with another household guard holding a familiar white mottled mare. I barrel towards Misty, and Matteo helps me mount with a speed Aislinn would be proud of. It's a miracle I decided to skip the dress today and wear comfortable linen pants and a billowy tunic, otherwise I wouldn't be able to ride in a saddle, and we'd waste precious time readying a carriage.

Once all the guards are mounted, Matteo turns to me and says, "Your Majesty, please ride in the middle. We'll lead the way."

I give an affirming nod, since I don't know the quickest way to the armory. Our horses set off at a gallop, and I situate Misty in the center of the pack, following Matteo's lead. Once we pass the castle gates I see the sprawled out city below us. The armory is on the far side of the city. It's dusk, but even the fading light doesn't mask the golden glow and dark smoke in the distance. Shit, even from this far away the fire looks massive.

We ride swiftly through the cobbled streets. Matteo and those in front shout warnings to clear the way. For the first time, I wish I was granted Rian's ability to use air. I would fly us to the armory in less than half the time. There's no point in dwelling on what could have been. I focus on staying in the saddle and keeping Misty in line with the others. She's not the fastest horse, but she has good endurance.

The closer we get to the fire, the more panic fills the streets. A few times our group has to stop abruptly and wait for carts or shouting people to move on by. Bright orange flames flicker above homes, and people frantically dart around with buckets.

We turn a corner to a particularly busy street, and intense heat buffets us. Misty startles, and I run a reassuring hand down her neck. From the front of the group, I see Matteo dismount and sprint to me. He offers me a hand getting down, but I manage to dismount without trouble. A marked improvement from a few months ago, when I bruised my knees and nearly twisted an ankle every time I jumped off Misty.

One of the guards leads our horses away, hopefully somewhere the smoke and heat won't be a problem.

A brigade of guards with buckets of water rush past us towards the blaze. Puffs of hot steam rise from the flaming wreckage where they toss them. I take stock of the armory and the nearby buildings. The structure of the armory is brick, but there must be plenty of wood inside to provide kindling. Where there used to be glass windows, there is now only flame. The wooden door is long gone, revealing a smoke-filled inferno inside. My attention turns to the surrounding buildings. Mostly brick or stone barracks, next to a wood tavern and homes on the other side. If the fire jumps, it could be catastrophic.

A city soldier runs up to us. She's wearing leather armor and has a sword at her side. "Captain Matteo, what are you d-," her eyes shift to me and she stops mid-question, giving me a deep bow, "Your Majesty, apologies."

"Please, there's no time for that," I say, "we're here to help."

The woman straightens and Matteo makes a rushed introduction, "this is the head of the city guard, Giselle Leonhart."

"Do you have a plan, Your Majesty, or are you just here to take in the sights?" Giselle has to yell to be heard over the sounds around us.

Until this moment, I wasn't sure I had a plan, only a fool's hope. "I'll try to contain the fire, keep it from moving to other houses. I'm," I hesitate, unsure if I should admit it, but better temper everyone's expectations right away, "not sure it'll work, but I'll try."

Matteo doesn't hesitate, doesn't appear disappointed. He raises his fist to his heart and nods. "We'll be by your side."

Giselle looks less convinced. I don't miss the skeptical look she gives me, the head-to-toe assessment, and the tightening of her lips after she's done.

I ignore her and focus on Matteo, giving him a nod back, moving closer to the searing heat of the flames. At my silent command, shadows spring up from everywhere. They're abundant and easy to control at this dusk hour. The surrounding area lightens as I steal the deep shadows from every dark nook, cranny, and corner. I gather the darkness around the burning armory like a protective circle and then build a bubble around it from the ground up.

The screaming and scrambling nearby cuts off. I hear someone shout, "it's the Crown Princess Elana! She's here to save our homes!"

"Our queen has come!" Another cry joins the first, and I see people out of my peripherals gathering behind me. Matteo takes a not-so-subtle step closer to me, eyeing the crowd warily.

"We'll take care of the people," Giselle says, drawing the sword at her hip and waving her hand at a few other city guards.

"You will not harm them," I say through gritted teeth as the wall of shadow slowly raises around the fire.

Giselle stares incredulously at me. "We need to be stern in deterring them from interfering."

I shake my head. "You and your guards will not threaten or otherwise harm these people, Captain Giselle. That's an order."

She lets out an indignant scoff and marches away, muttering something about weakness as she goes. It's only due to the roar of the fire that I can't hear the rest of her insult.

"Your Majesty, are you sure that's wise? The citizens are in a panic. Strong emotions like fear can easily turn to violence," Matteo says from my side.

I consider his words, but I still don't believe a show of force is the correct answer. "Put yourself in their shoes, Captain. These people are frightened. If you saw your home about to burn down, would you appreciate a group of city guards raising weapons at you and shouting threats when all you're trying to do is keep your entire world from going up in flames?"

Matteo's quiet for a few heartbeats. "I see," he says, "you're right. They could use some kindness right now."

"Exactly. We owe them empathy at the very least."

A sudden blast of heat breaks through a weak point in the shadow wall, and I redouble my efforts, shoring up the shield I'm creating. I'm hoping I can choke out the flames this way, reducing the fire's access to the air around us.

This is the most I've ever wielded the darkness. I'm starting to get light-headed from the effort. I raise my arms to direct the power as the bubble of shadow seals itself above the flames, locking the noise away with it.

A hush falls upon the crowd as we all stare, waiting for the flames to either die out or the darkness to disperse. My arms start to shake, but I hold them aloft, refusing to let the shadows fall. I have no idea how long it'll take to starve a fire.

"Wow," Matteo whispers from next to me, "your gift is incredible."

I don't spare the effort it'll take to respond, so I flash a quick, tired smile instead. Sweat drips down my forehead, stinging my eyes as it goes, but I still don't lower my arms. I feel the flames licking the top of the bubble, as if they're trying to escape, trying to find sustenance to feed them. I have to hold out a bit longer.

Slowly, so slowly, I feel the heat start to recede inside the bubble. The fire doesn't rage against the darkness anymore, and I take several deep long breaths.

"Sir," Giselle shouts from behind me, "you need to back up, give our queen some space. Wait, get back here!"

I hear the sound of swords being unsheathed, and Matteo leaps to protect my back.

"Halt! You may go no further," he says in a dangerously low commanding voice that I've never heard him use before.

The man must pause, because Matteo doesn't move. I try to keep my focus pinned to the dying fire, not to the distractions around me.

"Elana, if you wanted to get my attention, all you had to do was send a messenger hawk, not start a fire in the middle of your capital," the stranger says from behind me.

My body has an immediate, almost involuntary reaction to that smirking voice. My head whips around and my eyes nearly bug out of my head. "Aidan?" I cry.

At my momentary distraction, the shadows flicker, and the fire takes the opportunity to explode out of the cage I've trapped it in. I shield my face against the searing heat, but Aidan extends one hand and closes his fist. The flames immediately gutter out.

I suck in breaths like a greedy fish until I'm sure I can form a complete sentence. "What the hells are you doing here Aidan?" I snap, facing him down with my hands on my hips, still sweating and breathing hard.

Matteo and Giselle look between the two of us, as if trying to determine if the prince is a threat they can handle or not. Whatever they decide has them keeping their distance, but I catch Matteo's wary gaze and Giselle's openly curious one.

"Here I was, thinking I would help an allied kingdom out," Aidan says, with a twinkle of amusement in his expression. I openly glare at him.

"Not here, as in right here. Here as in, in this city and not halfway back to Luxoria?" I grit my teeth to avoid saying anything that would lead him to think I actually want him here.

"Ah, well your sister invited me to stick around and enjoy the sights of Sandral until the Resting Ceremony. So, not wanting to disappoint any princess, here I am."

"Aislinn asked you to stay?" My arms fall to my sides in shock. When did she speak to him?

"Yes."

Why would Aislinn invite him to stay? It's not like she's overly fond of Ocarin's crown prince. She tolerates him because of me, but she always called him the dangerous heir, the one to watch out for. So what changed?

"As a visiting prince, you're more than welcome to stay wherever you like within the city," I say, not wanting to appear ungrateful to the person who just put out the fire with ease.

Aidan dips into a dramatic bow, but a playful smirk tugs the corner of his lip up. "Of course, Your Majesty."

To my complete dismay, the sight of that smirk doesn't enrage me further, but rather sends a warm feeling to my stomach. Gods, get a grip, Elana. This is the man that kept me from saving my father on the battlefield. I can't afford to get warm fuzzies over him. Besides, it seems awfully convenient for him to show up right when there's a massive fire. A chord of suspicion winds its way through my stomach.

"It wasn't you, was it?" I ask quietly, almost regretting the question, but needing to know the answer. At Aidan's raised eyebrows, I elaborate, "did you start the fire?"

His playful demeanor sours, eyes darkening as he levels a stare at me. "No, Elana. I saw the smoke from my inn and-," he cuts himself off, eyes going wide before he lunges at me.

"Get down!" Aidan tackles me to the ground, rolling so he takes the brunt of the impact, but my breath still leaves me in a *whoosh*. A wall of fire erupts where we were standing, and cinders rain down on us, black pieces of metal pinging off the cobblestones. Pulsing black arrowheads. Aidan's fire stopped their trajectory and turned the arrow shafts to ashes, but the cursed arrowheads were unaffected.

"We're under attack, get to cover!" Giselle shouts from behind us, and boots pound the ground as guards scramble. Several people start screaming, and I silently hope no one was pierced by a black-tipped arrow.

Aidan helps me to my feet, then draws his sword that I didn't notice before. "If I lure the enemies out, can you purify their weapons?"

My heart plummets as I shake my head. "No, I can't use any healing or any light powers right now." I don't know why I tell him so nonchalantly when it took days to tell Aislinn. It feels right in a way I can't take time to explore.

His brows furrow, but he nods, then his gaze travels over my simple outfit. "Do you have your daggers or any weapons on you?"

Fuck. I hadn't even thought of bringing my twin daggers when I left. Realizing my error, my fingers feel empty without them. I shake my head again at him. "I didn't bring anything with me."

"Okay," he says, nodding as if to reassure me, or maybe himself, "I'll get them out into the open, see if you can use your shadows to disarm them. Don't let them get close to you."

I nod and take up a position behind him, plunging into my well of power and bringing a host of darkness with me. Once again the shadows around us bend to my will, snapping to my side, circling me in a protective ring.

Scrambling feet above us has me looking to the tops of the barracks and surrounding homes. "Aidan, they're on the rooftops."

His gaze snaps up as he spots an enemy, using a whip of fire to pluck him right off the slanted roof. The man hits the ground and my shadows descend upon him, wrapping him up like a snake and ripping the bow and arrows from his hands. Another smoking body falls near the first one, and I repeat the steps, disarming, then immobilizing.

Arrows whiz past Aidan's head, and he snarls at a soldier standing in the wreckage of the armory. A burst of fire incinerates the man before he has a chance to draw his bow again.

Swords clash behind me, and I turn, frantically looking for Matteo. I spot him, dragging a guard to the cover of a nearby stone building. He catches my eye and my heart lurches at the grief I see plastered on his face.

Giselle lets out a war cry, brandishing her greatsword as she meets a soldier in the street. Through a series of swift moves, she eviscerates him. I'm impressed. She's almost as deadly as my sister.

"Elana, focus!" Aidan's voice brings me back to my senses as he tugs me out of the way of a flying spear. The man's body is ashes before I blink. Two more enemies stand on opposite rooftops, arrows poised. I raise a solid wall of shadow right as they fly. The darkness swallows up the arrows, spitting them to the ground at our feet. Aidan sends two blasts of flame out, and the enemies go up in smoke.

We search the rooftops and alleyways, but no more arrows or soldiers come for us.

Giselle appears by my side. "I think we've got them all, Your Majesty."

I give her what I hope is an appreciative smile. "Good work, Captain. Can you have these two," I gesture at the enemies bound on the ground, "brought to the castle so we can question them?"

She nods and stalks off, barking orders at her men. I find Matteo crouching over someone lying on the cobblestone. I rush over to them and recognize one of my main guards from the last few days. There's a bloody hole in his neck. Blood slowly drips from the wound to the already large puddle on the ground. He's beyond saving, even if I could use my healing powers.

"I'm sorry, Matteo," I say, tears welling up in my eyes.

Matteo draws in a long breath. "It was a quick death. That's all we can hope for in the end."

"There could be more of them hiding. We need to leave here." Aidan hovers behind me.

I take stock of our surroundings, searching for enemies. Smoke still billows from the remains of the armory, but it's noticeably less than before the attack. Other than the horses, my small host of castle guards and the several dozen city guards, the streets are empty. The citizens must have fled when the fighting started. But Aidan's not wrong. We're out in the open and could be ambushed at any time.

Matteo stands. "Right. Let's go, Your Majesty." He wipes his bloody sword clean on his sleeve before sheathing it.

He nods to Giselle, who gives a sharp nod back. She's busy wrapping chains around the two enemies we've managed to keep alive.

Misty and a few other horses are led over. Matteo bends over and gently shuts the fallen guard's eyes. He raises his voice to address two nearby guards, "see that Jean gets to his family, but don't touch his wound, and instruct the family not to as well. We don't know if the poison is still in his system."

I watch as two of the castle guards split off from the group and move to the fallen guard, Jean, and carefully lift him, moving to their horses.

"Elana, do you need a hand?" Aidan asks me, and I realize he's asking if I need help getting into Misty's saddle. I consider the offer a moment before nodding.

The ride back through Sandral is a somber one. There are few people in the streets now, luckily for us, but Matteo still makes me ride in the middle of our group. Aidan rides his own gigantic black stallion next to me, but neither of us say anything. This is the second assassination attempt in mere days, and without Aidan having come to our rescue with the fire, I don't know how things would have turned out.

"You don't seem particularly surprised with what's happened. The enemy has tried that before, haven't they?" Aidan finally asks.

I sigh. "Yes, one of them infiltrated my court and tried to assassinate me a few days ago."

"And you still came out here today, alone?" Aidan's voice is a deadly growl.

"I'm not alone," I snap, "there's a host of guards with me."

Aidan scoffs. "And none of them are your sister. Gods, Elana, if you can't at least take Aislinn with you while you're gallivanting across the city, then-,"

"Aislinn isn't in Adrithia," I cut him off.

His head whips to me, and I catch his eyes, staring at me with a slightly open mouth. "Where is she?"

The last time I heard his voice this dangerously low he was threatening Calder's life on the Gods Peaks.

"I instructed her to take that traitor Aric Vernier back to Hotharia," I say.

"Let me get this straight," Aidan says through clenched teeth, "you sent your strongest warrior away before your coronation while you can't even use half of your power, only days after your first assassination attempt?"

I clear my throat and glance around at the other guards, but no one seems to be paying attention. They're all either looking around for signs of danger or whispering amongst themselves. "Yes, but keep your damn voice down about my power, Aidan. No one else knows."

He pinches the bridge of his nose with his fingers and groans. "Gods spare me from this stubborn princess and her reckless decisions."

"Excuse me? Who the hells do you think you are to call me reckless?" I snarl at him, feeling heat rush to my face.

A smirk dances across his face. "I'm the one who deals with the conse-quences of your recklessness, so I think I've earned the right to call you that."

"When?" I say, genuinely trying to think of a time that impacted him in any way.

"Hmmm, how about the time you jumped in between Calder's and my attacks? Or when you threw down your weapons in front of the shadow creatures during the last trial? Or when you pushed Rian to safety in the pool and almost ended up drowning yourself? Or maybe the time when you wandered off alone from camp and nearly were slaughtered by Calder? How about when you-,"

"Okay, enough!" I burst out, my face fully heated now. If it wasn't nighttime, I have no doubt the bright red color of it would be a beacon for curious onlookers. Several of the nearby guards turn to look at me, surprise and worry in their expressions. I clear my throat, and adjust myself in the saddle to sit taller, hopefully looking more regal, and wave their concerned glances off, muttering apologies.

When I finally gain the courage to look at Aidan, his shoulders are shaking with silent laughter. "Screw you, Aidan Ashfall," I whisper.

"Name the time and place, Magpie," he responds.

I send a whip of shadow to smack the back of his head in retribution. "Gross, and I told you not to call me Magpie anymore."

"So, what happened to your light power?" Aidan asks quietly a few moments later.

I debate the pros and cons of ignoring him, but ultimately decide to tell him the truth. I was the one who blabbed about it in the first place.

"I'm not sure," I say. "I stopped being able to access the light the day after the battle on the coast."

His eyes are on me, but I stare straight ahead. "But you healed those wounded soldiers the morning after the battle."

"Yes, and those were my last," I say. "I can't even feel the power within me anymore. The pool of darkness that I draw on is practically bursting, but the well that used to be full of light is just...empty. I'm worried Nura took her gift back after I failed to protect my father."

"In the entire known history of our world, no heir has ever had their gift taken away. It sounds like there's something blocking you from accessing it."

"No heir has ever had two powers before, either. Maybe this is their way of evening out the odds. Besides, what could block our power like that?"

Aidan shrugs. "I don't know. Have you tried communing with the goddesses?"

I sigh. "Yes, I've already tried that. It was incredibly unhelpful."

"Try again."

"It's not that simple," I roll my eyes.

"You have a temple here, don't you?"

"Of course we have a temple. But the goddesses don't always appear when asked," I say, getting annoyed.

Aidan lets out a long sigh of his own. "All right then, don't try. It's your power, not mine that's being blocked. And it's your life at risk, not mine, from these assassins."

I chew on the inside of my lip. We ride in silence after that.

When we're about to head up the solitary road to the castle, Aidan gives a tug on his horse's reins, directing him back towards the city. "If you have a need of me, Elana, send a messenger next time. There's no need to burn down half your city to get my attention."

I have to bite my tongue against the snarky retort that nearly bursts out.

"I'm staying at the Golden Lion Inn."

It doesn't surprise me one bit that he's staying at one of the most luxurious inns in Sandral. I give him a nod. "Good night, Prince Aidan."

"Good night, Magpie," he says with a half smile before his horse trots off towards the city center before I can chastise him.

Matteo's horse appears by my side and asks me in a quiet voice, "should we...stop him?"

I have to hold back the laugh. "No. He's the crowned prince of Ocarin, and our kingdoms remain allies, for now." I sigh heavily. "However, have someone discreetly follow him and report anything suspicious.

Matteo nods and our procession moves again. I turn in my saddle and watch Aidan's dark form disappear into the city.

# Chapter Ten

## Aislinn

If I can make it through this journey without chaining Donne to a tree and leaving him in the vast forests of Ocarin, it'll be a miracle. He's done nothing but complain since leaving Sandral. The man can't even sit on a carriage bench for more than a few hours at a time without waxing poetic about his sore arse. I swear to the Gods, if he doesn't shut up, I'll make sure he'll never sit comfortably again. Yesterday Tallisa offered to let him ride her horse while she drove the carriage. Mere moments later he claimed her horse was too "bouncy" and insisted they switch back.

We're all at our wits end with him. More than once I've contemplated locking him up with Aric, who I learned tried throwing him from the top of the ramparts a few years ago. I have no idea how he came into his current position as second to the captain, but it certainly wasn't through any actual acts of merit or leadership. *He's a citizen of Adrithia, he's a citizen of Adrithia*, I constantly remind myself.

Tallisa and Gregory both ride quietly, only talking when asked a direct question. To be fair, Donne won't shut up long enough to give them time to speak. I don't often make mistakes, and it's even rarer for me to admit my mistakes, but I'm one complaint away from falling to my knees and begging for Tallisa and Gregory's forgiveness for choosing to bring him along.

We're five days into this trip, nearly to the Ocarin-Hotharian border, where we will drop Aric off before turning back around. Getting into Ocarin was easy enough. All major and minor roads that cross into each kingdom are guarded by gates and guards of both kingdoms. Usually the soldiers at the gates are more of a formality, keeping the peace. But with the threat of war looming over us now, every single person, carriage, and cart was stopped, regardless of the direction they were traveling. Luckily, the road we travel isn't a busy road, so our crossing into Ocarin wasn't met with many delays. Since we've seen even less people on the road this far to the east, I doubt we'll have an issue at the next gate. We don't even need to cross into Hotharia, we'll release Aric on the border and head back home.

"You know, Princess Aislinn, if I had been in charge of this excursion, we would already be back in Adrithia. I know all the shortcuts," Donne brags when we stop for the evening.

"Donne, you couldn't find your way out of the castle's garden maze," Tallisa spits at him. I crack a smile, but repress the laugh that threatens to burst out.

"It was a moonless night! I'd like to see you make your way through that thorny maze with not even a torch," Donne snaps back at her.

I need to separate them before their bickering turns louder, something I don't think I can handle right now. "Tallisa, why don't you help Gregory gather some firewood? Donne, go keep an eye on the prisoner." I flash her a quick sideways smile, letting her know the sternness in my tone isn't for her sake.

She gives me a nod, and heads into the line of trees near the road. After some grumbling on Donne's part, he moves to the back of the prison cart, checking the lock and leaning against the side of the cart.

I've decided that we'll make the final push to the gate in the morning. Better to approach the unknown in the light. There could be several scenarios at play at the gate. One would be that the royal family will have someone stationed at the gate to bring Aric back to their capital, Forath. The transfer will be peaceful, and we'll be on our merry way quick as a snap.

Depending on how openly Hotharia wants to declare war, the second option is that there's an army at the gate. We assume that King Skade also aided in the attack on Ocarin, but we don't know for certain. If they did, the relations at the border could be precarious. My plan is to approach cautiously, prepared for attack.

"Your Highness, is there any chance we can convince you to allow the three of us to escort the traitor through the gate tomorrow?" Gregory asks as we unpack sleeping mats and a satchel of food.

"Nope," I respond matter-of-factly.

"Are you sure?"

"Gregory," I say, sighing as I shake out my bedroll onto a flat patch of ground, "there is no way in any of the hells I'll allow anyone to put themselves in danger while I sit back and watch."

He shakes his head. "Exactly, it's dangerous. And you're our princess. Second in line for the throne. We should be the ones protecting you."

I roll my eyes. "You do remember that I'm quite capable of taking care of myself, right?"

"Of course I know that. Everyone on the damned continent knows that, but you're important to our kingdom. The people look to you for strength and security. They don't look to us," he gestures at Donne and where Tallisa disappeared, "for shit."

I consider his words, slightly thrown off by his candor. The only guards who have ever spoken to me like that before were Matteo and Aric. Not like I listened much. But still, I respect Gregory's mettle. Which is why I say with rare gentleness, "as much as I appreciate your honesty and concern, I refuse to put others at risk when the risk is less for me. I stand a better chance against any foe, especially if we encounter any cursed enemies, because I fought them on the battlefield before. So, it will be me and only me taking Aric through the gate."

Gregory nods, but seems to deflate with disappointment as Tallisa returns with arms full of sticks and branches to firewood. "You tried to talk her into letting us take Aric to Hotharia, didn't you?"

He nods in her direction, and Tallisa lets out a short laugh. "I told you it wasn't going to happen, Gregory. She's as stubborn as a dragon."

"Excuse me," I say, dryly, "she's right here. And she happens to be your princess."

Tallisa shoots me an unconcerned, toothy smile. "I'm aware. I'm also aware that you don't mind what I call you."

"Oh?" I ask, one of my eyebrows shooting up. "And why do you say that?"

"Because you couldn't care less what people say about you, or about rank, or titles, none of that nonsense. Case in point, Gregory and I are here escorting you. We're two of the newest castle guard members, and here you are with us in tow on an important mission. Gregory's a known bastard, and I'm from a poor family in the slums of Sandral. You knew that, but you didn't care when you picked us for the journey. There were many more qualified guards you could have chosen, with more rank than us, but here we are. Given the chance to escort a traitor alongside our kingdom's princess."

I blink at her for a moment, shocked by her forwardness and observational skills. "When we get back, I'd like for you to guard my sister if I'm ever called away. She needs someone with a keen eye for detail."

She smirks, dropping the armfull of firewood onto the ground before dropping into the most pathetic curtsy I've seen. "It would be my honor."

Late that night, after I wake Tallisa to take over the watch, I'm plagued by unwanted dreams. Dreams of the temple, and a god looming over me, demanding I seek him out. I expel myself from the dream through sheer force of will, but his deep voice torments me even after my eyes open the next morning.

We leave our camp behind when dawn lights up the world in golden hues, and set out at a trot. We're all eager to make the return journey. Father's Resting Ceremony is eight days away. We've got plenty of time to make it home, but I don't want to be away any longer than necessary. Who knows what kind of trouble Elana is finding herself in.

"The gate is ahead!" Gregory's voice pulls me out of my worry. He rides by my side, while Tallisa takes a place at the rear behind the cart.

A sprawling gate comes into view, arching over the road ahead. A wall as wide and tall as our castle ramparts stretches on either side of the gate. "Right, be alert everyone."

The closer we ride, the more detail of the wall stands out to me. It appears to be crafted from a dark metal. Windows sit near the top, covered by slanted metal panels. It's not the most welcoming sight.

I've never been through this gate before, but I've traveled through other gates to Hotharia, and none of them have looked remotely this intimidating. A chill creeps up my spine and the hair on the back of my neck stands up. My knuckles go white on Hector's reins.

"Something feels wrong," I whisper, but we continue to move. No one crosses here, so there's no chance of us making it to the gate unseen. If we were about to be attacked, we could be picked off with arrows fired from the windows above. Our best bet is to move under the arch, where we're blocked by the thickness of the walls. "Keep your shields handy," I tell the guards.

"Your Highness, stop, please," Aric suddenly shouts from the cart. I haven't spoken to him since we left other than to ask if he needs food or water. He has a bucket in the cart that we've been taking turns emptying, so there's no reason for him to leave to see to his needs.

I give a signal to halt our procession out of arrow range, then leave Gregory to keep an eye on the gate as I angle Hector back to the prison cart.

"What do you know, Aric?" I ask coolly.

He's kneeling on the wooden floor, staring out the metal bars to the gate. "This is the gate I came through years ago when I first came to Adrithia, but it didn't look like this."

I eye the gate and surrounding structure. The metal is shiny, and the ground around it looks recently torn up. "You last saw the gate more than ten years ago. It could have been replaced for a variety of reasons."

"Look, I know you have no reason to trust me after everything that's happened, but I don't want anything to happen to you or these guards. Well except for Donne." he says, and I can't argue with him on that point. "There's something wrong here. Where are all the merchants, the travelers, the guards?"

I chew on my thumb nail while I think. "I feel it, too. There's something off about this situation."

Aric sighs, as if he's relieved I believe him.

"However," I say, and he stares up at me with wide eyes. "I see no way forward other than continuing."

"Aislinn, no," Aric says, then visibly swallows as he corrects himself at my glare. "Your Highness, you can't. We have to find another way. I don't know what their plan is at the gate, whether they mean to kill me, or you, or everyone, but I do know this is a trap."

A wicked smile curls my lips. "I know."

"Move, traitor," I poke Aric in the back with the tip of my sword. He startles and shuffles forward awkwardly. The chains around his ankles and wrists don't allow for much movement.

"Are you sure about this?" He asks as he walks. He's about an arms-length in front of me, a perfect shield in case of a barrage of arrows. My heirloom sword from Hale's trove practically vibrates in my grip. I've opted for a wood shield in my other hand to fend off arrows.

"Yes," I say confidently.

I turn back to check on the guards at my back. They're still mounted up out of firing range, as instructed, with shields at their sides, staring at the metal walls. They're to hang back with the horses in case anything happens. If it's clear I'll give them a signal, and if it's not, they know their orders.

At this point we wouldn't have enough time to turn back and find another path. There's another road leading to the border about a days' ride south of here, but that would cut it too close to making it home in time. So, the only option, as I see it, is to spring the trap.

I don't believe they'll hurt Aric, hence the human shield, but I also don't know that for sure, hence my actual shield. If they fire through him, I'll at least have some protection. Sure, I'd watch the traitor die, but I came to terms with that weeks ago.

The closer we walk, the tighter my grip on my sword becomes. It's singing in my grip now, as if it senses the same danger I instinctively feel. A group of soldiers mill about at the base of the gate.

Their uniforms slowly come into clarity. Three men are wearing the teal and gold colors of Hotharia and another three are dressed in the red and black of Ocarin. Some of the men talk amongst themselves, one leans against the wall, one holds a roll of parchment and quill. Everything seems normal.

And that's the biggest cause for concern.

"You're seeing this, right?" Aric whispers to me, slowing his pace slightly.

"Yes," I say, noting the stiffness in the soldiers muscles, their forced laughter, the hands resting not-so-casually on their sword hilts. I give Aric another nudge forward. "Keep walking."

We finally stop in the shadow of the gate. The soldier with the parchment, wearing Hotharian colors approaches with a bland expression. "State your business, please, miss."

I glance between the rest of the soldiers, who act too uninterested, their shoulders tense. A man wearing an Ocarin uniform steps closer, the one who had been leaning against the wall. His uniform is ill-fitted, with the top buttons undone and the pants riding up past his ankle.

"My name is Princess Aislinn of Adrithia," I call out, feigning my ignorance. "I'm here to release a spy, Aric Vernier, into Hotharian lands."

The parchment man makes a show of looking us over from head to toe, then scribbles something onto the scroll. "Very well, Your Highness. We'll take him from here."

Aric turns. "Please tell Elana-,"

"Nothing. I will tell her nothing from you," I snap, narrowing my eyes at his flinch. Gods, he really does look like a kicked dog.

One of the other soldiers approaches Aric, grabbing him gently by the crook of the elbow and leading him away.

He gives me one last pitiful glance. "I'm so sorry, Aislinn. I know I'll never deserve your forgiveness. But you must know I'll spend the rest of my days regretting my actions."

I stare at him, projecting the cold indifference I feel. He was my friend, our friend, for years, and while Elana and I spent that time opening up to him and trusting him, he spent that time spying on us. We let him into our home, our family, and he played us all for fools. Father paid the price of our ignorance.

Never again. I won't allow another stranger into my confidence like that.

Aric's shoulders slump as he's led away. Good riddance.

"Your Highness, the keys?" The guard with the parchment asks, holding out his gloved hand.

"Oh," I say, sliding my eyes down his frame in the same up and down look he gave me before, wholly unimpressed, "I don't have them. Aric's dangerous, after all. I suppose your king could unlock them for himself if he chooses to."

"Good idea," the guard answers with a serpentine smile as his eyes flick up to the top of the gate.

A sudden spike of worry pierces my gut at that glance. I have no time to think about it more, however, because the remaining guards rush to surround me, drawing their weapons. I almost scoff. Only five? What an insult.

A dozen more soldiers, dressed in full regalia, reveal themselves from their hiding spot on the Hotharian side of the arch. Ah, that's more like it.

The first thing I was taught in my training was how to defend myself. Once I mastered that, I was taught how to never defend myself ever again. By attacking first and getting an opponent on the defensive, I rendered the previous teachings useless. It's been years since I've had to use defensive moves, the last time was when I challenged Father for Hale's sword. I wonder if any of these soldiers will provide enough of a challenge for me to need to protect myself. I withdraw my blade, reveling in the sound it makes as it slides free from its scabbard. That sound means I'm about to dance.

I'm used to holding myself back. People have always been terrified of my skill and ferocity. Even our weapons master was apprehensive of instructing me. I chalked that up to his ego and not wanting a woman to surpass him, especially a woman in her teenage years.

I carefully watch the soldiers and give my shoulders a roll. The hilt of Hale's sword fits perfectly in my grip, as always, and sings with anticipation. It, too, was created for this deadly dance.

"I'm going to kill every last one of you," I say under my breath, and the words ring out like a promise spoken to the Gods themselves.

The men glance at each other, snickering. Clearly my reputation isn't what it should be in Hotharia. They see what they want to see. One woman armed with a single sword.

I can't wait to paint the ground with their blood.

A few men break off the pack and stalk forward at a slow pace. The swagger in their steps and laughter on their lips betray how easy they think the prey will be. They fail to see the predator in me.

When they're a few paces away, one of them pulls out a thick rope, twirling it around his hands as if he thinks he'll just slip it over my whole body and drag me away. Ah, so they intend to capture me, then? Interesting.

"Come with us, Princess. We promise we won't hurt you...much," the man with the rope says.

"And if I refuse?" I ask him in a high pitched tone, doing my best to sound meek and afraid. The three other men break away from him, surrounding me. As if it'll help.

"Come on, love, you're clearly outnumbered here."

Did he just call me...*love*? Oh, he's going to die slowly.

He closes the distance between us, and I move so fast his hands don't have time to clench. My sword is slick as I return it to my guard position. His fingers tremble as they drop the rope and grapple at his neck, which is spurting his lifeblood. The slice is deep enough to kill, but shallow enough for it to take some time. He collapses to his knees, making awful gurgling sounds.

The men around me yell, fumbling to pull their weapons out through their shock. A wicked smile curls my lips. Finally, I don't have to hold back. With a laugh devoid of humor I unleash myself upon them.

# Chapter Eleven

## Aislinn

Two go down immediately when they rush me from opposite directions - foolish. They weren't expecting me to go low, slashing their legs wide open. My sword is so unnaturally sharp it cuts clean through bone like a knife through butter. Their piercing screams echo off the metal wall as three more soldiers charge, metal armor clanging as they run. No more taking them off-guard, they're fully prepared for me now. I dance out of the way of one sword while catching one of the men in the abdomen. The second gets a deadly slice to his shoulder, and the third tries running me through, but his move is easily sidestepped. He leaves his body wide open when he strikes. He goes down as quickly as the first two, and I'm not even breathing hard.

The next few challenge me solo, but none of them offer up any kind of difficulty. I wipe my dark sleeve across my face, trying to clear the splattered blood from my eyes.

The rest of the pack seems to decide there's safety in numbers, because all but two barrel towards me at the same time. I use their movements against them, dodging when necessary, so their comrades take the blows meant for me. One of them manages a shallow cut on my left bicep, and I snarl at him, removing his head with one swift stroke.

Two soldiers remain. A shorter, younger one slowly backs up, the spear in his hand shaking. The other man wields two swords and is built like a tree, massive limbs with bulging muscles and a trunk-like neck that requires shirts to be cut specially to fit.

"Are you two going to come at me already? I have places to be," I flash a grin, but with the blood splattered over my face I'm sure it paints a gruesome picture.

"I think I'll just wait and enjoy the show," the large man says with a smirk. He points one of his blades into Ocarin territory, where Tallisa, Gregory, and Donne wait.

Angling my body so I still have the two soldiers in my peripherals, I look out at my guards. They're patiently waiting, right where I left them. Shouting comes from above me, and suddenly there are three large metal spears soaring through the sky. They move so fast I can barely track them with my eyes, but their trajectory has my stomach dropping.

"No," I whisper, running a few feet in their direction, but knowing it's hopeless. The spears find their homes, driving through my castle guards. Tallisa and Gregory raise their shields, but it doesn't matter, the spears shred through them like parchment. This isn't the skill of any normal human.

The king of Hotharia is here.

I close my eyes and don't watch the three fall. My heart squeezes. I'm no stranger to death, but seeing my companions slaughtered in front of me eyes hurts. When I open my eyes again, it's to the sound of horses hooves bolting. To my horror, Hector races towards me. Damnit, that stupid loyal horse. He should be running the opposite direction.

White hot rage burns through me. My grip tightens on the hilt of Hale's sword. I make the half turn to the last two soldiers left standing. The smaller of the two flinches at what he sees on my face, and drops his spear, backing away. The large man laughs and makes a "come and get me" gesture with a meaty hand. Oh, I'm going to enjoy this.

I charge, and he moves to block my incoming strike with his two swords. When I'm close enough to smell his rotten breath, I drop, skidding in the dirt, slicing my blade through his leg. It severs and the man goes down hard, screaming all the way. I rise to my feet and stare down at his writhing form. I raise my sword over my head and bring it down with both hands, right into his chest. His armored chest plate parts as the blade punches into his heart. I rip the sword free and give it a flick to clean the blood off.

The smaller man stands frozen, face a mask of fear, legs trembling. A dark spot slowly grows in the front of his pants. A better person, like my sister, might let him live. But we're at war now, and war holds no room for mercy. The best thing I can offer him is a swift, painless death to send him to the Gods. I make sure it's a clean cut, removing his head in one swing.

An anguished cry draws my attention to my guards. Tallisa and Gregory lie on the road, unmoving, but Donne, impaled by the metal spear through his left thigh, attempts to drag himself to one of the horses. His sobbing whimpers travel with the eastern breeze to my ears. "Please, no, please, I don't want to die. I'll do anything, please."

There's more commotion above, and Donne looks above the gate. Whatever he sees there has him crying more, and his pleading turns into panicked crying.

My lip curls in disgust. What a pathetic man.

The king of Hotharia must agree, because a metal spear soars through the air moments later, striking his neck, finally silencing him.

Hector makes it under the gate, snorting when he approaches me. I grab his bridle and give his nose a few calming pats. "You should have run away from here," I whisper to him.

My options here are slim. I consider trying to ride out of here, sticking to the side of the wall and then cutting into Ocarin from the end. But, there's no way King Skade wouldn't see me and impale me the same way he did my other three companions. Next, I wonder about sending Hector south and sneaking into Hotharia, then traveling north into the Gods Territory. I sigh, it has the same flaws as the first plan.

No, there's only one thing I can do. I flex my fingers and swing my sword, patting Hector, but leaving him under the safety of the gate.

Stepping around dead bodies, I search the walls nearby. There has to be a door. The soldiers above had to enter the wall somewhere. I finally find the outline of a hidden door, only visible thanks to the light reflecting off the inconsistencies in the metal. With blood-soaked fingers I slowly pry the door open, which isn't as heavy as it originally appeared. My hands slip several times, but I finally manage to work it open enough to allow me to slip inside.

Ahead of me lies a dark metal stairway. Boots pound the floor above me. I race up the steps on light feet, keeping my sword ready in case of attack.

At the top lies another door. I push it open gently to make sure it's not locked, then let it close again before anyone sees me. There's no doubt I'm at a disadvantage on top of a metal wall preparing to face the king who controls metal.

Taking two deep breaths, I ready myself. I might not survive the day, but at least I'll have some fun before I go.

Keeping a tight grip on Hale's sword, I kick open the metal door with a resounding *clang*.

A group of four men standing near the door startle and stare at me open-mouthed.

"Hello boys," I croon as I leer at each of them in turn. "I thought I heard rats scurrying up here"

I give them no time to respond before I'm upon them, and four bodies drop in my wake. Shouting comes from my right and race to meet the two soldiers in my way.

A loud metallic *banging* has me whipping my head around. Across from me, a large man with blonde hair and a thin cold smile stands in the frame of the door he just disintegrated. At last, I've gotten the attention of King Skade.

"Princess Aislinn. What an honor to have you visit Hotharia. I extend my sincerest thanks for returning my nephew to me unharmed," he says, giving me a quick mocking bow.

My eyes narrow as I take in his form. One question burns in my mind, above all others. I never thought I'd be the one to ask him, but I can't deny the opportunity now that it's arisen. "Why did you do it, Skade?" I don't give him the respect of using his honorific.

"I'm afraid you're going to have to be more specific, Princess. I have done a great many things in my time," he replies.

Oh, I bet he has. "Why did you betray the Astrellian Peace?"

He studies me with his iceberg blue eyes for a long moment, then finally sighs, throwing up his hands. "I admit, that was perhaps a bit rash, but these are times of war, Princess. I was given an offer, and I chose what was best for my people and my kingdom."

"Who gave you the offer? Who is the Empress?" I demand, pointing my sword at him like an accusing finger.

"Don't point that hunk of metal at me, girl," he snaps, flicking his eyes at my blade. His eyebrows pinch together and a muscle in his jaw clenches.

Still, he stares at my sword until his face turns red and his enraged eyes again meet mine. "What the Hells is that blade?"

A flicker of surprise has me staring down at Hale's sword. The hilt is reassuringly warm in my grip. Is it immune to King Skade's powers? How is that possible? Those blessed by Tolliver should have complete control over all metal.

Whatever reason for its immunity, it couldn't have come at a better time. I give Skade a smile as condescending as his. "What's the matter, Your Majesty, losing your touch?"

"You foolish child," he spits, "you have no idea what's coming for you, for the entire continent."

"Why don't you tell me what's coming for us? Don't you want to rub how little we know in my face?" I suggest.

King Skade flashes me a saccharine smile, then waggles his finger at me. "Tut tut, girl. As entertaining as that would be, I don't want to ruin the surprise and spoil all of her fun."

"Fine," I scoff. "The least you could do is tell me what her plan is." I flip my long bloodied braid behind my back, keeping it out of my face.

He gives another chuckle. "Sorry, I can't tell you that, either."

I flash him a toothy smile. "Of course not. You're clearly just her servant, and servants don't know shit." Before the words land I charge at him, swinging Hale's sword.

He gives me a snarl and blocks with his own greatsword. The two blades collide and send a shockwave up my arm. Skade advances while I take a few calculated steps back, allowing him to come to me. His swings are powerful, but predictable. He's not a bad swordsman, but he's also no match for me.

In two more swings I disarm him, sending his blade clashing to the ground. I don't wait for him to recover, instead thrusting my sword towards his heart. An ornate shield appears in front of him at the last moment, and my blade slides clean off it. The shield lowers enough for me to see his face, staring at his weapon. He lets out a little laugh. "Oh, you're good. As vicious as they say you are. I bet you'd have killed me right there if I'd allowed it. But you've forgotten one valuable thing."

I stare at him, letting the silence between us grow and, keeping a safe distance from his discarded weapon. If he starts to wield it without his hands, it'll be difficult to predict what he'll do with it.

"I couldn't shut you up moments ago, but now you don't want to speak? That's all right, I'll answer for you. You've forgotten what you're standing on," he gestures all around us to the metal wall.

Surely he doesn't mean to manipulate all the metal in the entire wall. The sudden metallic groaning under my feet says differently.

Oh Gods, I need to run, and get as far away from this wall as possible.

I sheathe my blade and rush to the edge of the wall, gauging the distance to the ground below. It's not too far, about as high as the gate at our castle, and I've fallen off that once before and survived with only a sprained ankle, so it's worth the risk now. I clamber up onto the edge and start to lower myself down.

The king's grating laughter brings my attention back to him. He shakes his head, wiping a nonexistent tear from his eye.

"Do you actually think you can escape? That's just adorable."

I let myself fall, loosening up my knees so the impact won't break my legs. Something hard slams into me well before I hit the ground, and my breath leaves me in a huff.

A giant metal claw protrudes from the side of the wall, fingers closing in on me. I unsheathe my blade and begin hacking, severing one metal talon, but it regrows in an instant, fortified by the metal behemoth surrounding it.

King Skade stands on the top of the shrinking wall, staring down at me with unbridled glee. The metal claw locks itself around me, shimmering bright silver in the sun. Chains appear around my wrists and ankles, and a cage slowly takes shape out of the metal claw.

A growing pit of despair envelopes me as home flashes before my eyes. I've let them all down. My sister, my mother, my entire kingdom.

# Chapter Twelve

## Elana

Father's Resting Ceremony is tomorrow. One more day, and my sister is nowhere to be found. I sent a battalion of soldiers out searching for her two days ago. So far, we haven't heard a word.

I chew my bottom lip, pacing in the room I've been using as my personal study. Mother finally stopped trying to make me use Father's old study. Instead, she told me to pick another room and we could furnish it together. The room I chose was a sort of sitting room that I used when I had my independent healing studies. So far, a beautiful light oak desk sits near the window with a few plush chairs and one large bookshelf. We haven't had much spare time to decorate.

"Elana, calm down. I'm sure Aislinn will waltz through the gates at any moment," Mother pleads, holding her temple.

I shake my head. "Something happened to her, I know it. She would never be late for this. She's in trouble, Mother, I can feel it."

I've felt unsettled for the past week. There's been a pit in my stomach since the day after the fire. The fire that we also have no new information on. The attackers we managed to capture alive won't speak to anyone, not even to me. When I attempted to interrogate them, the prisoners sat silently in their cells, staring at the back wall. Their eyes are pitch black, like the soldiers we fought on the beach, and they don't appear to have any emotional or physical response to anything we do to their bodies.

"There's nothing that can be done about it, Elana. Devon's Resting Ceremony is tomorrow, and we cannot not delay it," Mother steps in front of my pacing path, resting her hands on my shoulders. "I'm worried about her, too. But Aislinn would want us to go on with the ceremony as planned. We have the monarchs and their families from Ocarin, Aaranor, and Melinor attending tomorrow, so we must appear strong."

I step back, shaking my head. How can I pretend like everything's normal when my sister is missing?

The only silver lining in this situation is that the Hotharian merchants are here in the capital. They're being housed under supervision at one of Sandral's many inns. We've sent instruction to provide them with ample food and drink. They don't know why they've been summoned here, they only know they're being treated like honored guests. Who aren't allowed to leave. It was Mother's idea to try and get as many of them drunk as possible. "Drunk mouths move more freely than sober ones," she said.

We're planning on questioning them this evening, giving plenty of time to settle in and partake in the wine. Mother was furious when I told her I invited Aidan to question them with us, but I argued that Aidan has every right to gather information about Hotharia's treachery, especially considering his kingdom was attacked first. Since the fire, I haven't been able to stop thinking of him. I'm still furious at him, but there's a part of me, an annoyingly loud part, that wants him by my side.

"Shall we go over tomorrow's schedule and duties again?" Mother asks and I have to physically stop my eyes from rolling. We've done nothing but go through schedules and duties for the last several days. I'm tempted to remind her that it was Aislinn and I who made the plans, since our mother was lost in her grief.

"I believe I'm well-prepared," I say blandly.

Mother skewers me with a sharp gaze. "Where will you ride in the procession?"

"I won't be riding, I'll be walking, immediately following Father's casket," I reply.

The stone casket will be empty, since we don't have his body. A few days ago the castle's mason brought the lid here for our approval. Father's likeness was carved into it so realistically that Mother was a ghost of herself the rest of the day.

She nods. "And when will you make your offerings to Avani?"

"After Father's casket is placed inside the cave. I'll present the gifts and offer his soul to the earth goddess."

"And what will you offer?" Mother asks.

I sigh, inspecting a crack in the marble floor at my feet. "A drop of my blood, so his soul can be judged, and a piece of earth. Aislinn is supposed to offer the earth," I whisper. My fingers clench into fists at my sides, but I raise my voice so Mother can hear me, "if Aislinn doesn't make it in time, I'll make the offering instead."

"Your sister can take care of herself. She wouldn't miss tomorrow for the world."

I take no comfort from Mother's words. She's right, Ash wouldn't miss this for the world. And that's my worry...that only death would keep her away.

———— ✳ ————

"Mother, can you please stop glaring?" I whisper at her, sitting next to me on the settee in one of our informal receiving rooms where we wait for Rigel to bring him. From the corner of my vision, I spot her eyes rolling before I gently nudge her with my elbow. "He's a prince from an allied kingdom. We need to give him the respect his position demands."

"I know exactly who he is," Mother says sharply, her voice like a whip. "I'm surprised you've forgiven him already, considering he knew your father was going to die and did nothing to save him."

Her words send a flush of hot anger through me. "Of course I haven't forgiven him. But if the worst should happen and we meet Hotharia and the unknown enemy in battle again, we'll need his power on our side."

"A powerful ally during war, fine. But we shouldn't trust him any further than that. His mother is a seer, Elana. Seers are dangerous. How do we know Queen Amira isn't manipulating everything to her benefit?"

"They were the first kingdom to get attacked, and they lost many of their best warriors," I argue, recalling Aidan's haunting tale of his close friend dying in his arms after being cut with a cursed blade.

"A story they could have fabricated," she throws up her arms, standing in a huff.

I stand, too, facing her down with all the stubbornness of a Sable. "Gods, Mother, you sound paranoid. What benefit would Ocarin get out of everyone going to war with each other?"

She scoffs, waving a dismissive hand. "You haven't been at court as long as I have. The Astrellian Peace is tenuous at best. We dance along the edge of a knife because we know the destructive powers our monarchs hold. Who would stop the Ocarins if they decided to invade us? They have two rulers with the power of *fire*. They could burn down our entire kingdom. What could your shadows and sunshine do against that?"

I've had enough. Her skepticism has turned into paranoia since Father's death, and it's time I put an end to it before it impacts our relations with foreign kingdoms. "They are our allies," I say, punctuating each word with all the authority I can muster. "Aidan Ashfall is my friend. And you will treat him with respect, and cease this deranged rhetoric before you land us in scalding water with the rest of the kingdoms."

Mother regards me down her nose. "Fine, but don't complain to me when we're betrayed...yet again."

I roll my eyes and am about to suggest we both take our seats again, when Rigel sweeps in, bowing low.

"Prince Aidan of Ocarin is here," he says, and I can't help the smile that creeps up my face. "And his guest, Lady —,"

"It's General, actually," a woman's voice interrupts before she breezes into the room, "General Parisa."

She has stunning black hair tied in an elaborate braid, with hints of gold chains peeking through the silky strands. Her painted deep red lips are set in a thin line as she surveys me, then my mother, with dark brown eyes. I stop staring when I see her arm looped through Aidan's, with a hand resting on his bicep as she leans into him.

The shadows stir at my feet as I force a smile, wishing I possessed any ounce of my sister's composure. "Thank you, Rigel. Welcome, Prince Aidan, General Parisa. Please, take a seat."

I studiously avoid Aidan's face, instead looking at their garments. Aidan's black outfit is similar to what he wore on the mountain, and General Parisa wears a black suit that appears to be one piece, from her long sleeves down to her ankles, with designs of red and gold fire sewn into the fabric.

Mother and I sit side-by-side on the settee, while Aidan sits in the chair nearest me, and Parisa perches herself on the arm of the chair.

"Hello, Prince Aidan," Mother says coolly, finally addressing him, then turning to the woman. "You've brought your general into our home. Are you expecting trouble?"

Aidan leans back, tapping his fingers on the arm of the chair where Parisa doesn't sit. I keep my gaze firmly on his hand as I wait for his answer.

"No, not at all. Parisa is one of my closest confidants. She arrived here along with my family and a retinue of household members. She's merely here to observe and provide expertise in strategy if necessary," he says, voice as smooth as honey.

Mother's shrewd eyes lock with the general's. "Is it considered normal for princes to parade around with generals on their arms in Ocarin?"

Parisa gives my mother a sharp smile of her own, more teeth than any-thing. "Only when enemies are hiding *everywhere*. We want to keep our crown prince safe."

"Hmm," is all my mother gives as a response.

"How are you settling in?" I ask Parisa to break up the tension. Already my shadows coil around my ankles, ready to snap into motion at a mo-ment's notice.

Her dark eyes narrow on me, as if looking for cracks. The darkness pulls at its leash, and I mentally tug it back to heel. "We're settling in well, thank you. The accommodations are satisfactory."

As far as I know, Aidan and the other royals of Ocarin along with their entourage are staying at the Golden Lion Inn. Peak luxury in Sandral. If she considers it merely 'satisfactory', I wonder what the inns are like in Ocarin.

"When can we question the merchants?" She asks. "I traveled a long way and prefer to get this over with as quickly as possible."

"As soon as you'd like, we have a lot of work to do before the ceremony tomorrow," Mother says, ringing a small silver bell that I didn't notice was on the end table until now.

From the hallway, Matteo enters with three guards. He bows to us.

"Captain, our queen and her guests are ready to speak with the merchants."

I startle. "You're not coming with us, Mother?"

She shakes her head, her features softening when she looks at me. "No. I'm too noticeable, even by some merchants. And I'm technically supposed to be shuttered away, mourning the loss of my husband. Only able to venture out to offer sacrifices at the temple. Certainly not to be seen at a tavern, of all places."

"Oh, I see," I say. I understand, but wish she would bend the rules, even this once. I'm not sure I can do this without her.

"Try not to draw attention to yourself. It's the evening before your father's Resting Ceremony," she cautions.

"We'll take them in through a back entrance, Your Majesty, and we already have several private rooms where we can conduct the interviews," Matteo says, in an attempt to put us both at ease.

I remind myself that Aislinn trusts this man, so I can trust him too. He's not Aric. He won't betray us.

Mother gives a nod and Matteo leads us out to the stables. A plain carriage is waiting for us, much less recognizable than what my family typically uses. It's a simple cart, similar to the ones which are rented by the hour in the city.

I remain silent as I step into the carriage, staring out the window and definitely *not* thinking about the most gorgeous woman in the world currently clinging onto Aidan's bicep like he's a water skin and she's trapped in a desert.

The carriage is bumpy and uncomfortable. I sit facing Aidan and Parisa, who are crammed together on what must be Astrellia's tiniest carriage bench. It doesn't help that Aidan himself takes up most of the room the wooden box on wheels has to offer, with his broad shoulders and long, thick legs that extend well into my space.

"What's the plan for when we get to this...tavern?" I startle at Parisa's voice, breaking me out of my self-loathing reverie.

"Oh, umm I figured we'd question them one at a time. Hopefully they're drunk enough to talk. We paid off the barkeep to keep their drinks flowing."

Parisa stares at me, face an unreadable mask. Something most royals and close confidants have in common is their incredible skill at hiding all feelings. It's something I never mastered.

"That's it?" She asks. "That's your grand plan? Darling, Aidan told me you were intelligent."

My eyes snap to his finally, in time to see him shoot Parisa a dark look. "What's wrong with that plan?" I demand.

Parisa gives me a dramatic eye roll. "I thought you didn't want to get noticed?"

"I don't," I say.

"Then we need to blend in," she says, waggling her eyebrows suggestively, "and make sure they don't remember the night."

I let out a soft huff. "That's exactly why we paid off the entire staff of the tavern."

A slow smirk crawls up her face, showing off a dimple on her left cheek as she pulls a glass phial from a hidden pocket in her sleeve. "This will ensure no one remembers."

Inside the phial is a milky white concoction. She hands it over to me and I unstopper it gently, using my hand to waft the smell of it to my nose. Instantly I'm hit with a bitter aroma, followed by tangy notes.

"Dream cap mushroom?" I ask, swirling the mixture around, noticing a hint of purple. "And hamiberries?"

I know the abhorrent concoction well. It causes one to lose their inhibitions, to sink into a trace where nothing seems real. In the morning, a hazy cloud is all the participant will be able to remember of their prior evening. It was banned in Adrithia decades ago, but is still found through the dark market, a network of thieves and bandits who owe no allegiance to any kingdom or ruler. I've treated more than a few women in Sandral's seedier bars and brothels who woke up with bruises, headaches, and no recollection of the night before. It's a vile mixture.

"Ah, so you are good for something," Parisa says through a gleeful smile. "Aidan mentioned that you were an herbalist."

I shoot a glare at Aidan, who sighs and stares out the dirty carriage window. "What else did he tell you?"

"Oh, a few other things," she give a little laugh that doesn't put me at ease. "We can focus on that later. Now, let's discuss how we're going to blend in."

I give her a nod to continue. She gives me a once-over look. "We need disguises."

I look down at my plain pants and loose-fitting training top. "I'm already in disguise."

Parisa puts a hand over her mouth and suppresses a chuckle. "That is not the kind of disguise I'm talking about."

I'm not sure what she's referring to, but by the glee in her eye, I can tell I'm not going to like it.

# Chapter Thirteen

## Elana

As it turns out, I was absolutely correct. I hate this. Why did I let her talk me into wearing this…I'm not even sure I can call it clothing.

Parisa looks like she was born for this role, flitting between the merchants, a tray of drinks balancing on one hand, while the other delicately brushes across men's arms, or tips a goblet back into an eager mouth. She giggles behind a sheer red face veil. Her lean stomach is exposed, accentuated by beaded flowy red pants that sit low on her hips, and a matching top that barely covers her ample breasts. Beads and charms adorning her clothes make lovely music when she swishes her hips. According to her, it's common courtesan attire in Ocarin.

I stand uncomfortably next to a wall, holding a tray of drinks, each spiked with a single drop of the memory-loss concoction. Not enough to cause a blackout, but enough to distort inhibitions. My own outfit is slightly more modest than Parisa's at my insistence. A black top with short sleeves, and pants with a sheer gold skirt attached. My own black beaded veil sits below my eyes and has a piece which covers most of my auburn hair. The black ensemble barely fits over my curves, but the flowy fabric hides it well.

I shift so my billowy sleeves hide my exposed midriff, causing the beaded skirt to jingle. A flush permanently heats my face behind the mask, and I silently thank the Gods no one will recognize me.

Where Parisa pulled these clothes from, I'm not certain. All I know is she emerged from a room inside the tavern with them. "You look like you wish you were a part of the wall, Magpie," Aidan's warm breath suddenly tickles my ear. A shiver runs up my exposed spine as I spin around to face him.

"What the hells are you doing? You're supposed to be waiting inside the room," I snap at him, momentarily forgetting about my tray of drinks, sending some of the amber liquid splashing out of the mugs.

Aidan's eyes roam over my form and a slow smile forms on his lips. "And miss the show? Absolutely not."

His cedar scent surrounds me, and I'm suddenly more aware of my near-nakedness. My face feels like an inferno. I need to get his attention off of me, or else I might do something foolish like forgive him for letting my father die.

"Well, there's your show right there," I say, gesturing to Parisa, currently perched on the lap of the captain of one of the merchant ships. She's laughing at whatever he's saying, running her long fingers through his messy brown hair.

Aidan's eyes flicker briefly in Parisa's direction, then amusement lights his face. "Why would I want to watch my aunt seduce drunk men?"

My mouth drops open as my mind struggles to understand what he just said. "Your what?" I ask dumbly.

"Elana, she's my aunt," Aidan says, humor dancing in his eyes.

"I'm sorry, I don't understand," I stammer. Surely I didn't hear correctly. There's no way he could have an aunt who's as young as he is.

"She's my mother's youngest sister," he says through a grin.

My mind tries to wrap around the impossibility of it. "But, that can't be, she's too young."

Aidan lets out a full body laugh, clearly enjoying himself. "Oh, Parisa would love to hear you say that. She'd be a pest about it, of course, but a comment like that would put you in her good graces immediately. She's in her third decade."

I stare openly at her now, searching for evidence of her age. Tiny wrinkles or a stray gray hair, but there's nothing. There's no way in Hells Parisa is more than 30-years-old. I don't believe it.

"Your hot springs must really be magical if everyone in Ocarin ages like that," I whisper, mostly to myself as I admire her in a whole new light.

Once again, Aidan leans down and whispers next to my ear, "I'd love to show you sometime. You'd require even less clothes than these though, I'm afraid. You could wear the same thing you wore to the pool in the cave during the trials."

The underground oasis comes back to me, and I smile at the memory of the warm water, the little falls I stood under, and Aidan, lounging on the side of the pool looking more relaxed than I'd ever seen him. It was the most peaceful experience of the trials, at least until Kai, the Water God, tried to drown us all. After I pushed Rian to the edge I got caught in the whirlpool, where I was thrashed around until I lost consciousness. Once Calder gained his powers and saved us, the next thing I remember is waking up in Aidan's arms.

The ghost of his warm body cradling mine has me looking away and clearing my throat. I can't think about that right now.

Luckily, I catch Parisa's eye in the crowd. She gives me four fingers in the direction of one of the men, who's already stumbling to his feet towards the bar. Okay, my turn. I give Aidan a quick glance. "I'll meet you in the room."

I stride to the bar, putting some extra swagger into my hips and letting the little bells sing their tune of seduction. The clearly inebriated man turns as I approach, drawn to the sound like a moth to flame. His smile is sloppy, eyes glazed over with lust as his lips part to reveal yellowing teeth and blackened gums. Oh Gods, and the breath. It takes everything I have in me not to gag at the smell.

"Hello there," I say in my best slow alluring voice. I try to mimic what I saw Parisa doing, smiling sweetly under the sheer mask and letting my fingers caress his bicep.

"Hello sweet thing," he says, slurring his words, and moving a hand to cup my ass. I bat it away playfully, waggling my finger at him.

"Not here. I don't want an audience. Why don't we take this upstairs?" Parisa coached me on what to say while we were getting dressed.

I hand him a drink from my tray and give him a *follow me* gesture, enticing him to accompany me up the stairs and down the private hallway to the room we secured.

When I swing the door open, the man closes it behind me, giggling like a little boy. I move to set the tray down, and he surprises me by using the opportunity to grope me from behind. I let out a yelp of shock, and suddenly Aidan is there, wrapping his fingers around the merchant's neck as he lifts him off the ground.

"Keep your disgusting hands off her, you scum," he snarls, and the candles around the room flare brighter, reflecting the fire in his golden eyes.

The man struggles in Aidan's grip, trying to no avail to free his airway from the crushing grasp. I suck in a deep breath, composing myself and straightening the mask to ensure my face is still covered.

"Let him go, degenerate," I say to Aidan, using my favorite name for him since we promised not to use our powers or real names here. In case anyone not drugged stumbles upon us, we don't want them discovering our true identities. "He needs his voice to speak."

"He doesn't deserve to breathe the same air as you," Aidan says, with murder in his eyes.

I walk forward, putting my hand gently on his arm. "That may be, but we still need to find out what he knows."

Aidan looks at me, eyes softening slightly as he relaxes his grip on the struggling man. He tosses him with ease onto the bed.

"I don't like this plan anymore, Magpie," Aidan says through gritted teeth. His shoulders are rigid and he looks as if he'd rather rip the man's arm off and beat him with it instead of question him.

"Too bad, this is the plan," I whisper to him as I turn back to face the man, who's struggling to catch his breath. "We have some questions for you, sailor."

The man spits at my feet. "As if I'd tell yeh anything after yeh set yer dog on me."

The room noticeably heats up and I cast a sharp look to Aidan, who shrugs nonchalantly, even though steam rises from his shoulders.

"Want to find out if I'm more bark or bite?" Aidan's teeth gleam in the flickering candlelight, as he flashes a vicious smile at the cowering sailor.

I pinch the bridge of my nose. This is going to be more challenging than I thought. I walk to the side table, where my twin daggers wait for me. The hilts sit comfortably in my hands, reminding me of what I've been missing these past few weeks. I point one of the blades in the man's direction.

"Look, I don't want to hurt you, but my friend here does, so either tell us what we want to know, or I unleash him," I channel my sister. This is her specialty, not mine. From behind me, Aidan slowly withdraws his own dagger.

The man rocks back and forth on the bed, the combination of the drug and the booze clearly affecting him. His hands massage his neck, and I almost wince at the bruises already forming there.

"Who are yeh?" The man asks, squinting. Some of the candles near me flicker and sputter out, casting my face into more darkness. I silently thank Aidan for his quick thinking.

"We're your worst nightmare if you don't answer our questions," Aidan's tone drips menace.

"Fine," the sailor says at last. "Whadda yeh want to know?"

I almost sigh, but keep my relief in check. "You're from Hotharia, yes?"

He nods. "Born on the coast."

"What do you know of Hotharia's allies?" I ask.

His face scrunches, appearing genuinely confused. "Yeh mean the other kingdoms?"

I exchange a glance with Aidan. This doesn't seem promising. "No, not the kingdoms. Someone else. Perhaps you've seen foreign ships at port that don't bear the banners of any Astrellian kingdom?"

He looks down at the floorboards, eyes scrunched, clearly doing his best to think. "We've seen 'bout three or four colorless ships along the coast a few fortnights ago. Our Capt'n told us to mind our business, so we did."

"And that's all you know? You haven't heard any talk of Hotharia waging war against the rest of the continent?" I ask, knowing it's pushing, but also knowing he won't remember this conversation come morning.

The man laughs, spittle flying out of his mouth. "There's been peace for centuries, why would 'Otharia want ter ruin that?"

Why indeed.

Aidan steps up to my side, holding out three mugs of ale. I nod, recognizing the signal and agreeing with him that this merchant has outgrown his usefulness to us.

"Thank you for answering our questions," I say, taking two mugs and holding one out to the man. "A peace offering for bringing you in here so rudely and to send you on your way."

I hold my own mug out in cheers, and Aidan follows suit. The man eyes us warily.

"It's tradition in Adrithia to share a drink before parting ways," I lie, hoping it doesn't sound too ridiculous.

He shrugs and clacks his mug into our own before chugging his down. I sip from mine, knowing it's going to be a long night, and watch as the merchant drains his. Foam runs down his chin as he attempts to stand, but the high dosage of the memory erasing drug takes effect and he tumbles to the floor.

I grimace in disgust as Aidan pounds twice on the side door and three of my castle guards rush in, promptly picking up the man and carrying him out of the room. Matteo walks into the room and blushes as he sees my garb, turning away to stare at a wall.

"Everything go according to plan, Your Majesty?"

"Yes, although he didn't know much," I lament, shuddering as I realize I'll have to do that again.

"We should go right to the captain next," Aidan says. "If anyone knows anything, he will."

I give him a nod in agreement and we reset the room for the next round. The guards wait quietly next door as they deposit the first merchant into his own quarters. He'll awaken in the morning with a massive headache and no recollection of anything from tonight.

"Do you think Parisa is all right down there by herself?" I ask as Aidan and I straighten the bedsheets.

Aidan flashes me a smirk. "It would take a lot more than a tavern full of belligerent idiots to ruffle my aunt. She's a force of nature."

I smile at that, thinking it sounds familiar. My smile falls as I think of my sister. Where is she right now? Is she okay? I can't help but think the last thing I said to her was that I blamed her for Father's death. Worry claws its way up my throat, burning a path as it goes.

"Is Aislinn back yet?" Aidan asks, correctly guessing the origin of my worry.

"No," I say, and my wobbling throat threatens to close until I cough to clear it. "We haven't heard anything from her or the guards she took. I sent out a battalion days ago to try and find her, but there's been no word."

Aidan looks down, as if he, too, wonders what would or even could keep Aislinn away from home right now. It strikes a chord of doubt in my mind. Does he know anything? Has his mother *seen* what's happened to Ash? I need to know.

"Do you...," I trail off, taking in a slow breath as I work up the nerve to finish the question, "do you know what's happened to her? Has your mother *seen* something?"

A flash of hurt crosses his face before he shakes his head once. "No, Elana. I would have told you if she did. She arrived today, and said she hasn't *seen* anything related to the war or Hotharia."

I want to believe that's true, but after she saw my father's death and didn't reveal it to anyone except Aidan, I'm hesitant. Queen Amira won't be on my list of allies until she explains herself.

For now, it seems I have no choice but to accept Aidan's answer. "Okay. I just wish I knew what happened to her, and if she's all right," I say, chewing on my lower lip.

"I'm sorry, Magpie. I wish I could give you the answers you're looking for. Your sister is perhaps the most capable person across all of Astrellia. Whatever has delayed her, she won't allow it to keep her away for long."

I give a nod, knowing he's right. Aislinn will return to us. Anything else is inconceivable.

Once the room is back in order, I head out, seeking our next target. I descend the stairs as quietly as I can, hoping to go unnoticed until it's time to strike. Halfway down the steps I catch Parisa's gaze, giving her a barely perceptible shake of my head. Then, using three fingers, the signal we decided on for "next", I point at the captain. She barely dips her chin, but I know she's received the message.

I watch in astonishment as she sidles up to the captain, placing a full goblet of wine into his hand and somehow coercing him to drink it all. After several minutes of her teasing and flirting, she gives me the signal that he's adequately drugged. I move in on quick feet, bracing myself, knowing the same ruse won't work twice.

This time, I grab a mostly empty goblet from the bar as I stalk to him. Parisa monitors my approach, sees the goblet, and seems to understand my plan. She invites him to dance, and tugs him to his feet. He sways, unsteady, and I put myself in his path. When his arms flail for balance, one of them catches my wine goblet, spilling it all over me, him, and the floor.

"Oh dear, excuse me sir," I say, bowing low, an act that I have to grit my teeth to get through. "You must forgive my clumsiness."

The captain turns, a brief look of anger melting into sly supplication. "No, no, pardon me. The fault is entirely mine."

My head bows lower. "Please, you must allow me to assist you before the wine stains your fine trousers."

His eyebrows raise in mock question. He knows exactly where this conversation is going. "How do you propose to do that?"

I finally raise my head, giving him a suggestive smirk behind my mask even as I inwardly cringe. "By getting you out of those trousers, of course."

A grin spreads across his wide bearded face. "Well, in that case, lead the way, dearie."

Gods, I'm sickened by how easy this is. Parisa gives her best pouting face, sighing loudly and proclaiming, "some women get all the fun," before she allows herself to be swept into the arms of a nearby crew member.

I lead the captain to the stairs, but as I start to ascend, meaty fingers grasp my forearm.

"Hey, wench, before we go anywhere, tell me where my man is. I saw you disappearing with him earlier, but haven't seen him return," the captain growls suddenly, gripping my arm tighter, hard enough to bruise.

I leash my anger, instead letting my voice drop, lowering my eyelashes as I look up at him. "I'm afraid he was so exhausted after...well, you know, that he decided to retire for the night."

The man's suspicion turns to longing as his eyes drag up my form, lingering on my chest. "Is that so? Well, in that case, I hope I get the same treatment."

I give him a small smile even as I inwardly vomit at his leering. "Oh, you will. I promise it'll be like nothing you've ever experienced before."

He guffaws and releases my arm, cheerfully trailing after me to the room. Not wanting a repeat of the unsuspected groping, I hand him the key, gesturing for him to go first. He's more than happy to take the lead, unlocking the door, then taking one step inside and motioning me forward with a flourish. I step in the door, closing it behind me.

"Okay, whore, how 'bout you start on your knees," he says, placing his meaty palms on my shoulder and pushing down, right as the door swings shut behind me, revealing a very pissed-off Aidan.

"Excuse you?" Aidan demands, smacking the captain's hands off my shoulder with a move that resembles swatting at an errant fly.

"Oh, sorry, does she belong to you? Listen, bud, I won't rough her up too badly. As long as the bitch does what I say."

Aidan's fist comes out of nowhere, connecting with the man's nose. The *crack* of contact has me wincing as I recognize the sound of breaking bone. The impact sends the captain to the floor, face gushing blood, and Aidan doesn't give him a moment to breathe before he looms over him, grabbing the whimpering man by the neck and dragging him to his feet. The room steams as the temperature spikes.

In my panic, I shout, "Aidan!"

He freezes, taking in several shaky breaths before he loosens his grip on the captain's neck, instead shoving him backwards onto the bed. The man grips his bloodied nose with one hand while he stares at Aidan with eyes full of fear. From the way he trembles like a leaf, I'd say he's figured out who he is.

Gods damn it, I blew our cover. We'll have to make sure he gets double the dose in his mug, but I'm not overly concerned with that at the moment. Shadows stream from behind me, coiling like snakes around his legs, holding fast and locking him in place.

"Y-y-you're her...the q-queen," the captain stammers, going wide-eyed. With half a thought, I cast us into darkness, snuffing out all but a few candles behind us. The flames cast us into an eerie silhouette, our shadows stretching far up the wall, and furthering the terrifying vision we must present.

"Yes, I am," I say simply, but with enough inflection to cause him to tremble. "My friend and I have some questions for you. Let's start simple, shall we? What's your name?"

I didn't notice until now, but Aidan somehow moved through the shadows and now stands next to the man, his golden eyes practically glowing in the flickering light. His dagger flashes as he presses it into the captain's neck. "The lady asked you a question. I suggest you answer."

Damn, he's good at this.

The man's throat bobs as he swallows thickly. "Ronald. My name is Ronald."

"All right, Ronald. Tell us everything you know about the unmarked ships off the coast of Hotharia," I say.

Confusion wrinkles his brow. "The ships? Why do you want to know about the ships?"

I tsk at him as Aidan digs the tip of his blade in deeper, causing a spot of red to well. A very unmanly squeak emerges from Ronald's lips.

"Okay, okay, I'll tell you, just remove the blade, please. I can't talk like this," he pleads.

Some small part of me takes mercy on him, because I give Aidan a nod, and he reluctantly draws the dagger away. He hovers by Ronald's side, ready in case he makes a move.

Ronald touches his neck gingerly, then rubs the blood under his nose away with a sleeve. It's definitely broken, sitting at an unnatural angle. "A few months ago, around the time of the Crowning Ceremony, we started seeing unmarked ships anchored in our bay near Helmburg. It was only one or two at first, but shortly after Prince Calder left for his trials, a whole fleet showed up. Me and a few other captains got together and took our concerns to the harbormaster. He paid us a large sack of gold and told us we ain't seen nothing. That we weren't in any danger, and to steer clear. So, like the self-respecting merchants we are, we respected his instruction. About a week later, part of the fleet split off, sailing south with a few Hotharian warships."

Aidan and I exchange a glance. That must have been the group that attacked Ocarin, then later sailed to Adrithia's coast.

"The other captains and I decided it would be a good idea to find safer waters, so we started packing for a long trip. As we were recruiting crew and loading up our wares, we noticed some of the remaining ships dock at the harbor reserved for royal vessels and thousands of armed soldiers disembarked and marched towards the capital. We set sail that afternoon, passing ships that sailed north up the coast. We didn't want anything to do with whatever was happening there, so we turned our ship in the opposite direction, and ended up docking in Tierth at a really unfortunate time," Ronald finishes his story and takes a few labored breaths.

My blood runs cold. I stare at Aidan, who stares back, the same worries pulling his dark eyebrows together. Thousands of soldiers headed towards Forath? Where are they now? And where did the other ships sail to? Is this somehow related to why Aislinn hasn't returned?

A sickening feeling twists my gut. She's alive. She has to be.

"C-can I go now? I've told you all I know," Ronald looks between us, his knee bouncing with his anxiety, even as his feet remain bound with my shadows.

I don't respond, already my mind is spinning. My sister is clearly in danger. Should I leave Adrithia to find her? And where did those other ships go?

Aidan moves to the shadowy corner of the room. I hear him pouring ale, and most likely mixing the extra dose of drug in Ronald's too. He returns and hands a mug to me, which I accept absentmindedly, and one to Ronald. I command the shadows holding his legs to dissipate.

"One last question," I say, before he takes a drink. He waits with wide eyes, hand trembling slightly on his mug. "Do you know anything about other lands beyond our continent?"

Ronald lowers his mug, as if in relief. "Of course I do. I'm a captain."

"What exactly do you know?" I ask in irritation.

He quickly straightens and clears his throat. "There are several known lands. Smaller islands to the south, a three days' sail south of Adrithia. Then there's the land of Tyne to the far northeast of Astrellia. It takes several weeks to reach it, if winds are favorable."

I squint my eyes at him, trying to determine if he's lying. A shared look with Aidan says this is all new information to him, too.

"These lands have people?" I ask.

Ronald nods. "Oh, yes. There aren't many on the chain of islands to the south, but they're definitely there. As far as Tyne, there are few accounts of it, mostly whispers."

"What whispers?" Aidan demands, voice sharp.

"They're dark tales, full of death and mystery," Ronald's voice drops, taking on a spooky quality.

"Without the theatrics," Aidan sighs.

"Heh, sorry," Ronald shrugs, "can't blame an old sailor for his embell-ishments."

He clears his throat and starts again. "the last I've heard of a ship re-turning from Tyne was four decades ago. It was a trading vessel, set out for Melinor, but got caught in horrible storms, blowing them far off course. Their mainsail got shredded in the storm, and caused the ship to drift into an unknown cove. Their captain and half a dozen crew went to shore to purchase materials to repair the sail from a town just past the beach. The crew waited for days, but the captain and his men never returned. The first mate and the rest of the crew were unsettled. They never saw a single soul walking the beach or through the trees in the town. After waiting for a fortnight and using up most of their supplies, the crew decided to leave, having repaired the sail as much as possible. They barely made it back to

Ocarin to tell their tale. Their story isn't unique. Merchants talk, and it's well-known that Tyne is a hostile place, where few venture and even fewer return."

I wonder how much of this is sailors' superstition, and how much is truth. "How come we've never heard of these lands before? We were always taught that Astrellia is the only habitable land, which is why the Astrellian Peace is so vital to our survival."

Ronald shrugs again, taking a gulp of his ale. One sip shouldn't knock him out immediately, at least I hope. "I can't answer that. Us seafolk do well to keep our heads down and try to stay out of the crown's way. We pay our taxes, on time, every time, and go on our way. After all, we're only trying to make a living."

I roll my eyes, not caring in the slightest about his taxes. After catching Aidan's eye, I decide it's time to end this conversation. I hold up my mug. "Before you go, to show we hold no ill will, please enjoy a drink with us."

Aidan lifts his up to join mine and we stare at Ronald, expectantly. The captain stands up awkwardly, then smacks his mug into ours. "Cheers."

I take a slow sip from mine, while Aidan downs a few hearty gulps. Ronald tips his entire head back and empties the entire cup before I have time to blink.

"Your Majesties," he slurs, stumbling on his feet, "it's been my hono-," he slumps over on the side of the bed, unconscious.

"Well, that was...eventful," I say, trying to keep my voice from wobbling.

Aidan runs a hand through his unkempt black hair. "Are you all right?"

I nod once, but my hitching breath betrays my true feelings. "It's my sister. What if...what if she's in trouble? What if she ran into those soldiers from the boats?"

Aidan closes the distance between us in two long strides. He tugs me into his warmth, and I can't help but melt into him. "Aislinn will be alright," he whispers to my hair. "Wherever she is, she's okay."

My sniffles turn into body-shaking sobs as I try to hold them back. Aidan holds me, allowing me to sully his clothes with endless tears. "Aidan, the last thing I said to her before she left...it was terrible. What if I never get to apologize? What if she thinks I hate her?"

"She knows your heart, Elana. Perhaps more than anyone, she knows you. You didn't mean it, so there's no way she would believe it." His voice is soft as his cedar scent surrounds me, comforting.

We stay like that for a few precious moments, until I finally pull back. "Thank you," I whisper, eyeing the wet spot on his shirt. "And sorry for getting your shirt wet."

He leans down and presses a gentle kiss to my forehead. "You can get my shirt wet any time, Magpie."

I chuckle despite myself, and Gods it feels good to laugh again. "Keep it up, degenerate, and my mother will never invite you back."

He gives me a smirk, showing off his one dimple, as he taps twice on the adjoining door. Matteo and the guards enter, then drag Ronald's prone body out.

Suddenly, I'm hit with a wave of exhaustion. Aidan catches sight of my yawn and offers to continue questioning the crew with Parisa if I want to return to the castle. There's no need to deliberate. I take him up on the offer to retire for the evening. I instruct Matteo to leave a handful of guards here to keep an eye on things and help Aidan and Parisa if needed.

"Thank you for your help tonight, Aidan," I say. "I'm not sure I could have done it without you."

He smiles a gentle, rarely seen smile. "You could have. But you wouldn't have had nearly as much *fun*," the way he says the word sends a shiver down my spine and reminds me I'm barely wearing anything.

I blush. "I'm not sure what you'd call this night, but I definitely won't consider it fun."

"I call it a tease," he says with a chuckle, eyeing my revealing garments with an appreciative perusal that has my heart skipping a beat. "Goodnight, Magpie."

"Goodnight, degenerate."

# CHAPTER FOURTEEN

## AISLINN

The prison cart lurches over yet another root or stone on the path and my head collides with the metal bars of the so-called "window" behind me.

*Gods damn it, that hurt!*

I have no idea how many days I've spent in this fucking cart. All I know is I've surely missed my father's Resting Ceremony by now.

The thought seriously pisses me off. And I was already pissed.

King Skade constructed this prison cart for me on that first day, but quickly discovered that it would be impossible to get me into it, because even chained, I could still slaughter his men. It took two broken necks and a suffocation for him to realize it was a lost cause to force me into the box. He chained me to his horse and I walked behind it until the regiment was ready to take a break. When they finally deigned to give me water, I swallowed it all in several gulps, not caring if it was drugged.

It was, and that was how they finally got me into this Gods-forsaken cart. I haven't left it since. The Hotharians bring me water and food once a day, and there's a small bucket to see to my needs, which some unlucky soldier has to empty out.

My body aches with misuse. I long to stretch out my limbs, but Skade was devious in designing this cage. Not quite long enough for me to fully extend my legs, and not tall enough to stand. My options are to sit, kneel, or lay down with my legs curled up in order to be comfortable.

We've been traveling east. I can tell because the sun rises in front of the cart and sets behind it, and because it keeps getting colder. Hotharia is a bitterly cold kingdom. Even in summer, its many coastal mountains are still covered with snow. The end of summer, which it now currently is, is the warmest time of the year for the kingdom. I wouldn't exactly consider it warm, but during the day it's comfortable. Inside the all-metal prison cart, however, it gets sweltering. And when the temperatures drop at night, the metal grows so cold I swear I can see my breath in the little bit of moonlight that the windows allow in.

All in all, I've been having a miserable time.

The cart suddenly lurches to a stop and I'm sent careening sideways. My shoulder smacks painfully into the slab of iron at the front of the cart. I groan and slam my elbow into the metal, then shout, "hey, asshole, is this your first day driving a cart? I know armless men who could do it better than you with nothing but their teeth."

I expect to hear a man's roar of rage, for him to shake the cart or spit or do something. I don't expect the shuffling of feet outside the metal prison, then a mumbled, "I'm sorry."

It's a voice I recognize well. A bitter laugh bubbles out of me. Oh how the Gods must be watching with glee as I confront this poetic justice. "Traitor, is that you?"

A long pause before his quiet reply, "yes, it's me." He doesn't even try to correct me on the name.

Poor traitor. How sad he must be knowing he's responsible for even more Adrithian deaths.

"What are you doing?" I ask through a sneer that he can't see. "I figured you'd be halfway back to Forath by now."

Aric sighs, leaning his back against the side of the cart. If my hands weren't chained to the floor with little space to move around, I'd reach out and wrap them around his neck.

"My uncle asked if I wanted to return to the capitol with him. To finally see my sister again," he says, breathlessly. "But I couldn't leave you in the care of these men. Most of them want to outright kill you, but the others would enjoy torturing you first."

"So you're here to what, stop them? Join in? Assuage your guilt by ensuring your friends don't torture me to death?"

Aric turns, peering in through the window of the metal box at me. "Officially, I'm here to make sure you don't escape."

"And unofficially?" I wonder aloud.

He doesn't respond, and after a few moments someone calls Aric's name and he gives me a last look before walking towards where a group of soldiers are splitting some dried meat and fruit.

If he means to gain my trust, he's doing a terrible job of it. Maybe my smartest move here is to play along to see what he has to offer. Perhaps he'll bring me some extra water, or maybe even a blanket. *No*, I think, *that's too obvious*. Either way, I'll reap the benefits and let him think that I'm slowly forgiving him. Get him to talk about the soldiers he's traveling with, where they're going, and why. All useful information for when I inevitably break out of here and take my revenge. Now that the king has left, there's no one here who can stop me.

I sit back, resting my head against the wall. My mouth is dry, lips chapped and bleeding. I think of home, of my sister. And cake. I miss cake. You never know how much you miss something until it's gone, and right now I miss Gwen's cooking more than my warm bed, my feather pillow, and my bathtub combined.

My hand goes to my hip almost instinctively, and touches nothing but my breeches. No sword. Yet another thing to add to my list of losses. I don't know what happened to my heirloom sword after I was drugged and thrown into this cart. I wonder if the king confiscated it, or if he tossed it away after finding it useless to him, seeing as he's unable to manipulate it.

It's some time later when I hear the men pack up their belongings and mount their horses, ready to continue on. They're all men. Hotharia doesn't believe in women warriors, at least not in recent history. It's unfortunate that all of the first-born Verniers have been male in the last three generations, because the kingdom could desperately do with a female perspective. Instead, the women of Hotharia are relegated to tasks like taking care of the home, growing food, and, of course, raising children.

I shudder. It's not like I'm opposed to any of those tasks, but being told you can only do those things because that's all you're good for sounds like one of the Hells.

It's a completely backwards way of thinking. But, that's all the women of Hotharia know. They're taught that they're less than men, so they teach their daughters they're less than their sons, and so on. It's all they've ever known. It's a vicious cycle, one that I fear won't be broken until they get a female heir.

A shadow passes in front of the bars and then a small apple is tossed inside. It's bruised and deformed, but there appears to be nothing wrong with it. Aric's blue eyes stare at me though the bars.

"I told the men I stuck it in horse dung," he says, nodding at the apple. "But, I didn't."

I take a tentative sniff just to be sure. The sweet apple smell hits my nose, and my mouth starts to water.

I narrow my eyes at him, but slowly take a bite. It's crispy and juicy, and tastes like the most amazing thing I've eaten in weeks. I have to hold back my moan of delight. I hate the traitor and will never trust him again, but that doesn't mean I have to let this perfectly good apple go to waste. I can hate him as easily with a full belly.

Voices get louder outside the cart, and I hide the apple under my shirt.

"Eat shit, Adrithian bitch," Aric says in a tone that reminds me so much like Calder I'm shocked I never realized the similarities sooner.

Two of the Hotharian soldiers laugh as they walk past, clapping the traitor on the back as they go.

How many of their warriors did I kill at the border? One dozen? Two? Every dead Hotharian soldier is one less Elana will have to face on the battlefield. My discomfort is worth that price.

"Today is King Devon's Resting Ceremony," Aric says under his breath. "I thought you'd want to know."

My throat closes up, and every snide remark on the tip of my tongue dries up. It's midday, which means the ceremony will be underway soon. I think of my sister, and for the first time in my existence, I willingly offer up prayers to the Gods, pleading with them to give her strength and comfort.

I use my fingernail to dig into the skin of my left palm. I scratch the same spot over and over until the skin finally breaks, and a few drops of blood well up. I let them fall to the cold floor of the prison cart.

Then I close my eyes and whisper my own goodbyes to my father.

# Chapter Fifteen

## Elana

Today, I carry the mourning weight of the entire kingdom. And it's a burden I carry without my sister.

The train of my black dress drags on the ground behind me. Long, flowy sleeves affix to my shoulders. The bodice dips in the front modestly, and is fitted to my waist, but the plain satin skirts cascade in a sheet to my feet. A sheer veil covers my face as I look ahead. I'm eternally grateful to the Gods that the day is cloudy and slightly cool, with none of the end of summer's usual heat.

Mourners line the cobblestone path, tossing flowers and the occasional token or carved stone onto the street. Occasionally, I hear a wail in the crowd, but mostly I hear soft music and the clopping of horses' hooves. Several violinists are part of the procession, playing somber tunes. The wagon with Father's stone coffin steadily moves up the path, pulled by four black horses.

Mother walks next to me, as silent as I've ever heard her. The plan was for her to walk next to Aislinn, but she never showed up, and selfishly I didn't want to walk alone. So, here she is, wearing an elaborately embroidered black gown with the longest veil I've ever laid eyes on. She'd spent every free moment of the last few weeks embroidering the lace veil that covers her head and catches in the breeze behind her. It's a piece of artwork, and I can only imagine the tears she shed while creating it.

My parents didn't show many outward expressions of their love, but I often caught their secretive smiles towards each other, and occasionally walked in on them dancing in a room together, or sharing a kiss in Mother's gardens. Father would sometimes make a horrible joke that Mother would roll her eyes at, but upon turning away would crack a smile. When she fell ill years ago with a sickness that spread like wildfire across Adrithia, Father traveled all the way to Melinor to purchase a special live herb. The remedy that our master healer Clarisse was trying to make needed leaves from a fresh plant, so he learned how to care for the herb to ensure its survival on the journey back home. He told Aislinn and I not to move from her side until he returned, so we didn't. It was a miracle she made a full recovery, and she let Ash and I sleep in her bed with her for the next fortnight.

Aislinn. My sister should be here.

Anxiety spears through me, nearly causing my steps to falter. I'm more certain than ever that she's in trouble. Nothing else would have stopped her from being here. My breath comes in quick pants as I think of her, and all the possibilities of what could have happened.

"Elana, breathe," My mother whispers to me, keeping her head down. "Aislinn is okay. I know it."

How does she know that's what's sending me into a panic? I quickly suck in a sharp breath, then hold it for several seconds and slowly exhale. Of course she knows, she's my mother.

She grabs my hand and holds it, offering her comfort. I'm so shocked I nearly trip over the hem of my dress, but manage to catch myself before any embarrassment can be had.

Holding hands isn't the proper thing to do during this ceremony, but I swear I feel her fingers trembling as hard as mine for a moment. I gently wrap my fingers between hers. She gives me a reassuring squeeze as we walk. Unbidden tears well up in my eyes, but I swallow them away. I can't fall apart yet, not here.

We reach the shore of the lake which borders Sandral's western front, and turn north. Towering bluffs line the northern curve of the lake, and it's there that an empty cave waits for the arrival of my father's casket.

More people line the path, and more laments are played by the violin. Mother and I continue our walk behind the casket. Time passes, but I feel like I'm in a daze, my feet moving of their own accord. The only thing grounding me is the warmth of my mother's hand in mine.

At last, we reach the gradual slope to the cave entrance. The people lining the path here are more prominent. Adrithian nobility, including Lady Grimhart, and Duke Lyon's family stand to the side, bowing their heads and dabbing at their eyes as the procession passes.

I don't allow myself to look at any of them, instead staring straight ahead. Today is a day to honor my father, not worry about grievances with the court. The horses slow, and I see the mouth of the cave, yawning open before us. It's a massive opening, wide and tall enough for a carriage and then some.

Flanking the sides of the cave, I spot a dozen or so priestesses, as well as High Priestess Rosalind. They wear plain white robes and veils. Flanking the priestesses are the royal families of Aaranor, Melinor, and Ocarin. Rather than wearing solid mourning black, they're wearing splashes of the colors of their kingdoms. Red for Ocarin, purple for Melinor, and orange for Aaranor.

Unsurprisingly, Hotharia is absent.

I feel the heirs' eyes on me, but I do not acknowledge them. Today is not a day for politics and solidifying allies. It's a day to put my father's soul to rest, to usher him into the afterlife, where his soul will be judged and sent to one of the many realms beyond.

Mother gently squeezes my hand before letting me go. She walks to the side of Father's stone casket and leans over until her forehead touches the stone. I hear her whispering, saying her final goodbyes to him. She kisses the side of his carved stone cheek gently, and straightens, taking a few steps back.

Taking my cue, I move to the casket, placing my hand on the lid. It's cold. Cold and unmoving, which is the opposite of how he was in life.

My throat closes up, preventing me from whispering, so I settle for bowing my head and thinking my goodbyes.

*Father, already the world seems less without you in it. The castle hallways are empty without your booming voice, and the dinner table is dull without your conversation. We didn't have enough time, Father. I didn't have enough time to learn how to settle land disputes, or navigate the nobility. I'm lost without your guidance, and more than anything I wish we had more time. I want to be as good of a ruler as you, but I don't know how. For Adrithia, I'll give it everything I have, but I know it won't compare. I'll spend my whole life trying to live up to your greatness.*

My eyes sting, and I close them as tears well up and trail down my face.

*I miss you, and I'll miss you every day until my last day. You were the strength of this kingdom. And without you, a chasm is all that remains. I hope your soul is at peace. Farewell, for now, King Devon Sable.*

I suck in a shaky breath and step away from the coffin, letting my hand drop back to my side. With heavy footsteps, I walk alone to the mouth of the cave. Eight guards break away from the procession and carry the coffin. It must be heavy, but they don't balk at the weight. They carry it slowly to the back of the cave, setting it on a raised platform.

As they exit the cavern, I head inside, removing my veil, to address the goddess unhindered. There's a crystal bowl near the head of the casket, glimmering despite the lack of light making it in here.

I unsheathe one of my twin heirloom daggers from the hidden slit in my skirt. May all the Gods bless the tailor, who designed this garment perfectly. The soothing grip immediately puts me at ease, as if it senses my nerves and what I must do, and tells me everything will be alright.

In one swift motion, I drag the blade across my left palm, gasping quietly at the sharp pain of the cut. Crimson blood pools in my palm, and when there's enough of it, I flip my palm over, holding it over the glass bowl.

This has been done for generations. I remember my grandmother's Resting Ceremony, when Aislinn held me as father bled for his mother. As a child, I didn't understand why this was done. I do now.

My father's soul will be judged on his merits and how his deeds in life have affected the future. I'm spilling my blood to acknowledge that I'm his heir, and show that I'm willing to sacrifice a part of myself to his memory. If Aislinn were here, she'd be dripping blood into the same bowl. I smash down the thought as soon as I have it. *I will not think of her right now*, I repeat over and over in my mind.

"Goddess Avani, accept this blood so my father may be judged for his deeds in life," I chant, raising my voice to be heard outside the cave.

I let enough blood spill into the bowl to cover the base, then flip my hand back over, holding it out slightly so it doesn't drip on my dress. Moving on, I feel in my other hidden pocket for the round white stone I found on the lakeshore when I was a child. I remember the way Father laughed when he saw me digging through piles of rocks until I found the perfect one to bring home. There's nothing particularly special about it, other than its nearly round shape and pure white color, but when I saw it, I knew it was the one I wanted to keep. With a small smile from the memory, I place the stone into the bowl with the blood.

"Goddess Avani, please accept this gift to bring into your realm, as you have blessed our land with rock and stone, I give this small piece back," I have to fight to keep the trembling from my words, but I manage to get through them.

Now, all that's left to do is wait. I stash my dagger, replace my veil, and walk outside the cave, joining my mother, who stands at the mouth of the cavern, staring in. For once, anxiety rolls off her in waves. If the goddess accepts Father's soul to usher him into the afterlife she will give us some kind of sign. High Priestess Rosalind warned us that because his body isn't in the casket, we can't be sure what Avani will do. She could be offended and refuse us, leaving Father's soul in limbo until we make amends.

For several long moments, everyone stands there, staring at the cave in total silence. Even the violinists have ceased their playing. Then slowly, like a breeze picking up before a rainstorm, the earth begins to rumble. It starts with a barely perceptible shake, but turns into a roaring sound as a giant slab of stone rises up from the ground, sealing the mouth of the cave.

Beside me, Mother lets out a relieved sound. Rosalind steps out from the side of the cliff, raising her voice for all in the vicinity to hear, "Goddess Avani has accepted the soul of her devoted ruler, King Devon Sable. May he rest in eternal peace alongside the Gods!"

A cheer rings from the crowd, as people rejoice in their king's resting. Mother grabs my hand once again, squeezing it. "This is your kingdom now, Elana."

She means it as encouragement, I'm sure, but to me, it's as much a warning as it is motivation. This is my kingdom now. And I'm responsible for all its people. Let the nightmare begin.

# CHAPTER SIXTEEN

## AISLINN

When I escape I'm going to kill every last one of these brainless, spineless Hotharian assholes. They've been taking turns pissing on the sides of my prison cart, and one particularly idiotic dud even tossed in horse feces. It's really starting to ripen in this prison. I try not to inhale through my nose, because as much as I hate to admit it, I'm starting to ripen, too.

I've never been able to smell this much of myself before. It feels like a layer of dirt and grime sits on top of a layer of dust and sweat. It's purely inhumane, and makes me think about how we treat our own prisoners. I'd like to argue that we treated Aric better, but I think that'd be a lie.

It's the day after my father's Resting Ceremony, at least assuming the traitor was telling the truth. I rattle my chains for no other reason than to hear the nice clinking sound. There's only so much I can do to keep my mind occupied all day in here.

I try nodding off into a fitful sleep, but flashes of a looming god and a sense of foreboding, combined with the uncomfortable, borderline painful, prison cart keeps me from a peaceful slumber. These damn horses pulling the cart seem to hit every stone, root, or hole in the path, causing me to constantly bounce. It's a good core exercise, at least, to remain seated in one spot and avoid banging my head on the metal surrounding me.

I briefly wonder where Hector is, and if he's safe. I haven't seen him among the horses in the group. Did he escape, or was he captured by the Hotharians?

Of the ten soldiers *escorting* me, I've given eight of them names. I don't know their names, of course, so I've named them myself. There's the traitor, Big Beard, Little Beard, Scarface, Limpy, Rotten teeth, Baldy, and the worst one of all, Stubby. I admit, they're not the most creative names, but they're easy to remember, and have the added bonus of driving the men crazy.

I've only caught glimpses of the other two guards, but they haven't approached me yet. I'm not sure why. I'm quite friendly.

Letting out a long sigh, I count the links on my chains again. There are exactly 17 links from my hands to my feet, and seven between my ankles. Between my wrists there are five. It gives me enough room to hold a wooden bowl, but not enough to wrap around someone's neck. I already tried it. Could be a reason why Stubby's holding a grudge against me. That, and I apparently killed his brother at the border.

Several monotonous hours later, there's a commotion at the front of the group as my cart suddenly halts. I hear shouting and frantic hoof beats, then a brown horse gallops past my prison, and the traitor shouts for everyone to be calm.

There are frustrated voices arguing with him, but he gives clipped orders, and after a few moments everyone seems to busy themselves. How quickly he fits back into a role of authority.

I don't expect anyone to tell me what's going on, so I'm surprised when the traitor stops outside my prison cart and says, "the bridge is out ahead, and the river is overflowing. It's probably Prince Calder's doing, protecting the war camp."

War camp? He's taking me to a Hotharian war camp? "Wonderful, does this mean I'll finally be able to stretch my legs, or will I be drowning in here?"

He turns towards the river, then lowers his voice to just above a whisper, "this could be your chance."

My eyebrows perk up. "My chance for what?"

"Escape, Aislinn," he barely breathes.

I don't think I've heard him correctly. "What?"

His deep blue eyes bore into mine. "When you're in the river, use that time to get free and swim downstream as fast as you can. This river flows southeast, take it as close as you can get to Ocarin, then seek refuge there."

I rattle my chains, irritating the raw, bloody skin of my wrists underneath the manacles. "Aren't you forgetting something?."

I'm a strong swimmer, but even I know I won't stand a chance against the raging rapids while having my movement hindered.

He almost groans. "My uncle has the key."

I bite my tongue against my retort, it wouldn't have been a friendly thing to say to someone helping me escape. "In case it escaped your notice, there's no other way to remove these.

Aric shakes his head. "You're right. Shit."

Stumpy runs panting to Aric's side. "Sir, it's the prince!"

The traitor's focus snags on something across from the river, and then he kicks his horse forward. I press my face against the iron bars, but even then I can't see in the direction of the water.

"All hail our crowned prince, all hail Prince Calder!" Cheers erupt from the group, and with a jolt of movement, the cart is rolling again. We go up an incline, then down a slope, and I peer down to see we're on a bridge made entirely of ice.

Can't say I'm sad to see that terrible plan for escape dashed. Which, ironically, is what I would have been had I attempted it.

We continue moving at a steady pace after making the crossing, traveling around a large mesa until we reach the backside, and a path that zigzags up. The horses begin to climb. I stare out of the metal box when we reach the top, taking in the numbers in the assembled army. Judging by how close together the tents are and how large the mesa is, I estimate several thousand soldiers. It takes us several minutes to ride through the camp to the center, likely where the royal tent is set up. When the cart stops again, I know it's the last time for awhile.

There's commotion all around, and people rush out of every direction to greet my escorts, staring with unfettered curiosity and fear at my prison box.

Stubby, Little Beard, Rotting Teeth, and the traitor open the thick metal door to my cart. Sunlight streams in, and I blink against the brightness of it. A wave of fresh air hits my nose and I close my eyes for a brief moment, enjoying the crispness of it, even in the midst of the war camp.

"Let's go," the traitor says to me, motioning me to stand and follow him. His voice is cold, devoid of any of the kindness from earlier.

I sigh heavily and shake my chains, gesturing to where they're affixed to the base of the cart.

"Right," Aric says, disappearing for a moment, leaving me to sit in the cart and listen to the noises of the camp.

When Aric returns, he's holding a silver key. "My cousin has a set," he whispers, unlocking the chain and yanking me unceremoniously to the door.

Now freed, I contemplate rushing the traitor to escape, but I'm in the middle of thousands of enemies, armed and wary. Even for me, that would be a foolish move.

Instead, I stand slowly as I exit the prison cart. My legs wobble like a newborn fawn's, but I quickly gain my stability, allowing my muscles to adjust to my full weight again.

Aric leads me to a spot in front of Calder's grand tent, decorated with outlandish teal and gold.

"Kneel," Rotting Teeth says too close to my face and I gag on his rancid breath, which smells like a dead animal has been left in the sun to decay. I breathe in through my mouth to avoid vomiting.

"No," I say simply, refusing his request to kneel while I casually glance around the camp.

Several girls rush about with wash baskets and chamber pots, but otherwise there's not a single woman among the Hotharian warriors. I'm not surprised. What I am surprised to see, however, is the lack of the black-eyed enemies here. I'd expected the camp to be filled with them and their cursed weapons. I see none, which concerns me. If they're not here, where are they?

Stubby puts both of his meaty palms - his fingers were chopped off at the second knuckles, hence the nickname - on my shoulders, and pushes down, kicking out the back of my knees as he does so. Off balance, I collapse to my knees, letting out a hiss when they collide with the rock of the mesa.

Perhaps reason three that Stubby hates me is because I questioned whether his fingers were shortened to match his cock. The question earned me several kicks to my ribs. Men can be so sensitive.

Hotharia is a land built for harsh winters. Here, the snows pile thick in the cold months, sometimes covering homes for days until they can be dug out. Its terrain is mostly barren fields with rocky ground, and massive mountains with year round snowcover on the eastern coast. Hotharia is a difficult place to thrive in the winter, but its people are resilient. Some of them even attach slabs of thin long wood to their feet and slide down the mountains...for fun.

They're all crazy here.

Murmurs of the gathered soldiers quiet, and the crowd parts for Prince Calder. His strides are confident, as always, and he wears garish family colors like an honor. His golden hair gleams in the harsh midday sun as he accepts a goblet of wine from a servant and gives me an amused smile.

"What do we have here?" Calder sneers down at me. "Hello, Princess." He walks around me, as if I'm a wild animal on display at a carnival.

"Hello, asshole," I reply with a little smirk of my own. "Apologies for my state. I regret that I didn't have time to freshen up before greeting such an esteemed twat."

Calder's icy eyes harden, and he nods at Stubby. A gloved hand strikes my face, hard. I lean into the pain, forcing myself not to flinch or show discomfort. Instead, I laugh. "Is that all you've got, Calder? You'd have another man beat a girl for you?"

His sharp gaze narrows on me, the blues of his eyes seem darker than I remember. He passes his golden wine goblet to a servant and steps up to me with a hand drawn back. Sunlight glints off the sharp pieces of ice crystals between his knuckles as he brings his fist into the side of my face. Pain erupts, and this time I feel blood pooling in my mouth.

I run my tongue over my teeth, reassuring myself they're all accounted for. Then I spit the mouthful of blood onto the barren rock at his feet.

Calder jumps back in disgust. "You are no princess. You're just a bastard."

My mouth splits in a toothy, bloody grin. "And don't you forget it."

"Tie her up in the prison tent," Calder snaps at no one in particular, yet several men jump forward to do his bidding, including Stubby. Gods, this guy can't get enough of me.

"Cousin, welcome home," Calder greets the traitor with a true smile and the two of them walk away together, chatting like old pals. "My father told me to expect you, so I've had my men on lookout eagerly awaiting your arrival."

Guards haul me to my feet, and shove me forward. One of the men grabs my chains and tugs me along, to a shabby-looking tent near Calder's. Inside, there are several metal towers with rings on them. The chain that keeps my feet attached to my hands is fixed to the post, and I watch the key carefully as Stubby puts it in his pocket.

He fixes me with a leer. "I hope these 'commodations suit yeh, Princess."

I make a point of looking around, as if I'm assessing my surroundings. "Well, it's a bit lonelier than I hoped. There's no one here for me to talk to. Please tell me you'll stay." I give my best pouting face.

Stubby makes a noise of revulsion and backs away. "Not in a million years, you bitch. Enjoy your solitude."

He storms out, and I relax, sinking onto the bed of straw beneath me. After days of sitting and laying on nothing but unyielding metal, I'm grateful for the warmth and slight cushioning of the hay. There's another bucket off to the side, within my reach for when I need it.

I mentally catalog everything I saw outside. Several thousand men, positioned on a protected mesa, no sign of any cursed enemies, and the king is absent. From what I know about Hotharia, I'm fairly certain that we're in the north-central area. The land we travelled was fairly flat, meaning we're not too far east to run into the mountains. We didn't pass the capital city of Forath, either, so we aren't in the south. The river that we crossed could be the Gorde River, which runs from the Gods Territory all the way to the ocean on the eastern side of Hotharia.

I have no idea how I'll use any of this information yet, but if a chance arises for me to send a letter to Elana, I will.

I have to find a way.

# CHAPTER SEVENTEEN

## ELANA

"Everyone is prepared in the lesser hall, Your Majesty," Rigel says, standing inside the doorway to my suite.

Senara helps me affix my crown as I shift on my feet and try not to vomit on the floor. "And everyone is here?"

He nods. "All the monarchs and their heirs are present."

"Okay, good. Thank you, Rigel," I give him a wobbly smile, which he returns with a genuine one of his own.

"Is my mother coming, too?" I ask, smoothing back one piece of my hair that refuses to stay behind my ear.

"She is already there, entertaining the guests."

I can do this. I can do this.

There are dark circles under my eyes from my lack of sleep. After the ceremony, Mother and I returned home in the early evening and retreated to our rooms. I learned from Senara that my mother locked the door to her chambers, so not even her lady's maid could enter. The thought sends a pang through my heart that she was alone through her grief. Even though I had my own to contend with.

I spent the night rehashing every detail of the ceremony, down to the closing of the cave and our long walk home. Did my obvious show of emotion make me look weak or inexperienced to any of the other rulers?

Blowing out an anxious breath, I take one last glance at the looking glass, I hurry out of my suites and follow Rigel to our receiving hall. My guards flank me, a pair in front and behind me. Matteo must be in the hall already, because I don't see him among my escorts.

Mother insisted we host this dinner so I could get to know the other monarchs and start building relations with them before my coronation in two days.

Gentle music comes from the hall, which is almost immediately drowned out by a ringing in my ears as I step into the room. All eyes turn to me, with varying expressions of pity, wariness, and suspicion. I almost drop into a curtsy, but stop myself, remembering that these are my peers now.

My flowy navy skirt barely touches the ground, giving me ample movement as I approach the monarchs of Melinor, Ocarin, and Aaranor.

Mother surprises me by stepping forward and embracing me, giving me a quick kiss on the cheek, using the moment to say, "take a deep breath, daughter. You're exactly where you're supposed to be."

She lets me go, but stays at my side. Without thinking, I immediately seek out Aidan, and my heart starts pounding quicker as I take in his perfectly tailored black and red outfit. His gaze burns into me with an intensity that has the rest of the room fall out of focus. I almost start moving to him, but a familiar tall, gorgeous woman closes in first.

"Elana," she says, closing the short distance between us and wrapping me in a hug. Her avoidance of my formal title instantly puts me at ease. I hug her back enthusiastically.

She lets me go after a few moments, although worry etches deep lines between her eyes. Her voice is soft. "I'm so sorry about your father, and Aislinn. Have you heard anything about her disappearance?"

"Nothing official, but we have our suspicions," I whisper, swallowing hard at the frown that pulls her mouth down. "We'll talk later."

She gives me a nod. "If there's anything Melinor can do, let me know."

"Thank you, Rayna," I say, giving her a small smile back. My eyes catch on her stunning purple and gold dress, accentuating her umber brown skin, hugging her form and brushing the ground at her sandaled feet. Her hair is a halo of gorgeous black curls, her crown gleaming at the top of her head. A necklace of beads and metalwork hugs the base of her neck, matching the earrings that nearly reach her shoulder.

A man clears his throat behind her. Rayna grimaces before stepping to the side and gesturing at the couple. "Elana, these are my parents, King Mesfin and Queen Desta."

I give them a tentative nod. "Welcome back to Adrithia. I wish we were meeting under better circumstances."

Queen Desta gives me a warm grin. She's as tall as Rayna, with the same muscular build. Her clothes are more muted in color than her daughter's. Her hair is tied back and wrapped with matching fabric. "It's a pleasure to meet you, Elana. Rayna has told us many wonderful things about you."

King Mesfin steps forward. His outfit matches his wife's and complements his ebony skin. His crown sits on top of short black hair. I remind myself that he was blessed by the Air God Sepher. "We were sorry to learn of your loss. King Devon was a fine and honorable man. May your reign be as great as his."

"Thank you, King Mesfin," I say, not sure of what else could be said. He steps back, seemingly satisfied, and makes way for Rian, who approaches with a woman I only assume to be his mother.

Queen Nami is around my height, with her sleek black hair pulled into an elaborate bun on the top of her head. Her angular eyes are rich dark brown. Her orange robes accentuate her glowing tawny skin, and are layered with other colors, which cascade to her feet. Rian must have inherited some features like lighter hair and extraordinary height from his father, who passed away several years prior due to an illness. Queen Nami was blessed by the Water God Kai.

Her eyes scrutinize her son as he strides up to me, a lazy grin on his face, showing off his dimples. His ash brown hair is pulled back into a knot at the back of his head. I expect him to give me a hug, but instead he takes my hand and kisses the back of it.

He drops the grin and keeps hold of my hand with both of his. "Elana, I'm sorry for your incredible loss. My heart bleeds for you."

My face softens, and I feel like I've been transported back to the mountain. I didn't realize how much I'd missed my friends, nor did I realize I'd begun to think of them as friends.

"Thank you, Rian," I say, and he relents my hand as his mother steps to his side.

"My mother, Queen Nami," he says, and I dip my head in her direction.

"Your son is quite gifted with his powers, Queen Nami. He saved us all on the mountain with his ability to fly," I say, not entirely sure why, but I want her to like me.

After studying me for a few moments, she nods. "Yes, he has always had his head in the clouds. It doesn't surprise me that he ended up blessed with air."

The way she says it is almost distasteful. I blink in surprise at the harshness of her tone and glance at Rian, whose face turns crimson. A pang of pity washes through me on his behalf.

"Nami, dear friend, you don't mean to insinuate that there's anything wrong with being chosen by Sepher, do you?" Mesfin challenges her with a sharp smile.

"Of course not, Mesfin, but as we live on a mountain, air isn't exactly difficult to come by."

On the Gods' Peaks, Rian confessed to me that he never wanted to rule, that his passions lie outside of being King. I wonder if his mother's attitude has anything to do with him expressing those wishes to her.

Not wanting to further fan ill will between the neighboring kingdoms, I prepare myself to greet the final royal family. The instant I start to turn, my eyes meet Aidan's, as if my body instinctively knows where he is. My pulse thuds in my chest, and I feel it reverberating in my throat. I move one step, and he closes the distance between us.

He keeps his voice low as he murmurs, "Your Majesty." Gods, the fire in his gaze could set the entire room ablaze.

"Hello, Aidan," I say, trying to keep my tone neutral, but failing miserably as I hear the slight wobble.

His face breaks into a smirk as he angles his body to reveal his mother. "You've already met my mother, Queen Amira. My father, Edward, sends his regrets, but is unable to make it this evening." He announces coolly, making me wonder if something is going on there.

"Adrithia welcomes you, Queen Amira," I say in a practiced tone, then turn sharply away, to the formal dining hall.

Rigel stands there and gives me a nod. The staff is ready for us. "Dinner is ready, let's proceed to the dining hall."

Instead of waiting, I lead the way to the dining room. Mother appears like a shadow at my side and whispers in a clipped tone. "Rigel should have announced that, Elana. A queen does not announce supper."

I let out a long breath. "It'll be fine, no one will care."

"We are royalty. Etiquette is important."

I don't want to start an argument in front of everyone, so I give her an acknowledging dip of my head.

At the table, I head to the center, where the tallest chair sits. An attendant pulls the chair out for me and pushes it in as I sit. Mother sits on my right, and the others fill in around us. I settle into my chair, relaxing slightly until I notice who took the seat to my left. Dark hair to the nape of his neck, a large frame, and undeniable heat wafting off him. Gods, this is going to be a fun dinner.

Conversation is light as we start the main course, Rayna complimenting the ceremony yesterday, and Rian chiming in about how realistic the casket looked. Mother thanks them with grace. Nobody brings up the war with Hotharia, nor the disappearance of my sister, which I'm eternally grateful for.

All is pleasant, until Rian's mother, Queen Nami uses a moment of lapsed conversation to ask, "Elana, you simply must show us your powers. I've heard it's a sight to behold."

A piece of sauteed beef is halfway to my mouth, and I momentarily freeze before putting my fork down onto my plate. It's a simple request, one that I have no reason to refuse. Is it safe to tell them about the light? Maybe one will appease them, if I make a show of it.

The shadows are swift to answer my silent summons, rising up from the floor and cloaking the room around us. I command them to block out the hearth, plunging us into nearly total darkness, save for the candles flickering on the table. The room drops in temperature, and sounds from the rest of the castle cut off.

"Impressive," Rayna's father says from his end of the table, Queen Desta looking equally in awe. Next to her father, Rayna beams at me, her smile full of pride. Rian gives an appreciative nod, but his mother looks around, unaffected. I don't dare cast a glance at Aidan and his mother.

All at once, I instruct the darkness to retreat, sinking back into the ground and away from us.

"Yes, impressive, but what about your other power?" Queen Nami asks, leaning forward expectantly. "You were blessed by two goddesses, correct?"

I try not to blanch. To my surprise, Mother responds first. "Nami, surely you didn't come all the way here to see elemental tricks?"

Under the table, a warm hand grazes my thigh, and my eyes dart to Aidan, who shakes his head slightly. I can almost hear him in my head saying *don't tell her*.

"Are you that surprised, Maris? It's an entirely new power for Astrellia. There are no records showing anyone has ever had control over light and darkness before. It's only natural for us to want to see it firsthand," Nami says, and shit, it's difficult to argue with that logic.

Mother's lips go tight, the only indication of her annoyance.

"It's nighttime," I blurt, and feel the stares of everyone at the table. "I-I can't use the light right now because it's nighttime."

Queen Nami's eyes narrow to slits. "I thought it didn't matter what time of day it was. Didn't you write to Rian apologizing for misleading him, and that you could, in fact, use both powers whenever you wish?"

I try to think of some lie, but I've never been proficient at falsehoods.

"I think what she meant by that letter was to clarify that there are certain times of day when both powers could be used, right? Dawn and dusk?" Rayna speaks up, giving me a look that promises we will discuss this later.

"Yes," I say, latching onto Rayna's explanation like a lifeline, "that's exactly correct."

Nami studies me with a shrewd gaze. "Of course. Well, you'll have to make sure your coronation takes place at either dawn or dusk so you'll be able to wield them both."

The muscles in my jaw lock up and I feel Mother stiffen at my side. At my coronation? Why would I use my powers at my coronation?

Nami must spot my confusion, because she elaborates, "ah, yes, you were probably too young to remember the details of your father's coronation. He came into power fairly early on. When a new ruler is crowned, no matter the kingdom, all the monarchs come together and provide an offering of power to the Gods. You surely wouldn't want to leave out one of the twin goddesses, now, would you?"

The urge to glare at my mother is strong, but I manage to hold back. How could she not tell me about this? I swallow down my building anxiety with a sip of wine, trying for nonchalance. "Of course."

Nami stays mercifully quiet through the rest of the courses. Dessert is a delicious assortment of puddings, tarts, and cakes. I pack a modest amount onto my plate, trying a little bit of everything, until I earn a sharp look from my mother.

I ignore her and lift my fork to take my first bite of fresh apple tart. The apples were picked fresh this morning from our castle orchard. As if she strives to be my personal rain cloud on a sunny day, Queen Nami clears her throat. "Now that we're finished with our meal, could we please address more serious topics?"

With sheer willpower, I set my fork onto the delicate plate, the full bite still staring at me. "What would you like to discuss?"

"How did King Devon truly die? Why are the rulers of Hotharia not here? And who is this so-called enemy you warned us about?"

I already mourn the loss of the tart. There will be no enjoying it tonight.

Before I can say anything, however, Queen Amira launches into a detailed account of what happened in her kingdom. "Ocarin was attacked more than a month ago by an unknown force. They sailed to our shores near Kikar, and started killing their way through villages. They did not steal, they did not take prisoners. It seemed like their sole purpose was widespread destruction. Our advance army took heavy losses to stop them. The few enemies we managed to take prisoner refused to speak. They had tongues, but they did not use them. Not even when we utilized *harsher* tactics. It's like they were under a spell. Then, there were the weapons they carried. They were poisoned or cursed somehow. Blades of unnatural black, pulsing with a dark energy. One small cut was enough to cause the poison to spread, killing people within an hour."

Aidan's gaze is trained on his plate, as if remembering the effects of the poison on his friends. Rayna's parents exchange a concerned glance. Queen Nami, however, looks unaffected, despite Rian's brows furrowing with unease.

"When we beat back the invading forces, their ships sailed towards Adrithia. My son rode to Sandral to warn King Devon and Queen Maris of the impending attack, with one of their cursed blades as proof."

Amira turns to me, expectantly, and I realize it's my turn to pick up the story. I clear my throat. "We had a difficult time believing Prince Aidan's story at first, but there was no other reason for the cursed dagger to exist. We learned that the enemy was sailing to our southern coast, east of Tierth, and so our army left to stop them, with Father leading us."

I swallow the thick knot in my throat, then carry on, "my personal guard was supposed to send a call for aid from our army at Tierth, but we learned later that he never sent it. We arrived at the shore shortly before the enemy. The battle was brutal, and reinforcements never came."

Memories of the screams, the blood soaking the grass, the boy with blue eyes, Jakob, come rushing back to me. My throat threatens to close. I take a long drink of wine. Across the table, I catch Rayna's sad expression. She gives me an encouraging nod.

"We managed to rally after I was able to purify the enemy's weapons with my light. My father-," I break off again, taking in a shaky breath, remembering his order for Aislinn, Aidan, and I to run so he could split the earth under our feet. I can't do this. I can't relive that moment again. My mother's hand grips mine on the table, and she squeezes.

"King Devon broke the shoreline," my mother says, her voice low, but everyone is so quiet around the table it sounds like she's shouting, "but in doing so, he was attacked from behind, and fell to his death among the waves."

I can barely swallow as my vision blurs.

"Maris, we're so sorry for your loss," King Mesfin says, looking sympathetic. "Melinor will stand with you against this new threat."

My mother gives an appreciative nod, placing her hand over her heart in a sign of respect.

"That still doesn't answer where Hotharia is," Nami says without pause. Rian shoots his mother a disapproving glare, but her eyes are trained on Mother and me.

"Two of the ships the enemy used to attack Adrithia flew Hotharian banners. They wore Hotharian colors," I say with vehemence.

"They could have stolen the ships," she argues.

"Reinforcements never arrived because my guard was a spy for Hotharia. He never sent the request to our army in Tierth. And during his trial, we received a letter from King Skade, demanding he be returned to Hotharia safe and sound, or else there would be a second invasion," I respond, sharply.

Nami sits back in her seat, dramatically resting her chin between her thumb and forefinger. "I would like to see this letter."

I grit my teeth, but give her a clipped response, "that can be arranged." And what better time than now? Let's put this issue to rest once and for all. Rigel is standing at the edge of the room, and I catch his eyes. He disappears from the hall, heading to my study to grab the letter.

"Assuming this letter can be produced, then the Astrellian Peace is broken. We must have justice, and Hotharia will be made to answer for their crimes," King Mesfin says in a deep voice, pounding his fist on the table.

"This is indeed troubling," Nami says, and pauses, as if choosing her words carefully, "out of curiosity, how did you know when and where they would attack? You said you made it to the coast before the enemy."

My gaze shifts to Amira, then just as quickly I look away, not wanting anyone to become suspicious. I take another sip of wine as I try to think of a convincing lie. "Well, we had scouts stationed along the coast, because, umm, they were concerned about-,"

I'm cut off by Amira, who starts laughing, of all things. "Dear Elana, thank you for trying to cover for me. I'm afraid the responsibility lies with me, however, to answer that question.

I catch her look, and though there's humor on the surface, her neck is a tight line. "I have been keeping something from the other kingdoms since I was born. You see, the Ashfall family line has always been blessed by more than one god, although sometimes this gift skips several generations."

We all stare at her in silence as she closes her two eyes, but a third, vertical eye winks open in the center of her forehead. Gasps sound from around the table. Rayna stares, her mouth hanging open. Rian's mother is out of her seat, one hand clutching the arm of the chair she was seated at, as if for balance.

"You're a seer?" She shrieks.

# Chapter Eighteen

## Elana

This is not how I expected the evening to go. I didn't anticipate Rian's mother using her control over water to send her dessert wine at Aidan's mother across the dining table. The liquid flies straight for Amira's face, which is deflected with a dessert plate.

Amira, plate in hand, cocks her arm back, poised to throw. My mother takes the opportunity to delicately clear her throat. "Amira, if you don't mind, please find something else to throw. This set has been in the family for generations." She taps a delicate fingernail to her own plate, while eying Amira with one eyebrow raised.

Of the people in this room, my mother isn't a threat in terms of physical power, but she can go toe-to-toe with them in posturing.

Amira returns the plate to the table. "Apologies, Maris. We meant no offense."

"And none has been taken," Mother replies, going back to sipping her wine.

"How could you keep this from us?" Nami demands of Amira, angrily drumming her fingers on the table instead of finding objects to throw.

Amira levels a hard stare back at her. "Because it didn't impact you. My abilities in no way affected your life until now. I'm only revealing myself because it will help us in the war to come. But even my abilities only go so far. We need to stand together to face the enemy."

"You expect us to agree to an alliance after revealing this? You could have been using these powers against the other kingdoms this whole time and we would have been none the wiser. Why should we trust you? What else are you hiding?"

"I have never used this power to harm another kingdom." Amira turns to her son. "Aidan, tell everyone what you and Elana learned from the Hotharian merchants."

All eyes turn to Aidan and I once again. He casts me a look, as if checking to see if I want to explain. I give him a nod.

"We questioned the captain and some crew members from a Hotharian merchant ship a few nights ago. The captain confirmed the appearance of foreign ships in their harbor. He corroborated the timeline of when the ships ended up in Ocarin, then later in Adrithia. What was most concerning was that he told us of an entire fleet, but we only saw a handful of ships during our battles. There are dozens more out there, unaccounted for. He also told us that he saw thousands of men departing the ships at the royal dock and marching towards Forath. We suspect these ships are from a relatively unknown land called Tyne."

When Aidan stops speaking, the room is silent for several long heart-beats.

"None of this makes any sense," Rayna's mother says. "What does Hotharia get out of breaking the peace? And who are these invaders?"

Before anyone can answer, Rigel appears in the doorway, holding out a familiar rolled parchment on a silver tray. He presents it to me. "Thank you, Rigel."

I unroll the scroll and begin to read:

*"Princess Elana of Adrithia,*

*You do not know me, but trust that my words are not to be taken lightly. It has come to my attention that my nephew, Aric Vernier, is in your possession, and stands trial for treason against Adrithia. This cannot be, as Aric is and always has been a loyal citizen of Hotharia and part of the royal family. I implore you to release him into our care, lest our newfound army find another reason to attack your kingdom.*

*We expect his return within a fortnight, or else we will meet you on the battlefield once again.*

*King Skade Vernier"*

When I finish, I hand the parchment over to Aric, who quickly reads it, then hands it to his mother, who repeats the act, passing it down the table. When it reaches Nami, her eyes narrow as she scans his words.

After everyone has read it, Nami steeples her hands in front of her face. "This is a disturbing revelation. I need time to digest this, along with the clear betrayal of you keeping your seer abilities secret from us." She turns her predator eyes to Amira, who stares back with equal tenacity. "We will be going back to Aaranor immediately following the coronation, to consider this new information."

A feeling of immense disappointment crashes over me. This is not the reaction I was hoping for when telling the other kingdoms about Hotharia's betrayal. I swallow my disappointment and look at King Mesfin.

"What will Melinor do?"

"Long ago, my people suffered difficult losses in the attack on our king-dom. Because of that, the survivors spent years in misery while recovering. The hardships were immense," he pauses, sharing a look with his wife, then Rayna, "but the other kingdoms came to our aid. Our continent has always thrived when the kingdoms work together and help each other in times of need. Melinor will stand against Hotharia and this heinous breach of the Astrellian Peace."

Rayna's determined expression meets mine, and she gives me a confident nod. I return the gesture.

Rian's mother is the first to make excuses to leave. Rian gives one last apologetic look before following her out. Rayna's family is next, and she asks if she can visit me soon, to which I happily accept.

Aidan and his mother are the last, and the tension in the room is palpa-ble.

I look between the two queens and start to open my mouth to break the tension when Mother asks, "did you know my husband was going to die during the battle?"

I wince, my hands fisting in my lap.

Amira takes a long breath, breaking eye contact with my mother and staring at the wine goblet in her hand. "I knew it was one of several outcomes."

Mother narrows her hazel eyes at her. "Why didn't you say anything? Why didn't you warn us?"

"There were two ways the battle could have gone. One where everyone died, including my son and both your daughters, setting off a chain reac-tion that would have ended with the complete destruction of Astrellia, or one where Devon sacrificed himself to save his children and my son. I sent him this message, and he made his choice," Amira says, still staring at the goblet.

"You told him of the choice?" Mother asks sharply. I think back to the battlefield, and the message I received from Amira.

"The fire wyvern?" I question, and my mother's disapproving glare pins me to my seat.

Amira nods. "Yes, I can use fire to send messages across great distances."

"How do you know that he made the choice? There could have been another way. If he'd stayed on the side of the cliff that didn't fall into the sea, or if he'd made the choice earlier and prevented the attack sooner. There had to have been a way for him to survive," Mother insists.

Amira gives her a sad smile. "If he had stopped the attack before it started, you would have lost the city of Tierth, and hundreds of thousands of innocent Adrithians would have died. I saw that path clearly. Once the choice was made to meet them on the coast, the options narrowed, but became volatile. I gave Elana the message to go aid in the battle, because if she stayed at the healer's tent, then the battle would have been lost, and all would be dead. The only choice I gave to Devon was to fall, or allow his daughters to fall. I saw all three of our children rush to meet the second wave of attackers, and none of them live because of it."

My eyes sting once more as tears fall freely down my cheeks. I remember using the last of my light powers and thinking we'd won, then seeing the new ships and the onslaught of soldiers rowing to shore. Aislinn and I would have readily charged towards that second force to defend our kingdom, and Aidan would have followed us. I suck in a breath. Father shouldn't have had to die, but he did make the choice. I think I understand that now, but I still wish I'd been able to save him.

"I am sorry your husband had to die for your daughters to live. That is a decision that no parent should have to make, but if given that choice, I'd imagine it's one made easily. He was truly a good man," Amira drains the last of her wine, then stands.

Beside her, Aidan does the same. There are so many things I want to say to him, to both of them, but I also need time to absorb everything she said.

He doesn't give me the opportunity to speak, however. He grabs my hand and gives the back of it a warm lingering kiss, and whispers quietly, "Magpie, if you ever need me, you know where to find me."

"There will be no coronation tomorrow."

Duke Lyons stands in front of *my* throne, in *my* own home, holding a piece of parchment. A group of nobles is gathered behind him.

"Careful, Duke," Mother cautions, her voice low and threatening. "We've already sentenced one traitor this month. Your words toe the line of treason."

The duke has the audacity to look affronted, putting a hand on his chest while his mouth gapes in shock. "Treason, Your Majesty? I would never. I am a humble servant of Adrithia. I serve the best interests of all of its people."

"Let me see the petition," Mother gestures for the scroll, and Lyons hands it over swiftly.

She unrolls it, then keeps unrolling it. Gods, that's not a good sign. Her eyes scan down, reading the decree, then studying the signatures. The many, many signatures.

"So you wish to enact the garishly outdated Ascension Rite?" She hands me the parchment, and I quickly read. Indeed, the order is for whatever this rite is. And the signatures of most of the larger noble houses and more than half of the smaller ones are upon it.

My stomach nearly drops to the floor. This many people don't trust me to rule?

"That is correct, Your Majesty. An overwhelming majority of Adrithia's nobility is in favor of a regent serving in Elana's stead...until she marries, that is," he says, with a sly smirk, and I feel as if I'm being repeatedly punched in the gut. I call to the darkness around me, and it sings back a soothing melody.

"And have the nobility submitted the name of a regent?" Mother's eyebrow raises, the only sign that she's wholly unimpressed with the so-called Duke in front of her.

He gives a little bow and produces a second parchment from the inside pocket of his coat. "They have, Your Majesty."

She unrolls this one with as much agitation as possible. Breaking the seal with an angry finger, unraveling it in a single motion. "This has your name written on it."

Duke Lyons smiles, his greasy lips stretching wide up his long, narrow face. "Yes, it does. The nobility have endorsed me as their new regent."

There it is. My pulse hammers in my chest. This was his plan to seize power all along.

"No," Mother says simply, and his smile falters.

"No?" He questions, as if such a word were never spoken to him before.

"No," she reaffirms, passing the parchment to me. I don't even bother reading it.

"You-you can't say no, Queen Maris. That is the directive of the court," Lyons sputters, his cheeks turning a splotchy red.

Mother lets out a long sigh, as if she's tired of entertaining a toddler. "None of these signatures on here are from Sables, so therefore this is a request, not a directive. This land is ruled by the Sable family, no one else, as decreed by the Gods centuries ago."

"Of course we respect your husband's family's right to rule. The role of Regent isn't a permanent one. It wouldn't even have to be at all, if the princess would marry," Lyons suggests, and I nearly throttle him with my shadows.

"That is off the table, and you know it," Mother says sharply. "Queen Elana will wed when she sees fit."

The duke scoffs. "Well, do inform us when it is that she sees fit. There have been several perfectly acceptable offers presented to her already, and she's turned them all down."

"Don't make this about your bruised ego, Aldrich. Your son was not a good match," Mother waves a dismissive hand in his direction.

A humorless laugh sounds from him, and I cringe as the sound grates against my ears. "It's not only the offer from my son, Maris. I have personally overseen half a dozen marriage offers, and all have been perfectly reasonable. It seems you've managed to raise two daughters who refuse to do the one thing daughters are born to do, marry. Tell me, Your Majesty, what good is a queen who does not produce heirs?"

The darkness becomes a living cloak around me. Duke Lyons turns to me finally, his face paling.

"Let me get this straight, Aldrich," Mother says, quietly from my side. "You're intimidated by my daughters, so you enact some archaic formality to weasel your way into any semblance of power you possibly can?"

My jaw threatens to drop in shock of her completely commanding this situation. She's an absolute force of nature.

"Tha-that's not what's happening here. I'm doing this for the citizens of Adrithia. Because Princess Elana is too young to rule and hasn't had the experience in statecraft to successfully run our kingdom. The nobility agree with me. You have the decree with the proper amount of signatures," his face continues to redden.

"And if Queen Elana should refuse?" Mother challenges.

"Well, then she shall be queen of the peasants and no one else! We will take our personal armies and march to the countryside, and refuse to send aid if called upon." The duke shouts, gesturing angrily with his fist. "For the protection of our kingdom, this is happening."

Mother takes a long breath, eyes flickering briefly to Rigel, who stands off to the side of the room. "Since the nobility requires a regent, then I will assume the role until my daughter is formally crowned. We will postpone the coronation and reconvene after the Winter Solstice to discuss her ascension."

I bite my tongue against my frustration. Surely, she must have a plan, but to cancel my coronation now? Wouldn't that make more of a mess with the other kingdoms?

"Your Majesty, you can't be serious-," The duke takes a step forward, towards my mother, and my shadows spring to life, erecting a wall between them. He halts, then turns to me, face blanched of color.

"Take a step back, Duke," I command, rising from my seat and as I narrow my gaze on up.

He seems to fumble, shifting on his feet and taking a tentative step backward, while sparing a quick glance at the other nobles behind him. Several of them stare at the ground, refusing to meet his eyes.

Not all of them seem to be on board with his methods. Interesting.

"I meant no threat, Your Highness," he dips his head. "And forgive my questioning, but Queen Maris, you must still be grieving, so I assumed you wouldn't want to keep your position."

"Are you suggesting I am unfit to govern our kingdom because my husband died?" Mother's tone is sharp enough to slice through bone.

His head remains bowed as he says, "no, of course not. You are more than capable."

Mother doesn't take her shrewd stare off him. "Then we are all in agreement? I shall be regent of Adrithia until after the winter solstice, when we reconvene on Elana's ascension."

Duke Lyons turns to his supporters, who all back away from him. Finally, he seems to deflate. "Yes, that is acceptable."

"Good. Now, unless there's anything else you'd like to discuss with us, we thank you for your time and your continued commitment to Adrithia," Mother says, effectively dismissing them.

Suddenly, the doors to the Great Hall swing open and boots pound down marble. A messenger leads a set of guards across the expansive hall. Rigel rushes to intercept them, as the nobles part to allow them access to the dais.

Rigel exchanges hushed whispers, then does something I've never seen him do. He gasps. The man whose entire job is to appear calm and collected just...slipped. He coughs once to redeem himself and gives several nods to the messenger and guards. Then he turns to us, and his expression will surely haunt me for the rest of my life.

I swallow the painful knot in my throat and descend the steps towards them. Mother's hand grasps mine, and her fingers shake.

Rigel opens his mouth once, then closes it. He straightens his shoulders and says in a careful tone, "Your Majesties, the guards from the Ocarin-Hotharia border have returned. You need to come with me."

# Chapter Nineteen

## Aislinn

*"Seek me out, daughter of Sable. Before it's too late. Before all is lost," a deep male voice reverberates in my skull, cracking me open and baring my soul for him to see.*

*Around me, there's nothing. A vast emptiness. All I see is gray. A layer of thick fog. Where am I? And whose voice is that?*

*"Who are you?" I call out to the void.*

*"Find me, Aislinn."*

*I let out a growl of frustration. "Where exactly am I supposed to find you?"*

*"Stay your path and you will find me soon enough. Do not strain from your course, no matter how painful," the voice grows weaker with every word, like it struggles through the nothingness around me.*

My eyes wrench open, then squeeze shut against the blinding light.

Someone opened my tent flap. I peel back my lids slowly, blinking against the harsh midday sun.

A servant girl slowly approaches with something clasped in her hands. Flashes of my dream cut through reality. The sharp voice, the claustrophobic void around me, and the confusion.

I blink back into focus, staring at the servant girl with fiery red hair, not muted and muddled with brown like my sister's. It's so unruly it nearly bursts out of the knot at the back of her head. She's only the second person I've seen since they tied me here days ago. Someone gave me a bucket of cold water and a strip of dried meat yesterday and told me to make it last.

"What do you want?" I groan, adjusting my bindings so I can sit on the straw with my back to the post.

The slight girl, who must be in her mid-teens, holds out her hands like they're an offering. Within her calloused palms lies a piece of bread and a small chunk of cheese.

My stomach growls eagerly at the sight, but I command it to quiet. It doesn't, of course, and rumbles louder out of protest.

I stare at the girl, and my suspicion grows at the blatant fear in her expression.

"Why are you offering this to me?" I ask with narrow eyes.

She swallows with some difficulty. "L-Lord Aric instructed me to."

"You serve Aric?"

"Yes," she whispers, refusing to meet my gaze.

I sigh and take the bread and cheese from her shaking hands. "What's your name?"

She pulls her hand towards her chest like touching me will infect her somehow. Amusement pulls my lips up. "Are you afraid of me?"

The girl rubs her hands together. "They say you are the bastard spawn of a demon and Queen Maris."

Wicked delight curls through me for the first time in days and I let out a laugh. "Do they? And what if I told you that the truth is much, much worse?"

I bite into the bread, chewing slowly and savoring the taste despite my stomach demanding I feed it, right now.

"W-what is the truth?" Her voice quivers.

I give her a smirk as I swallow, leaning closer to her, as if I'm about to whisper a dark secret. "The truth, I'm afraid, is that I'm pure-blooded Sable. I don't know why I wasn't chosen."

I take a small bite of cheese, enjoying the sharpness combined with a slightly nutty flavor as I rest my head back and wait for the girl to leave.

She retreats, her steps hardly making any noise. "I'm Igraine."

A ghost of a smile graces my lips. "Thank you for the meal, Igraine."

I sigh as she leaves, slowly nibbling on the food she brought. It's awkward work, since my hands are still bound together with iron chains. It's an exercise in willpower not to shove it all in my mouth at once. I manage to make it last the entire day.

I stare at the scratch marks I've made in the stone with the sharp part of my manacles. Today is my sister's coronation.

The sun is starting to set, and in Adrithia, the feasts will be plentiful. Every tavern and inn will be overflowing with patrons. Thousands of lanterns will line the streets and citizens will revel until dawn, then sleep for a few hours and start it all over again. The nobility will feast at the castle, and then dance in the great hall until their feet bleed. Hopefully Elana will be among those dancing. Gods, I hope she's safe and not worrying about me.

I imagine the great hall, all decorated for the coronation with glimmering navy and silver banners. A quartet will play soft music in the corner of the room. The dessert table will be piled high with delicious cakes, pastries, and puddings. The mental image has me practically salivating.

The other heirs, except Calder, of course, will be in attendance. Rayna will be there. If Elana's lucky, maybe she'll even sing for her. Rayna's powerful voice has been imprinted in my memory since the first time I heard her sing at the summit years ago. If there was a god of music, surely they would have blessed her.

I picture her raven hair pulled back into an elaborate braided updo, adorned with gold pins to accent a deep purple gown. She probably hates it, like she does everything that isn't her sparring leathers. A smile lifts one of my cheeks as I remember during the last summit, when she was forced to wear formal clothes and she sat at the table fuming the entire time and adjusting the sleeves of her dress, which kept falling down her shoulders. I thought she was going to rip them off by the end of the day.

We've had so little time to explore what's between us. A few stolen moments at official events when our families or the other heirs weren't watching, then the exchanging of letters for several years.

Thinking back to that first letter she sent me, I almost laugh. It was a summons to a competition she had devised to determine which of us was the better warrior. I think we were between 13 and 14 years old at the time, and we hated each other. We sparred with swords, and I bested her in all four matches. I still remember how she stormed off, kicking sand as she raged.

After that, every time we saw each other she challenged me to feats of strength, or skills with weaponry. At nearly every summit we faced off in some elaborate trial. I beat her every single time. As the years went on, we both progressed in our talents, and I started giving her advice in the training yard rather than just beating her. Two years ago she finally beat me while performing archery on horseback. Her smile when her last arrow went straight through the bulls-eye while mine hit the edge lit up my entire world. And I haven't stopped thinking about it ever since.

The rustling of the tent flap awakens me once again. I keep my eyes closed, feigning sleep. It's a chilly evening, and my skin pebbles against the cold breeze brought in with the one, no, two figures. I make out two distinct male whispers.

"Okay, do it," one of them says in a deep voice, "she's asleep and tied up. What harm could she do?"

I fight back the smile. Oh, please find out.

"Why don't you do it?" The other voice is higher pitched and sounds younger.

"Because I outrank you, now go." I hear sounds of a scuffle, and a quiet *umph*, which I piece together is the older one shoving the younger one in my direction.

I focus on keeping my breathing even, my body loose. I'm laying on my side, with my knees pulled up to my chest to conserve my warmth. One arm is underneath my head and my other is resting next to my face, as far apart as the chain will allow. My wrists throb with a dull ache due to the blisters from the chafing cuffs. I compartmentalize the pain, shoving it back so I can focus on whatever the younger boy is about to do.

The shuffling of footsteps brushes my bed of straw. I breathe in through my nose and out through my mouth, slowly. Hairs on my neck prickle and my hands shoot out. Using my shackles, I knock the knife out of the boy's hand, and listen as it goes skittering to the front of the tent. Damn. There goes my plan for that later.

The boy yelps as my fingers dig into his wiry wrists, holding him fast. I'm surprised by the brightness of the tent considering it's the middle of the evening, until I spot the lantern in the hands of the older guard.

"What the Hells do you think you're doing, waking a lady from her beauty sleep?" I snarl.

The boy in front of me is no older than Igraine, with short brown hair and wide, fearful eyes. He tries to tug himself free from my bruising grasp, but I only dig my long nails in deeper.

"Unhand him, demon spawn!" The other guard says, dropping his lantern to clatter on the ground and withdrawing a longsword from its sheath. He looks no more than my age, sputtering in the flickering light. He doesn't know how to hold the sword properly, either. This is who Calder sent to try and kill me?

It physically pains me to hold back my laugh. "What are you doing in my lair? Besides trying to cut my throat while I sleep. "

"We weren't trying to kill you, we're only here to take a little bit of your hair," the younger boy squeaks out.

"Tristan, shut up!" The older one snaps.

"My hair?" I ask, dumbfounded, loosening my hold slightly on the boy's wrists so I don't accidentally snap them.

"You don't have the right to speak to us, demon," the older one sticks his blade out far from his body. It's such an amateur move I almost groan. If I'd wanted to, I could easily rip it from his grasp before his untrained muscles could even react.

Who the Hells instructed these children? And who sent them in here? It seems like a catastrophically poor choice.

"How about we make a deal? You get me a bowl of warm soup or whatever's cooking, and I'll cut the hair off myself and give it to you."

To show my good will I release Tristan, raising my palms to them in a gesture that shows I mean no harm.

"We're not giving you a knife," the older one says.

I sigh, pinching the bridge of my nose, then level a finger at his shaking blade. "If it'll make you feel better, you can point that sword at me the entire time."

Tristan and the other guard exchange a glance then nod.

"We'll be right back," the older one says as they both disappear through the tent. Tristan retrieves his dagger on the way out.

They return some time later with a wooden bowl of something steaming and a spoon. The older guard sets it on the ground barely out of my reach.

"Hair first," he grumbles, withdrawing his sword and tossing me a small, dull kitchen knife.

I catch the handle of the knife and inspect it. "This blade is dull as shit. I'd have better luck chewing a piece of my hair off."

"It's this or nothing."

I let out a heavy sigh, reaching behind my head and grabbing hold of my braid. Dirt and grime coat my blonde tresses, and the feel of it makes me shudder. I section off a small portion near the end of the tie, pull the strands tight, and use the dull, serrated knife to cut through several strands at a time. It's slow work, but eventually I hold a small clump in my palm.

"Satisfactory?" I ask, holding out the bundle.

Tristan moves forward to grab it, but the older guard barks out. "Wait! Drop the knife first."

I give him a little smirk, twirling the knife around in my hand before holding it out, handle first to Tristan. He carefully accepts the knife, then the clump of hair.

The older guard sheaths his sword and gives Tristan a nod to leave.

"Aren't you forgetting something?" I ask, gesturing to the bowl.

"Oh, right," the guard says, then with a smirk he kicks the bowl over. Hot stew spills all over the rock floor and the straw I'm lying on. I glare at the older guard, who pulls Tristan out of the tent.

"Why did you do that? We had an agreement," Tristan complains as they go.

"Shut up and walk. You've got a lot to learn, kid."

I glare out the tent flap, memorizing the older guard's face so I can kill him first when I escape. Part of me thought he was going to take the bowl with him, and I'd have accepted that, but to spill it onto the only place I can sleep, fury courses through me.

With my stomach empty, there's no way I can refuse to eat out of principle. Using the metal spoon, I carefully scrape as much unsoiled stew back into the bowl as possible. I'm not exactly in a position to care about dirt or decorum. I eat the few mouthfuls I was able to salvage, then toss the wood bowl to the front of the tent.

My wrists ache in protest of the move, and from the effort of sawing through my thick hair. The bloody blisters are only getting worse. I pour a little bit of water from my bucket underneath the manacles, hoping to clean off the dirt. I have to bite my lip from screaming out in pain.

Well, shit, that's not good.

# Chapter Twenty

## Elana

Several days after what was supposed to be my coronation, I stand at my mother's side, draped in mourning-black once again at the Resting Ceremony for the guards who were killed at the border.

Matteo was among the guards who escorted my mother and I to the three respectfully wrapped bundles that were brought back from the border. One-by-one Matteo unwrapped the coverings over their faces. I collapsed to my knees and wept with relief that Aislinn was not among them. Mother held me for a few moments, then tugged me to my feet and told me I had to act with decorum. Three families had lost their loved ones.

Of course I was devastated for their loss, and we're holding this ceremony to honor them, but I also can't help but feel an immense weight off my shoulders knowing my sister isn't among the dead.

The guards told us they found Donne, Tallisa, and Gregory some distance away from the wall. All three were killed by spears unlike any that have been seen before. Based on that and the newly erected metal wall on the border, Matteo believes that King Skade was there. No one else on the continent could have manipulated metal like that.

Besides the dozens of Hotharian bodies, there were no other signs of Aislinn. They did, however, find her horse, and brought him back with the others.

She's not dead. She can't be. It's an unacceptable scenario. I would feel it. The world would be somehow...less. But it's the same as it's always felt, so she has to be alive. She's in trouble, yes. But gone? No.

The two families of the fallen guards say their goodbyes. Donne's aristocratic family wanted to perform his Resting Ceremony at their lavish countryside estate, so they're not in attendance. Tallisa's mother sobs openly, held up by her husband, as the earth swallows up their daughter's casket.

I should say something to the crowd, but I'm at a complete loss for words. My tongue feels heavy in my mouth, and when I suck a breath in, my eyes start to burn. I wipe them with the back of my sleeve.

Mother pats me on the arm as she sweeps forward to console Tallisa's parents and Gregory's wife. She holds their hands in hers and says hushed words. They nod through their tears and give her wobbly, grateful smiles.

I watch her as she interacts with the families, shocked by her ability to compartmentalize, especially considering the letter we received from King Skade this morning. Affixed to the parchment was a lock of golden blonde hair. Aislinn's hair. The letter made no demands. All it said was, *"I have your beloved princess."*

I was ready to march to war that very instant, but Mother convinced me it would be impossible without the support of the noble families. Instead, we issued an official notice to immediately suspend all trade with Hotharia, and order any visiting Hotharian citizens to return home.

It's as close to a formal war declaration we can get until we hold court.

Mother insists on taking her own carriage home, so I sit in silence as I stew over the hectic day, and what's sure to be an exhausting evening. The monarchs and the heirs are dining with us again, where we'll hopefully smooth over their worries of the coronation's postponement.

Queen Nami and Rian departed after hearing there would be no coronation. She left a letter with Rigel stating she apologizes for cutting the visit short, but she must see to matters in Aaranor. Mother thinks she's still upset over Queen Amira's reveal.

King Mesfin and Queen Desta remained today, but announced their plans to leave before dawn tomorrow.

Selfishly, I'm hoping to have some time with Rayna and Aidan. I hardly got to speak with Rian, only speaking a few formal words when his mother was around. I won't miss my opportunity with Rayna.

I'm pacing the receiving hall waiting for my mother when the Melinorians arrive. I'm not sure what the protocol is for greeting them anymore, since I'm not to be crowned queen yet, so I give a slight dip of my head. Rayna rushes to me and grabs my hands before I have a chance to worry about etiquette.

"Elana, I heard about the bodies that were brought back from the Hotharian border. Did they...I mean was Aislinn-," she draws in a deep breath, unable to finish her questions.

I grip her hands tight. "She wasn't among the casualties, but she was taken prisoner by Hotharia. King Skade sent us another letter with a lock of her hair."

She shakes her head and pulls me into a fierce hug. I hug her back with the same intensity. I silently chide myself for not realizing she would have heard about the Resting Ceremonies. I should have told her earlier that it wasn't Aislinn.

"She's okay," I whisper to her shoulder. "I know she is."

After a moment we let go, and she gives me a smile, though it contrasts with her red, watery eyes. My mother breezes into the room as Rigel announces the arrival of Aidan and *both* of his parents.

King Edward is an imposing man, with long brown hair past his shoulders, and deep set brown eyes. He wears a jewel-encrusted ceremonial dagger at his hip, and boasts power even though he has no elemental abilities.

Like a moth to a flame, I instinctively seek out Aidan. I find him already staring at me, wearing a somber expression.

"Princess Elana, it's a pleasure to meet you," King Edward says, stepping in front of Aidan. "I heard you're in the market for a husband to appease your nobility. My second son, Aleksander, would make a fine match for you. He is intelligent, strong, and comes from the best bloodline. Together, we could unite our two great kingdoms."

My mouth hangs open, and I quickly glance between him and my mother to make sure I heard him correctly. Is this another of her schemes? I can tell from her narrowed eyes and tight mouth that this was something she did not expect.

"Thank you for the offer, but we are not entertaining any marriage proposals at this time," she says dryly. "On the matter of Elana's coronation, let's be clear the delay is not due to any fault of hers or lack of union. I'm simply not ready to give up my bedroom yet."

Her hazel eyes crinkle as she laughs, the other monarchs joining in. I can't tell if they actually think she's funny, or if they're humoring her. Edward nods his head emphatically and takes a step back beside his wife, who pinches the bridge of her nose as if she has a headache. Next to his father, Aidan visibly fumes, and I swear the room gets hotter.

"It seems you've had quite the eventful few days. Thank you for inviting us to dine with you." King Mesfin says.

"Of course, it's our pleasure. We're only sorry Queen Nami and Prince Rian had to return home so soon," Mother says seamlessly.

We're led into the dining hall, and spend nearly the entire meal discussing trade. It seems Melinor and Ocarin have also cut off all trade with Hotharia. Since the kingdom has a difficult time growing its own food due to the harsh climate and lack of fertile land, most of their sustenance is purchased from the other kingdoms. According to Mother, it's only a matter of time before Hotharian citizens begin to starve and rebel against their monarchs. With any luck, that's the most peaceful resolution to this conflict.

No one discusses war outright, but I can tell it weighs heavily in the unspoken glances between families and the pregnant pauses of conversation. It's not a decision anyone will make lightly.

After dinner I invite Aidan and Rayna to walk the gardens with me. Once we're outside, I lead them to the most remote garden, and wait until I'm sure we're out of earshot from the guards before I speak.

"Rayna, there's something I need to fill you in on," I say, taking her hand once again.

Her brows knit together, and she nods for me to continue. "After the battle on our coast, I lost the ability to use my light powers, which includes healing wounds left by the cursed weapons."

I wait for her judgement, her scorn, and her distrust for not telling her sooner, but it never comes. She merely squeezes my hand tighter in her warm grip. "That must be so difficult for you. I've never heard of a monarch losing their power, but could it mean something is going on with the goddesses?"

I wrinkle my brows at her in confusion. "What do you mean?"

"Well...," she trails off, as if thinking. "They were *forgotten* Gods. What if she didn't give you enough power, or if she can't maintain the connection to you for some reason?"

Biting my lip, I consider her words. No one really knows how the Gods grant us power, so all we can do is assume. "Maybe. Whatever the reason is, I need to figure out how to get my power back soon, or else this war will be one-sided."

Aidan and Rayna are silent as they exchange a look. It hits me then, really hits me. It's the first time I've said, and believed, that we're about to be at war. Thousands could die, thousands probably will die. Children will lose parents, and parents will lose children. Tears prick my eyes as I drop Rayna's hand. All of this is too much. My father is dead. My sister, captured. My best friend betrayed Adrithia. No wonder Nura took away my light. I'm clearly unworthy of her gift.

Words start flying from my mouth before I can temper them. "I can't lead a kingdom through this. How am I supposed to order people to fight and die for Adrithia when one of the Gods has turned her back on me? Even the nobility have decided I'm not fit for the throne. All because they want me wed and with child to ensure the survival of the Sable line. I don't know what the fuck I'm supposed to do."

My breaths come in short pants as I pace back and forth. I run my fingers through my long wavy hair, which is extra unruly from the humidity this evening. Shadows fly like wisps around me, as if sensing my agitation.

Rayna lays a comforting hand on my arm, stilling my anxious movements. "Elana, stop. We all struggle to prove ourselves to the noble families. Power-hungry people will always find ways to make our lives miserable. Listen to me...you are worthy. You saved us multiple times on that mountain. You're going to be a great ruler."

Warmed by her words, I nod my head and shake the thoughts free, for now.

After a few moments of silence, Rayna asks, "what do you think Hotharia wants with Aislinn?"

"They're likely going to use her as a bargaining chip in some kind of trade. Whether it's with Adrithia, or these invaders from Tyne, I can't say for sure," Aidan says, and it feels like a claw squeezes my heart.

"What are we going to do? We need to get her back," I say, staring between them.

"We need to host a summit," Rayna says, brows furrowed, as if thinking. "We need to give Hotharia a chance to surrender her before we formally declare war."

I scoff. "There might not be the time for that, Rayna. We have to do something now. Every day that goes by could bring her closer to death. I'll march into Hotharia myself if I have to."

Aidan's warm hand touches my shoulder. "Rayna's right. We can't simply charge in with nothing but our powers. We need the support of our armies."

I shake his hand off me. "*I* don't need any of that. *I* can sneak in by myself."

The shadows wrap up around me, slowly shielding me from view until I'm entirely cloaked in darkness. It's a trick I've been working on these past few weeks.

"As impressive as that is, Magpie, you can't take on an entire army by yourself. Someone's bound to notice a mass of shadow moving on its own," Aidan says quietly.

"I spent my entire life being the spare princess, I know how to avoid being seen." I let the shadows drop and glare at my friends. "If you two don't want to rescue her, I'll go alone."

"You really think I don't want to rescue her?" Rayna takes a step closer to me. I'd forgotten how tall she is, and now she bares down at me with a stare that could shatter stone. "I want nothing more than to save her. Trust me. But I'm not about to risk any of our lives to do it. *She* wouldn't want that. Do you even know where she's being held? Have you ever been to Hotharia before? Do you know the terrain? Have you faced a metal-wielder like King Skade?"

Her points are valid, but each one is like a knife to my chest. I glance down, unable to meet the ferocity in her eyes a moment longer.

"Elana, we don't even know who we're facing in battle. I'm not suggesting we abandon Aislinn. I'm saying we're woefully unprepared for a potential fight to get her back."

I let out a sharp sigh. Her argument is sound, and I have no doubt I would be in serious trouble if I tried to find and rescue her on my own. But, as Rayna pointed out, Ash would kill me herself if anything happened to me while I tried to save her.

"So, what, we convince our parents to host a summit and then sit around until they declare war?" I ask.

Aidan lets out a hum. "It's Melinor's turn to host a summit. Rayna, you must convince your parents. But that'll only help us so much. We still don't know who we're declaring war against. Who are these islanders, what do they want, and what powers do they possess?"

His questions are all leading. "What do you suggest we do, Aidan?"

He gives me a characteristic half smile. "We go to Aaranor and pester their archive keepers until they let us in to do some research."

Rayna lets out a noise of disgust. "You want to spend your time not training, or raising an army, but *reading*?"

I give Aidan a true smile. "That sounds perfect."

# CHAPTER TWENTY-ONE

## AISLINN

The wounds to my wrist are worse than I anticipated. The skin around the sores is angry, bright red, and hot to the touch. What's worse is that I'm pretty sure I have a fever. Inside my tent it's as chilly as ever, but my body is covered in a layer of sweat, adding to my already horrible stench.

Calder visited me yesterday, at least I think it was yesterday. I've been slipping in and out of consciousness, and lost track of the number of scratch marks I've made on the stone ground to mark my days. He asked if he should expect a visit from Adrithia's armies to rescue me. I laughed and told him I'm not worth it. I'm the spare now, so there will be no valiant attempts at rescue.

I'm sure they will want to, but there's no way the nobility will be on board with sending an army to rescue a powerless princess. I can only hope Elana won't be asinine enough to come here herself.

After Calder's visit, in which he kindly refilled my water bucket with ice cold water, I didn't see a single soul for a day.

I'm in the middle of an uncomfortable, restless sleep when a cool hand brushes across my forehead. I startle, blindly reaching and grabbing onto small calloused hands. A yelp of pain has me wrenching my eyes open.

A young girl with fiery orange hair shakes out her wrist a few paces away. "Igraine," I croak out, and my voice really croaks. Like a Gods-damned frog.

"Y-your wounds are infected, miss. I must treat them," she says, fear evident in her sparkling eyes. In one hand she holds a small wooden bowl with cream-colored paste.

My breath comes out in short pants. "I'll do it, hand it here."

She looks from me to my hands, as if deciding whether it's worth it to fight with me. "I have to apply it under your manacles, then I need to wrap your wrists."

"If you wrap my wrists, Calder will know someone's been helping me," I say through gasping breaths.

"They need you alive. The Prince asked Lord Aric to treat you."

I groan as I slowly sit up. My head spins and I nearly pass out again, but manage to keep myself upright. It takes all my strength, but I hold out my hands for her to work. "Why do they need me alive?"

She shakes her head as she works, first washing my bloodied wrists, then smearing some of the paste on them. "I don't know. I serve Lord Aric now, and I only know what he told me."

I grunt in acceptance, and breathe through the pain. It feels like she's flaying my skin. When I glance down, I see the paste has already turned pink from where it mixed with my blood.

"Are you a healer?" I ask, staring at her hands, which remind me so much of my sister's, during the many times she helped treat my various injuries over the years.

"I was training to be a healer before I was sold to the royal palace," Igraine says, pulling a roll of white cloth from her pocket and carefully wrapping it around my wrists.

"What do you mean, you were sold?" I ask through a wince.

She wraps the cloth under the iron of my manacles with practiced fingers. "My parents are textile merchants, but business has been slow the last few years, and they couldn't afford to feed me, and had no funds for a dowry to marry me off. The healer I was shadowing didn't have enough money to pay me to stay, so my parents sold me into servitude at the palace. I've been a scullery maid there for two years now."

The stabbing pain slowly starts to ebb into a more manageable constant throbbing. I breathe in deeply through my nose and exhale through my mouth.

When she finishes wrapping them, she hands me a cup. "Drink this. It'll taste awful, but will help with the fever."

I make the mistake of sniffing it first, and a barrage of pungent scents hit my nose like a battering ram. I scrunch my nose up in disgust. "Cheers, Igraine."

I tip the thick concoction back. From the second it hits my tongue, I'm filled with regret. I swear it's almost as thick as the paste she applied to my wounds. There's a sharp bite of ginger and garlic. Something tart like...cherries? I almost gag, but manage to force the mixture down my throat through sheer willpower.

Igraine fills a second cup of water from my bucket and hands it to me. I gulp it down greedily, eager to wash the grittiness out of my mouth.

"Well done. I've seen grown men come to tears while drinking that," Igraine gives me a sly grin.

I lay my head back on the post, breathing rapidly over the burn in my chest. "I may still cry."

"Get some sleep, I'll be back to check on you later," she gathers her things, then makes a swift exit.

I allow my head to roll back and my muscles to relax as the fever sweeps in to carry me to oblivion.

*"Aislinn Sable. You must endure a little while longer. It's not your time yet. Endure it," a deep male voice demands. It echoes across the void. Something prevents me from reaching out towards the mysterious figure haunting my dreams. Oh, right, my hands are bound.*

*I look down, but I have no hands. I have no body. I'm a soul floating without a home. A glimmer of something in the distance, in a shabby tent on a tall stone mesa.*

"Aislinn."

My name whispered quietly as if on a breeze.

"Aislinn, wake up," the voice says again. I know this voice.

I peel my eyes open. It's dark, but there's a low fire burning near the center of the tent. Its glow illuminates two figures crouched near my feet.

Igraine learned. Stay out of reach of my hands.

"Aislinn, we need to get you into dry clothes," the voice I recognized was Aric. Worry creases his brow as he stares at me.

My entire body is shaking. I'm curled on my side on the damp straw. Wait, why is the straw damp? I shift my legs, and, oh, that's why. I wet myself in my sleep.

Aric holds up a small silver key. "I'm going to unlock your chains while we get you dressed. Do not try to run. There are a dozen armed guards outside the tent, with orders to cut your feet off if you run."

"What happened to helping me escape?" My words are quiet and slurred, but he gets the idea.

"I swear on my sister's life that I will help you, but please trust me when I say now is not the time," he says, holding the key in front of him. "I'm not going to unlock these until you swear on Elana's life you won't try to escape."

I close my eyes for a moment, trying to think through my swirling thoughts. I may never be able to trust him again, but it's true I'm in no position to fight right now. "Fine. I swear on Elana's life that I won't try to escape tonight."

Aric nods and slides the key into the lock. The chains fall to the straw, and I breathe a shaky sigh of relief. Aric helps me stand, then removes the soiled straw. Igraine helps peel my clothes from my sweat-slicked body while Aric arranges a fresh bundle of straw. On top of the straw he lays a thick wool blanket, then turns his back to me while I get dressed.

Igraine helps me into fresh undergarments. I lean against the post for stability while she helps bind my breasts. The white long sleeve shirt she gives me is made from cotton, and the breeches are wool. Gods, the feeling of clean clothing is something I'll never take for granted again. My body shakes and I want nothing more than to curl around the small fire.

"I need to see your bandages," Igraine says, so I hold out my hands, wobbling on my feet. She lets out a heavy sigh, and a bit of her healer confidence comes out. "Sit down before you fall over."

Aric turns back to us and grabs my arm, helping to lower me to the straw. He pulls the blanket over my feet. Igraine holds my hands gently, unwrapping the pink fabric. The last layer is sticky, and she carefully peels it away from my skin. She turns them over, thoroughly inspecting every sore. She even brings her nose in close, inhaling near the surface. Whatever she smells has her furrowing her brow.

"How is it?" Aric asks, his face noticeably paler than usual.

"Not good. The wounds were left to fester for too long. I think I can cure the infection, but they'll take a long time to heal," she pauses, and catches my eyes, "and I'm afraid you'll have scars."

I give her a nod. "Scars don't worry me. As long as I can still wield weapons."

She almost smiles, then reaches behind her and hands me another cup of stinking mucus. "Drink up, Your Highness."

I attempt to roll my eyes, but a dizzy spell takes over and my entire head rolls instead. Aric kneels by my shoulder, takes the cup from Igraine, and tips it back to my lips.

"I need more healing ointment. I'll be right back," Igraine says, standing and disappearing through the front of the tent.

I choke down the so-called liquid and chase it with two cups of cool water.

"I'm so sorry, Aislinn. I never wanted any of this to happen. Calder wanted to kill you, but I insisted that you'd be a better bargaining chip. When his father arrived, he agreed with me, so now I can be seen helping you," he says, with some bitterness in his tone.

"The king's here?" I ask, fighting off another wave of the shakes.

"Yes, he arrived yesterday," Aric's voice is hushed, as if the ears of the enemy are in here with us.

"Why the war camp? What's happening with the army?"

Aric's cerulean eyes dart to the front of the tent again. "I'll tell you after tomorrow. There's a big meeting with his generals and warriors from the invading army."

I want to ask about the enemy, but my eyelids feel heavy, as if they're weighed down with an anchor. Instead, I gather my strength and voice the other question that's been burning in the back of my mind, "why are you doing this, Aric?" I ask. "For years, you could have chosen to do the right thing. So why start now?"

Aric sighs, brushing his blonde strands away from his eyes. "Because when I finally got back to Hotharia, the first thing my uncle told me was that my sister was waiting for me. And I realized that the brother she's eager to see isn't me. I was someone who watched out for her, and protected her from the cruelty of the world. She wouldn't recognize me now, not with the things I've done. So yes, I'm doing this to alleviate some of my guilt, Aislinn, but also because Ingrid deserves an honorable brother. One who is trying to make the world a better place for her."

"Elana will make the world a better place," I croak out.

"Aric stares at my wrists. "I know."

Sensing a vulnerability, I press him. "Help me send a letter to her."

He shakes his head, eyes full of regret. "I can't. The only messenger birds are monitored by Calder and his father. I can't get near them without drawing suspicion."

"So use some of those spying skills you honed while betraying my kingdom," I say with as much venom as I can muster in my weakened state.

Aric laughs, but it's a hopeless, humorless sound. "I was a terrible spy. Every time I had to send a message out, I would end up ill from the nerves."

Before I have a chance to respond, the tent flap opens and Igraine steps in, holding another bowl and more bandages.

She makes quick work of cleaning the wound, applying more salve, and dressing my wrists. Her eyes dart back and forth between Aric and I like she knows she interrupted a conversation. When she finishes, she hands me another bowl, this one filled with hot broth, and a slice of bread on top. She picks up my dirty clothes and gives me a little curtsy.

"Eat. I'll wash your clothes and have them back to you soon," she disappears through the entrance.

"Can she be trusted?" I ask Aric, my voice barely a whisper.

He meets my eyes with a glimmer of amusement. "Really? You're asking me that? I'm not sure any of us can be. But, she seems more trustworthy than most."

He relocks my chains, careful to avoid touching my wrists as much as possible. When he's done, I find the strength to hold the bowl of soup in front of me, breathing in the warm steam.

"Sorry in advance for this. I need to keep up appearances," he says quietly as he stands, then loudly scoffs as he makes his way outside, holding his nose dramatically. "Stupid bitch reeks. If I were you, I'd stay where you are. I can smell her from here."

Well, he's not wrong. I do stink, but thanks to the clean clothes, I smell slightly better than before.

My eyelids pull heavy again, and I pull the blanket up higher around me as chills run wrack through my limbs. I force myself to sip the broth, dipping the bread in to soften it. It's not fresh, but not hard as a rock yet either. The soup works its magic, and I eat every last bite before lying back down and letting the fever pull me back under.

# CHAPTER TWENTY-TWO

## ELANA

"This is preposterous!" Duke Lyons shouts. "You expect us to declare war on another kingdom and break the Astrellian Peace?"

Mother levels him with a stare I wish I could mimic. "You do remember our king was viciously murdered by allies of Hotharia, yes? I know your memory isn't what it used to be, but considering we laid him to rest less than a week ago...I'd think you'd remember."

The duke sputters, his face turning an angry shade of red, which only further accentuates his silver-streaked hair.

We're holding court in the hopes of consolidating our army and making a formal declaration of war. This would give my mother the power to call upon all of our warriors, from every corner of Adrithia to ready themselves. Mother met with our army leaders already, discussing strategy of where to host the camps and how to amass the necessary supplies.

In order for the preparations to go smoothly, all nobility must be in agreement, since they have a lot of power over supply lines. Food, weapons, and regional forces are maintained by the noble families.

We hoped this would be an easy declaration, especially after King Skade's latest letter bragging that he holds my sister hostage. Mother and I discussed our strategy for the meeting, and decided to lean heavily on the need for revenge for Father's death and Aislinn's imprisonment.

"Ocarin has already declared-," Mother starts, but the duke cuts her off.

"Why should we care about Ocarin?"

Shadows writhe around my throne and the duke's eyes go wide as he watches them with unbridled fear. "Because their crown prince fought with us at the coast. He risked his own life, and the safety of his kingdom to warn us about the oncoming threat. If not for him, the enemy would have stormed our coast and caught us off-guard. Who knows what kind of unchecked destruction they would have wrought."

"And now we're to be indebted to Ocarin because of their prince's choice? We are, of course, grateful for him, but we didn't ask for his *help*."

The way he says help has me gritting my teeth. Rayna departed with her parents yesterday, but not before convincing them to host a summit. She delivered the invitation to myself and Aidan before departing. Invitations to Hotharia and Aaranor were dispatched via messenger hawk.

*"Melinor stands with Adrithia and Ocarin against these heinous attacks. We are calling for an immediate summit of the kingdoms. These attacks must be addressed. We invite Queen Maris and Crown Princess Elana and any attendants to our home on the first day of autumn. We expect every kingdom to be represented at this summit, including Hotharia. May the Gods guide us."*

The first day of autumn was a little over a month away, which gives Aidan and I about a week in Aaranor to learn everything possible about Tyne.

Hopefully, Queen Nami won't mind our visit. We've already sent a letter to Rian asking for permission to enter the Great Archives. We didn't want to include any jeopardizing details in case the bird got intercepted. We'll explain our plans when we get there.

Aidan's parents left yesterday as well. They have to prepare for an extended absence before making the journey to the summit. All roads in Adrithia will be open to them, so they don't have to travel through Hotharia.

Queen Amira gave her blessing for Aidan to visit the archives, and in fact seemed adamant that he accompany me. *You'll need all the eyes you can get for your research*, she said, staring at me intently, as if there was something else she wanted to say. Shortly after she insisted that her sister, General Parisa, accompany us along with a few members of Aidan's elite squad. I was excited to meet this group of warriors he talked so highly of during our travel to the coast.

My mother was more difficult to convince. In the end, Amira helped us convince her of our safety. She'd had a vision where we all made it to Melinor safe and sound. Mother finally relented, but insisted I take Matteo.

"I support it," my full attention is brought back to the great hall when Lady Tessa Grimhart steps forward, standing straight as hundreds of eyes fall upon her. "I support the war declaration."

"A Lady of a lesser house," Duke Lyons spits. "Hardly a convincing vote."

"I also support the declaration," a woman's sharp voice cuts through the hall like a broadsword. I squint my eyes to find the supporter.

I'm surprised when Captain Giselle, head of Sandral's guard, steps forward. She wears her guard uniform, and gives a bow to the dais before she continues addressing the crowd, "I have seen firsthand what those monsters allied with Hotharia are capable of. If it weren't for the combined powers of Queen Elana and Prince Aidan, myself and many of my guards wouldn't be here right now. We must unite against that evil. Or else risk falling prey to it."

Her words seem to stir the nobles. Several others shout their approval, and one by one, the nobility falls into line. All except Duke Lyons, who glowers red-faced at the foot of the throne.

Mother calls for a vote, and a strong majority vote in favor of the war efforts. I let out a little sigh of relief, careful not to let it show in front of the court.

When Mother thanks the nobility for their attendance and dismisses them, I immediately slip into the crowd, finding both Tessa and Captain Giselle, and leading them into one of our sitting rooms.

"Thank you both for your support of the war declaration. I don't believe we would have gotten it passed if not for you speaking out," I tell them, wringing my hands together with my nerves.

"I only did what was right for the city," the captain grumbles. "Any good captain would have done the same."

I don't bother arguing with her that there were other captains in the room and none of them spoke up like she did. "Well, no matter why you did what you did, I'm thankful for it."

She gives me a nod.

"I did it for my son," Lady Grimhart says, flashing me a small grin. "Because he wouldn't be alive without you, Your Majesty."

I swallow thickly. "Please, call me Elana."

Her eyes widen. "Only if you call me Tessa."

"Deal," I say, giving her a smile of my own.

Next to Tessa, Captain Giselle sighs. "Then you'd better call me Giselle, if we're dropping the honorifics."

"Very well, Giselle," I say gleefully.

She eyes me suspiciously. "You seem way too happy about that, I take it back."

"Absolutely not, Giselle. You said it. No take-backs," I give her an exaggerated toothy grin. Tessa hides a delicate giggle behind a gloved hand.

Giselle lets out a low annoyed sigh, wrapping her arms in front of her chest.

"What's next for you now, Your- I mean- Elana?" Tessa asks, eagerly.

I consider my words, unsure if I should tell them the truth about where Aidan and I are going. The last time I was forthcoming with my trust, it ended up costing my father his life. But these women aren't Aric. And I'm going to have to start trusting people again, considering my social circle consists of my immediate family, my advisor, my lady's maid, and the heirs from other kingdoms.

I take a deep breath. "Prince Aidan and I are heading to the Great Archives in Aaranor to research who's attacking us and why. And then we're traveling to Melinor to attend a royal summit."

Tessa pales, biting her lip, while Giselle flushes with what looks like anger.

"You're leaving Adrithia, again?" Yes, that's definitely anger coloring Giselle's cheeks and injecting venom into her words. "We just lost King Devon, and now you're going to abandon us, too?"

I'm so taken aback by her words that I can't formulate a response. "W-well, I-I-,"

"You really had me fooled. You know, for one lousy second I thought maybe we got lucky and had another great ruler despite your young age and inexperience. I thought you cared about the kingdom. I certainly didn't think you'd abandon Adrithia when your people are in need of stability and leadership. Silly me," Giselle snaps, spinning on her heels and stalking to the door.

With half a thought I erect a wall of shadows, cutting off her exit and blanketing the room in silence. "That's not fair, Giselle. I'm not abandoning Adrithia."

She lets out a harsh breath and turns back to me. "You're leaving when we need you most."

"I'm leaving to save Adrithia. To save everyone!" I shout, my own anger surfacing.

Giselle doesn't say anything, merely letting me continue. "We know next to nothing about the enemy we face. All we know is they're allied with Hotharia. Would you rather we go against them blind?"

She doesn't answer, so I press on. "Trust me, if I could do this from Sandral, I would."

Tessa steps to my side, worry lines creasing her blemish-free forehead. "If you leave, it'll give Duke Lyons time to conspire against you."

Giselle's eyes narrow to slits. "What do you mean? What is that arrogant man up to? Does this have anything to do with why your coronation was postponed?"

I give her a nod. "Most of the nobles don't seem to want me on the throne. Duke Lyons tries to undermine me every chance he gets. He wanted me to marry his son, which I refused, and ever since then he's had it out for me. He even convinced the court to enact some archaic custom called the Ascension Rite and tried to declare himself the throne's regent until I marry and produce offspring. Luckily, my mother stepped in and claimed the regency, but still, my coronation was delayed until at least the winter solstice."

"He's despicable. I've heard from other noble families that he threatened them until they agreed to his coup," Tessa says, and I realize that I should have asked to see her days ago. She's a knowledgeable ally.

"Power hungry sexist snake," Giselle curses. "Tessa's right, if you leave now he'll only continue to try and usurp power."

I shake my head. "This could be our only chance to find out what these people from Tyne want and why they've allied with Hotharia."

Tessa turns to Giselle. "Captain, you're an influential person in this city. The citizens listen when you talk. It might not be the nobles, but you could sway opinions of the general public."

Giselle stares at Tessa. "What are you suggesting I do?"

Tessa turns red and gives a small shrug. "Oh, I don't know. Maybe you could dispel rumors, talk highly of Elana, hold a public meeting. You're respected, and having a voice of reason like you could only help her cause."

"That's not a bad idea, Tessa," I say, then glance at Giselle, waiting for her response.

She rests an elbow on her fist and rocks back and forth as she thinks. "I suppose I could be a vocal supporter. What would really help is if your mother hosted an occasional small court where she heard the voices of common folk."

It's a good idea, one that Aidan told me his mother has been doing for years. "You're right. That would be beneficial. I'll speak to her about it. Tessa, do you think you could help with some of the noble families?"

Tessa bites her lip. "I can try, but I'm only a lesser house, and I'm afraid I don't hold much sway over the influential families. But...I could help you in another way."

When she doesn't say anything, I give her an encouraging nod.

"Well...you see, I married into the Grimhart name. I was born and raised in Aaranor. My father is one of the Keepers of the Great Archives," she winces slightly as she says the words, as if they're not the most beautiful words I've heard in the last week.

"Tessa! Why were you holding out on me? That's the kind of information you lead with." A wide smile stretches my face as I give a little chuckle. Even Giselle's mouth is hanging open.

She sighs heavily. "He might not be able to help us. If the queen doesn't approve of us being there, then there's nothing he can do."

Queen Nami didn't seem to like me, but Rian, on the other hand...he'll help us. "I know a prince who owes me a favor."

Two days later, my mother helps me onto Misty's back. She stands next to my mare, patting her neck gently. She's always had a soft spot for horses.

"I still don't think this is a good idea," she tells me. "You should be taking more guards with you. And are you sure about allowing Lady Grimhart to go?"

I follow her pitying gaze to Lady Grimhart and Matteo, who is doing his best to help her mount her horse while wearing long skirts. Eventually, Tessa gives up her sense of modesty and hikes them up and over her patient horse's back. Matteo's face blossoms with pink at the sight of her long tan legs. I heave a heavy sigh. It's going to be a long trip for her. "I'm sure, Mother. About everything. Tessa's father should be able to help us in the archives, and more guards will only slow us down and draw more attention to our group."

Instead of bringing a retinue of guards, I'm only taking Matteo. With the addition of Tessa and our other companion, who I've decided not to tell Mother about, our traveling party was already too large. Especially since Aidan is due here with his aunt and two members of his elite guard at any moment.

Matteo holds the reins to Tessa's horse while she struggles to get comfortable. His face is still pink as he makes an effort to look anywhere but her face. I thought he'd be upset that we were bringing her with us, but he understood her importance in getting us into the Great Archives, and surprisingly didn't argue.

I feel comforted knowing Captain Giselle is stepping in to manage the castle guards and protect my mother while Matteo travels with us. Neither Matteo nor I would be leaving if we thought she was in any danger. Before she left, Amira had a vision of all parties making it to the summit safely, which is one of the reasons she was happy to let Aidan go.

The castle gates swing open and Aidan rides through with his cabal. My stomach nearly does a flip when I see him, riding his giant black warhorse like it's the most natural thing in the world to him. His traveling clothes are perfectly tailored to his sculpted frame. Oh Gods, I need to stop this line of thinking immediately.

I tear my eyes away to inspect the others riding with him. General Parisa rides next to him, and two men trail behind them, their heads on a swivel, surveying the castle grounds.

My gaze catches on one of them, and I'm positive he's the largest person I've ever laid eyes on. Dark, full eyebrows are pinched together, assessing everyone in our party. His narrowed eyes are onyx, and his long black hair is pulled behind his neck.

The other man is slighter, shorter than Aidan, with bright brown eyes and reddish brown trimmed facial hair. He wears a casual smile as he takes in the castle and my companions.

"Your Majesty," Aidan dips his head at my mother.

She gives Misty one last pat before turning to him. "I trust that you'll keep my daughter safe and get her to the summit on time?"

I roll my eyes, but he graciously responds. "Of course, Queen Maris. We wouldn't miss it."

She turns to me, and I reach one of my hands down to clasp hers. "Be safe, daughter. I'll see you soon."

I give her a wobbly smile. "See you in Melinor."

She releases my hands, and I give the reins a little tug, until I'm face-to-face with Aidan and Parisa. Matteo appears at my side, sizing up Aidan's guards.

"Aidan, you've already met Captain Matteo," I gesture to Matteo, who gives a quick nod. "And this is Lady Grimhart."

Tessa awkwardly holds the reins in front of her, and her horse stomps and shakes its head uncomfortably. I inwardly groan, but her bright demeanor doesn't seem dampened in the slightest. "Pleased to meet you, Your Highness."

Aidan watches her with an amused expression. "The pleasure is all mine."

He raises an eyebrow at me, and I mouth the word *later* at him, hoping to avoid the conversation and eager to get a move on.

"Elana, you know General Parisa, *my aunt,*" he emphasizes, and my cheeks heat.

She finishes eying Lady Grimhart with distaste before turning her eyes on me. They soften slightly as she gives me a challenging smile. "Hello again, Princess."

"Hello, General," I respond with a smirk of my own. Knowing she's Aidan's aunt, and having seen her nearly naked in a seedy tavern, I don't feel nearly as intimidated by her as when we first met.

"This is Novan," Aidan gestures to the smaller of the two men now by his side. Smaller is subjective, since he still towers over me. "And that's Vikal."

Vikal must have part giant's blood, because even though his brown horse is one of the massive warhorses, he still appears disproportionately large atop it.

"Hello, Novan and Vikal. Thank you for accompanying us," I give them a smile, but it withers under Vikal's harsh stare.

"Don't mind Vik, Your Highness. He's cranky because we made him get out of bed extra early this morning," Novan says, flashing me an easy grin that immediately puts me at ease.

I stare at the rising sun, bathing the landscape in its golden glow. "Right, well, we should set off before the sun gets too high. There's someone we need to pick up outside of Sandral."

Aidan gives me a questioning glance, but I urge Misty into a trot, giving my home one last look before passing through the gates. Mother stands outside the castle doors, watching as we ride away. She looks so small, framed by the silhouette of our home. I lift my hand in farewell. We'll see each other soon.

# CHAPTER TWENTY-THREE

## AISLINN

Hallucinations keep me company for an untold amount of time. Blurry, fever-addled visions of towering Gods, a great battle in the sand, blood staining the desert a deep red color. I dream of a man with shocking silver hair, eviscerating himself with his own sword. I see kingdoms rise and fall. I see Mother, weeping over Father's casket. I see Elana shrouded in shadow, facing down an army. Rayna, standing alone on top a golden, grassy hill, an ancient horn of carved bone clutched in her hand and tears running in rivulets down her umber cheeks.

When at last I pry open my eyes, I see Igraine's worried face. She hovers over me with a damp cloth, patting my forehead and neck with cool water.

"Miss, are you finally awake?" She whispers. Her bright orange hair is like a halo around her head.

My peripheral vision darkens until the rest of the tent falls out of focus and it's her worried face anchoring me to this world. Her methodical way of touching my forehead, inspecting my eyes, feeling my pulse at my throat, reminds me so much of my sister. I hold onto that, onto her. I will survive for her.

"I'm here," I groan out through teeth that won't stop chattering. "How long was I asleep?"

"Nearly a week. We weren't sure you'd ever wake up," Igraine says quietly, worrying her bottom lip between crooked teeth.

She holds a steaming bowl in front of my face. "You need to eat."

I stare at the incredibly unappetizing brown slop. My stomach clenches in protest. "Then bring me some chocolate cake."

In response, she scoops up a spoonful and holds it to my mouth. "You need to get better. It's the only way to fix Hotharia."

My head spins, but I try to focus in on her as I accept the bite, chewing, and chewing, and chewing until I finally grimace and swallow. I cough, my throat unused to working so hard. Igraine holds up a cup of water and I take a few sips.

"What do you mean 'fixing Hotharia'?" I ask her as I eat a second bite.

She eyes the tent flaps, then shifts closer to me. "There's something wrong with our men. The warriors who came here from the capital with King Skade. It's hard to explain, but they're not themselves."

"How so?"

Igraine sighs, filing another spoonful. "They just seem...different. They don't laugh or joke with the rest of the army. They follow orders and perform their duties and speak when spoken to, but they're somehow...less. I treated one man who had a leg injury from an accident during training, and he never showed any sign of discomfort, despite nearly losing the limb. The man didn't even flinch as I stitched his leg back together. He could have been in shock, but it was more like he was disconnected from his body."

My blood goes cold, and I shiver. This time not from the fever. This sounds eerily familiar, and I hate the thoughts I have. Gods, please don't let me be right. "These soldiers," I ask, swallowing another unpleasant bite, "do their eyes look different? Darker, perhaps?"

She stirs what's left in the bowl absentmindedly as she debates her answer. "No, I don't think so."

There's a brief sense of relief, but I don't believe in coincidences. I make a mental note to ask Aric about this as I force myself to finish off the last gritty bites of stew.

"So, you think the war has changed these soldiers, and you think somehow I can help them?"

Igraine takes the empty bowl and spoon, setting them down next to her as she checks my wounds. "Well, not you, exactly. I think they're under some kind of enchantment. And I think the only way to help them is to stop King Skade. He's always been a ruthless ruler, but he's only gotten worse since Calder left for his trials."

I narrow my eyes, trying to make sense of things. My head spins, and my eyes stay narrowed, threatening to close. No, I don't have time to sleep more. I need to figure out what's happening here.

"I think he's planning something horrible," Igraine whispers, staring off into the corner of the tent.

Whatever she says next is completely lost to me, as a cloud descends over me, pulling me into oblivion once more.

The next time I wrench my eyelids open, it's to grating voices inside the tent. Light streams in, illuminating my little prison.

"Ah, there she is," the grating, cocky voice belongs to none other than King Skade. I blink my bleary eyes into focus. "Enjoying the comforts of Hotharia, Princess?"

I wave a chained hand in his direction. "I was until you arrived. Now, if you don't mind, I'd like to get back to my dream. Where I was about to stab you in the face."

The already restrictive metal around my wrists wrap tighter and tighter, until my fingers turn blue. I grit my teeth, pushing the pain away, but panic grips me, too, and that's not as easy to ignore. *Gods, not my hands, not my hands, not my hands.* I silently repeat. I'm nothing without my hands. When it feels like my bones are about to shatter, I let out a scream of pain, unable to hold it in any longer.

The manacles loosen slightly, and I suck in a few calming breaths to push the pain down to a manageable level, flexing and wiggling my fingers to bring some blood back into them. I glare at the king, letting my hatred for him fill my entire body.

Another blonde head appears through the front of the tent, and Calder walks in. When his attention lands on me, his brows pull together, and he quickly looks to his father. It must be the flickering light from the small fire, but I swear the blue of his eyes appears darker than ever.

A glimmering reflection catches my gaze and I spot my heirloom sword, Hale Sable's sword, at Calder's hip. Every instinct within me rages upon seeing it in his possession.

*Not worthy. Not worthy. Not worthy.*

The words scream in my mind, but I work to keep myself composed. If they know how important that blade is to me, to my family, they'll no doubt melt it down and forge it into more chains for me.

"Go ensure preparations are underway for our march north," King Skade addresses his son without even sparing him a glance.

Calder's eyes find mine again, if only for a moment, before he looks at the floor, squeezing his fists as a muscle ticks in his jaw. "Father, instead of wasting our time torturing her and resources keeping her alive, why don't we just demand their surrender for her ret-,"

His words are cut off by a backhand across his cheek. "Boy, if I wanted your opinion on the matter I would have asked. Now go, before I make you."

Calder's face remains tilted for a moment at an odd angle from the blow before he drops his head and leaves the tent as quickly as he arrived, without another word.

I watch him go with a mixture of pity and satisfaction. I'd known Skade was a ruthless bastard, but I didn't know he beat his children. I almost feel sorry for Calder now...almost.

As far as childhoods go, Elana and I had a pretty decent one. Sure, our mother could be severe at times, and our father was busy running a kingdom, but neither of them would ever raise a hand to us. We may have had strict schedules and rules, but the punishments we faced for breaking the rules never led to injury. The same cannot be said for this royal family, it seems.

I'd known that most of the other heirs had difficult childhoods. Calder opened up to us once about his younger brothers trying to kill him when he was fourteen. Instead of punishing the younger siblings, his father told Calder to become better.

As far as the other heirs, well, Rian's mother has always been his harshest critic, and it only got worse when she was given the throne. Rayna's younger siblings have always made it clear that if the opportunity arose to depose her, they would take it in a heartbeat. Aidan was lucky to have Alek as a brother, who seemed to respect Aidan more than he respected the Gods. But, his father, King Edward, was a piece of work. The heirs have always struggled to prove themselves.

I was fortunate to have Elana and not some sniveling younger sister who strived to make my life miserable. Even when she was chosen instead of me, no matter how blindsided I was, I didn't feel bitter. Selfishly, I felt relieved. As the firstborn, I never got to choose anything. At least as second-in-line, I have more freedom.

A booted foot lands in my ribs, sending my breath out of me, and causing me to clutch my stomach, gagging on the pain. "Answer me!" Skade bellows.

I glare up at him. "Maybe you should try asking nicely."

Flecks of spit land on my cheek as he crouches down, grabbing me by my shirt collar with both hands, and slamming my head into the metal post.

Stars dance in my vision and I do my best to keep a hold of my consciousness.

"What are you worth to your family?" Skade asks, still holding on.

"Didn't you hear, Skade? I was passed over by the Gods. I'm worthless now." I taste the tang of blood in my mouth, and realize I must have bitten my tongue. So, I do the only logical thing I can think of, and spit a glob of it in his face.

Skade jumps back to his feet and roars as he swipes at his face. My manacles constrict again, squeezing my still-healing wounds until I scream. I think of my father. My sister. My Kingdom.

I'm not used to being bested. I've spent years being practically untouchable. Now, however, I feel a prickle of something I haven't felt in ages…fear.

I will not bend, I will not surrender, for them. I won't allow my father's sacrifice to be in vain. I won't allow my sister to lose hope.

I will fight. Because Sables do not surrender.

"You can have my screams," I spit another glob of blood at his feet, "but you will never have my surrender."

"I don't need your surrender, because I already have it," Skade says, and the chains that lock to my ankles writhe and constrict.

I breathe through my teeth, hissing as I feel muscles and bones in my wrist shift, so close to shattering.

"Sir," a man's voice shouts from outside the tent. "A commander from *her* army is here to see you."

Skade sighs dramatically, then the pressure on my limbs vanishes, and I gasp in breaths as my vision bursts with color.

"I'll be right there," the king says, giving me one last evil smirk. "And I'll see you later, Princess."

The thought, or maybe just the pain, has me shaking involuntarily as I stare at the ground and picture Elana, my mother, and Rayna. No matter what, I will not give up. I will get back to them.

# CHAPTER TWENTY-FOUR

## ELANA

We travel as swiftly as our horses will carry us across Adrithia and northwest into Aaranor. Their capital city, Numai, is nestled in the foothills of the vast Kangkaram mountain range which splits the kingdom in two.

This is my first time visiting a new kingdom. The only other time I left Adrithia was to travel to the Gods Territory. So I don't have much to compare the landscape of Aaranor to. When we first crossed into the kingdom, the geography was much like that of western Adrithia. Rolling hills, fertile farmland in between rivers and forests. The closer we get to Numai, the more the land turned rough. Hills turn into peaks and bluffs, while streams become rushing torrents, and then towering mountains come into view.

These aren't the singular peaks like in the Gods Territory. These are expansive mountains, one cut right into the next. The highest peaks are snowcovered, even though it's the end of summer. Many are covered with foliage until a certain height, where the trees fall away, revealing bare rock towering into the clouds. The sight takes my breath away.

As we ride through villages of all sizes, I notice only a few paths leading up through the mountains. The one we're on snakes its way around several large mountains before turning into the foothills.

On his warhorse next to me, Aidan rolls up a worn piece of parchment. I catch the scrawling lines of a map.

He notices my attention and flashes me a smirk. "One more day and we should be there."

"Oh thank the Gods," I let out a relieved sigh. We stopped in the last village to buy more provisions. When Aidan planned for supplies, he only figured there would be seven people in our traveling party, not eight.

We picked up Clarisse in a small village outside of Sandral, where she's made quite the cushy life for herself. Her home is modest and well-kept, and she employed a housekeeper as well as a cook. She had a large garden, which I can only imagine was full of medicinal herbs and flowers, and a pasture with several cows, a goat, and a flock of sheep.

Before we parted ways after the battle at the coast, she told me how to find her if I ever needed anything. Nearly a fortnight ago, I sent her a letter asking for her help, and told her to be ready to make a long journey.

While Aidan and I search for any information about the land of Tyne, I've asked her to research the goddesses and anything that can block powers.

If we're heading into another battle, I need to be able to counter those cursed weapons. And since the twin goddesses refused to send me any useful message at the temple, I decided to place my faith in research, which is where Clarisse comes in. She's the most knowledgeable healing master in all of Adrithia, but she doesn't have access to the expansive information within the Great Archives.

Blinding rays of the setting sun along with our horses' heavy breathing tell us it's time to stop for the evening. There are no villages nearby, so it looks like one last night of outdoor sleeping for us. To save time, we've only stayed overnight at inns when we've passed by at night...which happened twice during our trip.

I'm used to sleeping outside, thanks to the trials and the time spent traveling with the army, but Tessa is not. The first evening we stopped, she insisted that we didn't need to set up a tent just for her, but then she spent the entire night moving around in her sleeping roll. She even woke us all up once screaming because a bug crawled on her. Ever since then, as soon as we dismount, Vikal insists on setting up her tent first thing. I would think it was a kindness, but he grumbles about it the entire time, so now I've chalked it up to him really enjoying his sleep.

I get the very distinct impression that he doesn't like us Adrithians much. He mostly grunts and huffs whenever one of us tries to make conversation with him. Aidan told me not to take it personally, that it took Vik years to even smile at him.

Novan is the complete opposite. He goes out of his way to be friendly towards everyone. He's the first to offer assistance, and the last one to complain. On our third day of travel, we were stuck in a rainstorm that lasted the entire day and into the evening, but he was the first to point out the rainbow when dawn finally broke.

I dismount Misty, landing hard on my ankles and wincing. Behind me, Matteo helps Tessa down from her horse, and Clarisse is unpacking her bedroll.

Vikal has the tent halfway set up by the time I lay out my sleeping roll next to Clarisse's. Tessa asked if I wanted to share the tent with her, but it's small, really only meant for one, and I learned quickly that she kicks in her sleep.

"I'll take the first watch tonight," Matteo calls out, and he agrees on a watch order with Novan and Vikal. The one time I tried to take a watch, I was laughed at and told royalty doesn't take watch. Ever since then, I haven't bothered.

I know I'm not as adept at physical fighting as the rest of our party is, but that doesn't mean I can't keep us safe. With my powers, I can shield, cloak, restrain, and even inflict harm if I choose. Plus, I have my twin daggers with me. I pat my hips, where they're currently strapped to my sides. It's been weeks since I've trained with them, but my hands still grip the hilts as if it were the most natural thing in the world.

A heavy bedroll unravels next to mine. Aidan gently shakes out the folds, giving me an amused look as I stare openly at his audacity.

"Problems, Magpie?" He asks.

I blink a few times. "What are you doing?"

He looks around with raised eyebrows and a glimmer of mischief in his golden eyes. "Setting up my sleeping roll, I believe."

"No," I huff, setting my pack down next to me. "I mean, why are you setting it up right here?" I gesture to his spot, then mine.

"Do you want me to move?" He asks with a tilt of his lips. And Gods, do I ever appreciate those lips.

I blush and swallow hard, turning my back to him, trying to busy myself with unpacking my food so I stop thinking about his lips. "It's fine. You're already set up."

"Whatever you say, Princess."

I'm glad I'm facing away from him so I don't have to look at his smug expression. I grab a handful of nuts and strips of dried meat from my pack and take a seat by the fire Aidan breathed to life for us.

Warm breath caresses my ear and I inhale the scent of cedar. "Does this remind you of anything?"

I finally turn to him, surprised by how close he is. His presence is like a warm blanket, enveloping me completely. How I wish I could sink into his arms and allow myself the reprieve from my near-constant anxiety about my kingdom, my sister, and the ever-heavy weight of my father's loss. It's the last thought that has me straightening. What's between us has to stop. While I don't blame him for what happened anymore, I still haven't entirely forgiven him. He could have at least prepared us for the possibility of Father's death.

"No," I say, biting my lip against the lie, "it doesn't remind me of anything."

I expect him to appear hurt, but one corner of his lips curls up. My heart skips a beat. He looks as if he's just accepted a challenge.

"Elana, help me with some foraging?" Clarisse calls, waving at me.

I practically leap to my feet, knowing she doesn't need help when it comes to foraging. She's the one who taught me, after all. I don't say anything to Aidan as I walk off.

"Oh, can I please come?" Tessa leaps to her feet and grabs my arm. She drops her voice, as if she's embarrassed to ask. "I want to be useful."

The pleading in her tone has me softening. I'm well-versed in what it's like to feel useless, although I wonder if that's the only reason why she wants to get away. The Ocarins have been respectful, but not exactly welcoming to her. They seem to judge a person based on what value they provide the group. Matteo was accepted into the fold immediately for being a competent warrior. Clarisse, for her skills as a healer. I can only assume why they readily accepted me. But Tessa, her talents lie...elsewhere. Novan teased her playfully at first, perhaps trying to treat her like one of his companions, but she took offense to everything he said. Vikal makes a habit of pretending she doesn't exist, and Parisa, well...Parisa usually rolls her eyes the moment Tessa opens her mouth.

"Of course. I'll show you what to look for."

I lead her towards Clarisse, who's wearing an indiscernible expression.

"What do we need?" I ask, pulling open my bag of herbs, plants, and other healing ingredients. Between Clarisse and I, I'm pretty sure we packed enough supplies to heal any ailment our group could possibly befall. We've been fortunate not to need many remedies on the trip so far. A few nights ago, Novan brushed a firebush and broke out in nasty pustules. The next day, Matteo had stomach distress after eating questionable fish from the inn where we spent the night. Both ailments required minor treatment.

"Artemisia," Clarisse said simply, leading the way off the path and into the surrounding woods.

I give a nod and follow her, while describing artemisia to Tessa, "it's a silvery-green plant that has little hairs on the foliage. Look for long thin stems with small leaves. It usually forms in clumps."

We search the ground as we walk. Clarisse stops and points to a spot along a rocky ridge. "Lady Grimhart, I think I see some on that ridge over there. Would you mind grabbing it for us? Try to dig up the root, too, please."

Tessa beams and rushes over to the ledge. "Okay, I'll be right back!"

I watch her go until Clarisse clears her throat, drawing my attention. "Elana, we haven't had much time to ourselves to talk since we set out."

"We haven't," I agree, facing her fully, bracing myself for whatever conversation she's been itching to have.

"How are things going with you and the Prince? When I saw you last, you two seemed quite...close. Why are you trying so hard to avoid him now?" she eyes me with suspicion.

I clear my throat, glancing back at the camp and making sure we're out of earshot. "Yes, well, things change."

She gives me a dubious look. "Not attraction like that. You were both smitten."

I pinch the bridge of my nose, knowing she won't leave me alone until I tell her everything. She's like a dog with a bone, and always has been. She could always force the truth out of me whenever I'd accidentally mixed the wrong ingredients into a tincture, or when I misidentified ailments and gave the incorrect healing balm or antidote. Something about her makes me cave every time.

"He knew that it was a possibility that my father would die on the battlefield, and he never told me," I say, looking down at the ferns growing densely at my feet. "And he also stopped me from helping him, in the end."

She doesn't respond right away, letting the silence fester like a sore until I finally meet her eyes. They're full of pity, and I hate it. "Death is always a possibility on the battlefield," she says softly.

I don't speak. Clarisse seems to take this as permission to continue her tirade. "Your father chose his sacrifice. Aidan didn't force him to that ledge. Devon did what every parent would do, and gave his two children their best chance at a better future. I'm so sorry that you had to witness it, but there's nothing you could have done to stop it. You are not responsible for his actions."

There's nothing I'd enjoy less than thinking about the moment my father fell. I shove the memory of it deep into the darkest parts of my mind. Shadows curl around my legs, enveloping me from the knee down, as if offering me their comfort.

Clarisse watches the shadows move with rapt interest. "Have you ever considered that maybe the problem with your powers isn't because of the goddess, but rather self-inflicted?" She asks quietly.

"What do you mean?" I pull strands of the darkness into my hands, twirling them around my fingers.

She shoves her hands in the pockets of her trousers. "I mean, dear Elana, that you're holding onto your guilt like a shield, and I wonder if maybe it's affecting your powers."

A flash of anger surges through me. Perhaps this is why Mother kicked her out of the castle, for her incessant meddling.

"It's not," I say quickly, trying to dispel this line of thinking. "I mean, it's got to be the goddesses. I think Nura is punishing me for failing to save him."

Clarisse sighs loudly. "She has no reason to punish you-,"

"I don't want to talk about this anymore," I cut her off.

"Fine, then should we discuss your sister? Or the fact that the nobility undermines you at every chance, and now your mother is regent of the kingdom you should be ruling."

I turn away, wanting out of this conversation while I'm still in control of my emotions. The shadows around my hands become more solid between my fingers.

Clarisse makes a noise I've heard my mother make many times before, and I instantly regret bringing her on this journey. "You don't have to act like you're okay. Have you even let yourself grieve?"

"I laid him to rest. I grieved plenty," I respond dryly. "As for my sister, there's nothing I can do for her, as so many others have pointed out. My best shot at helping her is convincing the other kingdoms to go to war against Hotharia so we can get her back. And as far as Adrithia is concerned, most of the nobles are stuck up pricks, so I'm not too upset about being left out of that nightmare for now."

"Most of those nobles couldn't even spell nightmare, let alone run a kingdom. Speaking of nobles, what exactly is that one doing with us? She acts like she's never been outside before," Clarisse wrinkles her nose in the direction of Tessa, who's currently using two sticks to try and dig the plant up.

"Be kind, Clarisse. Tessa's very sweet," I chastise her. "She was one of the few who spoke up for Mother and I when we needed the support for our war declaration. Besides, she has connections that might get us into the Great Archives. And I have a feeling we will need all the help we can get."

Clarisse gives an acknowledging grunt. "Okay, okay, I'll try to be nice."

I roll my eyes, knowing that's not likely to happen.

"I got it!" A trilling voice calls from ahead, and Tessa rushes to us, a wide smile on her face, holding up the artemisia.

"Brilliant, Lady Grimhart, thank you," Clarisse says, a little too brightly. She takes the plant, shaking off excess dirt, and stashes it in her bag. Later she'll strip the leaves and roots, storing them until needed. Artemisia is widely useful in healing.

"Please, call me Tessa," she smiles warmly at Clarisse. "Do we need anything else?"

Clarisse looks at me, as if questioning if there's anything else to discuss away from the group. "I think that's it, Tessa. Let's head back."

The three of us walk back to camp, following the glow of the towering fire Aidan must be expelling some pent up energy on. A corner of my lips pulls up as I wonder what kind of energy he has pent up.

"Aren't we worried about bandits or enemies seeing that fire?" Tessa asks, wide eyes pinned to the flames stretching up over the trees.

I flash her a reassuring grin. "Aaranor's on the other side of the continent from Hotharia. I'm not worried about the invaders. And I highly doubt any common bandit would be stupid enough to attack a group of skilled warriors and an heir blessed by the Goddess Enya. If anything, that fire is a deterrent from potential visitors in the night."

She gives me a wide-eyed nod as we clear the trees and rejoin our companions.

"Ladies," Novan's lazy smile stretches across his face. "Did you find what you were looking for?"

Clarisse gives her bag a firm pat. "Yes, we did. Lucky for you, because I can make more of that stomach calming tea. Lucky for the rest of us, too. There's a reason we asked you to ride at the rear of our party."

Everyone shares a laugh, and even Vikal smiles as we hunker down and prepare to sleep. Tessa retreats to her tent while the rest of us settle into our sleeping rolls.

I keep my back to Aidan, though I can feel his gaze on me until my heavy eyelids droop closed.

A sound like soft thunder wakes me. It's dark, the fire is a soft glow near my head. At first I think I imagined the sound, until I hear it again, but I know instantly it's not thunder. I sit up, palming one of my twin daggers, squeezing the reassuring grip until my breathing slows.

A rustling noise to my left has me turning. Aidan is also sitting up, eyes trained on the starry sky, the hilt of his longsword in his hand.

Far above us, the moon is blocked out by two massive wings, and a long, serpentine body. The shadow falls over us, and I shiver, but not from the cold.

"Okay, now this reminds me of something," I whisper to Aidan, not wanting to wake anyone else up. I glance across the fire and see Novan leaning against a nearby tree, studying the dragon as it flies towards the mountains.

It's a stark reminder that although they're not commonly seen nowadays, they still exist. I think back to the dragon we killed during our trials. Did it have a family? Is the dragon flying above us a relative?

I can tell Aidan's wondering the same thing, with a tight jaw and eyes narrowed on the beast.

"Do you think it's friendly?" I whisper as its dark wings beat several more times and it soars out of view.

Aidan gives me a raised brow. "Why don't you go ask. I'll wait here."

I'm tempted to throw something at him, but the only thing in my hand is my dagger, and somehow I don't think that'll go well.

"We should get some sleep, Magpie," he says, but I'm wide awake now.

"I don't think I could sleep right now if I tried," I groan, wiping my face with my hands.

Aidan nods, then looks to the sky, and the lightest pink starts to color the clouds on the horizon. "Dawn is almost here anyway. How about some training instead?"

Because he told me once that training helps him clear his mind. And maybe he's more anxious about this trip than he's letting on. "Yeah, all right."

I stand up, slowly stretching my arms up over my head, then fold my torso forward, bending at the waist to stretch out my lower back. When I right myself, I find Aidan watching me with a gleam of mischief in his eyes.

"Ready?" He holds his hand out to me, and I take it with a nod, then says softly to Novan. "We'll be back."

Novan flashes a suggestive smile our way, and I ignore him as we head off the path and into an area with large boulders and sparse trees. It's the perfect area to train with fire.

Shadows nip at my heels in anticipation, as if they sense they're about to be released into the world.

"How long has it been since you trained your powers?" He asks me.

"Power," I respond, bringing a whip of darkness to my hand and solidifying it. "I've been...experimenting with it a little every day. But actual training, it's been a few weeks."

I don't actually remember the last time I used my powers in any real combat. Most of my experience with it has been one-sided, me sparring against trees or nothing.

"Well, then, let's get-,"

Without warning, I raise a cloak of darkness around us, blocking out the rising sun, pitching us into nearly total blackness. A single flame bursts to life to my right and I drop to the ground, barely avoiding the blast. I wrap myself in shadow, moving through the dark like a spector, until I feel him right in front of me. He must feel me, too, because he sends out another fire ball, and I leap out of the way. The flame briefly illuminated his hand, and I send my shadow whips at him. It catches his wrist, and I feed them, expanding the hold the shadows have over him.

A ball of fire appears in front of him, and now I can see his face. He watches the darkness in shock and fascination as it winds its way up his arm, across his shoulder, then down his right arm, where it pulls itself together and binds his hands together.

"Impressive," Aidan says, searching the darkness for me. His gaze stops on mine. "There you are, Magpie."

The stream of fire roars towards me and I leap out of the way, but another one cuts off my retreat. I send up a wall of shadow, but the searing flames cut right through it. I gasp and back up, but my back hits stone and there's nowhere for me to go. The fireball breaks apart, surrounding me, trapping me, but it doesn't burn. Aidan's keeping control of the temperature of his flames.

I try to raise more shadows, pulling from the well of energy within me, but Aidan appears before me, walking through the flames like it's nothing more than fog. His hands are still bound, but he wears a triumphant smirk.

"That was quite the show. Your control over darkness is something to behold," he says.

I give a nod to his hands. "Do you need help with those?"

His answering smile has my toes curling in my boots. "No, I think I like being tied up by you."

Oh Gods. My cheeks burn as his molten eyes bore into me. "You're a degenerate."

"Only around you," he says, wrapping his bound hands behind my neck and pulling me into his broad chest.

My breath hitches in my throat as I tilt my head up. This feels so natural, so perfect. Aidan leans down, and how I wish I could sink into his embrace and let myself forget everything since the masquerade ball. It was the last time I felt truly happy.

Aidan's breath warms my face as he gives me the softest kiss on my cheek, then brushes his lips against my forehead. I close my eyes and command the shadows to fall away, releasing his hands.

"I won't push you, Elana. You let me know when you're ready to explore *us* again," he whispers to my forehead.

Then, his heat is gone, the flames extinguished. An uncomfortable chill works its way up my spine as I open my eyes and see his back as he walks away, and it feels like my heart is being constricted. I suck in a few wobbly breaths, pulling myself back together, before trailing after him.

# CHAPTER TWENTY-FIVE

## ELANA

My mouth hangs open as I gawk at Numai. The city appears to have been carved directly from the mountains. The buildings are angular, from the squared walls, sometimes set into crevices in the rock, to the roofs, which range in colors from gold to burnt orange to sage green. Everywhere I look, homes reach into the sky, with suspended bridges and walkways between some of the taller ones. Stone steps are everywhere. It makes perfect sense now why Rian doesn't fear heights, because he grew up in the clouds. It's also no wonder why the Air God Sepher chose him.

"Well, there's a sight I could get used to," Clarisse says, gaping at the bright homes as we ride through a particularly colorful patch.

"Unfortunately, looks can be deceiving. I always found the city to be stuffy, and its people even moreso," Tessa says, wrinkling her nose at the sight. She's been uncharacteristically quiet this morning.

"Are you all right?"

She gives me a sad smile. "It's difficult to be back here."

"Want to tell me about it?"

She bites her lip. "It's not some tragic story or anything. I grew up here, in the city. My parents were both Keepers of the Archives, where they met and fell in love. I'm their only child, and was expected to take my place as a Keeper as well, but I never enjoyed it like they did. They lived for the tomes. Reading, cataloguing, transcribing, and writing their own pieces of history. That was their passion and purpose in life. It felt too claustrophobic for me. I wanted nothing more than to get out of the library as soon as possible.

I met my husband while he was passing through Numai on his way back to Adrithia. It was a total chance meeting, his horse nearly trampled me in the streets when I was chasing after some parchment I'd dropped. He helped me gather the pages, then asked me to dinner afterwards as payment," Tessa's eyes gaze down the street, as if she's remembering exactly where it happened.

She turns to me, sheepishly. "I'm sorry, I digress."

"Please, continue," I say, flashing her an encouraging smile.

"We were both smitten from that first supper. He proposed marriage, and just like that, I finally had my way out of the Archives. I went to my parents with the news, expecting them to be happy for me, but instead they were devastated. My mother cried, and my father wouldn't even look at me. To them, I was betraying the family. I tried explaining it, that we were in love, and wanted to start a family. But they only saw me abandoning them, and leaving the family legacy behind. When I got to Adrithia, I sent letter after letter with no response. They didn't even visit after my son was born. They only sent him a book on the history of the Archives. A few years later, I got one last letter, saying that my mother had died, and my father asked me not to come for her Resting Ceremony. I was heartbroken, but I honored his wishes. My husband died a few months later, and I was busy raising my son and managing the estate, so I never made time to come back to Numai. So, Elana, I'm not sure if I will be of any help or hindrance to you on this journey, but I wanted to try."

The revelation hits me like a sack of grain. There's every chance that we could be turned away from the Archives. I try not to let my devastation show, and my anxiety that this entire trip could be for nothing. Pushing those negative thoughts away, I meet Tessa's glistening eyes. My anger shatters into a million pieces. I do my best to push my disappointment far, far back, so she won't notice. "It's okay, Tessa. I understand why you wanted to come along. Maybe once we get inside, if you want to, you can try to talk to your father."

She nods her head emphatically. "Yes, that would be wonderful. I should still know my way around the stacks, too, so once you gain entry from the Keepers, I'll be able to help you find the texts you're looking for."

"We're approaching the castle," Clarisse calls from near the front of our party, and I look up, drinking in the breathtaking palace.

The first thing I notice is the hundreds of stairs in front of us, and my gut sinks. Once I get over the fact that my thighs are going to be experiencing a lot of pain soon, I take in the rest of it.

My gaze finds the ornate roof on the tallest part of the building. It has bright orange, elegantly curved sloped sections that meet in the middle, where a large golden ball rests on top. The towering sections of the palace are rounded, but not circular. Instead, it has eight sides, which gives it a rounded, but structured appearance. Red, green, blue, and orange is used in the ornate design of the arches and columns holding the many levels up. An incredibly skilled Avani-blessed ruler must have had a hand in creating this palace. Swaying bridges connect several of the towers. Large blocks of rock are used as the foundation and for the stairs, which are even more daunting up close.

Our party comes to a stop and in front, Aidan starts speaking to some-one. I ride up to see a beaming Rian.

I dismount Misty, thankful I don't injure myself this time, and rush over to the heir.

When Rian sees me, his contagious smile stretches further up his cheeks. "Welcome to Numai, Elana!"

He wraps his arms around me and lifts me up in a crushing hug. I pat him on the back a few times while I try to continue breathing. "Rian, squeezing...too...tight."

"Whoops!" He drops me to my feet and I suck in a long breath, holding my chest.

"I was practicing flying when I saw you riding into the city. I got your letter asking to enter the Archives. What are you looking for?" Rian asks, looking between Aidan and I.

"We need to learn as much as we can about the land of Tyne. If we're to win this war, we can't go into another battle blind," Aidan says in a low voice.

Rian stands straight again, his demeanor suddenly serious, a complete change from moments ago. "Right, then you'll need an audience with my mother."

A few stableboys rush towards us, grabbing the reins of our horses. Several palace attendants also step forward. Rian addresses them, "See that their bags make it up to the guest tower. And find suitable accommoda-tions for their companions."

The guest *tower*? I'm not sure I like the sound of that, but hold my tongue for now. It seems Aidan and I will be sleeping in the palace tonight while the others stay in an inn in the city.

I catch Parisa staring at Aidan, and he gives her a sharp nod. She gives one in return, then dismounts her horse and starts unbuckling her pack. The rest of our group follows her lead.

I watch as Vikal not only helps Tessa off her horse, but also grabs her heavy bags for her, slinging them over his back. She flashes him an appreciative smile, which he grunts at.

"Elana, you coming?" Rian calls to me, and I turn back to the stairs and see him and Aidan already several ahead.

"Why is it always more climbing?" I groan to myself as I start to make my way up the steps.

As expected, I'm the first to start breathing heavily. Rian talks nearly nonstop, not even winded.

"This city has stood since the founding of Aaranor, and is one of the oldest cities on the continent. Our very first monarch, King Cyrus, built the foundations for the entire city, and was one of the original founders of the Great Archives. Numai acts as the barrier to western Aaranor. It's a wild place, home to several warring clans that don't recognize my family's right to rule the kingdom. It makes relations tough, but they mainly stick to the far western coast, and with the mountains between us, we hardly venture there unless absolutely necessary. Most of the land is a wasteland, anyway."

I focus on my breathing while he points out the inn where our party will be staying. From this height, I see a sprawling complex designed around a luscious courtyard. We continue climbing.

"This has to be the tallest palace and the most stairs I've ever seen," I say through heavy breaths. My legs burn with exertion.

Rian flashes me a wry grin. "It is, actually. Although the palace in Forath is also built on a mountain, it's not as tall, nor nearly as impressive, as ours."

"Modest as ever, Yarrow," Aidan says with a roll of his eyes.

"Elana, I heard Aislinn is still missing. Any word of what happened?" Rian asks, turning to me with sorrow written all over his features.

I clear my throat and give myself a moment to breathe. "We're pretty sure Hotharia took her as a prisoner. But we haven't heard a whisper of where or why."

"I'm so sorry. Let me know if there's anything I can do," he says earnestly.

"Thank you, Rian," I smile at him.

We climb a few more steps. Aidan and Rian are hardly breaking a sweat, while I'm practicing my deep breathing techniques. "Rian, what can we expect from your mother? Will Queen Nami offer any assistance?"

Rian sighs heavily. "I don't know. She's furious at Hotharia for what they've done, and she told me it is a great injustice. However, Aidan, she's also angry with your mother for keeping such a dangerous secret. She's lost all trust in Ocarin. I've been doing what I can to smooth things over, asking her if she would have done the same thing if situations were reversed, but she refuses to even entertain the idea."

Aidan nods, keeping his eyes to the stairs. "What can we do to rebuild the trust?" He asks, referring to him and his mother.

"Honestly, friend, I'm not sure. It'll take a grand gesture. Something I'm not sure you're willing to give."

Aidan falls silent, and I take up the conversation. "Does one normally need permission from the Queen to access the Great Archives?"

Rian's answer is sour. "People within Aaranor are allowed free access to the library whenever they wish, as long as they're approved by the Keepers, but those from other kingdoms aren't trusted with the knowledge, so they need the monarch's permission as well."

"And you don't agree with that?" I ask, judging from his tone.

"No. Knowledge should be accessible to everyone. We shouldn't be gatekeepers of information that could help thousands of people."

I can't argue with that. The idea of keeping tomes away from those who could benefit from it doesn't sit well with me.

"Unfortunately," Rian says with resignation, "this rule has been in place for generations, so it'll be a difficult one to break when I become monarch."

I stare at Rian. He once told me he never wanted to become monarch. I still wonder what he would like to do instead of rule. Although I don't get the chance to ask. We're finally nearing the top of the stairs, and not a moment too soon. My chest feels like it's about to burst and I can barely feel my legs.

At the top of the stairs is a stone landing. Two women stand there. Queen Nami stands tall in the center, while an older woman with striking white hair and skin wrinkled with age but still showing her beauty, stands to her left. As we approach, Rian leaves our side and goes to stand by his mother's right.

Aidan and I dip our heads respectfully at the queen.

"Welcome, Princess Elana of Adrithia and Prince Aidan of Ocarin. Rian mentioned you'd be stopping by for a visit. And that you wish to use our Great Archives," Nami says, in a tight, slightly disapproving tone.

I nod at her. "Thank you for your hospitality, Your Majesty. If you grant us permission, we would like to use the Great Archives to find any information about the land of Tyne to the northeast of Astrellia.

Nami stares between us, giving no hint of emotion away. Instead of answering me, she gestures to the woman at her side. "This is my mother, Mai."

Mai's weathered face is spotted with age, but she holds herself straight with the help of a gnarled polished cane. I give her a nod of my head. "It's a pleasure to meet you."

A gust of warm wind blows my braid into my face, smacking me across my cheek. I give Rian a glare, but he laughs as he raises his hands and points to his grandmother. There's a twinkle of mischief and intelligence in her eyes that reminds me so much of her grandson.

"My mother was blessed by the Air God Sepher, as is Rian," Queen Nami says, turning on her heels and walking inside the massive double doors. The entranceway towers over anything I've ever seen before, tall enough to dwarf even the highest tower of my home. It seems unnecessary, but it certainly gives a grand impression.

Nami takes one of her mother's arms and leads her slowly up the stairs. Rian hangs back, giving Aidan and I a wide smile.

I drop my voice to a low whisper and ask him, "Rian, how does your grandmother have power but not the throne?"

"She abdicated to my mother about five years ago. It was a big to-do, and it's rarely ever done, but grams said she wanted to enjoy her remaining years in peace," he whispers back.

I try to hide my shock. I've never heard of a ruler abdicating their throne.

We follow Nami and her mother down a long main corridor, which I quickly realize is the throne room. There's no entranceway, no waiting room. It's one long hall, with a soaring ceiling. Nami takes a seat on her bench-like throne that's as colorful as her palace and carved with motifs of dragons, snakes, and all manner of creatures. Her mother, Mai sits down on a smaller, but no less impressive bench next to her. She stares at her son with one brow raised, but he remains at our side, as if drawing his line in the sand.

"I understand my son has given you an informal invitation to visit our archives any time you wish, but that invitation was never cleared with me," Nami says, eying us with a shrewd gaze that reminds me of a bird of prey.

"Oh, let them take the trials, daughter," Mai says, giving a dismissive gesture with her hands. "They traveled a long way to seek our knowledge. At least let them be tested by the Keepers."

Aidan and I exchange a wary look. "A test?" I ask.

"Of course. Knowledge is the most important and dangerous weapon we possess. And our Keepers protect it fiercely, as do the Gods," she responds with a gleeful smile.

Nami gives her mother a withering look, but returns her gaze to us. "Yes, it's true. The Keepers don't let merely anyone into the archives.

"All that knowledge and you just...lock it away?" I say, unable to keep the fury out of my tone. Information shouldn't be kept away from people.

"Knowledge is dangerous in the wrong hands," Nami counters. "We must ensure those who have access to it won't use the information against our kingdom or our continent."

I glare at her. "That's a pretty narrow minded way of thinking."

Rian winces, then flashes me a sharp look. His mother stares down her nose at me and I feel Aidan's presence shift closer. "Your opinion is of no concern to me. The Yarrow family has been entrusted with the protection of the archives for generations, and we will continue to do so for generations to come."

"Does that mean you're forbidding us from entering the Archives?" Aidan doesn't mince his words.

Nami stares between us. "Yes."

The air around me grows warmer and I spare a glance at Aidan, whose dark gaze is pinned on Nami.

"You would sacrifice the lives of the entire continent for your grudge against my mother?" Aidan snarls.

Nami's eyes pierce him back. "Believe it or not, Prince, not everything has to do with you and your family. I will protect the knowledge of *my people* against those who may do us harm."

"Neither me nor my mother have ever done your people any harm. We've been nothing but allies to Aaranor," Aidan snaps.

"Lies cut deeper than any physical wound," Nami says.

Aidan gives her a lethal smirk. It's an expression I've rarely seen on him. It means we're about to be in trouble. "Perhaps we should put that theory to the test."

The temperature spikes as waves of heat waft from him. Shit, we need to do something before this ends in bloodshed. I give Rian a frantic look, placing my fist over my heart.

He knits his eyebrows together at first in confusion, then realization hits him and he nods, encouraging me.

I take one step forward, putting myself in the path of building wrath between Aidan and Rian's mother. "Queen Nami, your son owes me a life debt, and I'm calling it in."

I swallow hard and wait for my words to sink in. It doesn't take more than a moment. She stares between me and Rian.

"Is this true?" Nami snaps at her son. The pressure around us in the room plummets, returning the temperature to normal. I shiver with the sudden loss of heat.

"Yes, it is. During the second trial on the mountain, Elana saved me from drowning in a whirlpool, nearly causing herself to drown. As such, my life is in her hands until I repay that debt. Allowing her and her companions access to the Great Archives will fulfill the oath."

Mai gives a solemn nod of her head. "A life debt must be repaid, Nami. We must let them enter the trials."

Nami fumes in her seat, drumming her fingers on the arm of the throne while she stares at her son with an expression that makes me wish I were anywhere else. Rian, to his credit, takes the scrutiny without flinching. After several long moments, she lets out a dramatic sigh. "Fine. Elana Sable, you have my gratitude for saving my son's life, and as such, we will allow you and your companions access to the Archives. However, before you enter, you must pass the Guardians' trial."

The win feels hollow at the prospect of another trial. I wonder what we'll have to do this time. Hopefully not fighting more dragons. I glance quickly at Aidan, and he gives me a shrug. "Very well, we agree to the trial. When do we begin?"

Nami gives a little wave of her hand, as if she no longer cares. "Tomorrow morning."

I stiffen, we can't miss half a day of research. Every hour that passes is vital, and could mean the difference between us finding the knowledge of the land and not. "We're eager to get started today. Is there any way we can begin the trial now?"

Nami narrows her eyes at me again. "No. Our Guardian needs to be notified so he can prepare the challenges for you and your companions. Tomorrow morning is the earliest."

Her tone invites no argument, so I bite my lip and merely nod. "Thank you."

With that, we're officially dismissed. Rian leads us out of the court and into a hallway with many passages.

"Thank you, Rian," I tell him when we're fully out of earshot.

He flashes me a smile. "Glad I was able to help, although I'm probably going to catch shit for it later." He glances at Aidan with raised brows.

"It's probably best that you and my mother didn't go at it in the throne room. Some of those pillars are a thousand years old, and we haven't had an Avani-blessed ruler in centuries to repair them."

Aidan gives a grunt of agreement as Rian leads us into a lush courtyard. There's a small pond in the center with giant lily pads covering most of the surface. Water-loving flowers grow all around it, and several large colorful fish swim in the depths.

We walk over the pond on a wooden plank walkway, heading to a shorter section of the palace.

"Is all of this your home?" I ask, taking in all the different buildings and towers.

He gives me a sly smirk. "Yes, I can't wait to show you everything."

Aidan's groan startles me from my awe. "And, here we go."

# CHAPTER TWENTY-SIX

## AISLINN

I haven't seen a friendly face in days. Not since King Skade showed up and demanded I set my own ransom. Strangers, usually armed and not talkative, have been bringing me food and water on a regular basis. Even though most days I can barely stomach it, I force myself to eat every bite, knowing I need to gain back some weight. Unfortunately there's not much I can do to keep my strength up in these conditions, other than stretching as much as my manacles will allow.

My fever broke two days ago, and my wrists hardly ache anymore thanks to Igraine's ministrations.

Outside the tent I catch fragments of hushed, anxious conversations. Something big is happening, and I'm dying to know what all the whispering is about. After Skade left my tent, the camp seemed to be in a near-constant state of frenzy.

I carve another line into the rock near the edge of my reach. I lost track of days during my fever, but I think I've been here for around a fortnight.

The tent flap opens and Aric steps through, carrying a plate. On it is a whole cooked fish and a potato. Oh Gods, it might be the most glorious meal I've laid my eyes on. I waste no time tearing into it.

"Where has everyone been the last few days?" I ask, staring past him to the tent opening.

"We're preparing to leave the mesa. This half of the army is marching northwest," Aric says, and I nearly choke on a fish bone.

"You're attacking Melinor?" I ask as a sinking feeling hits me in the gut. I take a moment to gawk at Aric. His facial hair is as long as I've ever seen it, and his normally tan skin is pale and sallow.

"There's going to be a summit at Oraphia. King Skade has already left with a small advance force. Prince Calder will be leading us, the third wave, to block them from retreating south," he says, staring at his shaking hands.

"Third wave?" I wonder, staring at him. "What's the second?"

He takes a deep breath before answering. "A large fleet is sailing up the coast of the continent and will land north of Oraphia."

I scrunch my nose. To my knowledge, Hotharia doesn't have that large of a naval fleet. "Aric, whose fleet is it?"

He swallows, shoulders hunching as he stares at the ground. "They're from a land to the northeast called Tyne. They're the ones who attacked Ocarin and then Adrithia. Their Empress struck a deal with Skade, who agreed to aid her in conquering Astrellia, and in return Hotharia will be the only kingdom untouched."

"Fuck." I feel suddenly ill. "Does their army have cursed weapons?"

He nods. "They do."

"And how many ships are in the fleet?" I ask, completely abandoning my meal.

"At least ten. Possibly more. I don't know the exact details. I'm only relaying what I've heard from other commanders and what I've managed to get out of Calder," he says.

I squeeze my fork as I try to think of ways to warn Melinor. All of the rulers and their heirs will be there. They could be wiped out in one swift battle. And if Elana can't use her light powers, Melinor's forces won't stand a chance against their cursed weapons.

"Are any of Tyne's warriors marching with you?" I wonder how many of them are in this camp right now.

Aric rocks back on his heels. "Yes. A small guard will be traveling with us, led by...one of their commanders."

He shifts uncomfortably, and before I have time to ask him anything else, he leans in close, saying quietly, "Aislinn, there's something you should know. This commander, he's-,"

The tent flap flies open and Calder stomps in, shadowed eyes narrowing in on Aric, who has gone as still as stone. From the dark circles surrounding his eyes, it looks like he hasn't slept in days.

Aric snatches the plate from my hands and tosses it over his shoulder. The half-eaten fish and rest of the potato scatter. My stomach rumbles in protest at the waste of food.

"I've always hated you, stupid bitch. It made me sick to pretend to be your friend," Aric's words cut, even though I'm aware it's a ruse to ease Calder's suspicion.

"Come on, cousin. There will be time to berate her later. Let's get her loaded into the prison cart," Calder says with a smirk that doesn't hold any of his usual venom. He just seems...exhausted as he tosses a small silver key to Aric.

Aric gives me a pointed look. "Wait until we're out of Hotharia," he barely whispers as he unlocks my manacles first, then unlocks the chains around my feet.

"Get up, bitch," he snarls and I glare daggers at him.

Rising to my feet takes significantly more time and effort than I expect. My muscles protest as I stand, my aching limbs not used to holding myself upright.

"Gods, you"re pathetic. Let's go," he snarls and tugs on the chains, forcing me to follow him at a brutally quick pace.

As we exit the tent I'm nearly blinded by the sun. I squeeze my eyes shut and blink a few times until they adjust to the light. Most of the camp is packing up supplies, and attaching packs to horses. Tents are being torn down, and fires are put out. Steam and smoke rises from everywhere.

Ahead, surrounded by half a dozen guards, I spot the bane of my existence. The dreaded prison cart.

One of the guards next to it must be one of the warriors from Tyne. He wears all black, his warm chestnut brown hair gleams in the sunlight. As we get closer, I realize he's slightly taller than me. My eyes immediately go to the black sword sheath at his side. I can barely make out the deep black metal of the cursed sword.

"Fuck," Aric mutters, frantically glancing around, and then ahead at the man. "Wait, Calder-,"

Whatever else he's about to say dies on his lips as the man turns, and my heart. Stops. Beating.

"Father," I hardly breathe. The word is choked out around the pure joy that threatens to overwhelm me as my thoughts race to catch up with what my eyes and my heart are seeing. *He's here. He's real. He survived.*

When his eyes find mine at last, I expect to see a hidden smile or a wink. A sign that he's here to rescue me and bring me home. That he dressed in the enemy's clothes to hide among them and only reveal himself when the time is right.

Nothing could have prepared me for the absolute gut punch when I see his eyes, because it's him. It's undeniably him. And yet, it isn't.

All hope turns to dust in my dry mouth as I lock eyes with him. And instead of seeing his soft brown eyes, I'm met with cold, inky blackness. Not a speck of color remains.

"No," I cry out, as sorrow grasps me in her greedy hold, threatening to pull me under. I don't understand what's happening, what I'm seeing. It's my father's body, but it's not my father. His appearance is straight out of my memories, down to the beard and mustache he kept neatly trimmed. He sports a new scar from his temple to his ear, but other than that he's exactly the same. Except for those pitch black eyes.

This is too cruel.

"Father, what have they done to you?" I shriek, trying to move towards him, but am viciously pulled back by Calder.

"Don't worry, you two can catch up later," Calder says, unlocking the door to the prison cart, then shoving me inside. I stumble and lose my balance on my way in. My shoulder makes painful contact with the metal wall, but I immediately crouch down and try to lunge out the door.

It slams in my face, but I pound on it with my bare fists, then I wrap the chains around my knuckles and continue hitting the door.

"Father!" I scream, punching it again and again, splitting my knuckles open and smearing blood on the door.

When the pain in my fists becomes too much to bear I flip to my back and start kicking the metal with the heel of my boot. It bends slightly under my barrage, but doesn't break.

I scream until my voice goes hoarse, then I lose it from yelling again and again at them to let me out. No one listens, so I turn my anger to the Gods, cursing them for this twist of fate.

The carriage lurches forward, and we slowly move northwest to Oraphia. To the summit, and where everyone I care about sits unprepared for the Hells about to be unleashed.

# CHAPTER TWENTY-SEVEN

## ELANA

The tour of Rian's palace took hours. We received a history lesson that would put my mother to shame in every room. I hardly remember my great-great grandfather's name, and which god blessed him, but Rian can recite every Yarrow and their powers going back centuries. He also told us which of his relatives commissioned each part of the palace, and how long the construction took. Much to my trepidation, he insisted that we take several of the bridges between towers. I held onto the ropes with both hands each time, and refused to stop and take in the view like Rian had suggested.

After a tense dinner with him and his mother, I nearly collapsed into the soft bed without batting an eye that it rested on the ground.

I peel my eyes open to bright sunlight and pull the covers back over my head, too comfortable to move.

"Time to wake up, Magpie," a voice whispers near my ear. "The Guardian awaits."

Aidan's voice caresses me from slumber. I stretch my arms slowly up, turning to get more comfortable in bed. A low, seductive chuckle startles me awake.

Aidan Ashfall is in my private quarters. I sit up on the bed and wipe sleep from my eyes, trying to clear my vision. A fiery bird with long tail feathers hovers in front of me, its wings beating slowly, sending out a shower of sparks with every beat.

Gentle fingers brush my wild hair back from my face. Aidan kneels by my bed, already dressed for the day.

"Oh Gods, are we late?" I ask, jumping to my feet.

"No, not late. But we should get moving if we want to spend the day researching," Aidan responds with a half smile.

The door to my bedchamber slides open and Rian's tall lean frame fills it. "My my my, what do we have in here?"

His eyebrows dance as he looks between Aidan and I.

I scoff. "I just woke up. It's too early for assumptions, Rian."

He holds his hands up in response. "You know I'm not one to gossip."

I'm not too tired to laugh, and a loud snort comes from me. "Oh, please. You're the biggest meddler I've ever met."

"You wound me" Rian puts a hand to his heart and fakes an injury. "Now, how about we get a move on? I heard from the staff that your companions have already begun their challenges."

The men wait outside while I get dressed, choosing soft breeches and a leather vest over a navy short sleeve tunic. I affix my daggers to my hips on reflex, and quickly braid my hair as I rush out the door.

Rian leads us to a small sitting room, where a variety of foods are laid out for us. We eat quickly, and my gaze dances between the stunning paintings in the room.

They range in sizes, some as tall as Aidan, and others no bigger than my head. Most of the pieces are landscapes. Most appear to be of Aaranor, with its lush mountain steppes a focal point. There's a few paintings of dragons, and one of the phoenix. I smile to myself, thinking of the Messenger of the Gods, and his sister, the Maiden.

One medium-sized framed canvas catches my attention. I recognize it immediately as the rope bridge us heirs braved during the trials on the Gods Peaks. A painting next to it depicts in great detail the view of the mountain range from the back of a dragon. It's breathtaking and incredibly accurate .Rian or his mother must have perfectly described the Gods' Peaks in order for such a lifelike rendition to have been created.

"Who is the artist who painted these masterpieces?" I ask. "I'd love to commission some work."

Rian smiles, resting his head on top of his steepled hands. "Ah, our court painter is renowned all across Astrellia. I doubt you could afford him."

I roll my eyes at his sarcasm, then point at the birds-eye-view of the mountain. "No, seriously, Rian. This piece is amazing, and I'd love to hire him."

Rian laughs and he takes a sweeping bow. "My dear Elana, I always knew you'd come to me for my *services*, I just didn't think it would be for my skills with a brush."

My mouth drops open with an audible *pop*, and I stare at him in a new light. "You painted all of these?"

"Yes, now please close your mouth. I don't want drool on my breakfast," he says with a twinkle in his eye.

"I never knew you painted."

His eyes suddenly lose their light, as if the twinkle were snuffed out. "Yes, well, not everyone in my family thinks it's appropriate for a Crown Prince to paint. They'd much prefer me presiding over court, planning soirees, or searching for a wife to bear my many children."

Aidan gives a snort of derision, then loudly slurps his miso. Rian sends a gust of wind into his bowl, and the soup explodes upwards, right into Aidan's face. He growls, and the liquid on his face steams and evaporates off his skin.

"You can do both," I say, interrupting their antics before they really lay into each other.

"I suppose. I wish I didn't have to," he says, looking at his painting of the mountain range with something like longing.

"I understand that," I say, taking a sip of tea.

"Someday, I hope to have a vivacious heir to pawn my responsibilities on like my grams did."

I laugh despite myself. "I'm sure you will."

Aidan wipes soup remnants from his face when Rian glances out the window and leaps to his feet. "We have to get going. The sun's almost up."

The Great Archives is unlike anything I've ever seen. The buildings are set behind the castle, which explains why I didn't notice them yesterday. The palace itself is so impressive, I was blinded to everything around it.

Seven towers reach into the sky, almost half as tall as the mountain itself. Much like the way the palace was built, it appears to have outgrown its original tower, and additional towers have been added through the centuries.

Unlike many of the other wood buildings in Numai, it's constructed of slabs of multi-colored stone. The rounded roofs appear to be ceramic.

"Admire the architecture later, Elana, we have to meet the Guardian," Rian says, practically pulling me along as I gawk.

Another set of massive doors swings open upon our approach. Aidan and I move inside, while Rian takes a half step back. "This is where I leave you for now. I've been forbidden from helping you complete the trial. Your friends also won't be able to help you, as they're in the middle of their own trials."

Aidan gives Rian a nod. "Thank you for getting us this far."

Rian nods back. "If I can offer one small bit of advice, go in with open minds."

I raise my eyebrows at him, but he only turns away and heads back to the palace. "I'll see you once you're done."

"Thank you, Rian," I wave at him as he departs.

Warm, reassuring fingers interlace with mine. "Are you ready for this, Magpie?"

I give him my best convincing smile. "Ready as ever, degenerate."

We were not ready. Because sitting behind a desk in front of us, blocking a massive stone door, is a giant.

"Aidan, please tell me you're seeing this," I whisper, staring up at the creature. He wears a dark green robe tied over one shoulder, with a large metal belt, adorned with gems the size of shields. His white hair flows down past his shoulders, and a bushy beard grows almost to his stomach. He wears leather bracers on his forearms and shins. Most shocking of all, though, is the pair of spectacles perched on the bridge of his nose.

I suddenly realize the need for such daunting doors. The giant holds a piece of parchment as tall as Aidan, and a quill that appears to have been whittled from a tree trunk.

"I see him," Aidan says, eyeing the creature with wariness, one hand on his sword hilt.

"I haven't seen you before. Names," a booming voice echoes in the cavern around us. The sound is so deep I feel it reverberate in my chest.

I've only heard tales of giants, never seen one in the flesh. I'm not sure how to correctly address him. "Hello sir," I say, tentatively. "My name is Princess Elana Sable of Adrithia, and this is Prince Aidan Ashfall of Ocarin. We're here to seek the knowledge of the Great Archives."

The giant sets his parchment and quill on his proportionally sized desk and stands. My neck cracks as I tilt my head back to meet his eyes. "Welcome, honored guests, to the Great Archives. I am Gilbrand, a scholar from the Vangu clan of the eastern Kangkaram mountains."

Gilbrand's voice echoes off the walls as he bows low, and Aidan and I follow suit, not wishing to offend.

The giant rights himself, sitting back on his stone chair that's the size of a small home. "Two things seekers of knowledge must have are intelligence and integrity. I cannot allow you to enter here until you complete our test, proving you possess both. Do you willingly submit yourself to this trial?"

I exchange a glance with Aidan. "It's your choice, Magpie. I'll follow your lead."

My anger with him seems to dwindle by the day. His unwavering confidence gives me the strength to face Gilbrand and say, "yes, we willingly submit to the trial."

"Very well," Gilbrand says, and claps his hands together, causing a barrage of echoes on the walls around us. The noise is deafening, louder than any thunderclap, and I'm too slow to cover my ears. Pain pierces my skull, and I drop to my knees with my hands to my head. Aidan groans and collapses next to me. I squeeze my eyes closed and lean into his warmth until the echoing gradually dies out.

I'm not sure what I expect when I finally peel my eyes open, but it's certainly not being alone in an empty room. Gilbrand is nowhere to be seen, and the stone desk and chair have vanished. Actually, it seems like we're in a completely new room. It's smaller than the one we were in moments ago, with barely enough space for Aidan and I to stand side-by-side and stretch our arms out. How are we in a new room when neither of us moved?

"What the Hells is going on?" Aidan growls, clearly as confused and agitated as I feel. His hand is on his sword again. Several fires pop up across the stone room, illuminating every corner.

"Do you see a door?" I ask, moving to one corner of the room while he takes the other.

It's a big square, but there's no door on any of the walls. I scan every surface and the solid floor, but it's completely bare. There's a metal plate on the ceiling, but a few bursts of Aidan's fire later we determine it's not helpful.

Aidan runs his hands along the far wall. "Feel for any warm or cold spots."

I mimic his movements, trailing my fingers along the cracks and crevices of the natural stone blocks. I'm halfway around the room when Aidan calls out, "there might be something here."

I meet him on his side, where there's a single stone slightly askew. He taps it with the hilt of his dagger and the stone moves slightly.

"Okay, maybe try pushing it in?" I say quietly, unsure why I'm speaking in hushed tones.

Aidan gently pushes the stone forward until it stops. The room rumbles, and I half expect a door to magically appear. Instead, the trap door springs open in the ceiling and water comes rushing out.

"Fuck," Aidan says, as the icy cold water splashes at our feet, immediately pooling on the floor.

"Quick, pull it out, pull it out," I say, gesturing to the stone.

"You know, I don't think a woman has ever said that to me before," Aidan laughs as he jams his dagger into the narrow crack to pry it forward.

I smack the back of his head. "This is no time to joke around."

While he works on the stone, I splash around in the frigid water, now ankle-deep, and try to find another loose stone. The spray of the water dampens my clothes and I shiver.

I unsheathe my own dagger and start tapping stones, trying to hear a different tone, but there are so many and I'm making little headway.

There's the telltale sound of metal snapping, and then Aidan loudly curses again. I look over in time to catch him glaring at his now much shorter dagger. "I think that block is officially stuck."

The water is now well up to my thighs, and I wrap my arms around myself to try and conserve my warmth. "W-what do we do?"

Aidan slides the broken dagger back into its sheathe and crosses the distance between us. "Come here, you need to stay warm."

I want to argue, to tell him I'm fine, but my chattering teeth won't let me. He wraps his arms around me, pulling me to his warm chest. The relief on my upper body is instant, even if the water is already pooling around my waist. Near our feet, there's a faint glimmering blue light.

"Stay right there and don't move," he instructs, holding onto me as he stares up at the ceiling where the water pours out. "Do you think your shadows could close the door?"

I look up at the thick slab of metal, blinking through the splashes of water that pelt my face. Shadows explode upwards around us, turning solid and slamming into the door, swinging it up. The flow of water is strong, and I throw my hands up to reinforce the shadows. My arms shake as I feel the weight of the water bearing down on the metal as the darkness pushes back.

I gain inch by precious inch, until the door finally closes. The tide of water is cut off for as long as I can maintain my shadows.

"Hold it right there, Magpie. I want to try something," he says, taking one of his hands from my waist and holding it up.

"Hurry," I grit out through chattering teeth.

A concentrated burst of fire hits the cracks between the door and the metal frame. Steam flies and I duck under Aidan's outstretched arm, keeping my hands raised, concentrating the shadows on the center of the door, and leaving the edges exposed.

It takes an eternity, but the metal eventually starts to melt, sealing the crack. Drops of molten metal splash into the water around us. I flinch, pressing closer to Aidan. He keeps the stream of fire up, moving slowly along the trapdoor frame. My arms quiver with the energy it takes to hold the water back.

"Almost there," Aidan says, grunting with effort. Heat pours around us in waves, and I'm suddenly grateful for the cold water nearly up to my chest.

I lose track of the moments, focusing solely on keeping my arms up, and my power steady. The pool of darkness within me steadily depletes. I haven't used this much energy at once since Aidan took me into the woods in the Gods' Territory and made me expel my power.

"Done," Aidan growls, letting his arm fall. "Okay, Elana. Rein in your shadows slowly."

I give him a weak nod, focusing on drawing back the darkness piece by piece, until one thin tendril remains. I let it fall. The metal door lets out a groaning noise and bows slightly in the middle. Miraculously, though, it stays in place.

My arms drop to my sides, feeling boneless, and I slump into Aidan's chest out of exhaustion. I catch my breath for a few moments, feeling his burning arms around me. "I can't believe that worked."

Aidan inspects the door. "I can't believe it did, either. But it won't hold for long. We need to find a way out of here, fast."

My teeth chatter together as I try to bury myself into his heat more. "Can't you warm up the water?"

"Believe me, I've been trying," he responds, running his callused hands up and down my arms.A metallic whine sounds above us, and the door shifts, allowing a trickle of water to pour out.

"I feel like we've been in this situation before," I say, thinking back to the second trial, when we all went for a swim in the underground pool.

A rumbling laugh bubbles from him. "You mean when you nearly drowned, and instead of saving yourself you pushed Rian to safety? Or earlier, when you ogled me from under the waterfall?"

A flush of heat floods me, warming my core in the frigid water. I tell myself staying warm is the only reason for this dangerous line I'm dancing on. I lift my head from his chest and stare into his shining gold eyes. "That's the first time I wanted to kiss you."

Aidan's eyebrow quirks up as he stares down. "Oh really? And how would you have kissed me?"

With a confidence I didn't know I possessed, my arms clasp behind his neck and I tug his head down to meet mine. Our lips crash together, and Aidan responds with fervor, his arms moving from my back to my ass, lifting me up. I wrap my legs around his waist and tilt my head, deepening the kiss. My tongue explores the inside of his mouth, and he lets out a groan that I eagerly swallow down. Gods, I missed this. His hands squeeze my ass, and I feel his hardness against me. A thrill runs through me as I fist one of my hands in his silky black hair.

There's a loud creaking above us, and another stream of water pours out, hitting Aidan's head. I gasp at the sensation of the cold water. It shocks me enough that I pull back from the kiss to see steam rising from his hair.

"Elana," Aidan whispers my name through heavy breaths, and the sound of it on his lips makes me want to ride him right here.

I still have my legs wrapped around his waist, and I don't want to let him go.

It's Aidan who pulls back. "Magpie, as much as I'd love to do this right here, right now, and you know I would," he pauses to catch his breath, "we should probably figure a way out of here."

"Right," I pant, "that's probably for the best."

Warm lips kiss the top of my forehead before he gently guides me away from him. I disentangle my legs, hating the cold that envelopes me in his absence.

I stare down at my boots, avoiding his gaze, when I spot the strange glimmer again. Near my feet, the shimmering blue light glows bright. "Aidan, look at our feet."

He bends over, shuffling his feet until he spots the blue glow. "What is it?"

"It almost looks like...like the Water God's symbol," I say, squinting down at it.

The surface of the water churns with our movements and the water splashing from above us, so Aidan sinks down and sticks his face under the surface. He comes up a moment later, wiping water from his eyes. "It's definitely Kai's mark."

I furrow my brow. "Okay, so what do we do?"

Aidan gives a shrug. "Try pressing it, I guess? That turned the water on. Maybe this is the switch to turn it off?"

That would make sense. I give him a nod and he sinks back below the surface, his hand covers the stone, then suddenly there's a noise like metal grinding together, and the water cuts off.

Aidan emerges from the water. "Did it work?"

We both look to the ceiling, where, sure enough, only a few droplets of water leak out.

"Looks like it," I say, then scan around the room, waiting for another door to reveal itself. When it doesn't, I let out a noise of frustration. "Please tell me we don't have to go through that door."

I point at the opening in the ceiling and Aidan follows my gaze. "Well, if it'll make you feel better, I won't tell you. I'll just toss you up there."

I level a glare in his direction. "No, you won't."

An expression of pure glee lightens his features. "Watch me."

# Chapter Twenty-Eight

## Elana

"**A**idan, put me down!" I shriek as he hoists me onto his shoulders, laughing. I have to hunch over so I don't hit the ceiling.

"Do you want to stay in this fucking freezing water until we both die?" He asks, spinning me around so I'm facing the trap door. I don't answer. "No, I didn't think so. So, Princess, if you would please grab onto the frame so I can toss you up there."

I want to argue, to pull his hair until he drops me, but I can't disagree that this seems to be the only way out. Letting out a huff of air, I stick my arms through the door, feeling stone on the other side.

"Can you light the space up? I can't see anything."

A fireball flickers to life in the room above my head and illuminates...an exact copy of the room with the water. Spectacular.

I put my arms through and push against the door frame, struggling to pull myself up. With shaking arms I manage to lift myself off Aidan's shoulders and wedge my elbows fully onto the other side.

I kick my legs out, feeling only air, as I dangle in the trapdoor. Through gritted teeth I ask, "can you help me out here?"

There's more laughter. "Hold on, I'm not done admiring the view."

My face burns with embarrassment and anger. My arms shake with the strain of holding myself in this position. "Hey, degenerate, either help me up or go drown yourself. Either would be helpful right now."

He chuckles again, but his hands cup my ass, and he's pushing me up through the hole. Once my butt is through, I sit on the floor and pull my legs through.

It takes me a moment to catch my breath. When I can breathe somewhat normally, I peer back down through the trapdoor in time to watch Aidan grip the edge and pull himself straight up and through. I raise an eyebrow at him when he crouches next to me on the stone floor.

"What?" He asks, peering down, then around, as if he missed something.

"You could have pretended to struggle a little bit, you know," I say, crossing my arms over my chest.

Mischief dances in his eyes as he gives me a wink. "Not possible."

I roll my eyes as we stand, taking in the identical room. With a sharp clanging sound that makes me jump, the trapdoor swings shut and then...vanishes.

"Okay...I guess we're going the right way," I murmur, rubbing my legs to bring some warmth back into them and staring at the spot the door used to be.

"Are you all right?" Aidan grabs my hand between his and blows warm air on it. "Fuck, you're freezing."

"I'll be fine." My legs and toes are slowly regaining feeling, and it's causing a sensation of stabbed by thousands of needles. I shift my feet, then stumble when I step on a rock that shifts under my weight.

A burst of fire surrounds us, and the heat is instantly welcome for my limbs. Aidan draws me to his chest, putting out his hand to the flames. "Thanks for the fire."

"Actually, this fire's not mine," he responds in a low tone.

I glance around the room, then down at my boots, at the stone that I stepped on. "Another test."

"I guess so," he responds in his serious tone that makes my heart beat quicker. "Stay close. I can block the fire, but I can't control it."

Not sure what he means by wrong, I store the information for later. "I think I stepped on the activation switch. Somewhere in the room must be Enya's mark. We just have to find it."

We both start searching the floor and ceiling. Feeling the effects of the heat, I stick to the center of the room. The inferno rages, blocking our view of the walls. After coming up empty on the search above and below, we stare at the fire.

"Can your fire, I don't know, cancel this one out?" I gesture to the flames licking up the walls.

Aidan cocks an eyebrow at me. "I don't think throwing more fire around is going to help this situation. Especially when only one of us is fireproof."

"Then what do you suggest we do?" I put my hands on my hips.

He heaves out a heavy sigh. "I guess I'll start touching rocks."

I watch as he moves into the flames, a shield of his own fire cloaking him from the blaze. He moves his hands over the wall, searching. Seeing his use of fire to form a shield gives me an idea. I pull darkness to me, silently commanding it to cover my arm. Once the shadows wrap themselves from my hand to my shoulder I solidify them. I approach the opposite wall from Aidan and stick that arm out, turning my face away from the heat. To my surprise, my hand feels cool. I take a step closer, until my shadow-wrapped fingers barely graze the flames, but still I feel nothing.

A wide smile stretches across my face as I turn to show Aidan, only to find him already staring back with a grin of his own, dimple on display. "You never cease to amaze me, Magpie."

I blush and turn back to the wall, cloaking the rest of my body in shadow. My vision darkens, but I lighten that portion of my shield enough to see basic shapes and muted colors. Slowly, I walk into the fire. The flames dance around me, flickering against my shield harmlessly. I start inspecting and pressing rock after rock, working in an up, down, over pattern moving away from Aidan. What started as a good idea quickly wears on me, my dwindling energy being sapped by the control it takes to keep up the shield.

When I'm nearly to the corner of my first wall I hear a muffled voice, and then the fire instantly cuts off. I shed my cloak of darkness, breathing hard, and see Aidan standing almost opposite from me, his hand on a glowing flame symbol. "Found it."

A simple wood door appears between us. It unlatches from the inside and swings open. Inside is a long, pitch-black corridor. A line of flame shoots out above us and illuminates the path.

It's not quite wide enough for both of us, so Aidan steps inside first, assessing the walls and floor as we go.

"That was an impressive display of control over your power. Not many Gods-blessed can create shields," Aidan says as we walk down the dank-smelling walkway.

"You gave me the idea," I say, shrugging. "It used up a lot of energy, though."

He flashes me a smirk over his shoulder. "We'll have to work on your stamina." I smile despite my annoyance and smack his arm. He chuckles and faces forward.

This corridor reminds me of the servant passages in our castle, and how Aislinn and I used the tunnels to sneak outside to explore the city, often leading to her getting into fist fights with drunk men while I tried to play mediator. It never worked. Aislinn's mouth got her into trouble more than a few times, and some burly man would always take offense.

"I hope wherever Aislinn is, she's all right," I say, breaking our comfortable silence.

Aidan reaches back and takes my hand, squeezing it reassuringly. "If Hotharia has her, I can't imagine them hurting her. She's a princess. She's too valuable for that. Plus, they would make enemies on all sides if they did. All of Adrithia would be up in arms. My kingdom will always support yours, and I'm sure Rayna would convince her parents to join us."

"I'm sure you're right. But I can't help but think I won't see her again. That she'll just be gone like my father, and I'll never get to say goodbye, or apologize for the horrible things I said to her before she left." Tears well up unbidden in my eyes. Besides my worry, there's a gnawing sensation that I'm not whole without her around. I've never been away from her this long. It feels like part of me is missing.

"The first chance we get, as soon as we find out where she's being held, I promise I'll help you get her back. Even if we have to decimate an army to get to her, I'll be right by your side, Elana, I promise. You're not alone."

I give his hand a squeeze, his words warming me through my still-damp clothes. Sadness hits me, though, as I remember his own kingdom. And mine. "You have obligations in Ocarin, Aidan. You can't stay by my side forever."

He tugs me to a stop, expression burning with intensity as he faces me. "I will turn to ash anyone who tries to keep me from you. I promise that. If we want to make this work, we will. No one will argue with two monarchs."

I stare at him, mouth open slightly. He gives me a gentle smile, using his free hand to tuck a stray hair behind my ear.

Without saying another word, he turns back around and keeps moving, our hands still clasped. We walk in a comfortable silence. My head spins. I never thought it would work between us because we're both destined to be rulers of separate kingdoms. But, what if we could make it work? How would it work? We could split our time between our castles, maybe even build a small home on the border to cut down on travel time. It could work. Relations would never be better between Adrithia and Ocarin.

Aidan curses, dropping my hand, and pulling me out of my reverie.

"What is it?" I ask, trying to push past him to see what's ahead.

He stops and angles his body so I can get a good look at the dead end about ten paces in front of us. "This doesn't make any sense."

I turn around, staring back the way we came. "Did we miss another tunnel, perhaps?"

"Not unless it was through another invisible door," he grunts, inspecting the stone in our way. "I can't see if there's anything on the other side."

He exhales in frustration, then pushes his weight into the boulder. The whole thing slides back, too easily, then stops harshly. Like a lever has been pulled, the stone lurches into movement, towards us.

"Oh fuck," Aidan says, pushing against it again, trying to stop it. It glides forward, completely undeterred by him. He grits his teeth, muscles straining, as he shoves his weight into the rock.

As expected, his efforts amount to nothing and the stone keeps moving.

"I'm getting real sick of these tests," I groan. "I'll run back and see if we missed any hidden passageways. Follow the boulder and see if you can find Avani's mark."

Aidan gives a nod and starts inspecting the walls and ceiling.

I rush down the hallway, my eye catching on every inconsistency in the walls, every slightly darker or lighter rock I see, but there's no other pathway. Aidan's fire guides me, until I nearly skid to a stop. Because sliding towards me is a spiked boulder.

"Oh what the Hells," I swear, trying to look past it, but seeing nothing. The rock merely grinds along, the threatening stone spikes aimed at my body. They're longer than my arm, and they're spaced three or four hands-lengths apart.

I spin on my heels and run back to Aidan. I'm breathing hard by the time I get back to him, both from the sprint and the anxiety coursing through my veins.

"What is it?" He asks, brows furrowing at the sight of me panicking.

"The exit is blocked off by another boulder moving this way, and it's full of spikes," I explain as I catch my breath.

"Fucking wonderful," he grumbles. "These books better be worth it."

I pin him with a sharp glare. "Knowledge is worth everything."

He waves me off, and together we check every brick, every stone, for Avani's symbol. The boulder scrapes forward, never ceasing.

"Should we try to stop it somehow?" I ask, seeing the other one come into view at the other end of the corridor.

"If I try to melt the boulder, it'll get too hot in this passage for us to survive. Not even your shield could hold out over the length of time it would take me to destroy it. I'm open to other suggestions."

I take a few moments to think while scanning the stones. Aislinn once told me that these powers are essentially limitless in what they can do. They're limited only by the creativity of the one who wields them.

An idea forms in my mind, and with half a thought, several dark shapes come to life in front of me. Triangles made entirely of shadow, but as solid as my shield was earlier. With a wave of my hand, I send one to each side of the boulder. The inky black shapes wedge themselves into the cracks between the boulder and the corridor, narrow side first. It takes a moment for the wedges to stick, but once they do, the boulder shudders to crawl, then it jerks to a stop.

"Nice thinking," Aidan says, turning the other direction. "Can you do it again?"

I follow him to the spiked boulder, but when we're halfway there a noise like shattering glass sounds, and the flat stone starts pushing forward again.

"Before you ask, no, that was my only idea."

Aidan shrugs. "I guess we'd better find that mark, then."

We search, slightly more frantically than before, listening to the stones as they push closer together.

"It's not here!" I complain, throwing up my hands. "We've searched every surface of this corridor."

Aidan runs his hand through his hair. The boulders are only about ten arms lengths apart now.

Feeling panic start to creep in, I summon darkness to me once again. It uses a tremendous amount of my remaining energy, but I solidify the shadows, fortifying them until they're as hard as steel, then push them out. The dark pillars slam into the boulders. I feel the rock pushing back, rebelling against my power. I hold them steady with all my concentration and dwindling energy.

"Keep looking," I tell Aidan, while I focus on keeping the boulders from crushing us.

Aidan lurches into motion, touching every stone once again. My forehead breaks out into a sweat and my arms once again shake. Damn, Aidan's right, I really do need to work on my stamina.

"I've checked every damn brick in this corridor," Aidan growls, then abruptly pauses. "Wait, Elana, drop your shadows on the spiked boulder for a moment."

"Are you crazy?" I shout back, panting. "That's the only thing keeping us from being impaled right now."

He's standing in front of it, inspecting the areas not covered by shadow. "It's the only place we haven't searched. Trust me, and release this one."

I allow that shaking arm to drop, doubling my efforts on keeping the first one in place. A fraction of a moment later, the pressure against the darkness ceases.

"I guess you found the-," I don't get a chance to finish my sentence, because suddenly the hard ground beneath me gives way, and I fall.

A scream rips from my throat and is lost in the wind as I tumble through nothing but air, flipping end over end. My hair tears free of its braid and whips me in the face ferociously.

"Aidan!" I shriek, reaching for anything I can grab onto in this freefall.

There's a brilliant explosion of orange light, and a creature bursts to life in the sky. It resembles a horse with massive feathery wings. Aidan rides on its back. As soon as he spots me the horse swoops in my direction, catching me between its wings. I flinch as I expect the horse's bright body to burn me, but the flames are cool to the touch.

"How is this possible?" I ask, staring at the wings that leave trails of fire in its wake.

"It's similar to the wyvern my mother uses to send messages across great distances. I've been practicing, but haven't mastered an apparition this size until now," Aidan says. I'm stunned into silence as I stare at the details of the horse. Hooves like embers, a mane and tail like a wildfire, but the body and head is smooth and solid. This is a feat unlike any I've known to be possible. "We need to find Sepher's mark, and fast. I'm not sure how long I can keep this up."

I give him a nod and take in our surroundings. We seem to be in a completely open area. There's nothing but empty sky in every direction, and the wind whips at us viciously. The horse flaps its wings and we soar faster, only to be buffeted by winds so harsh they nearly blow me backwards off the creature. I clutch onto Aidan's hard abdomen to steady myself.

"Hang on, I'm going to take us lower," Aidan shouts to me. I cling to him even harder as the horse brings its wings in and angles down. Wind buffets us and we sail through fluffy clouds.

There's a screeching noise behind us, then a pair of razor sharp talons grab the space above my head, catching a few strands of my hair and yanking them out. I duck down, and catch a glimmer of a shining white symbol on the underside of the beast's nearly iridescent wing.

I narrow my eyes at the creature, but it blends in so well with the gray clouds, appearing nearly invisible, and I immediately lose track of it.

"What the Hells was that?" Aidan yells.

"Some kind of bird, I think. It's difficult to see it, but I think it's got Sepher's symbol on its wing."

Before Aidan has a chance to respond, the bird appears in front of us, hovering like a target. Long feathers trail behind it, not unlike those I've seen on the phoenix, but instead of standing out among the clouds, this bird blends in. Soft white and pale blue feathers shimmer, but the whole bird appears to vanish and reappear among the clouds. From the angle we're hovering, it's easy to see a glowing mark resembling a cyclone on the underside of its wing.

I point it out to Aidan. "If I can get us close enough, can you grab it with your shadows?"

My exhaustion is evident in my shaking limbs and light-headedness. I feel inwards at the nearly empty well and hesitate telling him, but lying in a time like this isn't going to help us. "I'm pretty drained, but I can try."

Aidan gives me a serious look over his shoulder. "Okay, but be careful not to deplete your energy. If you think it's going to be too much, pull back."

"I will," I respond, and then fist my hands in his tunic tighter, allowing myself a brief moment to appreciate his hard muscles.

The horse shoots forward, and the creature made of wind lets out a shrill cry and flaps its wings at us. We're hit with gale-force winds, sending our horse tumbling back, the flames flickering. My stomach does flips as I scream, clenching my thighs and gripping tighter so I don't fall.

Aidan lets out a frustrated shout and the horse glows beneath us, its fire rejuvenated. We level out, and my stomach settles with the smooth movement.

A light breeze and a feather-light brush of feathers is all the warning I have before talons dig into my shoulders, yanking me from the back of the horse.

"No!" Aidan yells, reaching for me, but his hand falls just short of my legs. His face is taut with horror as he shouts my name. I slam my fists into the bird's talons, but they hold fast. I'm dragged up into a dense layer of clouds and I lose sight of Aidan.

The bird holding me caws triumphantly while I dangle in the air like a fish on a hook. I could use my twin daggers to cut myself free, but I don't want to plummet to my death if Aidan can't see me.

Every moment we're in the sky is a moment we're using up our energy, and there's likely at least one more test. We still haven't encountered the test for the metal god, Tolliver. I need to end this now.

Shaking, I draw upon the last kernel of my power, pulling darkness around the bird. Bars of shadow interlock around the creature in a simple yet effective cage.

The bird lets out an angry screech, flapping its wings and pecking at the darkness to no avail. Winds batter around me, whipping my hair around my face. In its frustration, it releases its grip on me, and I drop until I catch myself on one of the bars.

I pull the rest of my darkness to me, binding the bird's wings together momentarily. I stretch out, brushing soft feathers, but realizing with a sinking in my gut that I can't quite reach the bird's wing. I don't give myself time to think, relying on a burst of courage as I launch myself off the bars, grabbing hold of the feathers surrounding Sepher's glowing symbol.

The bird lets out a horrible cry and vanishes, as does the last of my power, and once I again plummet to the ground.

"Elana!" Aidan's frantic voice shouts, then the fiery winged horse is beneath me, and his warm arms wrap around my waist. I grip his shoulders tightly as I breathe in the cedar scent.

"I got you," he says, brushing my wild mane of hair away from my face. "Nice job with the cage."

"Nice job with the fire horse," I laugh, patting the flames beneath me.

The clouds clear, and the scene around us changes. We're no longer in the air outside, but in a massive chamber with metallic walls. The horse lands, fiery hooves creating sparks moments before it flickers and extinguishes, causing Aidan and I to tumble to the metal floor.

We're both breathing hard. I don't think I recall seeing Aidan this exhausted, not even on the shores of Adrithia when he battled the cursed army.

We pick ourselves off the ground, staring at the odd room. Each of the four walls, the ceiling, and the floor, are made of the same shiny metal. A round metal column stands in the center.

"Do we think this test will activate on its own?" I ask as I walk to the column, running my hand across it.

The daggers at my hips start vibrating when I find a crack in the metal. When I push it, a hand-sized portion of the pillar recedes.

"Never mind, I found the switch," I call to Aidan, "be ready for anything."

My hips practically pulsate, and I remove my daggers from their sheaths and glare at them, as if the metal will grow lips and tell me why it's reacting. In the black reflection of the blade, I see a silvery flash on the wall, but before I get the chance to scream, my blades rip my arms to the side, and there's the grating sound of metal against metal. Then, the resistance breaks, and my dagger slides through a sword like butter.

A metal figure looms over me, pulling back his broken blade. It has the shape of a man, but silver armor covers nearly its entire being. It wears a spiked helm, but either has no face, or it's so shrouded in darkness that it can't be seen. In its gloved hands, a broken longsword shimmers and regrows from the hilt.

"What the Hells?" I ask, taking a few steps back.

Aidan's sword flashes from behind the metal guard, and there's a sharp noise of contact, but it doesn't flinch. It spins around, swinging its sword wide, and Aidan deflects the strike. He swings again for the guard's body, but again his blade practically bounces off.

"Elana, find Tolliver's symbol! I'll keep this monstrosity busy," he says as he dodges another attack.

I rush around the room, searching for what I assume will be a glowing silver mark. The room itself is so damn shiny, it's hard to tell if there's anything glowing or not. I make a lap around the room to inspect the walls, then move onto the floor, then the ceiling. The entire time, Aidan's sword clashes with the metal guard. The last place I check for the mark is the column. But there's not a single blemish to be found.

I turn to where Aidan fends off the assault of the guard. It moves slow, but its blows are powerful. There's not a scratch on its armor. Aidan's attacks appear to be useless. My daggers buzz, then yank my hand up, as if pointing at the guard. As Aidan ducks out of the way of a wide swing, the metal torso follows his movements, giving me the chance to see its back, where a small mark that resembles a shield shimmers.

"Aidan, the mark is on its back!" I shout. "Keep distracting it."

He gives no reply as I rush forward, set on ending this while its back is to me. I reach out my fingers, but when I'm a few paces away, my blades move of their own accord, slicing to the side.

The guard's longsword twists at my neck. My daggers deflect its path, then my fingers twirl, spinning the blade around and opening up a slice through the guard's wrist.

From behind it, I see Aidan rush forward, but when he's a mere breadth away from brushing it, the guard's torso twists, and Aidan barely has enough time to raise his sword to deflect an attack.

But the action puts the mark right in front of me. I lunge for it, only to receive a vicious kick to my chest, which sends my flying backwards. My shoulder hits something solid, maybe the pillar, and I lose my grip on one of my daggers as I hit the unyielding ground, smacking my head and knocking the air from my lungs.

I blink, seeing nothing but darkness for a moment. Then blurry shapes come into focus. Aidan runs towards me, the guard is a half-step closer. Aidan shouts my name, then a wall of flame erupts before me, pushing the metal figure back. Aidan slides through the fire, kneeling next to me, pulling me into his lap as I try to breathe through the pain radiating throughout my body.

"Elana, are you all right?"

I can't respond. I can hardly draw in a full breath. Aidan's own breathing is labored, and I see the fire shrink, despite him using his hand to feed more of it.

"Fuck. Hang on, Magpie. I'll get the creature's attention back on me. I'll figure something out. Just keep breathing," he presses a quick kiss to my hair before standing, swinging his sword as the fire dies out completely. He charges at the guard.

I suck in a few ragged breaths and the pain starts to subside as I run through my injuries. Dislocated shoulder, concussion based on how much my head is swimming and the blood that's dripping past my ear, and probably some bruised ribs. Painful, but nothing life-threatening.

Slowly, I sit up, supporting my arm so as to not cause more pain in my shoulder. There's a shout from the other side of the room, and Aidan puts a hand to a cut along his bicep. He bares his teeth at the guard and charges again. He's going to get himself killed attacking like that.

I shakily rise to my feet. My vision swims, but my grip tightens on my dagger. It pulsates in my hand, gently tugging me to where Aidan and the guard fight. As if it, too, senses the need for us to end this as fast as possible.

As we get close, the guard spins, and my hand jerks out, lighting quick, slicing clean through the bracer and the guard's wrist of its main sword hand. The blade and the gloved hand tumble to the ground. The guard's remaining hand reaches for my throat, but Aidan is already placing his hand on its back.

The guard halts, then like a warming block of ice, sinks to its knees. I watch in equal parts horror and fascination as it starts to melt into the floor, dripping into a growing puddle that starts to drain through the floor.

My vision doubles, and I drop my dagger. It clatters to the floor as I, too, start to fall, my vision darkening.

Warm hands catch me, but whatever happens next is lost as unconsciousness overwhelms me.

# CHAPTER TWENTY-NINE

## AISLINN

We've been on the move for several days now, and my thoughts are a constant tempest of turmoil. I haven't seen my father again. I'm starting to think I hallucinated him. But no matter how much I try to convince myself it wasn't him, a sinking pit in my gut tells me it is. The way Aric reacted proves it as much as Calder's gloating.

The prison cart is just as much a thorn in my side now as it was during my first journey. I sit in my usual spot, along the side, as it gives me access to watch the landscape. By my best estimations, we've been heading straight west. If I'm correct, it would mean we're heading into the Gods' Territory, which is certainly a death sentence.

The Gods don't take trespassers into their land lightly, especially not entire armies. If they don't kill us, the countless dangerous creatures there will. Giant scorpions are one thing, but there are monsters far worse lurking in the forbidden forests of the territory. I think back to the giant felines, the goddesses in animal form, I encountered the last time I traveled through with Elana. If Calder thinks his troops will pass through unscathed, he's in for a rude awakening.

I bump along inside the metal box, draining the waterskin I was given yesterday. The sun is starting to make its descent to the horizon, so the barren rocky fields are awash in a golden glow. It would be beautiful, if I had the capacity to appreciate beauty right now.

It's not much later when the cart slows to a stop. I sit up on my knees and press my face to the bars, trying to catch any glimpse of my father. There's a flurry of movement as soldiers set up their sleeping rolls, tents, and cooking fires, but I can't make out familiar chestnut hair anywhere.

I watch the camp until the torrent of movement becomes a trickle, and people settle into their spots for the evening. My knees ache on the cold metal when I finally sit back against the wall, wrapping my hands in my armpits to keep my fingers from freezing.

"I'll take over the first watch. Go get some sleep," Aric's familiar voice comes from behind me. Then there's the sound of shuffling feet as the relieved guard walks away.

"Calder left camp tonight to meet up with one of his father's messengers, so I was able to sneak back here," he whispers to me.

He shoves a wool blanket through the bars, little by little. I accept it greedily, not above taking provisions from my enemy to stay alive, if I can even consider Aric an enemy anymore. After I wrap myself in the warm material, he hands me a plate with some kind of grilled meat and dry potatoes.

"Do you have any water?" I ask, shaking my empty canteen. He trades me for his full one, and I take a few long pulls from it. I scarf down a few bites of the warm food, not wanting it to get cold, since I have a feeling this conversation will sour my stomach.

Finally, I work up the nerve to ask, "was that really my father?"

Aric grips the bars, staring in. "Yes, at least, I think so."

"How?" I grit out, swallowing back the bile that forces its way up my throat.

"I don't know, and Aislinn, I swear I didn't know any of this when I passed information to Hotharia. I hadn't actually heard from or spoken to anyone for years...until several months ago, when my uncle became obsessed with Adrithia's military movements."

"Get to the point, traitor. I already know what you've done," I snarl, not wanting to rehash the past while I'm trying to make sense of what Father is doing here.

Aric sighs. "I don't know much, but what I do know is that he showed up with the Tyne soldiers, as their commander. Scared the Hells out of all of us, but it quickly became apparent that he's...not the same King Devon we knew."

"What does that mean?"

"He's different. I'm not sure he remembers who he is or how he came to be the commander of the Empress' regiment. His eyes are as black as the rest of them, and he hardly ever speaks or expresses any kind of emotion. But it's his voice, Ash. His face, his hands, his fighting style. It's without a doubt him. Even though his memories, his personality, everything that makes him who he is seems to be wiped away."

"Who is the Empress and what does she want?" I ask, on the verge of breaking down into sobs and trying to contain myself.

"I wish I knew. I've never met her. No one here has, except for Calder. And my uncle, of course. All I know is that she conquered the land of Tyne, and now she's trying to do the same here. But I can't tell what her motive is. Whenever I ask Calder about the Empress, he gets evasive and tells me I'll know when I need to. I don't even know her name."

Tears prick my eyes, but I hold them back. Crying will serve me no purpose at this moment. "I need to speak with him."

Aric shakes his head. "No, Aislinn. I don't think that's a good idea. Didn't you see him before? He didn't recognize you. Whatever happened to him after he fell changed him. If he realizes I'm helping you, he'll tell Calder, and I'll be killed before I can help you escape."

"Aric," I say, sharply. It's the first time I've said his name out loud since I discovered his deception. It gets his attention, he stiffens as he stares intently at me, deep ocean blue eyes reflecting the moonlight that streams in through the bars. "He's my father. I last saw him falling from a cliff, and I just found out he's alive. Please, I need to speak with him."

"Princess, I don't-,"

"Pretend you need his help with something. Lie to him, anything. Please, I need to see him."

Aric stares at me for a few long moments. I return his hard look, silently pleading for him to agree. It's the same expression I used to give him when we were younger, and El and I would hatch some diabolical plan to steal desserts or sneak out and visit Sandral's taverns. When he averts his eyes, I know I've won. His shoulders sag and he heaves a heavy breath. "Fine, I'll get him over here, but I can't guarantee you have long, so you better figure out what you're going to say."

Shaking his head, he stalks off, defeat heavy in his gait. My leg bounces as I wait. I pick the dirt out from under my fingernails absentmindedly as I think of what to say.

"The prison cart is this way, Commander," I hear Aric's formal tone. It's one he uses when addressing royalty.

I sit up, staring out the window until the familiar frame of my father appears out of the shadows. He walks next to Aric with a blank expression. His midnight eyes blend in with the nighttime landscape.

As they approach the cart, Aric waves his hand in my direction. "As the Empress' ambassador here, you can see with your own eyes that the prisoner is well confined. She speaks, too, if you wish to question her about her confinement conditions."

Oh Gods, that has to be the worst excuse for getting Father over here, but it works, and he steps closer.

As he gets nearer, I'm struck with a sense of unease. His cold, blank expression holds no warmth. The laugh lines that used to rim his eyes sag, and that damn scar practically glows against his pallor.

"Do you know who I am?" I ask, silently cursing myself when it comes out shaky.

"You are a prisoner of Hotharia's," Father responds in a toneless voice. Hearing it is worse than the fever, worse than the unbearable pain in my wrists from the infection.

I clench my fists, digging my nails into the skin of my palm. "What's my name?"

He stares into the prison carriage, showing no emotion, but stepping closer. Close enough. "You are a prisoner of Hotharia."

The knife twists deeper into my gut. I steel myself and lunge forward, grabbing hold of his shirt collar as I stare into his black eyes and whisper viciously, "it's me, Father, Aislinn. Your daughter. You are King Devon Sable, ruler of Adrithia. Remember me. Remember our home!"

He does nothing, he doesn't even defend himself or try to release my hand. He stands there, unfocused, uncaring. There's zero recognition in his eyes. My heart plummets.

"What the Hells is going on?" Calder's harsh voice calls. "You, bastard she-demon, release the commander!"

Ice grows between my fingers and the fabric of Father's shirt. I let go with a gasp, pulling my hand back to my chest and shaking off the cold crystals.

"Cousin! How could you have allowed this? Your king instructed you to keep him away from her," Calder rounds on Aric.

Aric bow, looking apologetic. "Apologies, Your Highness. I thought it would torture her to see him...like this."

Calder stares at his cousin for several long moments, then barks a bitter laugh. "Oh, that's diabolical. Did it work?"

He rounds on me, searching my face. I slouch and do my best to appear distraught. My performance must be adequate, because Calder laughs. "Well done, Aric. Come, let's go have a drink and enjoy the evening."

I watch as he and Aric turn and start to walk away. Calder calls over his shoulder. "Commander, come drink with us."

Father spins to join them, not sparing me another glance. I'm left staring at their backs. I keep waiting for the moment of recognition, a hand gesture, a nod, a backwards wink, anything to prove he remembers himself, remembers me. It never comes.

I sink down, my back sliding until I'm sitting on the cool metal floor. Using the wool blanket, I curl up as best as I can, trying to avoid laying on the chains.

My mind is in turmoil as I chase sleep. Thoughts of my father plague me. What happened to him after he fell? How did he end up aligned with the Empress' army?

There's one thing I know with certainty. That man, if I can even call him that, is not my father. The only thing left to do is figure out if he still exists somewhere. And if he doesn't, I need to dispose of the imposter before my sister or mother sees him. Because if they do, it may just kill them.

# CHAPTER THIRTY

## ELANA

I'm utterly at peace, wrapped in warmth and lying on a plush bed. I think I should stay here forever, where I'm cozy and -

Pain rips through my shoulder. I scream as I bolt upright, blinking my eyes furiously into focus. Aidan's concerned face hovers over me, his strong hands gently pushing me back to my sweat-drenched sheets.

"Magpie, please. The healers need to see to you," Aidan's voice is strained, as if he's been shouting for hours. "They set your shoulder back into its socket, but need to check your head."

The only sound I make is a whimper, before I collapse back onto the fluffy pillow as nausea and pain overwhelms me. Then, a damp cloth is pressed to the side of my head and a sharp throbbing sensation radiates from the spot. I grip Aidan's hand, breathing through the stars that burst behind my eyes. It doesn't work, and my vision swims as I'm pulled into darkness.

*A presence like the starry night sky surrounds me, but I am not afraid. There's tranquility in her shadows, so at odds with the fear and urgency in her tone as she speaks to me with a voice like velvet.*

*"Heir of Adrithia, you must prevail. We chose you for this task, and you alone can prevail. Evil is returning to our land. She once caused immeasurable suffering across Astrellia. You cannot allow her to do so again. Wake, Elana, wake."*

I force my eyes open to a candlelit room. No, not candles, but dozens of glowing flames flickering in the comfortable space around us. There's a weight on the side of my bed, and a curly mess of dark hair reflects orange in the light.

A sense of foreboding washes over me, like there's something important I need to remember, but whatever it is stays firmly out of my reach. My shoulder aches, but it's nothing like the pulsating pain in my skull. I put practiced fingers to the wound. There's a small cut and a fairly pronounced lump around it, but no stitches.

My movement startles Aidan awake, and he glances around the room, scanning for threats, before his eyes fall upon mine. The rest of the room falls away, and his pinched expression is all I see.

"Gods, Magpie, I was so worried," he says on a brief exhale.

I flash him a quick smile. "I'm fine."

"You weren't."

I shift uncomfortably on the bed under the weight of his scrutiny. I've always hated being coddled. When I was ten I broke my leg climbing a tree, trying to keep up with Aislinn. Clarisse set the bone, but I was confined to my bed for weeks. Everyone in the castle went out of their way to cater to me. They brought meals to me, cut up my food, and even let me have extra desserts, all while I was confined to my quarters. I hated every second of the extra attention, and as soon as I could stand without pain, I escaped my room and found my father in his study. I insisted that my lessons continue, and there would be no more special treatment. The only concession I argued to keep was our family dog, Rufus, sleeping in my bed.

The heaviness of Aidan's stare sends a pang through my chest. I've never seen him look so distraught. Dark bags sit under his eyes, and a purple bruise stands out on his cheek. I reach out and graze my fingers across it, eager to steer the topic of conversation away from me. "What happened to you?"

He takes my fingers in his and plants a gentle kiss on them. "I may have gotten into a fight with Rian about the competency of his healers."

I breathe in a gasp, and put as much scorn into my words as possible. "You did not."

"I did. Then, I may have threatened to burn down the Great Archives floor by floor until he found Clarisse."

I can't help the short laugh that escapes me, albeit painfully. "I don't blame Rian for socking you. In fact, I'm inclined to give your left cheek a matching mark. Threatening to burn centuries of knowledge is not acceptable behavior, you degenerate," I chastise, only slightly joking.

He chuckles. "Of course you defend Rian while I defend you."

"Well, who would I be if I made things easy for you?"

"You wouldn't be my Elana," he says, then kisses my hand again as he stands, filling a glass with a water pitcher on a nearby table and presenting it to me. I nearly melt back to the bed. He called me *his*. The word feels momentous. And, more importantly, it feels right.

I accept the glass from him and drink it down in one gulp, relishing the cool liquid on my tongue. I'm almost afraid to ask how the rest of the trial went. "Did we pass the test?"

Aidan gives me a smirk. "Of course. Once we completed the final trial against the metal soldier, the room changed, and I found myself back in the foyer of the library with the giant. We passed and are free to use the Great Archives whenever we wish."

I'm tempted to rub my temple, to relieve some of the achiness there, but I don't want to pull on the skin and cause my head wound to reopen. "So, where is Clarisse?"

"They're still in their trial," Aidan replies, crossing his arms over his chest.

"What?" I practically shout.

"Rian is outside the Archives waiting. As soon as they complete the tests, he'll bring them all here."

Shaking my head, I wonder aloud, "why did Rian not warn us about how involved the challenges would be?

Aidan shrugs. "You'll have to ask him. I wasn't really in a chatty mood when I brought you in here."

I nod, also wondering when I should confront Tessa about her omission of that bit of knowledge, too.

Looking around the room, I notice late afternoon sunlight streaming in. I furrow my brow. I didn't think I was asleep for more than a day. "How long was I unconscious?"

"Not long, a few hours," he says, sitting back down next to me. I scrunch my nose. Only a few hours? That doesn't seem right. My pain should be a constant, throbbing companion in that short amount of time. I don't recall taking anything to dull my senses, although I suppose they could have forced me to drink a tonic while I was unconscious.

Aidan opens his mouth to speak, but the door bursts open, and Clarisse rushes inside, dark green cloak billowing behind her like wings as she charges towards me. She's followed by a flustered-looking Rian, and the rest of our traveling party.

"Out of my way, Prince," Clarisse waves her arms dramatically at Aidan, who bristles, but surprisingly complies.

The healer's experienced hands go to my head first, gently moving my hair and peering at my scalp. She places several fingers under my chin and lifts it so I make eye contact with her.

"Close your eyes," she instructs and I comply. "Open them."

I open them, staring at her emotionless face. It's the same expression she taught me to adopt when assessing a patient. No matter how horrific the injury, you must present a calm, confident expression to reassure them.

Content with my head, she moves to my shoulder, grabbing my arm and moving it up and down slowly, then forward and backward. I wince at the motions, but no sharp pain brings bile to my mouth like it did earlier.

She tells me to lie back on the bed and when I do she continues her examination, lifting my shirt to stare at the angry bruises on my battered body.

Satisfied by her inspection, she delivers her prognosis. "You'll heal."

Coming from her, that's practically praise. "No head trauma?"

"No, I don't even think it'll leave a scar," she says loudly, then leans in and whispers to me, "you seem to be healing at an accelerated rate. Are you sure you don't have access to your light powers?"

I shake my head. "I haven't felt anything since the morning after the battle."

She nods, then takes a step back. "You need rest, and lots of it. Not only for your body to heal, but also for your energy to rejuvenate quicker."

"We both nearly exhausted our powers in there. The trials were nearly as dangerous as the ones we faced on the mountain," Aidan stands a few paces away, crossing his arms in front of his chest, keeping his eyes on me.

"What happened?" Parisa demands, pushing her way to the front of the group. "It was supposed to be a test of intelligence, not physical strength.

Our trials were a series of puzzles inside of a maze. It took forever, but our lives were never in danger."

"Was this your mother's doing, Rian?" Aidan asks through gritted teeth.

Rian's tan skin is noticeably pale, but he shakes his head adamantly. "No. She has no authority over what happens in the library. The test is different for everyone, tailored to each person or group entering. I gained access when I was five. I don't remember my trial, but it certainly didn't harm me."

"How?" I nearly whisper, but everyone turns to me as if I shouted. "The powers we fought against represented each of the main Gods. But beyond the Gods' Territory, that kind of power doesn't exist."

"It was the Gods," Rian says with a shrug.

"What's that supposed to mean?" Parisa demands.

Rian shoots her a raised eyebrow. "The Gods have long protected the Great Archives as they do the Gods' Territory."

Parisa throws her hands up in frustration. "That tells us nothing. How do the Gods protect the archives? Why do they protect it?"

Rian's gaze meets mine, then lands on Aidan. "There are some secrets that are not ours to reveal. Some power holds our tongues."

Recognition hits me like a battering ram. The same bit of magic that prevents us from revealing information about the shifter siblings serving the Gods must also protect the Great Archives. Aidan gives Rian a nod. He, too, understands this.

"Leave it alone, Parisa," Aidan says, and for a moment she seems like she's about to argue, but sighs and bites her tongue.

"You're lucky," Clarisse suddenly says to me, patting my uninjured shoulder gently. In the next heartbeat she turns her sharp eyes on Aidan. "As are you. If anything permanent had happened to her, I'd be holding you personally accountable. And I may not know how to fight, but I know 117 ways to poison a man. Now, everyone get out. Elana needs to rest."

Her no-nonsense tone has a smile stretching across my face. One-by-one the group starts to file out. Only Aidan stays rooted in place, until Clarisse stands and takes him by the elbow.

"You too, Prince. I have a feeling she won't get much sleeping done if you stay here."

My cheeks heat with embarrassment and I pull the sheet up to my nose. Aidan's worried gaze finds mine, and I give him a reassuring nod as Clarisse shuts the door.

Once I settle back against the pillow, sleep finds me easily, and once it does, it doesn't release me until rays of sunlight stream in through the massive windows.

I peel my heavy eyelids open, blinking away the confusion that comes with a long, dreamless rest.

"Are you awake, Your Majesty?" A high-pitched voice asks.

Groaning, I wipe my eyes and sit up. Tessa stands near the foot of my bed with a silver tray laden with food. My stomach gives an eager growl at the sight.

"I am now. And I told you to call me Elana," I say, putting a gentle hand to the side of my head, where a scab has already formed over the cut. My shoulder is still sore, but there's no throbbing pain anymore. How long was I asleep?

These wounds are healing way too quickly for it to be anything but my power. But when I search inside, grappling for the familiar warm glow, I can't find it. The darkness is there, weakened, but growing stronger. There's no light. When Clarisse mentioned I was healing fast I didn't believe her, but now...there's no refuting it.

I voice the question to Tessa as she sets the tray down on my bed. "It's just after dawn, Elana."

"The day after Aidan and I passed the Archives challenge?"

"Yes. The others are breaking their fast with Prince Rian in the dining hall. I wasn't sure if you'd be up for the company yet, so I brought food to you."

Tessa pours steaming liquid from an ornate kettle into a porcelain cup and hands it to me. "This tea is a special Aaranorian blend."

"Thank you." I take a sip of the tea. It's bitter, but the initial bitterness is chased away by light floral notes. I'm pleasantly surprised. "This is good."

She gives me a smile. "It was my mother's favorite."

Remembering the story she told me of her parents, and growing up in the Archives. I set the cup onto the tray. "You didn't think to warn us about the trials?"

Tessa looks at me with sparkling saucer-like eyes. "I-I'm so sorry. Prince Rian is correct, there's only so much we're allowed to say about it. And because the challenges vary for everyone, I didn't know how to warn you."

Groaning, I gently rub my temple, where a dull ache is setting in behind my eyes. "In the future, Tessa, please give us all of the information, even if it ends up not being helpful. We walked in there blind."

"Yes, of course. I'm sorry," her shoulders hunch and she stares at her feet, sniffling.

"It's fine. Let's not dwell on it," I say, eager to put my frustrations behind me and get to work researching. I eat a few bites of rice porridge, until I feel comfortable. Then Tessa helps me dress in a simple gown, with a lightweight corset that ties in front. I strap my daggers to my thighs under the skirts. There's no way I'm going anywhere without them anymore. Not after they saved my life.

Our group enters the Great Archives by mid-morning. Rian escorts us, but can't stay for long. He'll join us after he attends a war-council, where he'll argue in favor of joining our kingdoms in the fight.

Gilbrand the giant is once again standing guard in the foyer. We gather around his large desk in a loose clump. His eyes roam over our group, giving Aidan and I a brief smile. He inclines his head respectfully at Rian, then his gaze snags on Tessa. His mouth drops open in shock. "Is that you, Little Tessie?"

I whirl to see tears in her eyes. She rushes forward, and Gilbrand kneels down, his height now only about double mine. "Uncle Gil!"

Uncle? I think to myself, openly staring as he wraps his massive arms around her. "I never thought I'd see you again, child."

"I didn't think I'd ever be back," she says, breaking away from the hug. "How's my father?"

Gilbrand gets back to his feet, wiping unshed tears out of his shiny eyes. "He's...tired. Doesn't move as well as he used to. He's getting on in age."

Tessa nods her head, staring downcast at the floor. "I'm sorry I left."

"Don't apologize for living the life you want," Gilbrand says gently, then he turns to our group. "Welcome all to the Great Archives. I'll lead you inside and find some Keepers to help you in your research. Once I let you in, you'll be able to come and go as you please, and you'll be trusted with the secrets of the Archives. Knowledge is often a heavy burden to bear."

Tessa walks by the giant's side, the two of them speaking in hushed tones, likely trying to catch up on the years they were apart. Aidan, Rian, and I follow, and our group files in behind us. A set of double doors swings open for us, and we step into an absolute haven.

# CHAPTER THIRTY-ONE

## ELANA

The Great Archives lives up to its name. As far as I can see in front of me and above, are rows upon rows of shelves. Each filled to the brim with stacks of parchment, some rolled, some bound, some stacked neatly.

There are no flames inside, instead natural light filters in through minimal windows, and what I assume is a skylight at the top of the tower. A grand staircase spirals up, and up, and up, more than a dozen levels. Another staircase leads down, lit by lanterns with what looks like glowing moths inside.

Here and there, I spot Keepers wearing brown robes, flittering between shelves, carrying armfulls of tomes. But mostly it appears devoid of visitors.

"Wow," I breathe.

"I know, isn't it magnificent? I don't think I'll ever get used to the smell of this place." Rian takes a deep inhale, and I do the same, reveling in the scent of ink and parchment and books. "This is the main tower. There are two others, one on each side."

He gestures to two elaborate doors which must lead to the second and third towers. I have no words, so I merely shake my head and continue staring.

"Aidan, I feel compelled to warn you," Rian starts, gripping Aidan's shoulder, "if you try to use any fire in here you'll draw the wrath of the Gods. So do your best to keep your hot-headedness in check."

Aidan gives him an exasperated look, which quickly turns into a smirk. "Fine, blades only, then."

Rian rolls his eyes. I walk over to a nearby shelf lined with books bound with leather and pull one out at random. *The Reign of Queen Calanthis of Hotharia* is a relatively thin tome. I gently open it to its first page. Thanking the Gods for the foresight of this transcriber, I read the scrawling synopsis. Apparently this Sepher-blessed monarch only ruled for a decade before she was killed by her eldest son once he gained his power from Enya. Not much of importance happened during her rule, but she was known as a fair and venerable ruler. I carefully re-shelve the text, then stare at the lines of shelves and no apparent organization system. A sinking feeling claws its way into my gut. This is going to be impossible.

I rejoin the group, who has started to separate, each seemingly lost in the lure of the Archives. I'm about to ask if Tessa can help us find a section on geography when Rian clears his throat.

"Feel free to explore, but try to stick together. It's not uncommon for new visitors to get lost in this place. I'm going to find some empty tables." In two long strides, Rian disappears behind some shelving.

"I'm going to find my father," Tessa says suddenly from my side. "He should be able to help us, but I think I should find him alone."

I give her an understanding nod of my head. "Of course, Tessa. Good luck."

She gives me a wobbly smile, takes a deep breath, and heads up the nearest staircase, moving with a purpose I hardly ever see from her. She's comfortable here.

There's a shuffling sound, and I suppress a scream as a creature scampers towards me. A long, scaled, serpentine body writhes as it moves on short but quick legs. Its sharp talons strike the stone floor with scraping noises. It's the size of a large dog, with a head similar to a dragon's, only more rounded. Great big eyes, set behind a wide mouth, are locked on me. Despite my initial fright, the creature doesn't actually move menacingly. It's relaxed, moving with a certain easy-goingness.

"Elana, get back," Aidan says, shoving me behind him, putting his hand on the hilt of his sword. Matteo steps to my side instantly, withdrawing a long dagger.

Behind us, I feel Parisa and the others tense, drawing in closer. The creature lets out a wary shriek, slowing down and staring back and forth between us uncertainly. It cocks its head to the side as it lets out another chirping noise. I instantly know it means no harm.

"No!" I shout at the members of our party drawing their weapons. "Sheathe your blades. It's no threat to us."

Aidan's hand stills on his hilt. He turns to me, brows creased with concern. "We don't know what it is."

Glancing between everyone, I see raised weapons in all hands except Clarisse. I turn back to the creature, which retreats slowly. I need to take charge of the situation before they attack out of fear. "I said, put them away. Now."

Matteo immediately abides by my order, the sound of his blade sheathing sharp in the relative quiet of the Archives. I glare at Aidan for a long moment, challenging him to argue. He searches my face, then the creature's. At last he lets out a breath and relaxes his stance, sheathing his longsword.

Parisa, Novan, and Vikal follow his lead, putting away their weapons, although based on their frustrated stares, they're not thrilled with this order.

"Your mate is correct, Enya-blessed one. This creature will not harm you," Gilbrand's deep voice reverberates through my chest. I startle at the sound. I'd forgotten he was nearby.

"We're not mates," I say, stumbling to respond before he gets the wrong impression. "We're...friends, allies...it's...complicated."

I wince at the embarrassment. Next to me, Aidan can hardly contain his laughter. The giant merely lets out a drawn-out sigh, as if we're taxing his patience.

"Humans are such complex creatures for such small beings," Gilbrand rubs his beard as he steps to the creature, bends over, and gives the back of its scaly head a few quick scratches with a single finger. Its tail starts whipping back and forth, just like a dog's. "This is an archive wyrm. There are dozens across the library. They help us pull tomes, catalog, and return them to the proper shelves. They're quite intelligent and helpful residents."

A slow smile pulls at my lips as I watch the wyrm butt its head back against the giant's hand, as if begging for more attention. Another one scampers up from between some nearby stacks, approaching tentatively. It's a cream color, and significantly larger than the darker one near Gilbrand. It cocks its head side-to-side as it comes within an arms-length of me. Its long scaled tail ends in a fan, and several short sail-like spikes line its back.

"Hello, little one," I say, bending down to put myself at eye-level. Next to me, Aidan tenses, but I ignore him as I reach my hand out, introducing myself.

The wyrm stretches its neck out, its nostril slits expanding as it sniffs my fingers. It shuffles closer, bumping my hand with its snout. I can't contain the soft laugh that escapes me. "I think he likes me."

"That one is a female," he says. "Females are larger and more outgoing. The males tend to be more skittish."

"Do they have names?" I ask.

Gilbrand makes a contemplative noise. "Several of them do, but most don't. The named ones tend to attach themselves to certain Keepers, acting like their assistants, but it's not common. Ask her to bring you a tome."

I give Gilbrand a dubious glance, but he only gives me a nod. I turn back to the wyrm. "Could you please find me a tome with references to someone called 'The Empress'?"

The wyrm tilts her head even further, then her eyes widen and she rushes off, tail wagging behind her as she goes. Aidan gives me a disbelieving look, and Gilbrand rubs his beard as he watches her hurry away.

"You'll be in good claws. She's a smart one. Now, if you'll excuse me, I must return to the gates," he bows his head to us and returns to the entryway.

"Do you think that creature will actually bring something useful back?" Novan asks from behind me.

I stare in the direction the wyrm disappeared and smile. "Yes. But even if she doesn't, we're going to smile and tell her she's doing a good job." I shoot a glare in his direction, so he knows I'm serious.

His eyes bulge as he raises both palms out in a placating gesture. "If you say so."

"I've found us the perfect workspace!" Rian re-emerges on our left, waving us over.

We follow him up one level and behind some stacks, to a well-lit area near some amber glass windows. Several tables have been pushed together, and nearby there's a plush couch and an oversized armchair.

"Here we are. Make yourselves comfortable, and I'll-," he's cut off as the female wyrm nearly barrels into him, a large book in her mouth. She digs her talons into the stone to slide to a stop in front of me. Her head bumps my hand gently, as if urging me to take the book from her. I grab hold of the tome's spine, and she opens her toothless maw and deposits the book into my hands. I expect it to be slimy, but it's surprisingly dry.

Her head, about level with my waist when she stands at her full height, brushes my side and I give her a few scratches behind her head fans.

"Thank you," I say, and suddenly she's scampering away.

"I see you've met the Archive wyrms," Rian says with an amused voice. "As you can imagine, they're quite helpful. If you ever need one, but can't find one, they can be summoned with a whistle."

He demonstrates, whistling a short tone. There's the sound of shuffling, and then half a dozen wyrms race out of the stacks towards us, stopping in front of Rian, with eager tails wagging. I note that the pale wyrm who brought my book is nowhere to be seen.

"Hello friends, can you please help us find every text with any reference to an island off Astrellia's north-east coast? As well as every text referencing an island named Tyne?"

The wyrms take off at a sprint, each rushing in different directions.

"Wyrms can understand complex requests, so be as detailed as necessary when asking for something. When you're done with them, ask that they re-shelve them. You'll want to avoid stepping on their tails, and whatever you do, do *not* damage any books in their presence, or return any damaged books to them. They may appear adorable and docile, but if they attack, they attack together, and there won't be anything left of you to heal," Rian explains. "Obviously no food or drink is allowed in here, and try not to get lost. The stacks and levels can easily get disorientating."

"Wonderful," Clarisse says, sitting in one of the chairs at the table. "How long are we allowed here?"

"The Archives are always open, so come and go as you please. Oh, and one last caution. Never remove any texts from this building."

Just then, two wyrms return. One with a large bound book, and the other with a scroll. Rian accepts them and sets them on the table. We spend the next hour receiving and organizing every piece of literature on the subjects of islands, Tyne, and the Empress. The eager wyrms produce dozens upon dozens of tomes, scrolls, and loose papers. One even carries a stone with something sketched onto it.

When the wyrms finally start to slow, we have five piles. There's a stack for written works before the war and the founding of Astrellia, most of which appear to be in various stages of deterioration. Then there's a stack on each of the topics, and lastly, texts we can't read. These must predate the common language of Astrellia.

Getting down to work, we split up the piles and start reading. I discreetly ask my new friend, the cream-colored wyrm, for all texts on the twin goddesses, and anything that mentions healing powers, and she delivers, bringing me a small pile, which I hand off to Clarisse to research. Maybe the goddesses Nura and Nisha aren't as forgotten as we assumed them to be.

For several hours, there's only the sound of flipping pages, and the occasional scribble as someone discovers something interesting and writes it down. We spend most of the day reading and taking notes. After supper, we reconvene and share anything noteworthy. Rian returns from court and sets a small metal sign on our tables, which reads "still working". He claims it will stop the wyrms and Keepers from re-shelving our tomes.

I absentmindedly scratch the pale wyrm's head, who's sitting next to my chair, as I stare at the text I'm reading. It's about a wealthy gem merchant from Melinor who called herself the Empress of Emeralds, because she discovered the most fruitful emerald mine since Astrellia's founding. I sigh, rolling up the parchment and tying the ribbon around it with care.

"Will you take this one back for me, please?" I ask the wyrm and she happily accepts it and dashes away.

"I think that one's attached to you, Elana. You should give her a name," Rian says, nodding after the wyrm.

I smile after the creature. "I'll think on it." The wyrm swerves out of the way of a familiar form heading our way.

An older man walks next to her, and the resemblance between them is uncanny. They share the same soft face and kind eyes, although hers are a few shades darker. Where Tessa's hair is a deep brown, her father's is silver, streaked with black, betraying his age. It seems she's found, and hopefully made up with, her father. Vikal's head pops up when she approaches, and he watches her steps with interest.

"Excuse me, everyone. I don't mean to interrupt your research, but I wish to introduce my father, Keeper Shin."

"Hello, Keeper Shin," I say, standing to introduce myself, then the rest of our party. He gives Rian an acknowledging nod, which Rian returns.

Shin bows low to me, then to Aidan. "It's an honor to have more future monarchs in our Great Archives. It's vital to have educated rulers on the throne, for knowledge is power."

"I couldn't agree more," I say with a smile.

"Please, won't you join us for a little while? I know your time is valuable, and you must have important work to do here, but we would be delighted to have your assistance," Aidan asks, giving him his best diplomatic smile.

Shin's eyes crinkle. "Oh, you flatter an old man."

"Papa, you're not that old," Tessa chides with a smile.

He pats her arm, then walks to an empty seat, his eyes alight with interest. "What can I assist you all with? Tessa has filled me in on the path of your research."

Aidan nods to the stack of unreadable texts. "It seems some of these predate Astrellia's common language. We're hoping someone can translate them?"

Shin reaches across the table and plucks the top scroll off the stack, unraveling it with practiced ease. His eyes skim a few lines, then he hums to himself. "Ah, yes. Interesting."

He picks another from the pile and scans it. "Yes, I thought so."

We stare at him in barely contained anticipation. He merely hands the two scrolls to his daughter, who skims them as he picks up the stack of parchment next in line and starts thumbing through the sheets.

I hold my breath, catching Aidan's raised eyebrows. A muscle ticks in his jaw as his impatience starts to get the better of him.

After several long moments, Shin lays the papers on the table. "As you suspected, these texts were written before Astrellia's founding. Tessa and I can translate them, but it'll take time."

I let out a relieved breath, giving him a nod. "Thank you both."

Tessa and Shin take the empty seats at the table, between Vikal and Rian. Tessa blushes fiercely when Vikal pulls the chair out for her.

Her and her father work efficiently, but it's still a slow process, so we all get back to our own research.

When rays of sunlight streaming in through the colored glass stretch across the floor, growing dimmer, we break for supper, choosing to eat in the palace because of its proximity to the Archives.

Rian leads us out the doors, and I slow my pace until I'm walking next to Tessa. Her father chose not to join us for dinner, and instead headed home for the evening. "Your father seemed thrilled to see you again."

She gives me a wide smile. "Yes, I think he was. He almost didn't recognize me, but once he did, it was like no time had passed. It took us a while to catch up, sorry we didn't join you sooner."

"It's fine," I say, waving off her concerns. "Really, I'm happy that you two made up."

"As am I. It feels good to be back."

That reminds me of something I wanted to ask sooner. "Is Gilbrand really your uncle?"

She laughs, and it's a light trilling sound. "Oh, we're not related by blood. But he helped raise me. He was a mentor my entire life, and for that, he is like family to me."

It reminds me of the relationship I have with Clarisse, who's walking a few paces ahead, casually conversing with Parisa. Those two have developed a sort of kinship that I don't quite understand, but they seem to get along, so I try not to think about it.

Rian brings us to a private dining room, where we're served a variety of specialty Aaranorian dishes such as a soup-like dish with pieces of meat, an egg, and thin, transparent noodles. We tear into our food as if we haven't eaten in days.

Someone clears their throat loudly from the doorway. "Who the Hells are these barbarians?" A young woman asks, and Rian instantly stiffens, all of his casual friendliness vanishing in a moment. The stranger has striking black hair, and resembles...oh.

"Watch your tongue, sister. Among these people you call barbarians are the heir of Ocarin and the heir of Adrithia. Show them some respect," Rian says curtly.

Her scrutiny passes over Aidan and lands on me, angular eyes narrowing as she assesses me. I try to keep my face passive, but I've never been good at schooling my features like my mother or sister.

"Didn't your father just die? So shouldn't you be a queen, instead of just an heir?"

My shadows awaken, stirring back to life with a vengeance despite being nearly depleted in the trials yesterday. I have to restrain them, so they don't go for the princess' throat. I put on my best bored face. "I'm sorry, and who are you? Heir to...nothing?"

She glares at me, her nose wrinkling in disgust. "Rian, Mother wishes to speak with you." As quickly as she came, she exits the room in a huff.

We all turn to Rian, who sighs and covers his face with his hands, groaning. "Everyone, I would love to introduce my sweet sister, Sareena."

"Apologies, friend," Aidan says, gently patting him on the shoulder. "She seems like a treat."

Rian gives a sarcastic chuckle and excuses himself to go hunt down his mother. He tells us to eat our fill, and he'll be back soon.

"So, did anyone find anything useful?" Aidan asks while we're finishing our dessert, a chewy doughy ball with some cold fruit-flavored cream inside. It's delicious.

For a few moments, no one seems to want to say anything.

Surprisingly, Vikal speaks up first. "I found a list of exports to the land of Tyne dated just after Astrellia's founding. Unfortunately, I don't think their bundles of colored silks are useful to us."

"It's interesting that we used to trade with them," Tessa says, staring at Vikal encouragingly.

"I wonder when that stopped," Parisa mutters, and no one seems to have an answer for that.

"Anything else?" Aidan asks.

My research into the Empress unfortunately came up empty-handed. The only references seemed to be nicknames given to Astrellian monarchs who got too big for their breeches, or a character in some children's story.

I wait for anyone else to say anything, but it seems our research didn't yield much.

"Well, it's only the first day, and there are plenty more texts to cover. Let's not allow our hopes to be dashed so soon," Clarisse says, as if sensing our disappointment.

Tessa nods her head emphatically. "Yes, exactly. The fun part has only begun!"

I share an amused look with Aidan. Oh yes, I'm sure five more days of reading will be everyone's idea of fun.

# Chapter Thirty-Two

## Aislinn

There are few things I hate in life more than sitting in this Gods-damned prison cart. In fact, there are only five things. I've made a list.

1. A dull blade (what's the point of a dull weapon, afterall?)

2. My mother's nagging about finding a suitable husband (I can still hear her aggrieved sighs when I turn away each suitor)

3. Over-ripened tomatoes (I despise equally having them thrown through the prison bars at me, and being forced to eat them since it's the only food they've offered me in days)

4. The foul breath of the guards who only drink shitty ales (does no one here chew on mint leaves? Gods, the stench)

5. Calder's stupid fucking smug face

That's the extent of the list.

Nearly seven days into the journey and I'm bored out of my mind. There's only so long I can occupy myself by imagining creative ways to end Calder's miserable existence.

To pass some of the time, I let my thoughts wander to my family. To my sister, who is likely traveling to Melinor and her first Summit. I think of my mother, who is likely shoving marriage proposals down Elana's throat and lecturing about the importance of continuing the Sable line. Eventually, my mind drifts to Rayna. She must be busy preparing to host the other kingdoms.

I wish I were able to warn her about the danger approaching.

For the first time since we departed the mesa, a familiar face brings me a meager dinner.

"Igraine!" I whisper, grabbing the bars and smiling widely at her. "I didn't think you traveled with the war party."

She gives me a pitying look. "Sir Aric didn't want anyone to see us speaking on friendly terms, so he told me to stay away."

"And what makes tonight different?" I question, glancing around at the surprisingly empty camp.

"They've set up a fighting ring to boost morale. Nearly everyone in the camp is there."

A fighting ring? In the middle of a war party? What a strange way to boost morale. However, this could provide me an opportunity to speak with my father. Precarious hope blooms within me.

"Igraine, is Tyne's Commander still traveling with us?"

She stares at me through the bars, chewing her lip, as if debating whether to tell me the truth. "Yes."

"Good. Then I need to ask you a favor."

"No."

I blink at her, unsure anyone has ever said that to me before. "What do you mean, 'no'?"

"You have a crazed look in your eyes, and I want nothing to do with whatever you're planning," she insists, crossing her hands over her chest.

Gripping the metal bars of my prison, I struggle to come up with a way to convince her. "Please, Igraine. That Commander is, or was, my father."

Her eyes go wide, glancing over her shoulder, as if she can see him through the trees. "That's the king of Adrithia?"

"Yes, well, at least he *was*. I need to know what happened to him. If it is still him." I'm not used to pleading, but I put every ounce of pain I feel into my words, hoping she'll take pity on me.

She furrows her brow, glancing over her shoulder several times, but finally, after a long sigh, I can tell she's given in. "Fine, what do you need me to do?"

"Tell Calder that I challenge him to a duel."

Her mouth pops open and she stares at me as if I just told her I was a seer. She leans in close to my bars and hisses, "are you trying to get me killed? I'm a servant. I can't issue a challenge to a prince!"

I shake my head. "Make me sound bad. Tell him that I was screaming obscenities or threatening you or something. Call me a bastard. He won't harm you."

Igraine pulls back, worrying her lip. When she scrubs her hands across her face and groans, I relax. "Okay, I'll ask. But if he refuses, there's nothing I can do," she says, then rushes away.

I shove the rest of the food into my mouth, hoping it gives me a boost of strength I'll surely need. Is Calder arrogant enough to accept my challenge? All I can do is wait.

While I eagerly await a response, I focus on stretching my sore muscles, maneuvering as much as possible in this cramped cart. I haven't been able to properly exercise in weeks, leaving me at a disadvantage, but having seen Calder fight before, I'm not too concerned.

I'm rolling my neck back and forth when I hear multiple sets of footsteps approach. Peering outside, I see a very put-out-looking Calder. Aric stands behind him, glancing between us with concern etching his features.

"I heard you have a proposition for me?" Calder asks with a scowl.

I give him my cheeriest smile. "I heard you have a fighting ring out there."

"I do," he says curtly.

"Good. Then, I challenge you."

Calder is silent for a moment, his dark eyes narrowing before he bursts out in laughter. "You wish to challenge me? Why the Hells would I agree to that?"

"Because you want everyone here to know how strong you are. You want your men to respect you. You want them to never question your power," I say, shrugging my shoulders.

His humorous expression turns serious. "They already respect me."

"I'm sure you can't hear the grumblings from the front of the line, prince, but I can assure you the discontent is there," I lie. "They may respect you, but they don't fear you. And fear is the only thing that will ensure their undying loyalty. There's no better way to invoke their fear than to prove you can defeat the strongest warrior on the continent."

"You're not the strongest warrior. My father is," he scoffs, then his eyes roam over me, taking in my state, seemingly evaluating his chances of winning. "What do you get out of this? You can't win against me. I'm blessed by Kai. You wish to be humiliated for nothing?"

"If I beat you, I get an hour alone to speak with the commander of the Empress' forces."

"An hour? Absolutely not. You can have five supervised minutes as long as he agrees."

I work my face into a deep scowl, letting him think that I'm making a big concession, when in reality five minutes is all I need to determine if he's still in there.

"When I win, you will get on your knees in front of my entire battalion and tell them that I am the greater warrior," Calder says with a smirk.

I roll my eyes, but reply, "done."

"Cousin, bring her to the ring," Calder hands Aric a silver key, then spins on his heel and storms off.

Aric waits until Calder is out of earshot before laying into me. "Aislinn, what the Hells are you thinking? I know you're, you, but you've been confined for weeks. And Calder won't hesitate to use his power against you. I doubt he'll even take the chains off."

"Oh please, his ego will force him to unchain me," I say, standing up and walking out of the cart for the first time in nearly a week.

"This could be your chance," Aric whispers. "You could overpower me and steal one of the horses, then ride to Melinor, to the summit. Find your sister and warn her of what's coming. We'll be in the Gods' Territory tomorrow. You could get through first, or go around. If you're travelling by yourself you should be much quicker."

My mind goes to my sister, to Rayna, unaware of the army that's heading towards them. Her people, innocent in all of this and about to be thrust into the middle of a war. How many unnecessary deaths will be on my hands if I don't take this opportunity? How many could I save if I left now? Would I even make a difference against an army?

I think of my father, and the duty I have to him. I owe him peace.

In what may become the most foolish decision of my life, I shake my head. "I can't."

Aric groans. "Why not?"

"Because I need to find out what happened to my father. If any part of him still remains, or if he's nothing more than a puppet." I glare at Aric, daring him to argue. Surprisingly, he doesn't.

He leads me away, to the front of the battalion, where I hear a cacophony of voices shouting, mixed with the sounds of fighting.

"Do you have a plan on how you're going to beat him? Because you're not exactly in the best shape right now," Aric says under his breath.

I flash him a grin that's all teeth. "I have a plan."

Aric stares at me expectantly for a few moments before letting out a sigh of resignation. He keeps a firm grip on my arm as he leads me through the throng of soldiers. Some of them curse when they see me, some spit or throw food or drinks. I block it out, focusing on the bright blonde head standing near a makeshift ice throne at the far end of the crowd.

Calder smirks upon seeing our approach. He raises his arms, and the fight between two men practically the size of sun bears immediately ceases. They clap each other on the shoulders, faces equally bloodied, and give Calder a bow before returning to the audience.

I have to fight back my eyeroll when Calder dramatically sheds his overcoat, accepts his spear from a waiting attendant, and waves Aric and I into the makeshift ring. Hundreds of men shove forward, each vying for the best spot to watch, no doubt wondering why their prisoner is facing down their prince.

"Warriors of Hotharia!" Calder calls, lifting one of his hands, calling for silence. "Our depraved prisoner, Princess Aislinn of Adrithia, has dared to summon me to this circle."

He points at me with the sharp end of his spear as he pauses for the loud shouts and jeers that erupt from the crowd. Once it dies down, he raises his hand again. "Because I am your honorable prince, I will not allow this challenge to go unanswered. May you all bear witness to the might of Hotharia, and our Gods-given right to win this war."

He smiles triumphantly at the cheering, waving his hand several times before spinning his spear around in an elaborate show of skill.

I let him have his moment, twirling his stick.

When he finally looks at me, I hold up my manacled hands, shaking the chains. "Surely you'd allow your opponent a fair fight? I am not Gods-blessed as you are, so at least allow me free use of my limbs."

Calder glares at me and appears to chew on the inside of his lip, but upon hearing the mutterings from his people, he gives a cocky smile "Of course. We are honorable above all else."

He digs in his pocket and pulls out a second key, which he tosses at Aric who unlocks my feet, then moves to my wrists and whispers without moving his mouth, "I hope you have a plan."

The metal clangs to the ground and I roll my shoulders, feeling lighter and more nimble already. I rub at my wrists and shake them out, reveling in the lack of biting metal as I go over my plan. It's simple, really: win.

Speed is my biggest advantage. As is the fact that Calder can't perform any wide scale attacks on me without threatening his own soldiers. He tried it as his first move, probably hoping for a flashy way to quickly defeat me, but instead ended up washing away a quarter of the onlookers and causing several injuries.

He didn't allow me any weapons, but I don't need any. I have my eyes on his spear. I duck under his attack, getting in close. I wrap my hands around the shaft and kick hard, sending him sprawling back. The kick takes more out of me than I anticipate. My time in captivity has apparently hindered me more than I thought. Calder catches himself on the ground, weaponless. I smirk as I twirl the spear in the same sequence he showed off before. His lip pulls back into a wordless snarl.

Spears aren't my favorite weapon. I prefer closer combat, but with Calder's water abilities there's an advantage to giving myself a little extra distance to move.

The first thing he does is craft himself an ice spear. He lunges for me, striking out with a predictable move that I parry with ease. His weapon shatters with the impact. Calder stumbles back, looking shocked, but another one shimmers to life in his hands, quickly replacing the broken one.

We trade blows, and every few impacts Calder has to replace his weapon. I'm tiring faster than I hoped, while Calder maintains his barrage of strikes, showing no signs of exhaustion. Sweat trickles down my back and my weakened muscles scream as I barely dodge a set of moves that I could have easily blocked if I were at my full strength.

While I spin out of the way of one of his strikes, he whips a hand out and freezes the ground under our feet. I have minimal experience on ice, nothing compared to the people of Hotharia who experience winters so cold their rivers and lakes freeze solid.

Where my feet slip, Calder's glide, and when I fall, he presses his advantage, jamming the icy handle of his spear into my neck. I bring mine up to block. His weight on mine is immense, and the wood bows under the prolonged pressure of the ice.

I breathe through my teeth, pushing with all my strength, while Calder roars, pushing his ice closer and closer. Satisfaction darkens his gaze, and the ice underneath me starts creeping up, slowly encasing my back, my shoulders, my head, and my thighs.

Panic sets in, seizing my muscles in a grip I haven't felt in well over a decade. I swallow against the fear. I need to get my shit together. I conquered this emotion long ago. Drawing in a deep, calming breath, I gather my strength.

With a savage kick, I free my leg from the clutches of the ice and bring my knee up as hard as I can, hitting Calder in the groin. He lets out a wheeze of pain, and the ice around me cracks and breaks. He sucks in a few sharp breaths, his face a brilliant shade of red, resembling a fully ripened tomato.

I take advantage of his momentary debilitation and scramble out from underneath him. It takes a second for me to catch my breath before I launch myself at him. I'm met with a wall of ice. Flipping the spear around, I keep my core tight as I thrust it as hard as I can into the ice barrier. It shatters into hundreds of shards, scattering across the icy ground. Calder is still doubled over, breathing hard. His eyes shine with unshed tears.

Abandoning all caution, Calder summons a massive wave, pushing it towards me. There's no time to dodge. I flip the spear and slam the sharp head into the ground, then drop to my knees, grabbing the pole right above the earth. I take in a deep breath of air and brace myself as the wave crashes into me.

It hits with a force akin to being thrown from a horse. My breath is knocked from my lungs, and it takes all my willpower not to gasp in air. My weakened body screams out in protest, but I force it to endure. The spear remains firm in the ground.

Finally, the water subsides and my head breaks free. I suck in a greedy breath.

Screams erupt behind me, and I almost wince when I think of the spectators. Calder's back on his feet, but his face is pinched with pain. Catching my breath, I rip the spear out of the wet ground, then rush him before he recovers further. His ice weapon is nowhere to be seen, and he barely avoids my strike in time.

I press him, moving quickly to end this before I exhaust myself. He summons a shield of ice, which I batter relentlessly, searching for a weakness. Again and again I strike, until my limbs shake from the effort. I feign a misstep, pausing to collect myself, while he withdraws his shield and lunges for me with a crude axe of ice. I whirl, knocking the axe aside and delivering a swift blow to his temple with the butt of the spear.

His eyes widen, then roll back. He topples, unconscious before he hits the ground. I fall to my knees, catching my breath.

The shouting around me intensifies, and suddenly a dozen men surround me, weapons drawn. I drop the spear from my shaking hands, then do my utmost to appear as unthreatening as possible, keeping my eyes on the dirt in front of me, and staying still with my hands at my sides.

Aric shoves through the line of guards, taking stock of the situation. He shouts for a healer as he leans over Calder, his ear over his mouth. A man and a woman rush over and start tending to their prince.

Then Aric instructs the guards to get me to my feet as he latches the chains back around my hands, then ankles. He and a few others lead me back to my prison cart. Aric locks the door behind me.

"I hope the five minutes are worth it," he whispers before turning away.

# CHAPTER THIRTY-THREE

## AISLINN

After the first minute, I know without a doubt that my father is gone. His body stands before me, but his personality, his mannerisms, everything that makes him who he is, is gone. Empty black eyes stare past me. He never looks directly into my face, even as I rattle the bars of my prison cart.

"Father, if you're in there, if you can hear me, I need you to give me a sign. Anything," I whisper, scanning him from head to toe.

"I do not know you, prisoner," his voice is monotonous, so unlike my father's.

I need to try again. He has to be in there, somewhere. "I am your daughter, Aislinn Sable. Your wife is Maris. Your youngest daughter is Elana. You are the king of Adrithia."

His gaze remains unfocused as he stares at the back wall of my prison. "I belong to The Empress. I am her commander. Nothing more. My only duty is to fulfill her wishes. I will conquer this land in her name and earn her revenge."

Something snaps my control and I reach my arm through, grabbing his shirt collar and yanking, slamming him into the metal bars of the prison cart. His chin smacks the unyielding metal, but he makes no noise of pain nor effort to get me to release him. "So you would forsake your wife, your children, and your kingdom for this foreign Empress' demands?"

"She is everything to me. My life is hers. My will is hers. Without her I am nothing," he says simply, as if he's said it a hundred thousand times throughout his life.

"What do you remember? How long have you been...aligned with this Empress?" I try another tactic.

His head tilts, as if he's listening for something far away. "I have known her my entire existence. She plucked me from the sea, and gave me life."

My breath catches in my throat, but I swallow my emotion down and press him. "Before the sea, what do you remember? Do you remember the cliff? The battle, and falling?"

"There was nothing before the water."

"Yes there was!" I snap. "You were on a cliff. You saved our forces, but you fell in the process. Think, Father, remember!"

"There was only darkness and water before she found me."

I shove him back, releasing his shirt, and running a frustrated hand through my tangled hair. "Before that. You had an entire life before the water. Please, please remember. Remember me."

"The Empress gave me life. That is all. There is nothing to remember." His voice is cold as ever, and it slices me deeper than any blade.

Disgust and nausea roils through me and hot, angry tears prick my eyes. I blink them away.

"Do I really mean nothing to you?" I ask, staring at the bars instead of his face.

His black eyes flick to my face quickly, then dart away just as quickly. "You mean nothing."

My chest caves in on itself. I suddenly struggle to breathe. Somehow, I gather enough strength to say, "then leave. I have no more need of you."

The enemy wearing my father's body like a puppet turns and walks away without a second glance.

My vision blurs as I scream until my voice is hoarse. I don't care that the guards around my prison yell at me to shut up. I punch and kick the walls and door of my cage until every muscle aches and the skin of my knuckles cracks and bleeds.

What the Empress did to my father, I don't know, but it's my duty as his heir to ensure he has lasting peace. Squeezing my eyes closed, I force myself to recall his booming laugh, his comforting presence, and his sage wisdom. When the tears flow, I don't stop them. I let them fall, coating my cheeks in my sorrow and fury.

Hours later, I'm spent and lying on the cold metal, too exhausted to lift my head. I scratch another notch into the floor. Another day has come and gone.

My eyes slowly drift closed.

For tonight only I allow myself to imagine I'm back home, sprawled out on the settee next to Elana, listening to Father tell stories of his childhood while Mother rolls her eyes and complains his tales aren't fit for ladies.

Just for tonight, I'll delude myself into believing I'm surrounded by love and happiness. In the time before the Crowning Ceremony, when my world truly went to shit.

# Chapter Thirty-Four

## Elana

My fingers may be permanently stained with ink. I rub them together, shuddering at the gritty, tacky feel. Midday sun streams in through the large window as I pour over a scroll on the history of temples. My eyes strain against the words. After days of nothing but staring at words in this place, I have to admit that the Great Archives is losing its charm.

Even cheery Rian has been grumpy, going back and forth between attending court and helping us research.

Tessa, however, is in her element. She flits through the stacks, finding obscure titles for us to read, while making friends with every wyrm she sees. She has spent the last few days reconnecting with her father, who spends as much time with her as possible.

Matteo, Parisa, and Novan seem to have exhausted their curiosity of the Archives after the first few hours. They flip through pages, groaning and sighing as they read. Surprisingly, Vikal eagerly takes anything Tessa hands to him.

So far, we've learned nothing of import. While many of the titles are intriguing and sound promising, we're discovering fables and folktales more than academic or historic texts. Not much survives, even here, of the time before the Astrellian Peace.

My eyes glaze over the words in front of me, and I blink furiously as I roll up the scroll. The history of temples briefly mentioned The Empress, but Shin explained that it was a poor translation from the language that existed before our common tongue, and it should have read "Goddess".

Ceridwen, the archive wyrm that's taken a liking to me, uncurls herself from her ball at my feet, as if sensing that I have another text for her to re-shelve. Her beady eyes blink awake at me, and she stretches her neck and long tail out.

"Here you go, sweetie. All done with this one," I say, holding it out to her. She opens her maw and accepts it gently before scampering away.

I feel eyes on me, and look up to catch Aidan's gaze from across the table. He's shaking his head slightly and smiling at me. I glance around the table to see if the others are staring, too, but no, he's the only one. Tessa, Parisa, and Novan, are staring down at various texts, the latter is so engrossed in the work that his face is less than a handbreadth away from the parchment. Clarisse took Matteo and Vikal into the city this morning to prepare supplies for our journey to Melinor. We leave the day after tomorrow.

"What?" I ask Aidan, suddenly feeling self-conscious.

"You would befriend a terrifying creature and name her Ceridwen," his face is alight with humor.

"She's cute," I say, as if that justifies it. When his only response is a chuckle, I shrug my shoulders, feigning indifference even though my cheeks heat. His intense golden gaze stays on me. The sun reflects a bronze color on his dark hair, and I have the sudden urge to run my fingers through it. To feel his arms around me, strong hands caressing my skin. A slow smirk spreads across his face as he watches me with predatory focus, and Gods, I want those lips on my-

"I think I've found something," Novan says, snapping me out of my lust-addled thoughts. He folds the corner of the page he's looking at.

Tessa gasps and reaches across the table, snatching the book out of his hands.

"What are you doing?" She hisses, smoothing out the page gently, while glancing around the archives. "You must never dog-ear any of these pages. If the wyrms catch you damaging anything in here, they won't hesitate to attack."

I watch Ceridwen approach with a wide grin and a toothless maw, beady eyes bright and eager to return to me. It's hard to imagine this creature with a violent streak, but I'll take Tessa's word for it.

"What did you find?" Parisa asks, leaning over to read the text Tessa now holds protectively.

"It's a merchant vessel's logbook. The captain logged the imports and exports of years of their trade with Tyne," Novan says, pointing at a few passages.

I stare over Tessa's shoulders at the nearly illegible handwriting. "So we used to trade with them? What happened? When did they become hostile towards us, and why?"

Tessa sets the book back on the table and flips through it carefully. We're all silent as she pages through. "There are dozens of accounts of trade here, but it abruptly cuts off years after the first recorded trip, and it looks like the vessel was decommissioned immediately following."

"Is there a year?" Aidan asks, brows furrowed.

Tessa's finger traces over several lines. "It appears to be around two hundred years after Astrellia's founding."

"Decommissioned?" I wonder aloud, then bend down to speak to Ceridwen. "Can you bring us any texts on decommissioned ships from around eight centuries ago?"

She cocks her head at me once, then twice, before she rushes off, disappearing down the stairs.

"Do you know what else happened around 800 years ago?" Rian asks, grabbing one of the other texts that he had set aside earlier. "The invasion of Melinor."

"The battle that wiped out most of the ancient Asheeri warriors? Didn't the invaders come from the north?" Parisa asks, drumming her fingers on the wood table.

Rian nods his head emphatically. "Yes, exactly. There's not much known about the invaders. They seemed to attack for no reason. The first thing they did was set fire to the coast. As if their sole purpose was destruction."

He flips to a page near the end of the tome in front of him, pointing to a passage. "This is the firsthand account of Queen Makeda during one of the last battles against the enemy. She describes them taking no hostages and making no demands, *'They fight as if they had nothing to lose, and only death to gain'*."

Aidan and I lock eyes, and I know we're thinking the same thing. I stare down at the book in Rian's hand as I respond, "that sounds eerily similar to the soldiers we fought."

"Okay...so, you think something happened in Tyne to make them attack us after centuries of successful trade?" Novan asks, looking between Aidan and I, trying to piece together our scattered thoughts. "And you think they're attacking us again now?"

"It's a possibility," Aidan says, as I nod.

Everyone is silent for a few moments. Novan scrunches his face up as he asks, "why would they wait this long to attack again? This is centuries later."

"We decimated their forces. Maybe it took centuries to recover?" Aidan shrugs.

Novan's question bothers me. It wouldn't take eight centuries to recover. I could easily see a century or two for the population to bounce back, and crops and resources to regrow, but not eight. No, there has to be something else.

A feeling of cold dread crawls up my spine. "Is there any mention of cursed or poisoned weapons?"

All eyes turn back to Rian as his eyes trail over the passages. "No. Queen Makeda sustained a wound in the battle that she was unable to recover from, but it doesn't mention any unusual weapons."

My stomach churns and I'm afraid to voice my thoughts. As if voicing them will make it true, and shatter the Peace our kingdoms have fought for. I swallow against the discomfort and ask, "what if the invaders only came back because they had these weapons? We already know that Hotharia is working with them...what if King Skade created those poisoned blades?"

Silence falls across the table as my companions chew on the idea. Parisa and Aidan exchange a long look, neither looking pleased.

"I'd hate to think Skade has been planning this under our noses for years, but it does seem...plausible," Parisa admits.

"Unfortunately, we don't know how long Hotharia has been in contact with the invaders," Aidan says, running a hand through his hair.

Rian interrupts, clearing his throat. "I hate to be a storm cloud on a sunny day, but all of this is speculation. We can't bring our best guesses to the Summit. We need something more concrete to convince the kingdoms to ally against Hotharia and condemn Skade and the royal family."

"So, more reading," Tessa says, sounding all too eager. "I'm going to go find my father. He might have suggestions on where we should focus our energies for our remaining time here."

I give her a nod and she hurries off. Ceridwen appears where Tessa vanished, with several scrolls in her maw. I smile as I take them, scratching behind her ear spikes, then tossing her a small fish from a jar that Keeper Shin gave to me the day we arrived. The preserved fish are a favorite treat of the wyrms, and Ceridwen practically dances every time I reach for the jar.

Opening the first scroll, I read through, making notes in a bound journal next to me. I finish scanning it and move onto the next one.

"Has Clarisse found anything about your powers yet?" Aidan's voice is as soft as a butterfly's wing as he sits next to me, leaning in.

"No," I whisper back, the sinking feeling settling in my stomach again. Whenever I think of my powers, I think of my father. "She hasn't found anything about healing or light powers anywhere. And the mentions of the twin Goddesses have mostly been fables. She has a few texts left, but I'm not holding out much hope."

Aidan places a comforting hand on my thigh. "We'll figure it out, Elana. And even if we don't, your shadows are spectacular."

I flash him a grateful smile, and take his hand, squeezing gently. Gods, this feels right. I spent so much time being mad at him that I'd forgotten how good we are together. While I'm not sure I've forgiven him for holding me back on the cliff, the anger has mostly subsided.

"Speaking of your shadows, Magpie, I'd love to see what you can do with them," Aidan says with a devilish smirk.

I respond with a suggestive smile, "if we weren't in the Archives right now, I'd show you exactly what they're capable of."

A quill smacks the side of Aidan's face and he whirls, glaring daggers at Rian.

"Would you two please just fuck it out already?" Rian flashes a crude gesture at us and my cheeks heat, embarrassment lighting up my features.

"Hey Yarrow, why don't you mind your own fucking business?" Aidan's smile is no longer playful. His eyes flash with molten malice, and before he can make a move to get us banished from the Archives I pull my foot back and kick him as hard as I can in his calf.

"Stop causing a fuss, you degenerate," I hiss.

His hot gaze snaps to me, all fury vanishing in a heartbeat, replaced with a wicked humor. "Apologies, Your Majesty. Consider the fuss over."

I roll my eyes and return to my reading. This scroll ends the same as the last. My brows furrow as my suspicions are beginning to come to fruition. I pick up the last one and quickly skim the last few dates.

"According to these," I hold up all three scrolls, "all trading vessels that had been trading with Tyne for decades were decommissioned at the same time. Around the invasion of Melinor.

"But there's no mention of why?" Novan asks.

"No. Nothing." I sigh heavily, sinking into my chair, wishing more had come from my revelation besides more questions.

"We're missing something," Parisa says. "How can there be no information about why major trading vessels were decommissioned? And nothing about the invaders that nearly destroyed a kingdom. It's like our ancestors kept us in the dark."

The sound of shuffling feet has me turning around. Tessa and her father are rushing towards us, a large leather-bound tome in Keeper Shin's hands.

"I believe," Tessa says between gasps for breath, "this tome might contain some answers."

"Great, let's crack it open," Novan says, reaching for it. At his words, Ceridwen jumps up and hisses, her retractable teeth snapping into place in a menacing snarl. I startle at the  razor sharp canines that appear to be dripping viscous fluid. Novan pulls his arms back and shows his palms in a surrendering motion. "Metaphorically, of course. I would *never* crack a book."

Ceridwen gives him a vicious hiss before shaking off and curling up under the table again, though her slitted eyes remained trained on him. Novan barely breathes, casting wary glances at her every few moments.

Tessa shakes her head at Novan as Shin sets the bound pages on the table. "We won't be able to open it, I'm afraid."

I stare at Tessa, confused by her words. "What do you mean?"

"It's a locked tome. It can only be opened by one of the five monarchs," she winces as she says this, as if worried I'd be upset about another reminder of being kept from my throne.

"I've never heard of such a thing," Rian says, staring at the book with rapt attention.

"It's quite rare to encounter." Shin runs a hand over the cover. "We Keepers generally leave them alone if we do manage to discover one. Some knowledge is too dangerous to be revealed."

My eyes narrow on him. "Knowledge shouldn't be kept from people. The more we understand about the world and our history, the better we become."

"Be cautious, Your Highness. You may find that once you learn what's contained within these pages, you'll wish you could put it back," Shin says, but backs away from the tome, nodding slowly. "However, it's not my place to decide in this situation. I'm merely a steward of the text. You must determine whether the knowledge is worth the potential suffering."

Tessa gives her father an odd look. I suddenly understand why she was so adamant to leave this place all those years ago.

"You're sure none of us heirs can open it?" I ask Tessa, eager to put my annoyance with Shin behind me.

She gives me a long look. "The lock requires a drop of blood to open. There's a pin on the top, if you wish to try."

I stare at the locking mechanism, eyeing the pin. It seems clean enough. The last thing I need is to develop an infection. I carefully press my finger down at an angle, to avoid accidentally stabbing too deep and hitting bone. The pin is sharp, and stabs into the pad of my finger without much effort. I pull my finger off the pin, wincing at the bite of pain, and let a drop of blood drip into the lock.

We all hold our breath for a moment, then another.

When it's clear nothing is going to happen, I let out a sigh and set the book back down.

"My mother will open it for us," Rian speaks up.

Aidan raises his eyebrows at him. "She didn't seem too keen on helping us before. Are you sure she'll open it?"

Rian nods. "She loves a mystery. She'll want to know what's in this book as much as we do."

Aidan, Rian, and I find ourselves outside of Queen Nami's study. Several guards stand outside the door, but allow Rian to knock unhindered.

Rian's sister opens the door only enough to fit her body into the space. She sneers down her delicate nose at her brother, even though he stands nearly half a head taller than her. It's quite a feat. "What do you want, Rian?"

"We need to speak to Mother. It's important," he says, looking past her, to where his mother pours over parchment at her desk.

"We don't have time for whatever this is, Rian," Sareena gestures at us. "Mother and I are making preparations for when you leave for the Summit. She's leaving Numai in my care."

Her smug attitude grates on me, but Rian brushes it off as if she's nothing more than a fly. With a heavy sigh, he lets loose a gust of wind that pushes her back into the wall and holds her there. He swings wide the heavy doors and ushers us in. When we're all inside, he releases Sareena, who snarls at him.

Queen Nami doesn't look up from her desk as she dips a quill into an ink pot and writes on a piece of parchment.

"Mother, we need your help," Rian says, before either her or Sareena can say anything.

The queen says nothing, merely continues writing. Rian clears his throat and tries again. "We need your blood."

She finally looks up from her stack of papers, steepling her fingers together as she assesses us in turn.

"Why, exactly, do you need my blood?" She asks with interest.

"We found a locked tome that will only open with a monarch's blood. We think it has information on who is attacking Astrellia."

Her eyes are bright with intrigue as she silently studies her son for a long moment. Finally, she pushes her chair back and stands. "Very well, let's go unlock it."

She sweeps from the room without another word or a second glance. I don't even have time to hide my shock at her willingness to help. Sareena glares at Rian as she follows her mother out the door. We trail after them, and I practically have to run to match their swift pace.

At the library entrance, Queen Nami greets Gilbrand warmly, who bows low to her in return. It's the kindest I think I've ever seen her. Aidan shoots me a surprised look that tells me he's thinking the same thing.

Once inside, Rian leads the way up the steps to our working area. I notice our companions have cleaned up the table, although they're nowhere to be found. Ceridwen, however, naps in her usual spot under the table, at the feet of my chair.

Nami approaches the table, gaze locked on the large tome.

"Interesting, that a locked tome would appear to you, when I've spent most of my adult life seeking out rare books and forgotten knowledge here," she says, almost sounding impressed. She inspects the thick dark cover, brushing her fingers lightly across raised markings, then picking it up and examining the spine and the latch holding it together. "I've only heard of locked tomes, never seen one. This is fascinating."

She gives no preamble before she jams her thumb down on the pin attached to the latch, letting a few droplets of blood flow into the lock. I expect there to be some flash of light, or perhaps an errant wind, but there's nothing. Only a clicking sound as the latch unlocks.

Queen Nami sticks her thumb into her mouth and sucks the blood clean as she opens the cover. I lean in, as does the rest of our group.

As soon as I see the scrawled text I sigh heavily. "Of course it's not written in the common tongue. I'll get Tessa and Keeper Shin to translate."

"That's not necessary. This is the ancient Aaranorian language. Not all monarchs have forgotten their old tongues. I will translate," Nami says, flipping through the pages. I'm not sure if that was an insult directed at me, but I feel the sting of it regardless. I don't think there's a person alive in Adrithia who can still speak or read old Adrithian. Maybe after all this is behind us, I can find someone in the Archives to teach me. "This appears to be an agreement between the land of Tyne and the sovereign kingdoms of Astrellia. A prison log."

Her finger traces a few paragraphs of text. "A single prisoner was exiled from Astrellia and sent to an uninhabited island off the coast of Tyne around the time of the founding of the Astrellian Peace. The kingdoms paid heavily in riches in order for Tyne to accept the terms."

Queen Nami turns the page, reading carefully, translating as she goes. "According to this passage, the prison ship ran aground and sank off the coast. The crew and prisoner went down with the ship, all presumed dead."

"Does it give any details about the prisoner? A name, a title, anything?" Aidan asks, his arms crossing over his chest as he props his chin on his thumb and index finger.

The queen turns the page, then lets out a startled gasp, dropping it to the table. From beneath the thick wood, Ceridwen lets out a low, rumbling hiss.

"Mother, what?" Rian asks, resting his hand on her shoulder as he looks down at the book, searching for the offending words.

She places a hand to her heart and closes her eyes, taking in several calming breaths. "There is no name, only her title."

We all look at her expectantly. The tension in our corner of the Archives hangs over us like a tangible thing, and I want nothing more than to brush it off. But, like everyone else, I stare at Queen Nami, pale and frozen until she sets us free.

"They exiled a goddess."

# CHAPTER THIRTY-FIVE

## ELANA

"A Goddess?" I whisper on an exhale. "An actual Goddess?"

Queen Nami doesn't answer, holding up a finger while she sits in my chair, reading with greater focus. We hover in anxious silence for several minutes, before she lets out a heavy sigh, pinching the bridge of her nose and sitting back in the seat.

"Mother, what did you learn?" Sareena asks, shoving past Rian to gently touch Nami's shoulder.

"There's very little information here. The word 'Goddess' in our ancient language is commonly mistaken for 'Empress', but in this case, it's definitely referring to one of the Gods. There's no mention of a name, or an associated element. Every precaution was taken with transporting the goddess, however. It seems the captain was chosen for his sailing vessel, the fastest ship across Astrellia. He didn't tell his crew what they were transporting, only that it was of great importance," Nami flips back a few pages and points at a passage. "The goddess was bound in a human form using chains crafted by Tolliver to contain her powers.

"I wonder how many other Gods we don't know about," Rian grumbles, and I can't help but agree with his frustrations. We were taught the five Gods were all-powerful, and the only divine beings of our world. But in the last few months, we discovered two lost goddesses, Nura and Nisha, and now apparently a third unknown goddess. It seems our history isn't as straightforward as we thought it was.

Sareena shifts on her feet. "So, there are more Gods. I don't see what impact this has on us. According to this," she gestures at the book, "the goddess was banished and died. What does that matter in our situation?"

"You're assuming the goddess perished," I say, and a prickle of trepidation works its way up my spine. "What if she didn't? What if she's been hiding out on Tyne for generations? We found several shipping manifests merchants trading with Tyne that stopped around 800 years ago. There was no explanation for why, but it lines up with when Melinor was invaded."

"So you believe that a goddess in human form has lived for generations and rallied an army hundreds of years later, only to be beaten back, but managed to survive for another 800 years, and is now returning once again to exact her revenge?" The queen turns her steely gaze on mine, and I straighten my back almost by instinct.

I share a glance with Aidan, who nods encouragingly to continue.

"Yes," I say, balling my hands into fists at my side. "Maybe she washed ashore in Tyne, or was pulled from the ocean. She could have allied with the people of the land and launched an attack against Melinor," I take a deep breath and fix my gaze on Nami as I speak, "but she failed. So she waited, and bided her time until the moment she could make an alliance with one of the Astrellian kingdoms. She needed someone who was blessed by Tolliver, to help her make weapons. Someone who had always desired more power, who resented the Astrellian Peace. She found King Skade."

Silence falls in the wake of my words. I swallow thickly and wait for her response.

"That's a lot of conjecture, Princess." She stares me down, as if waiting for a crack of weakness to show. I give her nothing. "But, I suppose it is possible."

I hold my breath, waiting for her to say more. The shift in her demeanor and expression gives me a sliver of hope. Hope that maybe she will fight alongside us in the battle yet to come. I don't want to push her, but I need to know where we stand. "Does this mean you believe us? That you'll ally with us against Hotharia?"

She eyes me without malice before turning back to the bound pages in front of her. "I will not make any formal declarations yet, but I admit this revelation is disturbing. I must confer with King Skade at the Summit. Perhaps his hand was forced, or he is being impersonated. If, however, he has allied with a goddess against the continent and killed your father, he must face judgement."

Some of the tension loosens from my shoulders at her words. Not an alliance, but a path to one. Rian glances over his shoulders and gives me an encouraging smile.

"We need to leave for Melinor immediately," Aidan says. "King Mesfin needs to prepare in case Hotharia doesn't show up alone."

Nami straightens, turning to her children. "Prince Aidan is correct. They must be warned. We depart tomorrow at first light. Rian, you and I must address the court as soon as possible. Sareena, ensure the city leaders are aware of our departure."

Rian nods, facing Aidan and I. "Your companions are welcome to share the road with us. If any of them would like to remain in the city, they may do so, too. Perhaps more research could be helpful."

"We would be honored to travel alongside you," Aidan says with a respectful incline of his head to Nami.

"We will look for you at dawn, then," Nami says, giving us a nod before spinning on her heels and rushing out.

"What can we do to help?" Tessa's voice startles me, and I turn to see her, Parisa, and Novan walking out from between several rows of bookshelves.

"What the Hells were all of you doing?" Aidan asks sharply, crossing his arms over his chest. "Please tell me you weren't hiding from the queen."

Parisa scoffs. "We weren't hiding, I merely suggested that we would all benefit from some exercise. So, we took a casual walk through the Archives while we waited for you to return, but it looks like you made it back before us."

"Oh really? And your disappearance wouldn't have anything to do with Queen Nami's personal vendetta against you?" Aidan's brows are raised, but there's humor dancing in his expression.

"Nephew, you insult me! Surely you know such petty squabbles from when we were children are far beneath us now?"

I look between them, wondering what happened between Parisa and the Queen. I'll have to ask Aidan when we're alone. Tessa appears to be as confused as I, but Novan's tight lips are fighting to hold back a smile.

"Of course not, Aunt. Such distinguished, mature women surely don't hold grudges for that long."

Parisa narrows her eyes in exaggerated outrage, taking several steps to close the distance between them, placing her hands on her hips. "'Mature'? Did you just call me old?"

Aidan laughs. "I'd never dream of it."

Parisa cracks a smile.and smacks his arm playfully. "I knew you'd never have the guts."

"That's because he's not an idiot, General," Novan says with a wide grin, shouldering his way past them, staring down at the table. "Now, since we heard everything, we know we have a lot of transcribing work to do before tomorrow. Tessa, do you think your father would help us?"

Tessa nods her head emphatically. "Oh yes, I'm sure he would. Perhaps some of the other Keepers as well.'"

Her brown hair bounces as she races away to find him.

When she returns with three Keepers, including her father, and a stack of blank parchment, they waste no time transcribing anything which can be remotely considered useful. Shin and another Keeper work to translate the text from the unlocked pages, while the rest of us work vehemently on our other stacks.

Clarisse, Matteo, and Vikal find us in the early hours of the evening. We give them a shortened version of everything we learned, and our plan. Clarisse frowns at the few texts left in her stack, but makes no complaint as she sits down and opens the first one up.

"Your Majesty," Tessa's tentative voice asks from next to me. "I'd like to stay here and continue researching, if that's all right? I'm afraid I'll only slow you down on the road, and I'm of more use here."

She has a gentle, hopeful smile that tugs on my insides as she looks between her father and me. "Of course you may stay. We need to learn as much as we can about this banished goddess. If there are answers here, I have no doubt you'll find them."

Her smile grows wider, and I catch a joyous look on Shin's face too.

"Vik," Aidan's deep voice says from beside me. "I'd like you to stay here and assist Lady Grimhart. If you find any vital information that you don't trust to send via messenger bird, then ride out and find us."

I expected Vikal to be upset with this order to stay behind, but he glances quickly at Tessa and gives Aidan a nod. From the pink tinging Tessa's cheeks, I can't imagine she'll be upset with his company at all.

After hours of reading, I finally close the cover of the last tome. I set my quill down and massage a cramp out of my hand, taking in the stack of parchment in the center of the table. Tessa, Shin, and Clarisse are all who remain around the table.

The Ocarins and Matteo left a few hours ago to finish preparations and pack our horses for the journey.

Tessa catches me stifling a yawn. "You should get some sleep, Your Majesty," Tessa whispers from across the table. "There's nothing more you can do tonight."

I stand up and stretch my arms up over my head, feeling a satisfying pop in my back. "Are you sure you'll be all right here after we leave?" I ask.

"Of course. I'm quite happy to stay here. I'm not really made for travelling," she says sheepishly.

Giving her a smile, I glance down at my feet, where Ceridwen is poised to escort me to the door, her serpentine tail wagging back and forth slowly. "I have one more request for you. Please take care of Ceridwen while I'm gone."

At that, Tessa beams. "It would be my honor."

I'm on my way to the stairs with my wyrm companion when Clarisse catches up to me.

"I would like to stay behind as well," she says, and my heart sinks. "I still haven't found anything about your powers, so I need to stay. Besides, I don't think your mother would appreciate seeing me."

I can't imagine making this trip without Clarisse. Not having Aislinn by my side, not having Clarisse, or even Tessa, whom I've come to trust and value as a close friend. The thought makes me bitter, and reminds me of another time when she left me with no explanation.

"Why didn't you stay at the castle, all those years ago? You should have fought harder against my mother. I looked up to you, and one day you were just...gone," I say, without really meaning to. The words slip out before I have a chance to bite my tongue. "Didn't you even care?"

Clarisse's eyes narrow, and her shoulders tense. "I helped deliver you into this world, of course I care. You were the first royal baby I ever delivered. It was a difficult labor for your mother, and even more difficult when you were born. We weren't sure you were going to make it, but you did. I spent so much time with you that first year, you felt like my own child. So don't say that I don't care. I always have. I wish I was able to stay at the castle with you."

I look away, embarrassed at my outburst, and feeling like her pupil again. She's not to blame. It was my mother's decision to banish her from my home. My face scrunches up suddenly as I process something else she said. "What do you mean I was the first royal baby you delivered? I thought you delivered my sister, too."

Clarisse freezes, closing her eyes, then turning away from me, busying her hands. "You were the first."

"Who delivered my sister, then?"

"I did." There is no hesitation in her voice.

My mind reels. Were the rumors about my sister right this whole time? "Are you saying that Aislinn is a bastard?"

She turns around sharply, giving me a look that can cut glass. "Your sister is a true born Sable, as are you. Never doubt that."

I try to wrap my mind around other possibilities, but come up blank. "Then tell me what the Hells you meant. You're not making any sense, Clarisse."

She sighs. "Clearly, there are secrets your mother is still keeping. They are not mine to reveal. Ask Maris."

With that, she turns away and marches back to the table. I gape after her, feeling unsettled. How could I have been the first royal baby born if Aislinn is a true Sable? Is she even my sister?

I shake my head, trying to free that thought from my mind. Of course Ash is my sister. There's no reality in which we could be anything but sisters.

# CHAPTER THIRTY-SIX

## AISLINN

I never thought I'd return to the Gods' Territory inside a prison cart. We crossed the border two days ago, and everyone has been on edge since. The warriors have been unusually quiet, and tempers are running at an all-time high. I saw three fights break out between the ranks yesterday alone. At night, wild animals howl and stalk the camp, fraying the Hotharian's nerves. Every night I hope to see the glowing green and yellow eyes of the goddess cats as they tear through the camp, but my hopes have gone unanswered.

Last night Calder put up an ice wall around the captain's section of the camp, which infuriated the rest of the army. My guards have been complaining about it all morning. According to them, his leadership has been lacking, and ever since he injured his own people and then lost to me in the fighting ring, many of the soldiers have lost their respect for him.

I haven't seen a shadow nor heard a whisper of my father since that evening after the fight. Although I prefer not seeing him, I need to know his movements if I'm going to fulfill my promise to grant him eternal rest.

To my immense relief, Igraine slipped through the lines a few nights ago while Calder was distracted and sent a messenger bird to Melinor warning them of the impending danger.

My mind stays on my family nearly constantly now. I worry about them when I'm awake, and I dream about them when I sleep. At times, when the darkness creeps in and my body aches more the constant dull throb, I curse myself for not leaving when I had the chance. What did I truly accomplish from challenging Calder? My heart already knew that Father was gone. If I had left when Aric said, I could have been halfway to Oraphia by now.

Pushing my guilt aside, I work on my stretches, gripping the metal bar with one hand and turning my torso away. It's late afternoon, and thankfully the heat of midday is starting to subside.

When the horse pulling my metal prison suddenly lets out an anxious whine and halts. I huff my annoyance at the jarring motion, but shake my head and continue my routine. I've devised a system for stretching so my muscles don't become weak from disuse. One thing I learned from fighting Calder was that I've been too lax. Even imprisoned, I should still be formidable.

I've counted to nine when I hear a startled, high-pitched cry coming from somewhere behind the prison cart. When the single cry turns into a chorus of screams, I shake my arm and shoulder out and peer through the bars, seeking the source of the distress. I quickly draw back, heart racing, as an explosion of flame blasts through the nearby trees.

The horse the cart is hooked up to startles and bolts, throwing me against the door.

I right myself and press my cheeks to the bars, trying to catch a glimpse of what's throwing fire at the army. Could it be Aidan? And if he's here, my sister won't be far behind. Hope blooms in my chest, until I hear a blood-curdling cry, "dragon!"

Turning my attention to the sky, my pulse skips a few beats. A shadow blocks out what I swear is half the sky as a giant winged creature soars above the trees. It opens its jaws and lets out a roar that shakes the bars of the prison cart.

"Oh Gods," I whisper. We're all going to die, and if I can't get out of this damn cart, I'll be among the casualties.

The dragon swoops down, burnt orange scales glimmering in the sunlight. It opens its maw and another burst of fire explodes from it, setting a hundred soldiers ablaze in a second.

I need to escape, right now. If I stay in this cart, I'll die. I reach behind my head and pull out the secret weapon I've kept tucked away in my hair. It's the metal spoon I was given during one of my first days of captivity.

Slowly, during these past fortnights I've been whittling it down, sharpening the handle and shaping it into what it is now. The rounded part of the spoon is now the handle, while what was the grip is now as thin as a hairpin, and deadly sharp, with an angle near the bottom, perfect for what I'm about to do.

I reach through the bars of the cart, stretching my arm down, and fit the sharp end into the lock. Letting out a deep breath I sink down until my ear is pressed against the cool metal. It'll be easier if I can hear the mechanism inside.

Carefully turning the spoon around, I feel a slight catch. I rotate the spoon, keeping it level. Back home, there isn't a lock that I haven't picked. I learned the skill at a young age, when my parents thought locking me in my room would keep me inside. It had the opposite effect, and now no door can hold me.

I move the spoon carefully, avoiding any sudden movements that could cause it to slip off the release. Finally, there's a click of the mechanism unlocking, and I breathe a swift sigh of relief, pulling the spoon out and swinging open the door.

I spare a glance at my short length of chain connecting my wrists. The Hotharians didn't bother with my ankle chains again after the fight with Calder. I imagine Aric had something to do with that decision, perhaps to help me escape when the time was right. Carefully, I fit the spoon handle into the hole until I find the catch. It takes a fraction of a breath to maneuver the pick correctly and then the manacles tumble to the floor of the prison cart. I breathe a quick sigh of relief.

A deafening roar has me looking to the sky, where the orange dragon is joined by an emerald one. Together they fly in a wide circle, then dive back down, the green one peeling off to attack the front of the army. I race around to the front of the cart, where the old mare is stomping her feet nervously.

Two guards see me and raise the alarm of my escape, but everyone is either too busy fleeing for their own lives or scrambling to find weapons suitable to fend off a fully grown dragon.

"Halt!" The braver of the two guards unsheathes his sword. He seems to realize I only carry a spoon and is eager to prove himself, rushing forward. "Get back into the cage."

I try to look startled, holding my hands up, spoon in my sleeve. When he's a few paces away I lunge, closing the distance between us, ducking under his sword swing and jabbing the spoon in his throat. I yank it out and am already moving for the second guard before the first hits the ground.

The second guard unsheathes his broadsword and swings for my neck, but he's off-balance and the move is sloppy. I drop, kicking out, and he tumbles into the dirt. I slash out with my makeshift blade, opening up a wound on the inside of the man's thigh. He yells as blood pours from his leg, as quickly as if he were to wet himself, which he also appears to be doing. He'll pass out from blood loss soon thanks to the artery I just severed. He shakes his head, staring at his leg in disbelief, before his head lolls to the side. He doesn't get back up.

Heat assaults my back and I suddenly remember the giant dragon Hells-bent on roasting this entire army. I pick up the fallen guard's sword and run to the horse. She's my best chance of making it out of this mess. I unhook her from the cart and she needs little motivation to run.

I'm tempted, so tempted, to take this horse and head straight for Melinor, but there's something I need to do first.

I tug on her reins and we race to the front of the army, where we dodge small fires and fallen bodies, some charred to bits. Trees burn and everywhere men are screaming. I scan every face and every body we pass. None of them are my father. A shadow passes over me, and I jerk the horse's reins to the left, narrowly missing a jet of fire that scorches a path we were heading for. Several groups of warriors fire arrows at the beast, which bounce harmlessly off its shiny green scales.

"Take cover!" A familiar voice shouts over the din of the battle. I yank the horse in that direction.

I spot Aric hiding behind a boulder, sheltering against an onslaught of fire. I wait to approach until the dragon moves on, targeting a group of warriors firing arrows.

Aric jumps when he sees me, but quickly recovers, checking around to see if anyone takes notice. I leap off the horse's back, keeping hold of her reins so she doesn't bolt.

"Where is he?" I shout.

"Who? Calder?" Aric yells back.

"My father."

Aric shakes his head. "He's gone. The Tyne half of the forces split off yesterday. They said they received new orders from their Empress, but

Calder didn't want to disobey his father's plan, so we're continuing on our planned route to Oraphia."

Disappointment wracks through me. I close my eyes, knowing I missed my opportunity to lay my father to rest once and for all.

"All right," I try to shake the dismay from my shoulders. Now's not the time to dwell on that. "Where's Igraine? We need to get out of here, now."

Aric looks past me, and I turn to stare at a burnt husk of what I imagine was once a grand tent. "She was serving Calder his supper when the creature attacked."

"No," I whisper, feeling a sharp pang of grief in my chest. I stamp it down. These emotions serve me no purpose right now. "You're sure she was in there?"

He nods, and I notice he's paler than usual, and something like regret shines in his eyes. "Calder got out, but I didn't see anyone else."

Hatred burns through me. "Where is he?"

His startled gaze meets mine. "Aislinn, you have a horse. Leave here. Go find your sister."

"Why?" I snarl, gripping the reins tighter. "He wouldn't hesitate to kill me. Why should I give him any more grace?"

Aric's gaze drops to the ground. "I know he's done horrible things, but he wasn't always like this. But I still believe there's good in him. He could change things for the better in Hotharia if given the opportunity."

I, too, remember a time when Calder was a different person. A time when he would joke with the rest of us heirs, and sparred with us. We used to sit together and imagine our trials and what life would be like when we earned our powers. But those are mere memories, and not the reality we face today.

I shake my head, a humorless smile on my face. "You're right, he wasn't. But he made his bed when he sided with the people who murdered my father. And it's time he faces the consequences of his choices."

"Killing him won't change anything. All it'll do is justify King Skade coming after you. Then where does it end?"

I want to laugh. "Do you think this will end without bloodshed? You helped start this war by allowing my father to die. Now you've suddenly grown a conscience?"

Aric is quiet. His shoulders rise and fall with rapid breaths. Nearby, an explosion lights several more trees and sends up a chorus of screams.

"Fine, Aislinn. Do what you want. Calder ran to where the horses were tied up, that way," he points at a particularly fiery area.

"Are you coming?" I ask, mounting the horse again, who snorts angrily, as if she senses my intention.

Aric shakes his head. "If I make it out of this alive, I'm heading back to Hotharia. I'll take my sister and run."

I give him a begrudging nod, knowing I'd do anything to keep my sister safe. I grit my teeth against the peace offering I'm about to give. "I wish you well, Aric. I don't forgive you, but I do understand why you did what you did."

His eyes are wide as he gives me a shaky smile and a nod. I dig my heels into the horse's side and leave Aric behind, sincerely hoping this is the last time I ever see him.

I push the frightened mare through the smoke and ashes. I have to cover my mouth with my hand to avoid choking on the acrid air. My eyes burn against the unpleasantness as we gallop forward.

At last we break through the smoldering cinders, and I take in a deep breath of clean air. A group of horses are tied to trees ahead of me. A flash of blonde hair, and I see Calder racing for them, and he's dragging someone with him.

White hot rage simmers through me again as I see an injured Igraine being dragged by the arm. Tears are coursing down her cheeks, making tracks down her soot-stained face. She's limping, and it looks like her arm is severely burned.

The green dragon circles overhead, diving in their direction, only to pull back when Calder yanks Igraine in front of him. My brief sense of relief at seeing her alive is replaced by fury as I realize that fucker is using her as a shield. I abandon all sense, jumping from the horse and sprinting towards them.

I duck as the tip of the dragon's taloned wing brushes the top of my head. In that instant, the world around me freezes. The fire stops crackling, the screams cut off mid-yell, Calder's retreat pauses, even the dragon is caught mid-air, wings outstretched and jaws open to reveal teeth the length of my hand.

I skid to a stop, taking heaving breaths and looking around wildly.

The same low, booming voice that's been haunting my dreams suddenly echoes around me.

"Aislinn Sable, you come to meet your destiny at last," a man descends from the sky. He wears a long, billowing cloak. His face is shrouded, but he's distinctly masculine. His body is covered in shining silver armor, woven so tightly together it almost looks like scales. It shimmers and ripples when he crosses his hands over his chest. "I am the Metal God Tolliver, and you have traveled far to finally claim your birthright."

My mouth drops as I stare at the imposing figure. "W-what are you talking about? I wasn't chosen to rule. My sister was."

"You are chosen. By me. However, only one heir could travel to our mountain and complete our trials. That had to be your sister. But you, Aislinn, are still an heir."

My mind reels. "H-how could that be?"

The god sighs heavily. "Because I demand it. Tell me, do you know why the Gods have chosen only firstborn heirs for generations?"

"Are you about to give me a history lesson in the middle of all this?" I ask dubiously, gesturing at the frozen world.

There's a grating noise as Tolliver leans forward, eyeing me with distaste. "History teaches us about ourselves. There is a reason why we guard the Great Archives so fiercely."

I blink, momentarily taken aback by his seriousness. He lets out a gruff noise and rights himself. "Power used to be everywhere, Aislinn. The elemental Gods gifted our powers to the mortals long ago. With it, you thrived as a species, and you worshipped us as your creators. You built entire temples in our names and created religion to honor us. Only, we didn't create you. Your true creator grew jealous at the worship we were receiving. She sought to strip away your power, and force your kind to revere her. We tried to warn her, saying that the power had been a part of the land and you humans for so long that taking it away would have dire consequences, but she didn't listen. She used her power to eliminate the trait from your kind. Overnight, an entire new generation was born without the elements. It was a devastating blow to your growing race. My siblings and I, the elementals, couldn't do anything to stop her. She created us, too, after all. The only Gods she did not create were her sisters, the twin goddesses.

Nura and Nisha came up with a plan for us to fight her. We each blessed one human family with our abilities. We gifted a piece of our immortal beings upon the family, to ensure the gift would last for generations to come.

We don't choose the firstborn from the royal family because we think they'll make the best leader, or because they deserve it. We choose them because they possess the most potent piece of our being. Simply put, the firstborn's potential is greater than their siblings'. With each generation, that gift becomes slightly less potent. Some generations, like your grandmother, are able to surpass previous ones. But it's becoming increasingly rare. We've had to continue to pour our power into your bloodlines generation after generation to ensure that your offspring are born with the ability to receive our power."

"Why not let your power die out naturally? Why keep it going after all these years?" I wonder.

"Do you want your kingdom to fall into ruin, and all of your people enslaved to a goddess, Aislinn Sable?"

My eyes widen and I firmly shake my head.

"If my creator wins this war, that is the fate which will befall the continent. All of our power was needed to expel her from this land the first time, and all of the elements will be needed once again to end her. I am here to gift you my abilities so that you, too, might stand against this goddess."

A feeling, unlike anything I've ever felt before, washes through me. I feel it in my bones, under my skin. Energy fills me, and I gasp with the raw intensity of it.

I take several deep breaths, centering myself and getting used to the way the power fills me. Tolliver hovers, studying me, until I'm able to speak again. "Don't I need to pass some trial like all the other heirs?" I ask the god, feeling slightly disappointed that I didn't earn his favor.

A harsh bark of laughter. escapes his lips. "You broke yourself out of a metal prison, forged your own makeshift weapon out of a spoon while starving and injured, and killed two people with it. Consider me thorough-ly satisfied that you are the best choice for this gift. Now, go retrieve your family's sword and get to the green dragon. She will take you to Melinor."

"Did you just tell me to ride a dragon?" My mouth hangs open. The sword makes sense, but the dragon?

As quickly as he appeared, he vanishes. I stare with my mouth agape at the space he just occupied. The world jerks back into motion. Overhead, the dragon lets loose a rattling roar. My focus snaps to Calder, still dragging Igraine along by her uninjured arm. A group of his guards circle around him, as his gaze finds mine. His surprise quickly dissolves into a vicious sneer as he pulls Igraine to his chest, daring me to attack him.

I feel it then. The connection to my heirloom sword. It's slung across his back. I can't see it, but I know it's there. I mentally reach out to the silvery threads of the tether and yank. The sword and scabbard rip free from Calder's back and sail towards me. My hand reflexively grasps the hilt.

A smile stretches across my face. I'm once again holding my ancestor's blade, and it feels like a piece of me has been returned.

Seeing the sword in my grasp, and perhaps realizing how it got there, Calder pales.

"*At last,*" a voice says from right next to me, and I swing the blade to attack, but there's no one there.

I shake my head and brush off the odd sensation, fixing my gaze back on Calder.

"Get her! Apprehend the prisoner!" Calder yells at his surrounding guards.

Two of them charge me, swords swinging. I allow them to get close, to swing at me, before I rip their weapons from their hands with half a thought, sending them into the chests of their fellow guards. I bring my sword down in an arc, removing the closest guard's head from his shoulders, and then run through the other.

*"Behind you!"* The voice cuts through my concentration and I whirl as a wave of water batters into me, sending me flying.

When my back makes contact with the ground I sink my sword into the earth, stopping my momentum.

I leap to my feet, dodging a wooden spear aimed at my chest, and send a discarded metal shield into the torso of the man who threw it.

I'm already running by the time he collapses, dead. Calder sends shards of ice at me, which I deflect with my sword, shattering them into cold dust. He backs up, shoving three more of his men at me.

Two of them have swapped their metal weapons in favor of wooden spears, but there's enough metal lying around this forest to sustain me against an entire army. They go down before they can even pull their arms back. The third drops his axe and bolts in the opposite direction. I reach out to his armor, grabbing it with my power and slamming it to the ground. He doesn't get back up.

Above me, the great flying beast circles back around, its orange wings creating a wind that sends the towering trees knocking into each other.

Tolliver's order to ride the dragon to Melinor sends a wave of unease through me. It would be the quickest route, no doubt, but I'd just as likely become its next meal.

My sword jerks to my right and blocks an arrow that nearly hit me. *"Focus, Princess. We're still in the middle of a battle."*

I whirl around, looking for the source of the voice. "Who said that?"

Another arrow flies for me, and I whip the metal arrowhead back around to the person who fired it. A man's wailing cry lets me know it made contact.

*"Can you hear me?"* The voice asks tentatively.

"Yes," I say, still searching for the source of the voice, but come up empty. There are no living soldiers nearby. Bodies lay scattered around me.

"*I…I can't believe it,*" the voice sounds overcome with emotion. "*After all these years, nearly 384, to be exact, I was beginning to think the seer was lying to me.*"

"Are you a god?" I ask, speaking quietly. The voice doesn't sound like Tolliver, but what else could communicate in this way besides one of the Gods?

There's a sound like choked laughter, and then comes the response, "*thank you for that, but no, I'm not a god. I was once like you are now, Tolliver-blessed. You can call me Hale.*"

"Hale?" I sputter, staring down at my blade in utter shock. "As in my ancestor, Hale Sable?"

The sword vibrates lightly in my hand, as if happy with my response. "*Yes, exactly. Well, I suppose that's not completely accurate, since I'm merely a piece of your ancestor. The most important piece, but still just a piece.*"

I'm too stunned for words. My mouth is open, gaping at the hilt.

The voice continues speaking, as if it didn't flip my whole world upside down. "*I am Hale Sable's soul.*"

# CHAPTER THIRTY-SEVEN

## AISLINN

I must have hit my head. Or maybe I'm actually dead. Perhaps one of the dragons killed me, and everything up until this point has been the shitty afterlife. Or maybe I'm in another infection-fueled fever dream.

My sword moves of its own accord, cutting deep into an attacking man's shoulder. Warm blood splatters my face, and I flinch. Okay, this is real. He screams and drops, unsuccessfully trying to stop the bleeding.

*"Now's not the time to explain. I will tell you everything, but you must survive in order for me to do so,"* the voice of Hale Sable warns.

Getting a hold of myself, I whirl around, catching an axe mid-swing that I felt was there. I send the weapon flying, and dispatch the man with my sword. Spinning to make sure no one else is charging me, I find no one else in the vicinity. Calder is gone with Igraine.

"Fuck," I say, looking for his horse, but it's nowhere in sight. He must've released the other horses, too, because they're no longer tied up. The mare who pulled the prison cart is also long gone.

Cursing again, I start running in the direction I think he went. The ground violently shakes as something massive crashes down behind me, and a hot breeze assaults my back. I halt in my tracks, not wanting to appear like prey running away. Slowly, I turn and come face to snout with the glimmering green dragon.

I don't move, don't dare make a sound, and I certainly don't look it in the eyes. Its smoldering breath blows my matted braid back. I wait. Wait for the inevitable crunch of my bones when it takes a bite, or to feel my skin melting when it turns its fire on me.

After a moment, the dragon lets out a huff and pulls back, curling its long neck and shaking its head.

"Get on, Princess, if you wish to save the girl and reunite with your sister," a raspy, deep feminine voice calls, straight from the dragon's mouth.

I startle, nearly losing my grip on my sword, something I never do. "What?" I ask, stupidly.

"*Go with her, Aislinn,*" Hale Sable's voice insists.

"Why does everyone want me to ride a freaking dragon?"

"*She's not a dragon. Once you get on her back I'm sure she'll explain.*"

Staring around, I look for any other option. A stray horse, anywhere.

"Hurry up, human, while I can still smell them," the dragon says through bared teeth, and I hustle, sheathing my sword in one fluid motion and using my momentum to run up the dragon's leg. I grab one of her spikes and situate myself between several prominent ones.

"You might want to hold on."

There's no harness, nothing to hold on to, so I grasp the spike in front of me and hope it's enough. Her shoulders, where I've situated myself, are wide, at least as wide as two full-grown horses. I grip as best as I can with my thighs.

She bends down and spreads her massive leathery wings, using her legs to leap as she pushes them down. We sail upwards, and my stomach plunges with the movement. I bend down and hold on tight as we gain altitude.

With several powerful flaps of her wings we're soaring high above the trees. Feeling more secure in my positioning, I slowly sit up, watching as we leave the scorched ground behind us. The orange dragon remains, circling the entire length of what was the camp, blasting an occasional jet of fire at whatever enemies still live. I find myself hoping that Aric survived, that he will make it back to Hotharia to rescue his sister. I also hope to never see him again.

"There," the dragon descends sharply, and I feel my body start to lift off her back. I frantically grab her spike once again and clench my legs together, hoping it's enough to keep me seated during the dive.

She levels out and a burst of fire explodes from her maw. I lean over, trying to catch a glimpse of what she's attacking when she drops below the trees and lands harshly. I lurch forward, but catch myself so I don't go flying off her back.

"Get the girl, but leave the Prince alive. He must answer to the Gods," the dragon hisses, and I take it as my cue to jump from her back.

Quickly orienting myself, I draw my sword and sprint to Calder's horse. The poor thing is panicking, flames licking at his hooves. Calder douses the flames, but the horse continues to buck and stomp, refusing to move. Igraine sits in front of Calder, face pale, eyes half-closed, and I have no doubt that if it weren't for Calder's arms caging her in, she'd have fallen off by now.

"Calder!" I yell, getting his attention. "Let the girl go, and we'll leave you in peace."

"Do you think I'm an idiot, Aislinn? I know as soon as I surrender her you'll use your stolen power to kill me!"

In any other circumstance, he wouldn't be wrong. But, with one very ferocious dragon at my back instructing me to leave him alive, I'm treading carefully.

However, his quip about my power irks me. "What makes you think the power is stolen? Tolliver appeared to me the same way Kai appeared to you."

"Bullshit! You stole the power, exactly like your sister did. Your whole family is a bunch of liars and thieves, and we're purging the continent of you and your ilk."

I take a moment to inspect him. His gaze is dark, the circles under his eyes are stark against his sallow skin. I've never seen him look so unwell. Gods, there must be something wrong with me, because I'm pitying him. He used to be my friend. All of us heirs were. What happened to him?

"What has your father done to you?" I don't realize I ask out loud.

"Nothing," he snaps, and Igraine winces as spittle hits the side of her face. "He is paving the way for a new world. One where The Empress rules all, and our family is in a place of power."

I shake my head. "You already were in a place of power, Calder. I don't understand why your father is doing this to our continent."

"You wouldn't understand. His destiny isn't to rule over one kingdom, but them all. He's called to a higher purpose, and your feeble mind couldn't even begin to comprehend the plans he has for Astrellia. With The Empress at our side, my family will rule for an eternity."

Blinking at the impressive level of shit spewing from his mouth, I try again. "Calder, I won't try to stop you from going wherever you think you need to go. The only thing I'm asking you is to let the girl go. She is innocent and needs to be treated for her injuries. I can get her to a healer quicker than you can. Please, let me help her."

"Why do you care so much about one pathetic servant? Is she a spy for Adrithia?" Calder asks, wrapping an elbow around her neck. A low rumble sounds behind me. The dragon lashes the ground with her tail threateningly. I'm glad she's on my side.

"No," I say, trying to sound impartial. "I only met her when she healed me from the infection. If you keep her, she'll only slow you down."

Appealing to Calder's morals didn't work, so it seems I'm going to have to speak bigot if I'm going to have any luck. I hope Igraine will forgive me for what I'm about to say. "What good is a servant who's too weak to perform their duties? She's useless to you."

Calder's glazed eyes turn ravenous. "You haven't answered my question, Aislinn. Why the fuck do you care?"

I narrow my eyes at him. "She's a person, Calder, and she's in pain. Of course I care. If you still had a soul, you would, too."

His eyes widen and he releases her. "Fine. Take her."

I dart forward before he can change his mind. I reach for Igraine's hand and help her down from Calder's horse. She's in worse shape than I thought. She can hardly walk, so I walk next to her, putting my arm around her waist so she can lean into me.

When she sees where I'm leading her she hobbles to a stop, eyes going wide with fear. "No, I can't ride that beast."

"She won't harm us," I look from the dragon to her burns, cursing myself, "I promise. The god Tolliver told me to go with her."

Irgaine gives me a skeptical glance and when she hesitates long enough for me to question whether she would rather go with Calder, the green dragon lets out a low whine. "I did not mean to harm you, child. I am sorry."

Her voice sounds remorseful, and it strikes me as odd. A dragon, feeling regret? Igraine stares at the creature for a long moment before giving a quick nod, allowing me to lead her along.

We're nearly to the dragon when I look over my shoulder at Calder, who watches us and the dragon with disdain. There's a well-made dagger at his waist that piques my interest. I barely have to tug before it flies off its holster into my waiting hand. I call back to him, slipping his dagger into my empty thigh sheath, "you took my blade. Fair is fair."

He scoffs and spurs his horse in the opposite direction. I help Igraine climb onto the dragon's back, who helpfully stretches out her leg to make it easy for her. Would have been nice if she'd done that for me before, but I'm not about to mention it.

The dragon makes an effort to fly smoother so as to not agitate her injuries. Again, would have been nice to have gotten the easy ride.

Igraine groans in pain, trying to get comfortable on the dragon's shoulders.

"Is there anything I can do to help you?"

"No. All of my supplies burned up. I've got nothing to dull the pain or speed the healing," she says through gritted teeth.

"We need to get to Melinor as fast as possible. My sister can help you," I promise. Even if she can't access her healing powers, she is still one of the most talented healers in our kingdom. My heart races with the possibility of seeing her again soon. Her and Rayna.

Hours later, we're still in the Gods' Territory. I know, because I can see the mountain range where the heirs' trials took place in the distance. That, and the land below us is still rich with life and energy. It oozes from the towering trees, and lush green foliage. I spot Melinor on the horizon, illuminated by the golden light of the setting sun. There, the landscape turns into a grassy savannah, and eventually a desert.

I enjoy the views while watching over Igraine. She fell into a pain-filled slumber hours ago.

Deciding I've had enough listening to nothing but the wind rush past me, I break the silence. "All right, one of you better start talking, dragon, or sword."

A rumbling sigh comes from the dragon's throat. "It's difficult to speak like this. So, for now, I'll tell you my name. You may call me the Maiden."

"The Maiden?" I ask, gaping at the back of the dragon's large head.

"Yes. And you met my brother, the Messenger, back at the Hotharian camp."

So the orange dragon...is her brother. I chew on this fact, when my sword suddenly buzzes at my side.

*"You already know my name, but I suppose you'd like to hear how, and why, I became a sword?"*

"Yes, I would," I say tentatively. "But first, am I the only one who can hear you?"

*"It seems so. I was hoping all of my bloodline would be able to understand me, or even those in our family blessed by Tolliver, but there have only been two since I reforged myself, and they weren't able to hear me at all,"* Hale says, and there's a deep sadness in his voice.

"So you've been in this form for 350 years?" I ask, my stomach dropping imagining the

*"It'll be 384 in winter...but who's counting? Most of that time I've been in a dormant state. I awaken when those who wield my weapons need assistance, but otherwise I'm sleeping. At least until you and your sister have come into possession of my trove, that is. You've kept me busy, and your sister even more so in the last months. She really possesses no fighting skills. Keeping her alive is a feat. At least when you came into possession of my sword, you were competent."*

I bristle at being called merely competent when I had bested the most talented fighters in my kingdom to earn the sword, including my father. "What do you mean, 'competent'?"

Hale lets out a low chuckle. "*Well sure, you're good, Aislinn, but I dedicated my life to studying the art of sword fighting, and even I had several masters who could beat me, until Tolliver gifted me my power. You may have beaten the best warriors of your kingdom at that time, but far greater ones have lived than you could ever imagine. Besides, your father wanted you to possess me, to make you even stronger. I don't think he really gave his all during that match.*"

I furrow my brows and stew. There's no way Father would have let me win. I refuse to believe it. I take a deep breath and release the frustrations I feel. "We're getting off-topic. Get back to why and how you became a sword, please."

"*Oh, right, of course. Apologies for the tangent. It's been awhile since I've held a conversation,*" Hale makes a sound like he's clearing his throat. Does a piece of incorporeal soul even have a throat? I don't know, but perhaps the action is so mundane it's subconscious. "*As you know, I was once Adrithia's king, blessed by Tolliver. I ruled for several decades in peace. My son completed his trials and was blessed by Kai, the Water God. The line was secure, and the next generation was well on its way to being born. I never got to meet my grandchild, though, because a seer came to the castle to visit. He was well-known across Adrithia. One of the kingdom's last seers. At least of those that made themselves public and offered their services to others. He was a friend to my family, and gave us many visions that helped our people. He warned us of fire, drought, and disease. He was a trusted member of my royal entourage.*"

I nod for him to continue. I've heard before that there used to be more seers, and that they used to serve the ruling families, but it's still fascinating to hear a firsthand account.

*"I wasn't expecting anything dramatic when my friend came to visit, but he arrived in such a panic that I immediately received him. He told me he had a vision of the future. Of a time when the continent would come under a great threat, and one of my ancestors would be woefully unprepared to meet her destiny. If she failed to stop the war, then devastation would come to the continent. All peoples of the land, regardless of kingdom, would be enslaved. Astrellia would fall."*

*"I wanted to brush him off. My wife wanted me to ignore it, telling me it wasn't likely to come to pass, and it was our descendents problem, not ours. But my friend was insistent, hysterical, even. He kept telling me I could do something about it, that I was the only one who could help. I knew I had to take him seriously. I asked him how the Hells I could possibly help a future generation, and so over the next few months, we formulated a plan. A plan that required my death."*

*"My wife and son begged me not to go through with it, but how could I do nothing when the fate of the entire continent was on my shoulders? The knowledge was a burden too great to bear. It was an easy choice, in the end. Ending my life so the future could have a chance."*

He doesn't say this with pride or self-importance, but with resounding sadness. I ache for him, for his sacrifice.

*"With my powers, I constructed a forge. Tolliver must have known and believed in what I had planned, because he allowed me to mine the rarest and most precious raw metal from the Gods' Territory. When I melted it down, I poured my power into it. With each hammer strike, I imbued my will. My family gathered to say their farewells and watch as I forged my soul into the trove. The longsword, which you hold, and the twin daggers,*

*which were passed onto your sister, Elana. I finished the daggers first, and felt weak from using so much of my power. But, the greatest weapon was yet to come. I gave everything to this sword. My love for my family and my desire to protect the future sustained me until the final tempering. I felt my body die, and suddenly my consciousness was here, within this sword. I imagine two relatively equal pieces of me reside within the daggers, but I've never been able to rejoin them."*

He's silent, his story told. I don't know what to say. How can you thank someone for their sacrifice and apologize that they had to do it in the first place?

"Hale, I," I start to say sorry, then stop myself. If I'd given my life to help someone in the distant future, I wouldn't want someone to apologize to me for it. "Thank you. For what you gave up to face this evil alongside us."

*"Anyone would have done the same,"* he says, and I have to stop myself from arguing. Because, no, they wouldn't. Not everyone would give up what they have to help someone they've never met and potentially never will meet. In fact, very few would.

"The ancestor who needs your help, is that my sister?" I ask, remembering what he said about someone needing his help.

Hale hums. *"I believe it is. She certainly was unprepared to take the trials."*

I let out a noise of agreement. She should have been allowed to train alongside me. I'll never forgive my mother for purposely keeping her weak.

A strong wind hits us from the side and the dragon -the Maiden, I guess- flaps furiously to stay level. She rumbles deep in her chest. I feel the vibrations from where I sit. "I must land. I tire."

I risk a glance at the ground. A full moon illuminates the thick grasses of Melinor's savannah region. The dragon aims for a small lake, starlight reflecting off it like a beacon. She banks to the left, and I wrap one arm around Igraine to steady her.

She makes a startled sound as she wakes, grasping onto the spike in front of her. "Holy Gods. Where are we?"

"We just passed into Melinor. We're landing, hang on," I try to sound reassuring.

Our landing is less smooth than the takeoff. Igraine nearly topples from the Maiden's back, but I grab her at the last moment and keep her seated. When the dragon lands, I jump down and help Igraine to the ground.

The Maiden is breathing hard, her shimmering green scales moving quickly with her rapid breaths. Damn, I guess she did push herself too hard. I'm about to tell her to get some rest when her whole body shakes and shrinks. I gape as I stare at a woman in a dark green robe. Her alabaster skin shines in the moonlight. A curtain of long black hair frames her face and two striking, snake-like green eyes.

"You're a shifter," I say, dumbly, still gaping at her.

Something like humor dances across her features for a moment. "That I am."

"How...is that possible?" I ask. "I thought all the shifters were wiped out centuries ago."

A flicker of emotion darkens her face. "Most of us were. My brother and I have dedicated ourselves to serving the Gods, who in turn protect us. Which is why our existence has remained a secret for generations. Those who know of us are enchanted to never speak of us."

Elana must know about them. I wonder what her reaction was to meeting these mythical beings. "Why did you help us?"

"I already told you, I serve the Gods, and they requested I ferry you to the Summit." She unfastens her cloak, and sets down a large pack she must have been hiding beneath the cloak. I don't recall her carrying anything in her dragon form, but shifter abilities are not ones I understand, so I don't question it. I'd rather not risk her ire.

Instead, I busy myself by helping Igraine to the pond. She moves slowly, and I can tell every step brings her agony. She clenches her teeth and breathes through the pain.

After we clean her burns, we return to where the Maiden is fast asleep. She started a fire in our absence, and laid out some fresh fruit, bread, and various nuts. Even more surprising is the blanket she left out for each of us.

I rub my wrists, where the manacles used to be, and where scars remain. I try to stay awake to keep watch, but the temptation of sleep is too strong, and I fall into a restless slumber.

# Chapter Thirty-Eight

## Elana

"This is one of the best views in the entire city," Rayna says, standing atop the palace's white stone steps that lead down to the heart of Oraphia.

The Melinorian palace is unlike anything I've ever seen. Set in the center of the sandy desert, the capital city surrounds an expansive bright blue lake, which empties into the Dread Bay. The city, too, is beautiful, with light colored stone buildings, and unlike the rest of the desert, lush green foliage thrives here. I recognize crop trees such as date palms, apricots and figs, lining the streets.

Our trip took us eight days. Turns out traveling with a full company of Aaranorian guards slows you down. It wasn't terrible traveling alongside Rian's mother, but it was tense at times. Rian was more subdued than I've ever seen him, and his mother kept us on a strict schedule. There was no arguing with her. She was in charge of our party, and that was that.

Once we got into the heart of Melinor, we started traveling during the early mornings or the evenings after the sun went down. We rested at oases along the road, where there were small towns or groups of merchants set up with supplies. All life in the unforgiving desert revolved around water. In that, we were fortunate to be traveling with a monarch blessed by Kai.

The ever-shifting dunes were beautiful to behold, but they whipped up sandstorms in the blink of an eye. We got caught in one terrifying storm which required us to huddle together so Rian could encase our group in a shield of air, keeping the sand from burying us.

Then there were the mirages that had me constantly seeing sources of water when there were none.

Needless to say, I have never been happier to see the desert finally give way to this spectacular city.

"This is where my people held back the tides of the enemy centuries ago," Rayna says, staring at a marble statue depicting Queen Makeda, the warrior queen who reigned during the time when Melinor was attacked. "You really think the war from back then and the one now were led by the same...exiled goddess?"

Rayna is leading Aidan, Rian, and I on a tour of her city. At least, that was our excuse for getting out of the palace this morning so we could speak candidly. Today is the second day of the Summit, and all monarchs and their heirs are in attendance, except for the Hotharians.

Yesterday, Aidan, Rian, and I presented our findings from the Archives. Queen Nami validated our findings, but still remained skeptical about the goddess. To be honest, it's difficult for me to believe, too, but my gut tells me it's the truth, no matter how ludicrous it sounds.

"Well, I'm not completely convinced, but we haven't found anything that refutes it...yet," Rian says, staring up at the face of the statue. "Hey, did you ever notice that you kind of look like her?"

Rayna rolls her eyes. "Of course I look like her, you nitwit. She's my great great great great probably many more greats grandmother."

"Rayna, do you know anything about how your ancestors beat the armies?" I ask, ignoring Rian's antics.

She shakes her head, her braids swishing back and forth. "Not really. What we know is that our armies and the Asheeri warriors were able to beat them back with sheer force, but it wasn't easy. Many lives were lost, and by the time reinforcements arrived from the other kingdoms, almost all the Asheeri were wiped out, and we lost our queen and her crowned heir.

Rayna walks to a neighboring statue, depicting a fierce warrior on horseback. Her hair is braided much like Rayna's, and she holds a spear in one hand, and an elaborately carved horn in the other. There's a bow slung on her back and a quiver at her side.

"The Asheeri were our elite fighting force. They resided outside of Oraphia, in their own Keep, but were always loyal to the crown. I wanted to be one of them when I was a child, even going so far as to learn how to fight on horseback like them. When my parents told me that all the Asheeri warriors were dead, I cried for days. You know, there's a horn in our Great Hall that is said to have belonged to the last chieftess of the warrior clan. Legend says that when the horn is blown in great calamity, the Asheeri will rise again," Rayna says wistfully, before lowering her gaze and shrugging, "but it's only a story."

"Your Highnesses," a messenger races toward us, eyes focused on me, a rolled up parchment in his hands. He bows as he presents it to me, then rushes away as quickly as he came.

It's tied with a piece of leather cord and no formal wax seal. It could be from Tessa or Clarisse, if they found anything that would require secrecy. Maybe they've also sent news of Ceridwen. It was more difficult than I thought it would be to leave her. She tried to follow me out of the Archives after I said goodbye. Whatever magic that bound her there was the only thing that kept her from coming with us. Blinking away the sadness at leaving her, I quickly unroll the parchment and begin to read.

My stomach lurches with every hastily-scrawled sentence. My joy at reading my sister's words again is overshadowed by the immense sense of dread at her dire warning.

"Magpie, what's wrong?" Aidan asks, studying my shaking hands with a worried gaze.

I suck in a sharp breath and breathe out, composing myself enough to speak. "It's from my sister. We need to get back to the palace. Now. We need to convince your parents to evacuate the city and prepare for war."

I give Rayna the letter, and she reads it quickly, with every word her frown deepens. "Fuck. Let's go."

She hands off the parchment to Rian, who in turn gives it to Aidan as we run back to the palace.

*"Dear Elana,*

*I'm writing this to you, but my message is for the entire Summit. I only hope my letter makes it to you in time.*

*I am a prisoner traveling with a force of several thousand Hotharian soldiers, and a few hundred of the enemy we faced at the coast. They are led by Prince Calder Vernier and will be approaching from the south. King Skade is already on his way to the Summit, and with him travels a force of Hotharia's elite. A third army is sailing to the northern coast of Melinor, and plans to march south until they get to the city. They have more than a dozen ships. Skade's presence at the Summit will serve as a distraction so his armies can surround the city.*

*Their goal is to lay siege to Oraphia and force the kingdoms to surrender. Get the citizens out of the city. As quickly as you can.*

*I was able to send this message via a servant I befriended, and I trust you to verify the authenticity of my writing.*

*I promise you, I will escape. See you soon, sis.*

*Kick their asses for me,*

*Aislinn"*

I finish reading aloud with a quivering voice, then I present the parchment to Mother, who is on the verge of tears, showing emotion for the first time since we've reunited.

"She's alive," she whispers, holding the letter to her chest for a moment, closing her eyes, before passing it along to the other monarchs. Queen Desta, sitting to her left, lays a comforting hand on my mother's shoulder as she takes the letter, reads it, and passes it to her husband.

"We are sure this is legitimate?" King Edward asks, looking skeptically at the parchment as it makes its way around the group.

"Positive," I respond in a flat tone which hopefully demands no argument.

"I only question it because we have no evidence this is true. Skade is not here. There's no army at Oraphia's doorstep. She could have misheard these plans. Or maybe they were feeding her false information in hopes of sowing further discord," Edward presses, looking at each of the monarchs in turn.

Aidan glares at his father with malice. "It sounds to me like you're the only one sowing discord here, Father."

"I'm simply stating a fact, son." Edward gives a shrug, not concerned at all by Aidan's obvious disdain for him.

Mesfin ignores this outburst, and instead turns to a middle-aged woman with striking white hair, standing behind his throne. "Send our fastest riders to the northern coast, and ones to the east and south. Three in each direction. If armies are coming for us, we need to know about it."

She gives a quick nod and hurries off.

"Father, if we're to empty the city, where will the citizens go? I'd rather not put them in further danger by sending them out to the Dread Bay, or risk them going closer to Hotharia." Rayna's shoulders are tight, her features pinched in worry.

Mesfin steeples his fingers and rests his chin on them. "We'll send some to the cities along our southwest coast. Rayna, your siblings are at the academy in Zagran studying the arts of statecraft. They can help manage the refugees. Space will be an issue, however. None of those settlements can harbor this many refugees."

"Aaranor will gladly welcome your people," Nami speaks up, startling me. "We have plenty of space, and we've had excellent harvests the last several years. We can feed and shelter your people."

Mesfin dips his head, putting his fist to his chest in thanks. "Thank you, Nami. Melinor is in your debt."

We spend the next several hours making plans for evacuating the citizens. The city guard, much like the guards in Sandral, will escort them. The plan is to have most of Oraphia emptied by tomorrow afternoon. Mesfin also sent messengers to muster the armies of Melinor. Nami offers Aaranorian aid as well, but we all fear they won't arrive in time.

The day passes in a blur of preparations, focusing on protecting the citizens and those most vulnerable first.

That night, I lay in bed, tossing and turning. Memories of the last battle overwhelm my senses. I hear the screams, the clashing of swords. I smell the tang of the blood-soaked dirt in the healer's tent. I feel the twin daggers in my grip, my only protection as I made my way to the center of the carnage. I see Father, stabbed through the back and falling to his death. I taste the tears, hot on my cheeks.

I sit up in my bed, breathing hard, and wiping the wetness off my face. Knowing I'll never get to sleep now, I walk to the domed windowsill, where moonlight pours in. Two potted palm trees sit on either side, and there's a plush bench in between them. I sit on it and stare out at the oasis below.

Aislinn is alive. She's well enough to warn us of impending dangers. A weight has been lifted from my chest with this knowledge. I feel lighter than I have in weeks. But, there's also the leaden sensation of what's to come. The fight ahead of us.

After hours of debating, the monarchs decided not to leave Oraphia. We understand the risks, but no one wanted to abandon the grand city to the Hotharians and the invaders.

Deciding I've had enough of staring at the water, when I could be in it, I throw a sheer covering over my thin black knee-length nightgown and head down the stone steps to the water's edge.

The pool glows in the moonlight. There's no breeze, so the water perfectly reflects the moon and stars above. On our tour of the palace and the city earlier, Rayna told us that the oases maintain a comfortable temperature year-round, and we were welcome to swim in them. I dip a toe into the water, pleasantly surprised to find it warmer than the cool air. I scan the courtyard, making sure no one else is around before I let the shawl drop. My nightgown is modest, and will only weigh me down in the water. I pull the thin straps down my shoulders. It pools onto the stone at my feet, and I step out of it, walking into the pool.

I swear, water has healing properties, because as I wade into the deeper section, a sense of calm overwhelms me. My head tilts back and I allow myself to float. My unbound hair halos my head as I stare up at the night sky, reveling in the quiet.

Is Aislinn looking up at the sky somewhere? Did she keep her promise from the letter and free herself? Or is she still held captive? I sigh. That peaceful feeling didn't last long. I let my legs sink to the bottom of the pool and inhale deeply, filling my lungs before diving down into the water. My ears pop against the depth, but I stay there, enjoying the slight strain on my chest as I hold my breath.

When we were young, Aislinn and I used to see who could hold their breath longer. Ash almost always won, but never by long. Her being better than me at nearly everything was expected. It never bothered me. She was born for it, for the athletic stuff. I was born to be married off and forgotten. What strange, horrible turns our lives had taken.

The last of my air bubbles leave me and I kick off the rocky bottom of the oasis. My head breaks through the surface and I draw in several quick breaths, tilting back to look at the stars again.

"Elana," a panicked voice whispers from the shore.

I gasp and duck into the water up to my neck, wrapping my hands over my chest to cover my nakedness, spotting a person standing on the edge of the pool, breathing heavily. Aidan's golden eyes are wide, his mouth open, as if he had been shouting my name.

"Aidan." I don't know what else to say, so I say his name. He's dressed in an open silk robe, and a pair of what looks like silk shorts. Sweat beads on his chest, shining in the moonlight, leading to the chiseled planes of his stomach and lower.

My gaze returns to his in time to see him swallow hard, searching my face, then the area around us. Once he seems satisfied that there's not another soul nearby, he visibly relaxes, his tense shoulders dropping, his frown flattens. "I was worried. I saw you from my rooms. Your head was underwater, and I thought-," he trails off, and I have a feeling I know what he was thinking.

"You were remembering the trials? In the cave?" I ask, and he nods. I understand his worry. I think about that terrifying whirlpool every time I see water. But I refuse to let the fear stop me from doing something I enjoy.

Needing to wipe the concern from his face, I feel a sudden burst of confidence, dropping my arms and swimming to him. My wet hair plasters to my chest and down my back.

Aidan eyes me with rapt attention, drinking me in as if he's been wandering the desert dehydrated for days. "Won't you join me, degenerate?" I ask, holding my hand out to him.

His gaze darkens as the worry slowly vanishes, replaced by hunger. He shrugs the robe off in one smooth motion, then moves to step towards me. I hold up a hand, and the shadows swirl at his feet, preventing him from taking another step.

"Uh uh," I chastise mockingly, feeling bolder than ever before. "I'm not wearing anything, so neither can you."

Wicked delight sparks across his face as he smirks. "As you wish, my Queen. But perhaps it's time you show me what else your shadows can do?"

Oh. Gods. I bite my lower lip, then with half a thought expand a wall of shadows around us and the entire oasis. Then, I turn my full attention on Aidan, moving my eyes slowly down his body. My shadows move up his legs, trailing lightly across his skin, eliciting a low groan from him. When they get to the waistband of his shorts, I solidify the shadows into several hands, and in a movement smoother than I could do with my own hands, tug the shorts down over his muscular thighs.

I curl my index finger at him in a 'come here' gesture and he steps into the pool. He moves with predatory grace, all while keeping his gaze locked on mine until he stands directly in front of me.

"Thanks for joining me, Prince," I tease, longing to feel his soft hair between my fingers again.

"Your shadows didn't exactly give me much choice, Magpie," he replies. Then, something like confusion knots his dark brows together. "You're not still angry with me?"

I let out a long breath. "No," I say truthfully. I don't know when the switch happened, but it's time I acknowledge this chasm between us. The chasm I created. "I'm not. It was wrong of me to blame you for his death. I'm sorry, Aidan."

One of his warm hands cups my cheek. "Grief clouds even the sunniest days. I understand how devastating loss can be."

I give him a tentative smile, wondering if he's thinking of Nadia, or his friends he lost in the battle at Ocarin. He returns my smile with a small one of his own. Gods, I can't even describe how much I love seeing his half smile. Knowing there's no ill will between us anymore brings to life a little glimmer inside me.

Aidan's warm gaze turns mischievous, and he lunges for me, scooping me into his arms, one arm under my knees and the other holding my back. He cradles me to him for a moment before sinking us into the water until I'm floating, securely in his grasp. He turns in a circle, spinning me. I laugh and enjoy the weightless feeling, my hair dragging behind me. One of my arms rests on his back while the other glides through the pool.

"Gods, I love your hair. You should wear it loose more often," Aidan says quietly, watching my auburn tresses flow through the water.

I blink at him, surprised. "Really? To me, it feels like a nuisance, always getting tangled and never lying flat like my sister's."

"You're perfect, Magpie. I love every piece of you exactly the way you are."

I swallow, barely breathing, and I'm not sure if it's his words making me feel terrifying things, or the spinning, but I start to get dizzy, and a familiar ache builds within me.

He slows, then stops, our spinning, holding me close while searching my gaze. It's sweet and relaxing.

I don't want sweet and relaxing right now. I've had enough of waiting for him to make a move, so I readjust myself, wrapping my legs around his waist and wrapping my arms around his neck until I'm straddling him, keenly aware of our lack of clothing. His hardness rests near the apex of my thigh, sending a shiver of anticipation through me.

"If you don't want anything to happen tonight, Magpie, you're going to have to unhook those legs," Aidan groans as I wiggle my hips. The water around us starts steaming. The sight brings a smirk to my lips as I continue to tease him.

"But what if I want something to happen?" I ask, slowly grinding my hips against him.

He groans low in his throat, and I can tell he's holding himself back. "You're sure?" He growls into my neck as he kisses the soft skin there.

In answer, I lower myself onto him, letting out a soft moan when I'm fully seated. "Yes," I whisper, breathlessly. After a moment to adjust to his size, I roll my hips, taking him deeper, while Aidan takes the opportunity to kiss down the column of my throat, then lower. He teases my nipple with his tongue, biting down gently. I gasp at the raw heat that courses through me from the sensation. At the sound, Aidan finally unleashes himself. His hands grip my thighs as he slams into me. My fingers fist into his silky hair and I tug his head up to meet mine, claiming his lips with a fury.

This isn't sweet like our first time. Everything he gives, I demand more, greedily pushing both of us to the brink.

I fall over the edge, gasping and clutching his shoulders as I ride him through the waves of pleasure. Aidan bites my lower lip gently and groans into my mouth as he follows me into oblivion moments later.

Exhausted and satisfied, we sit together in the shallow part of the pool, staring up at the twinkling stars.

I wish my mind could turn off, but thoughts and questions still plague me. "Aidan, how come your mother hasn't seen anything about the siege? She saw the battle in Adrithia, and the one in Ocarin as well."

Aidan sighs. "I wondered that, too. When I questioned her on it, she told me that if she'd revealed anything before Aislinn's letter, Queen Nami would have assumed it was false information and convinced Mesfin to ignore it."

"So, how long did she know Aislinn would send a letter? How long did she know my sister was alive and held captive by Calder, who's probably torturing her as we speak?" I ask, anger filling me at Amira's apparent secret-keeping.

"I wish I knew." Aidan's voice is heavy, and he sounds tired. "She's always been like this. Not very forthcoming with what she sees, unless it's a dire situation. She says that knowing the future is a great burden, and it changes so often that it's not always worth telling. Maybe she saw a consequence of her telling us what she saw."

I bite my tongue against what I want to say, that she could have warned us about Aislinn being captured in the first place, or maybe even my father dying. She has no right to withhold these visions from us.

We sit in silence until I start fidgeting against Aidan's side, scratching an errant itch on my leg, then adjusting so I'm not sitting on a sharp rock, then finally giving up sitting altogether when I touch some slimy weeds in the water.

I pull on my nightgown from where I discarded it at the edge of the water, then throw on my shawl. When I turn around, Aidan's silk robe is on, and I almost mourn the sight of it. He's facing the oasis, arms crossed over his chest. Moonlight reflects the warm tones of his dark hair.

Stepping up behind him, I wrap my arms around his waist, burying my face in his back, breathing deep. He laughs and unhooks my arms, pulling me around to face him.

"I can tell your beautiful mind is racing, Magpie. Care to share what has you out here in the first place in the middle of the night?"

Suddenly, the weight of the last few weeks weighs heavily on me. The anxiety I feel for my sister, and knowing several armies are marching here as we speak, feels like too much.

"Aidan, I'm so fucking terrified. I can't do this again, this battle. I can't watch more people I care about die. I know I can't sit around and not fight, either, but Gods, I still have nightmares about that day," I say, tears hot as they train down my cheeks.

Aidan looks pained. He bends over, gently cradling my face with his hands, and kisses the tear tracks. "If you don't want to fight, no one will make you. If you want to stay in the palace and protect your mother and the others who can't fight, that's an honorable thing, Elana. No one will make you enter another bloody battlefield again. But, if you find the will, know that I will be there with you. Every step you take, I will guard your back. I will be your shield and your sword if you need it."

I stare up into his golden eyes, his face revealing more emotion than I've ever seen from him. "How do you do it? How do you find the strength to end people?"

His eyes shutter before he answers. "By killing, I ensure the safety of those close to me. I protect my family, my friends, my people, and my heart," he gaze practically burns into me, holding me captive.

"Your heart?" I question, barely breathing.

"You, Elana. You have my whole heart. It's been yours since the trials. Since that Gods-damned whirlpool when I almost watched you drown. Possibly even before that, when you stared down two enormous goddess cats, and insisted on crossing the rope bridge first. Everything you did drove me absolutely insane."

"You have my heart, too, Aidan. I'm sorry for the distance between us, and I'm sorry that I partially blamed you for my father's death. You saved me that day, and you've been saving me every day since. I would have fallen apart a thousand times if it weren't for you."

Aidan holds me, and I hold him, and everything is going to be alright with us, with the world, as long as we're together. Gods, I love him. With everything I am, I love him.

# CHAPTER THIRTY-NINE

## AISLINN

Never in all my life did I ever think I'd not only meet, but become allies with a shifter. I also never imagined talking to my sword, but that seems like the least crazy part of my situation. The Maiden wakes Igraine and I before dawn, telling us to prepare for another long day of flying. She quickly packs up our supplies, slinging the sack around her shoulder.

Igraine is in bad shape. She's pale, clammy, and weak. I wonder if an infection has started to take hold of her fire-ravaged body. Twice, I've caught the Maiden staring at her with concerned looks. Both times I've had to refrain from snapping at the shifter, reminding her that it's her fault Igraine is injured.

The Maiden offers to hunt fresh game for us since it's still before dawn and I can't see in the dark, unlike her. She disappears into the tall grass, moving as quietly as a serpent.

I sit in the grass next to a shivering half-conscious Igraine, wondering if Elana has received my letter, and if they've managed to evacuate the city.

*"I know you're worried about your family, Princess, but you should be practicing with your powers in every spare moment,"* a disembodied voice calls out to me.

"Good morning to you, too, Hale," I think back to him. The sun hasn't risen yet, and already my ancestor is intruding on my peace and quiet.

*"Why don't you try making something out of the dagger you took?"* Hale suggests, ignoring my obvious sarcasm.

I sigh and pull out the dagger I swiped from Calder. The metal feels good in my hands. It's high-quality, likely made by Skade. But it's too lavish for me. Bright blue stones adorn the grip, and it has an elaborate swirling pattern which reminds me of rolling ocean waves.

Reaching out mentally, I reach the energy, tethered within my core. I gently tug on it, and suddenly I'm connected with all the metal around me. The coolness of my swiped dagger, and the warmth at my hip, pulsing with life.

Hale's spirit hums his approval. *"You feel it, don't you, Aislinn? The connection with the metal all around us. In the ground, in people, and animals."*

I can feel it. The tangy element sings to me, and my power sings back. I'm suddenly desperate to hold it, and mold it to my will.

Pulling the dagger from my side, I hold it over the flickering flames of the fire. I command it to its liquid form, pulling the metal from the ornate hilt like I'm dragging my fingers through a pool of water. The gemstones drop into my waiting hand, and I pocket them.

The metal responds to my call, puddling in the air before me. I shift it to my will, shaping it into a new form, stretching and lengthening it, rounding it out, sharpening the tip and creating fine, feather-like fletchings. I slowly spin it, smoothing out the imperfections until its shape is without blemish. A sleek, silver arrow.

A gift for Rayna.

I jump to my feet as a rustling of the grass startles me out of my concentration. Firelight reflects off a pair of glowing green eyes as a sleek black fox appears carrying an antlered hare in its mouth.

"Maiden?" I question, pointing the tip of the arrow at the predator as it hovers around my shoulder height. The fox gently spits out the hare, then in a flash a woman stands in front of me once again, one brow raised in warning at the arrow.

Quickly snatching the arrow from the air, I stuff it into the empty sheath at my thigh, giving her a shrug.

The Maiden informs me she doesn't eat meat in her human form, so Igraine and I split the roasted hare as the sun rises.

Soon, I'm helping Igraine back onto the Maiden's large scaly back before climbing up myself.

"Maiden, where do your belongings go when you change form?" I ask, noting the pack she was wearing is nowhere to be seen on her dragon's body.

"My other form carries it with her. It's the same reason I still have clothes when I change from animal to human," she grumbles in her raspy voice. "I can make small changes to each form without switching bodies, but for vastly different forms, I pull a different body forward."

I consider this, confusion wrinkling my forehead. "But how does it work? You have more than one body, but they always stay with you?

"It is not for mere mortals to comprehend. This is the magic of Gods," she snarls back at me, effectively shutting me up.

———————✳———————

We battle a fierce wind most of the day as we soar through the sky. Well, the Maiden battles it. I shut my eyes against the blowing sand and keep a hand on Igraine to stop her from blowing right off the dragon's back.

The ground beneath us is a swirling mass of orange as sand rips across the landscape, reforming the shape of the dunes.

After flying for half the day through intense heat, and exhausting winds, the Maiden tires. She gradually loses altitude, battling the strong gusts which threaten to knock us sideways.

"We need to find cover so I can rest," she hisses, scanning the ground.

"On your left flank!" I shout, pointing down past her head to a rocky alcove, where several palm trees and spiky plants grow in a clump.

She dives for it, then turns into a gradual circle so we don't crash into the ground. She lands a distance away. Igraine tumbles off her side and I help her to the cover of the rock slabs that form a shallow cave. The Maiden flares her massive wings, blocking some of the wind and blowing sand as we make our way to the shelter.

"It's empty," the Maiden says through her gritted jaws. "I smell no other creatures here."

I give her a grateful nod as we hunker down out of the wind, spitting up gritty sand. The Maiden joins us a moment later, a woman again. She grabs a waterskin out of her pack and hands it to Igraine first.

We sate our thirst and share some preserved food the Maiden packed. There's nothing else to do here besides think of the upcoming battle. The anticipation of a fight makes my knees bounce. I wonder if I'll get to go toe-to-toe with Skade again, or if I'll get to fight this supposed goddess. Maybe I'll see the husk of Father's body again and finally bring him peace.

The power churns inside of me, ready to be wielded, shaped, and formed. Unfortunately there isn't much metal out here for me to practice on, but I do experiment with the arrow, reshaping and hardening it under Hale's instruction.

Beside me, the Maiden shifts, eyeing the arrow warily. I remember the stories Father told Elana and I as a child, ones where the shifters were all hunted down. I wonder if the Maiden lost any kin to those brutal hunts. Not wanting to upset the only person who can see us safely to Oraphia, I put the arrow away.

"Will you be joining us in the fight against the goddess' army and those traitor Hotharians?"

Igraine stirs out of her rest at this, whispering, "not all Hotharians are bad people. Many didn't want to participate in this war. Most of us common folk just want to live in peace."

I let out a long breath. "You're right, I'm sorry, Igraine."

"I will leave you at the gates of the palace, no further." The Maiden's voice is sharp, leaving no room for complaint. I do so anyway.

"So you won't fight with us?"

Her snake-like blazing green eyes narrow on me. "No. This is not my fight. My duty is to the Gods. My kind has seen so much battle that I have no taste for it." Her gaze slides over to Igraine, and regret shines brightly there.

I should let it go, but it's not in me to abandon a strategic advantage without a fight. "This is everyone's fight. Skade made it so when he allied with the exiled goddess."

"Who rules outside of the Gods' Territory is none of my concern. I keep the peace inside of their land, and nothing more."

Sighing, I let it drop for now. There's still time for me to convince her, afterall. I won't give up so easily when her involvement could secure our victory.

# CHAPTER FORTY

## ELANA

Sitting next to Aidan is going to be impossible today. I break my fast alongside my mother. Neither of us speaks much. I think the letter from Aislinn rattled her more than she wants to admit.

In the palace's great hall, I find my seat, thankful that Mother and I are the first ones to the meeting today.

Rayna and her parents walk in moments later, followed by Rian and his mother. Aidan and his parents are noticeably late, but when they walk in, I can't seem to take my eyes off him. I wring my hands in front of me, then drop them to my legs, then fold them together. I have to stop myself from launching at him and demanding he take me to the oasis again. Or perhaps this time we could finally make love on a real bed.

I chose a navy gown that hangs off my shoulders, and from the way Aidan drinks me in, I'd say it's appreciated. His eyes drag slowly, almost lazily, over my form, from my toes to my unbound hair, which falls in waves over my shoulders. A smile lifts one corner of his lips as he finally meets my eyes. A shiver passes through me at the intensity of his gaze.

"Set out another chair, Mesfin. There's going to be one more joining us today," Amira says, pinching the bridge of her nose and wincing as if trying to clear a headache.

Mesfin shoots her a raised brow, but turns in his seat and nods at the woman standing behind him, who disappears into the hallway, returning a short time later carrying a chair. She sets it between Nami and Desta.

We start the day with an update on evacuations. About half of the city has left, according to Mesfin. Dozens of wagons full of provisions are being sent along with the evacuees, so they don't deplete the stockpiles of the cities where they seek refuge.

Nami sent word to Sareena to open their food reserves to help provide for those temporarily displaced. Mother offers to send some Adrithian provisions as well to ease the burden on Aaranor. It's harvest time back home, so luckily there will be plenty to go around. Life won't be pleasant for the refugees, but they'll survive, which is better than the potential consequences of remaining in Oraphia.

I wring my fingers together under the table until a hand grazes my outer thigh. Somehow, I manage not to jump out of my seat in shock. Aidan's warm hand takes mine, and just like that, my fidgeting stops.

Moments later, the double doors to the hall fly open, and an imposing man marches in. Everyone falls silent, and immediately the energy in the room turns hostile. I recognize Calder in his blonde hair, his sharp nose, and cold, bright blue eyes. King Skade isn't especially tall, but his broad shoulders make up for his lack of height. His gold crown matches the rest of his lavish outfit perfectly. He's a man who wears his importance and demands respect before it's earned. He sweeps across the grand hall, his gold cloak billowing out behind him.

"Friends, apologies for my tardiness," he says

"You are not our friend," my mother spits. It's a rare show of emotion, and it takes me off-guard. Discreetly, I move closer to her, ready to intervene if Skade attacks. I don't know that shadows could stop metal, but they do wonders against the human body, and he's still made of flesh and bone.

He sits in a flourish, smiling and nodding at each person around the table until he gets to my mother.

"Dear Maris, I am so sorry for your loss, and I do apologize for being unable to make it to your husband's funeral. That skirmish at the coast was such a terrible misunderstanding that I hope to clear up today," his voice oozes charm, but his eyes are as unfeeling as ice.

"I have come to negotiate a surrender," he says as he takes the empty seat next to Queen Nami.

"Excellent. I'm so glad you came to your senses," King Mesfin says, gesturing for Skade to continue. "What are your terms?"

Skade shakes his head. "Oh no, dear, I'm afraid you've misunderstood me. I'm not here to surrender on behalf of Hotharia, no. I'm here to accept your negotiation. Your city is currently being besieged. I have an army to your north and an army to your east. Soon, there will be an army to your south. There's nowhere to go, old friend."

Silence falls in the wake of his declaration as the monarchs take in his words.

"You think it's that easy to waltz in here and declare war against four united kingdoms?" Nami hisses.

"Well, yes, that's exactly what I did." Skade repeats, slowly, enunciating each word as though he's speaking to a child.

I don't need to look at Nami to know she's seething. The air around us plummets in temperature, and a fine mist hangs over our heads.

"I believe what Nami is wondering is if you're feeling all right, Skade?" Amira asks dryly, an eyebrow raised in his direction.

"Quite well, Amira. I understand your skepticism, but you'll want to hear my offer before making any rash decisions."

"You should know, Skade, that the only offer we will accept is you being brought to justice for your part in Devon's death," Mother says, with a coolness in her tone that matches the temperature in the room.

"As I said, a terrible misunderstanding. You see, we sit here on the precipice of the future," Skade rocks forward, animatedly. "We have the opportunity to serve a true visionary. One who will bring our continent everlasting peace and prosperity."

"You speak as if we didn't have peace before, as if you weren't the one to break that peace," Mother snaps, drilling her fingernails on the table loudly.

"Our peace was tenuous at best. And we were kept apart from the elemental Gods that lord over us. The Empress offers freedom from their tyrannical rule. She does not come here as a God. She's here as an equal, as mortal as any of us. And she has promised us a true peace, not ruled by Gods who choose to give favor to only a select few. All her subjects will be equal."

I cast a glance to my right, catching Aidan's eye, seeing my own disgust reflected back at me.

"Why is she not here to offer this herself?" Amira questions.

Skade lets out a little chuckle. "So eager to meet the one who will lead us out of darkness? Well, not to worry, she will be here soon enough."

"How soon?" Mesfin's voice takes on a dangerous tone. A general preparing for battle.

"Hmm, a fortnight, maybe? Two? I'm not entirely sure. But, she's on her way, with the rest of her army. Thirty, maybe forty thousand strong."

My heart stutters. That's not possible. How could a force that large cross the sea? How many ships would they have built? I do my best to conceal my horror. There's a chance Skade is lying to us. Maybe he thinks if we're scared enough we'll surrender.

I try to think of Adrithia's army, and how many we could muster after the battle at the coast, where we suffered heavy losses. The rest of our army is maybe eight, nine thousand strong. I don't know about the other kingdoms. And now's not exactly time to ask.

"We have the power of the Gods on our side. Each one of us blessed with their power is worth more than a thousand mortal soldiers," Mesfin says, openly glaring at Skade.

Skade sighs and waves his hand in a dismissive gesture. "Inferior gods. I'll admit, the power of Tolliver is quite strong, but the power of the Empress is unmatched."

There's only so much the elements can do against overwhelming numbers and their damned cursed weapons, especially if I'm unable to use my light.

"Our kingdoms have beaten back the forces of this so-called Empress before, Skade. What makes you think this time will be any different?" Nami questions, leaning away from him like he's contagious.

"Last time you weren't fighting against me. Tell me, what wars have you heard about where the winning side fought without metal? You can't raise any weapons against me and you know it. How do you anticipate winning? With your fists?" Skade laughs, but the sound is without any humor.

He continues before anyone else has a chance to speak. "If you refuse to surrender to reason, then perhaps some extra motivation is necessary. Aislinn Sable is currently my captive. I will return her, safe and sound, in exchange for your complete and total surrender."

Rage boils through me in a flash. The room darkens, shadows lengthening, as I try to breathe through my fury. From across the table, I see

Rayna's fists shake from where she holds a water goblet. The ground gives an unhappy rumble.

"You dare threaten a princess of Adrithia?" My mother seethes.

"That's exactly what I'm doing. But, honestly, you should be happy, Maris. She's not the important one. Your heir is sitting right next to you. If anything, I'm doing you a favor. I heard Aislinn is incredibly difficult to marry off. Think of it as I'm helping you get rid of that little problem."

In a blink, Mother's delicate wine glass goes flying across the table, shattering as it makes contact with Skade's adorned doublet. "Your children may be expendable to you, bastard, but mine are not."

Skade looks down at his ruined shirt and sighs. "What a waste of a perfectly fine coat. I suppose I'll have to punish your daughter for your actions later."

Beside me, Mother goes as white as a bed sheet. Swirls of darkness wrap around me, coiling like serpents about to strike. Aidan grips my hand under the table, offering a reassuring squeeze. I know he'll back me up if I decide to make a move. My chest aches from all the words I hold back.

"You have until dawn tomorrow to give me an answer." Skade pushes his chair back, standing with an air of assuredness and striding to the door with exaggerated swagger.

My delicate control snaps, and my shadows egg me on, pushing me up out of my seat before my brain can catch up. My mouth is opening before I'm fully aware of what I'm going to say. "Hey, Skade."

He turns around, halfway out the door, one blonde eyebrow raised in question.

"I have your answer," I say, and my fingers curl into fists of their own volition. The darkness waits excitedly, twitching in anticipation. "Go fuck yourself you bastard."

Two massive hands made of solidified shadows slam the double doors in Skade's face. All I hear is his bellow of fury as the darkness reshapes into a shield, blocking the doors from opening.

Aidan, Rayna, and Rian are at my side in an instant, each of them poised to strike in case he uses his power to blast through them. We hold our breath for a few tense moments, waiting for his reaction.

Slowly, my heartbeat returns to its rhythmic pace, while the darkness dissipates, sensing the danger is past. I blow out a long breath, counting to eight. The heirs around me relax as well, and we return to our seats.

I expect my mother to be furious with me, but she surprises me by giving me an approving nod.

"Well, I suppose he has his answer now," she says dryly. "Elana, I don't suppose next time you feel inclined to curse at the bastard who has an army at the doorstep, you could run it by the rest of us first?"

My cheeks heat and I look at the table, but there's no heat to her words, only a sparkle of mirth.

Mesfin clears his throat. "Now would be an ideal time to discuss battle strategies. Amira, have you *seen* anything that might be of use to us?"

Amira grins as she says, "I thought you'd never ask."

# CHAPTER FORTY-ONE

## ELANA

Dawn breaks, and suddenly I'm thrust back into my nightmares. I'm standing in Rayna's chamber, fully armored in sleek black leather, sans any metal except for my twin daggers, which sit securely at my sides. I refuse to be parted from them, even if I am to fight Skade. My heart hammers in my chest, and I can barely breathe enough air.

"Deep breaths, Elana," Rayna says, laying a comforting hand on my shoulder. I showed up at her door before dawn, after Aidan left my rooms to prepare his guards. "Remember what Amira said, we have the safest task."

I shoot her a raised brow. If it was really that safe we wouldn't have all four heirs and a dozen guards escorting us.

"Here, I made something for you," Rayna pulls me over to a tall dressing curtain. I stare at the angled pieces of stone bound with fabric sitting on a small table.

"Thank you," I say tentatively, unsure how I should react.

She lets out a breathy laugh. "It's armor. It's something Skade can't manipulate, because it's made of rock."

I tap my fingers against the hard material, noting its smoothness and light weight. "Is this ceramic?"

"Kind of," Rayna hums. "It's more durable than ceramic. I've been experimenting with using this as armor since we returned from Adrithia. It was too brittle at first, then too heavy. But, with Aidan's help firing it, I think it's finally ready. Against metal, especially Skade's, it can only take one hit. It'll crack and be useless after that, so you'll still have to be careful."

One hit could mean all the difference. I smile at her. "It's perfect, Rayna. Thank you. Would you help me put it on?"

She smiles back and instructs me to raise my arms. She ties a few pieces to my chest and back, then places two curved guards on my shoulders.

"I didn't have time to make them pretty to match your leather."

I let out a strangled laugh and run my fingers over the plates. They're formed almost perfectly to my body, but still allow me to move freely. "Rayna, these are incredible. I couldn't care less how it looks."

"I made sets for Aidan and Rian, and our parents, too." She bites her lip in worry.

Before I get a chance to respond, there's a knock on the door, and Rayna calls out to enter. One of her guards stands beside Matteo. Something in my chest eases upon seeing him. Since arriving in Oraphia, he has allowed me more freedom, probably knowing I'm surrounded by the most powerful allies across Astrellia.

"Your Highnesses, it's time," Rayna's guard says.

Rayna and I exchange a long look, then a hug, before we move to the door. The four of us heirs are escorting the last citizens out of Oraphia. With the blockade of enemy forces falling into place overnight, the people who couldn't get out in time became stranded. Rayna, Rian, Aidan, and I are in charge of getting them out.

Rayna and I make our way to the palace gates, where several hundred people gather with their horses, wagons, livestock, and even some pets. Rian and Aidan are already there waiting for us. I immediately appreciate how good Aidan looks in his ceramic armor.

Rayna clears her throat and we all turn to her expectantly.

"Is everyone here?" She calls to the group of Melinorian city guards who will be escorting the group the entire way to Aaranor.

"Yes, Your Highness. These are the only remaining citizens."

A group of guards spent the last day going door-to-door in the city, ensuring everyone evacuated and no one was left behind. Some weren't happy about it, and had to be dragged out and forced to leave, but upon hearing war was imminent most went willingly.

"And the palace staff?"

He shakes his head. "Some are leaving, but others have elected to stay behind with your family."

Rayna sighs and nods. I can't imagine it was an easy choice for the staff. In many cases, they probably chose to separate from their families to remain behind and continue their work at the palace.

Over the past several days, Rayna has been working tirelessly, nearly exhausting herself, to construct tunnels under the city and on the far side of the blockade. We're going to lead them through the tunnels and to the other side safely.

Rayna waves a hand at the ground in front of us, and the ground splits to reveal the entrance to a tunnel. It's wide enough to fit at least two wagons side-by-side, and slopes gradually into an inky darkness.

Aidan steps to the tunnel's entrance, and two lines of fire light down the length of the walls. It's a heatless fire, bright, but not too overwhelming to scare the horses.

"I'll travel at the front of the group. The other heirs will spread out to ensure your safety. Please try to stay close together as much as possible so I can reinforce the walls around us. We'll be on the other side within several hours," Raya addresses the citizens, before confidently walking into the tunnel. Citizens start filing in after her. I count at least fifty before trailing after her, giving Aidan a nod as I pass him. Rian will enter after me, and then Aidan will guard the rear of the group.

Inside the vast tunnel, the flickering of Aidan's fire illuminates the path well, and I can almost see to the front of the pack, where Rayna strides, checking and reinforcing the walls. Once the entrance levels out and I leave the natural sunlight behind, I'm struck by the pungent smell of damp ground.

I make small talk with the people as we go, reassuring them, and talking about how stunning Numai is, since that's where they'll settle for the time being. I do my best to keep my spirits high, to ask them questions about themselves and their families. Keeping them talking will hopefully keep their minds off their current situation. When a sound like a battering ram rings out above us, shaking the ground, and children start to cry, I tell them about my friend Ceridwen, and how I befriended the Archive wyrm. The children are especially interested in that tale.

Echoes of stone crumbling on the surface has my heart lurching even as I explain what retractable teeth means to an especially inquisitive youngster.

I wonder what's going on above us, and if the noise was Skade's forces launching an attack on the city walls. A lead weight has found its way into my stomach, and there it sits while I worry about the battle waging in our absence.

What if they need us? What if they're being overrun? What if Mother's in danger? I practically begged her to leave last night when we were discussing the day's plans during the Summit. Mother told me I was insane to ask her to leave while I stayed behind. But, of the two of us, I can wield darkness, and she can't. If not for Amira insisting that she would be safe, I would have tied her down to a horse's saddle and made her guards escort her out.

Screams come from somewhere near the back of the group, and little pebbles fall from the ceiling. I clench my fists, but continue moving, encouraging those around me to stay calm. I have to trust Aidan or Rian to take care of whatever is happening back there. I can't leave these people. My shadows itch to be used, to protect the people in my care.

I let out a steady breath and launch into a loud, animated retelling of my time on the mountain. Several people scoot closer to me, their fearful eyes glowing in the flickering orange light, eagerly listening as I describe each trial in detail, only leaving out the parts between Aidan and I, and the instances when Calder tried to kill me. And, of course, withholding any knowledge about the shifter siblings.

After several hours of me rattling on, my throat becomes hoarse. I drink deeply from my waterskin and try to think of my next topic, when a commotion starts near the front and works its way back to us. We come to a slow stop. Whispers from the front are relayed back, and it sounds as though we made it.

Several agonizing moments go by. Everyone around me creeps forward, peering over heads, standing on tiptoes, before we're finally moving again. Every step we take is an incline now, and the tunnel gets a little brighter with every footfall.

Finally, the scent of grass and fresh air hits my nose and my shoulders loosen with my relief. Rayna stands at the entrance of the tunnel, smiling at her people, waving them through the exit, and wishing them luck on their journey ahead. Some stop to say things to her, others bow or curtsy, but all of them smile.

It's a slow process, and it's another hour before we see the end of the line, and Aidan trailing the last of the citizens. There's an elderly woman leaning into him. She wears a traveling cloak, worn sandals, and a wide smile. Striking silver hair haloes her head. When they get to the exit, he helps her onto a nearby wagon and wishes her luck. Her smile is mostly gums, and she holds his hand for a few moments longer than necessary.

"Eh, looks like you found yourself a backup option?" Rian waggles his eyebrows at him suggestively. "You know, for when Elana finds out what an asshole you are and leaves you for me."

I sputter, my cheeks heating to the point I almost press my cool water-skin to them. "E-excuse me?"

Aidan rolls his eyes and shoves Rian playfully. "Joke's on you, Yarrow. She already knows I'm an asshole. The woman twisted her ankle when we heard that explosion. I couldn't exactly leave her behind. Rayna would have killed me."

Rayna gives him a hard look. "Gods damned right I would have. Now, what do you say we head back before there's nothing to head back to?"

We all exchange determined glances. I know we're all thinking about the sounds of battle. The plan was to avoid engaging with Hotharia's and the Empress' forces until they engaged with us. Which can only mean they began their assault.

Rayna turns around, closing and concealing the tunnel behind us with loose dirt. We don't want enemy forces to discover it and make their way to the palace gates. A large rock platform rises from the floor, similar to the ones Rayna created during the trials.

"Everyone, get on."

We don't argue, hopping onto the platform and crouching down. We move quickly back the way we came, not stopping for anything. I close my eyes and lean into Aidan, who wraps an arm around me. None of us know what kind of situation we're about to walk back into.

When we near the end of the tunnel, the walls rattle with whatever's happening above. We race up the incline, and Rayna motions for us to stay back while she checks to make sure the entrance isn't overrun.

She slides a head-sized portion of rock away, and peeks through.

"Oh Gods," she whispers, then opens a door-sized hole in the exit. "We need to go. Hurry!"

I nearly trip when I see what's got her in a panic. As far as I can see surrounding the palace, there's a towering wall of ice. On the other side of the wall, explosions sound, shaking shards of ice free to smash on the stone ground. Even the elaborate metal gate, framed with beautiful tan colored stone, is completely encased in ice.

Amira warned us last evening that this would likely happen. That the enemies would break through the city walls and surround the palace.

Nami rushes down the steps of the main palace entrance towards us.

"Rayna!" She calls, looking more fierce than I've ever seen her in her battle gear, and a naginata similar to Rian's strapped to her back. "I could use your help."

"What can I do?"

"I need your help reinforcing the ice. If I hollow out my wall, can you fill it with hard stone?"

"Yes," Rayna nods.

Nami takes a moment to catch her breath. "Okay, let's get started. Start with the gate. That's where they've been hitting the hardest."

"Mother, what happened? How did they get into the city? The walls were supposed to hold for longer," Rian says as we follow the two, working together to shore up the walls.

Nami gives her son a worrying glance. "Skade happened, like Amira predicted, he just happened a lot sooner than we anticipated. That bastard tore holes in the battlements like they were parchment, and then they used catapults to turn them to rubble. Their army forced their way into the city and overwhelmed us. The Melinorian army fought hard, but soon the attacks were coming from all sides. We retreated back to the palace with the wounded and what remains of our forces."

"Wounded?" I ask, anxiety ripping through me as I think of who could be injured, and how severely. I don't have many healing supplies in my rooms, but I could still be of some use.

"Mostly those from the front lines. I don't believe any Adrithian guards were there, nor were any of the guards from the other kingdoms. The Melinorian healers are seeing to them now, and I assure you, they're quite capable," Nami explains, as if sensing my worry.

I relax slightly. We're halfway around the perimeter of the palace. Rayna breathes hard. She used her powers for most of the day, keeping the tunnel open, keeping us safe, and now she's straining herself yet again.

Suddenly, a metallic clanging sound interrupts my thoughts, followed by a whoosh.

"Watch out!" Nami shouts, raising her hands above her head as the shadow of a wagon-sized shape comes into view, soaring over the wall, heading in our direction. Nami and Rian react first, the queen sending a tower of ice to intercept the rock heading for us, while Rian summons a burst of air, knocking us down the length of the perimeter. I lose my footing in the wind and tumble into Aidan. His arms wrap around me protectively as he fights to keep his balance until we're well out of the path of danger.

The ice shatters under the force of the barreling stone, and shards rain down on us. The rock drops to the ground, shattering the beautiful stone of the palace yard and sending dirt and bits of rubble in every direction. It carves a short path of destruction before it comes to a rumbling halt.

Rayna's hand covers her mouth, tears welling in her eyes. "I couldn't stop it."

Nami gives her a sad look. "It's not your fault, Rayna. They've been catapulting metal instead of rock to do more damage."

Rayna's stunned look turns into one of anguish, then fury. "Let's build it higher."

Nami gives her a nod and the two of them get back to it, reinforcing the wall even higher and thicker than it was before. Rayna works with focus and determination, showing no signs of exhaustion. I'm struck with an admiration for her. She reminds me of Aislinn.

By the time we return to the palace gates, both of them are sweaty, but are doing their best to hide their tiredness. Luckily, we don't encounter more catapults. We head straight to the throne room, where several guards heft open the defenses to let us pass. Wooden spikes adorn the doors, and large logs brace the inside of every entry and window.

I've never seen a palace under attack before, but I wasn't expecting such...chaos. Men and women scatter, some belting out orders, the rest rushing to obey. A few people are huddled in corners heads down. I don't know if they're praying or hiding.

A commander of the Melinorian army approaches us, wearing full armor. "The war council is meeting in the lesser hall."

We're led to the back of the throne room, past Parisa and Novan who give Aidan an indiscernible look, past Matteo, who dips his head towards me with a relieved expression, and out a smaller set of doors to a large chamber overlooking one of the oases. Rayna's father sits on a tall-backed chair, and the rest of the monarchs sit around him. Aidan's father is notably absent, but I haven't seen him since the last meeting yesterday. Several generals sit around the stone slab table.

Mother sits next to Amira, studying wooden pegs on what appears to be a map of the city.

"Rayna!" Mesfin's booming voice startles me. "Please tell me at least one of us had luck today. Did the last of the citizens make it past the blockade?"

"Yes, Father, they're safe," Rayna says, moving up to the table to peer down at the map. "So they've taken the city?"

"We were overwhelmed, as Amira predicted. Their catapults and Skade's power are great," Mesfin despairs.

"Sound the horn. We must call for the Asheeri warriors," Rayna says.

Mesfin lets out a long sigh. "Rayna, the Asheeri are all dead. They were annihilated during the last war. You know this."

"But the legend says they'll return again-,"

"The legend is a children's tale, not a prophecy. Even if a few warriors still live today, you would have them rush into the city and be slaughtered again. The Asheeri cannot help us now." Mesfin tries to soften his words, but they land like a blow to Rayna. She balls her fists at her sides and stares at the table, giving no response.

A shadow passing by the window catches my attention. Dark wings blot out the sun; they're so massive. Was that a flash of green scales? I blink, staring harder, but the shadow is now gone.

"We have to flee the city," Nami's voice breaks through the uncomfortable silence.

"Absolutely not," Mesfin argues. "We will not abandon Oraphia to ruin. This is our family's ancestral seat. For more than 900 years this palace has stood and withstood the test of time, even through the last war. We cannot leave it to be destroyed by those traitor Hotharians."

"We cannot hold them back indefinitely, and we can't beat them in battle." Nami pinches the bridge of her nose. "I am sorry, Mesfin. It's not an easy choice to leave one's home. But as long as your family survives, so does the heart of Melinor. You can rebuild."

"It's not just a home, it's a history of our people, Nami."

"Your people are safe, but they need a ruler," Mother interjects. "They need you and your daughter to lead them out of these dark times. Don't make the same mistake as my husband. Don't martyr yourself."

I shift uncomfortably on my feet until Aidan's hand finds mine. My breaths come a little easier with the contact.

Desta leans over in her seat and rests a reassuring hand on her husband's arm. He meets her gaze and a silent conversation passes between them. Their expressions hold a lifetime of love and devotion. I squeeze Aidan's hand tighter.

Mesfin pushes his chair back as he stands. He stares at his daughter. "We will lead everyone out through the tunnels. All of the remaining palace staff, the rest of our army, the wounded, all the heirs and monarchs. Go southwest to Aaranor-,"

There's a sudden commotion outside of the doors leading to the throne room. Guards inside rush to the doors, ready to defend. They slam open, and my heart nearly stops.

"You're not running," a familiar voice interrupts, and I blink away the shock at what I see, who I see, filling the doorway. "Not while I'm here."

# CHAPTER FORTY-TWO

## AISLINN

"You're sure you won't help us defend Melinor?" I ask as the Maiden makes a circle over the city. Even I have to admit, the situation looks dire. The city's walls are mostly destroyed, and the Goddess' forces surround the palace in a great black mass. The sheer number of enemies at the gates churns my stomach. It's difficult to tell from the height, but the palace appears to have been fortified by a wall of ice. My sister and the other monarchs must be inside. We seem to have arrived just in time.

Spotting the catapults, I know it won't be long before the palace is overrun, too. I need to get down there, immediately.

"I've told you, this is not my fight," the Maiden responds in her raspy dragon voice. "I will drop you off inside the walls, but then I must return home."

I let out a sigh, but I can't exactly blame her. She helped Igraine and I get all this way. We've been flying nonstop since we left our camp in southern Melinor. My entire body aches from sitting for so long, but I push my discomfort to the back of my mind. There will be time to rest when the enemy is destroyed, and the city saved.

*"The other Tolliver-blessed one is down there."* Hale says, and my sword pulses at my hip with what feels like fury.

I reach out with my power and feel a surge of energy by one of the catapults near the gate. There he is.

"Hold tight, I'll have to make a quick descent."

Grabbing hold of Igraine's shirt with one hand, and the Maiden's back spike with my other, I can't stop the feeling of my stomach flipping as we plummet. She flares her wings and banks sharply as we approach, landing hard on the cream-colored stone of the palace grounds. The courtyard shatters against her weight, sending bits flying.

The Maiden mutters something about small spaces as I slide off her back, reaching to assist Igraine, who's barely conscious. She lets out a moan of pain, but limps at my side as I back away from the shifter.

"Thank you for getting us here, Maiden. I hope we meet again," I give her a grateful dip of my head.

"You're welcome. Now, get that young one inside and to a healer before I eat you whole," she rasps.

I back up, helping Igraine take a few steps as we watch the Maiden shake her entire body, from her head to her whip-like tail, and launch into the sky. Arrows and spears fly for her as she gains height, but I use my power to bat them away harmlessly. Her dark green scales glitter in the mid-afternoon sun as she disappears into the clouds.

"Let's get you inside," I say, taking one of Igraine's arms around my shoulder and moving slowly to the front gate.

I pound on the wooden door until a small section slides open. An arrow with a shiny metal head protrudes from it. Using my power, I rip the arrow from the bow string.

"I am Aislinn Sable, Princess of Adrithia. I've come to aid my sister and the kingdom of Melinor. Let us inside," I demand, using all the authority I've been taught throughout my life.

The man slams the small window closed. I wait several long moments before my temper flares. I bang on the door several times with my fist. "I'm here to see Queen Elana Sable of Adrithia. I have an injured person with me. Open this Gods-damned door!"

"*Maybe you should've said 'please','*" Hale chuckles to himself, and I roll my eyes.

The door opens again, and another person peers through, but before he can speak, his eyes go wide and his mouth drops open in horror as he looks at something beyond me.

"*Incoming!*" Hale's warning shouts in my mind, and then I feel it.

I spin around, already bracing. A massive spiked metal sphere sails over the fortified ice wall and right for the front steps of the palace.

"Oh fuck," I have time to whisper, holding up my hands. My power reaches out, connecting with the metal, but the force of it throws me back a few steps into the door.

"*Hold it, Aislinn. It's yours to control,*" I feel Hale's voice like a comforting hand on my shoulder.

Gods, this thing is fucking heavy. My arms strain as I push back against its trajectory, stopping it midair. I'm shaking all over from the sudden use of my power. I allow myself one quick breath before I shove, pushing the metal back, sending it soaring in the direction it came from.

The ground rumbles as it hits...something...on the other side of the wall. I exhale in relief and exchange a raised brow with a pallid Igraine, then nearly tumble backwards as the doors open.

"Your Highness!" Strong arms steady me, and I turn to find Matteo standing there with half a host of Adrithian guards, making me wonder if they forced the doors open themselves. I recognize many of the wide-eyed faces staring at me.

I give him a smile. "I told you to call me Aislinn, Captain."

"Old habits," he gives a shrug and a boyish grin.

"Matteo, my companion needs to see a healer. Are there any here? My sister, perhaps?"

Matteo takes one look at Igraine and his face pinches with concern. He waves two guards over. "Take her to the healers and see that she gets immediate care."

Igraine takes a hesitant step to my side, as if she just realized she's in a room with a bunch of people who aren't too fond of Hotharians.

"Igraine, it's alright. They'll take care of you. I promise to check in on you as soon as I can."

She gives me an uncertain look, but allows herself to be led away.

"She saved my life," I call after them, "make sure they save hers."

The three of them make their way to a side door. I turn my attention to the rest of the room, searching for my sister, Mother, Rayna, anyone. "Where is the queen?" I ask.

"Your mother is in a meeting with the rulers of Melinor, Aaranor, and Ocarin. They're this way," he takes a step back and motions.

"My mother?" I ask. "No, I mean my sister."

Matteo lets out a groan before clearing his throat. "Apologies, Aislinn, it's not really my place to explain. You'll want to speak to your family about that."

Catching the meaning between his words, I'm guessing I'll have to kill Duke Lyons when I return home. Whatever happened has his name written all over it.

We make our way through the crowded throne room, where people scatter, preparing defenses. It's chaos.

As we approach a set of wooden doors at the far end, I catch the tail end of a conversation, "we will lead everyone out through the tunnels. All of the remaining palace staff, the rest of our army, the wounded, all the heirs and monarchs...,"

Oh Hells no. There's no way they're turning tail and abandoning their capital city. The guards stationed on either side of the door attempt to stop me, but with half a thought they're pinned to the walls by their heavy armor. They try to shout at me to halt, but I brush past them as if they're nothing more than a cobweb.

I shove open the door with both hands. "You're not running. Not while I'm here."

The first person I see is my sister. She stands from her seat, mouth wide, and face blanched, but otherwise appearing healthy. A knot loosens in my neck that I never realized was there.

"Aislinn," my mother whispers, a sob choking her voice. My eyes find hers next. Tears fill her eyes upon seeing me. She does a full-body sweep in that way of hers. Usually reserved for making harsh judgements, I'm shocked to see nothing but relief lining her features.

Elana abandons all courtly decorum and races to me. I open my arms and she crashes into me. She knocks me back a half step and I laugh. It feels as though the pieces of the world have realigned. The hug lasts one moment before Mother is there, and all three of us are embracing.

"You're safe," Mother whispers, her arms around both of us.

"I'm safe," I say to reassure her, although I can barely believe it myself.

"*The daggers*," Hale whispers, but not to me. "*Reunited, at last.*"

When we pull away, my gaze next seeks out Rayna's. I find her on the opposite side of the table, smiling gently, eyes bright. Gods, she looks gorgeous, framed in the afternoon sunlight from the window behind her. I long to go to her, but first we need to drive away the enemy at the gates.

It's at this precise moment I become wholly aware of my disheveled appearance. My clothes hang off me, hardly fitting due to my recent weight loss. My tunic is torn and caked with mud and dried blood, and my hair has been tied back in a messy braid that's been whipped around on the back of a dragon for several days. I can't even imagine how I must smell. Shit, maybe I should have begged the Maiden to drop me off in the lake before bringing me here.

I exhale a breath, pushing the unhelpful self-conscious thoughts from my mind. "Calder is leading another army this way from the south. He kept me prisoner among his forces until I broke free days ago. They were traveling through the Gods' Territory when they were attacked by some...friends of the Gods."

The shifter's magic prevents me from revealing them, but Elana's face alights in recognition, and I catch Mesfin and Nami exchange a knowing look.

"Anyone that can't fight, like your staff and the wounded, needs to get into boats," I say earnestly.

Mesfin startles. "You want us to send our people through the Dread Bay?"

"Yes." I hope the sternness in my tone doesn't come across as aggressive, but we don't have much time left before the enemy figures out a way inside the fortifications. "Queen Nami and Prince Rian can go with them. They'll use their power to shift the winds and tides."

There's a pause as everyone considers this idea.

"We can get your people to Numai," Rian speaks up from across the room, without waiting for approval from his mother, who surprisingly gives a solemn nod in agreement.

"What about the rest of us?" Aidan crosses his hands over his chest. "I'm not running from Hotharia."

"We fight," I shrug. "Until we drive them back. Which we will, now that I'm here."

Aidan gives me a raised brow. "You want to send away two of our Gods-blessed fighters, and you still think we can win?"

"I know we can."

A saccharine smile lifts the corners of my mouth. I do love the opportunity to be dramatic.

With hardly a thought, every weapon in the room lifts to the ceiling. I'm impressed that most of them have traded in their metal weapons for wooden ones, but still, several respond to my call. A sword, a dozen arrows, Rian's naginata, even Elana's twin daggers rise far above our heads. I make them spin, dancing midair, twirling around like a deadly cyclone. Then I slowly bring them down, returning them to their wielders. Elana's daggers hover in front of her slack-jawed face, waiting for her to grab them.

"You were blessed by Tolliver?" Mother asks, gripping my arm firmly.

"Yes," I say. "When I was in the Gods' Territory."

Once again, my gaze finds Rayna's. Her expression is one of wonder and pride. I give her a wink.

"This is good," Rayna says, moving from her spot at the table, approaching me. Determination sharpens her features. The hard set of her lips, the slight narrowing of her eyes. "With your power, we can reclaim Oraphia."

I give a short, decisive nod.

"You should also know what it is we're fighting against," I start, about to launch into a condensed version of everything I learned during my time as a captive and from Tolliver.

"We know we're fighting a goddess who calls herself an Empress," Elana says, surprising me. I wonder how they learned that.

"You know she's a creator goddess named Maenia?"

Elana blinks several times, exchanging a look with Aidan. "A creator goddess?"

"According to Tolliver, she created the elemental Gods. That's why they can't destroy her, because she created them."

"And the twin goddesses?" Elana asks, biting her lower lip in concentration.

"No, she didn't create them. I believe they're siblings. At least, that's what I think Tolliver meant," I say, trying to remember his exact words in that moment when my mind was occupied by everything else happening.

Mesfin pushes his chair back. "Did you learn anything that will help us stop her?"

I shake my head. "Tolliver wasn't exactly in the mood to answer questions, but he did mention every elemental power would be needed."

"Mother, did you *see* anything that could help us in this battle?" Aidan asks Queen Amira, who's been quieter than I've ever seen her. She's typically the one leading discussions and negotiations.

Ocarin's queen taps her fingers on the table, staring out the window. "Even with Princess Aislinn's return, the battle will be difficult. The outcome has changed a dozen times in the last day. We must prepare for anything, and that includes fleeing. Mesfin, you must be ready to abandon your home should it come to that. She is correct about sending those who cannot fight away. I have seen clearly that endeavor ends well."

"There are few ships left in the harbor, and we'll have to fight our way there. The harbor is just outside the palace grounds. Rayna, can you create a tunnel there?" Mesfin turns to his daughter, hopefully.

Rayna furrows her brow in concentration, but hesitantly shakes her head. "I won't know where to create the exit. I'd run the risk of tunneling right into the lake."

"We could extend the ice and rock wall to provide some cover?" Nami suggests. "But, we'd need to keep Skade away while we do that."

"Sounds like you need a distraction," I say, cracking my neck. "I know exactly what to do."

# Chapter Forty-Three

## Elana

My sister's wonderful distraction plan involves her taunting death. Of course it does. We just got her back, and she's already flinging herself at the most dangerous thing possible. Mother nearly exhausted herself trying to convince her to be careful. I gave up before I even tried. There's no talking Aislinn out of anything she's set her mind to.

Now Aislinn, Mother, and I are alone in the war room. We've been filling each other in on our journeys as quickly as possible. Ash looked ready to march off to Adrithia to give Duke Lyons a piece of her mind when Mother told her why I haven't been crowned yet. And I was shocked into silence when my sister recounted how Aric helped her survive.

Everyone else has rushed off to go help the wounded prepare for the journey by sea. Oraphia sits on the banks of an expansive river, which is fed by a massive lake. The river flows westward through the desert, where it eventually becomes the Dread Bay, a terrifying stretch of water known for shipwrecks due to unpredictable tides, fast-moving currents, and the many sharp rocks and islands off the coast. But, with Rian and Nami's powers, it should be a breeze for them to navigate safely.

"Mother, you need to be on that ship with Rian and Nami," Aislinn insists. "We can't have our focus be divided worrying if you're safe."

"Aislinn, I'm not some helpless damsel. You know I've had training-,"

"Basic training," she interjects. "This won't be an easy fight. I'm not even sure I want Elana in the battle, but she's got her powers, her daggers, and Aidan and I to protect her."

I give her a glare. "I'm not going anywhere, not without you. Not again."

She smiles back at me. "I know, and I won't ask you to. We need those shadows of yours."

Mother sighs, putting her hands on her hips, digging in for a long argument. "I will not be running away from the battle like some coward while my daughters fight for Astrellia.

"Mother, I will say this only once. Either you put yourself on that ship, or I'll put you there," Aislinn's tone takes on a dangerous quality, one that tells me she means business.

Our mother recognizes the tone, too, because she narrows her eyes, and digs her heels in. Gods, if this turns into a battle between their wills we'll be here all day. I glance between them as they stare each other down with nearly identical eyes.

Before this gets out of hand, I sigh and step in. "You are our queen, but you're also our mother, and we've already lost one parent. We can't lose another. Plus, you'll be needed in Aaranor to help the people of Melinor receive supplies. And you'll be closer to Adrithia in case anything happens. You're better at negotiating than either of us, and the displaced people of Melinor will need an advocate until Rayna and her family can get there."

"Desta is staying here. As should I."

Aislinn shakes her head. "Queen Desta has trained as a warrior since she was a child. She's an accomplished fighter and an asset to the forces."

"Mother, please. Go with the others. Ash is right that we'll only worry about you."

Her shoulders drop as the fight goes out of her. "How do you think I'll feel? The last time my family went off to war, my husband never returned, and we laid to rest an empty coffin."

Ash reels back as if she's been punched. I swallow hard, remembering what it was like to witness it. I can't imagine how Mother must have felt. She didn't get the chance to say goodbye.

"I will go," she relents at last, "but you will look out for each other. If things start to turn against our favor, you will get yourselves out of danger. I don't care who you have to leave behind. That is an order from your queen. Our family can't take more loss."

"Yes, Mother," I say, and Aislinn nods her agreement.

"All right, I'll go pack my things," she says, but Aislinn's hand reaches out, stopping her in her tracks.

"Wait. Before you go, I think Elana and I are owed an explanation."

Mother's eyebrows rise as she waits for Aislinn's request.

Ash gives me a look, swallowing, and if I didn't know better, I'd say she was nervous. "Tolliver told me that I was a true born Sable, but also that I wasn't the firstborn. How is that possible?"

"Aislinn, not now-," Mother starts, but Ash cuts her off.

"We deserve the truth."

At this, our mother looks pained. Her shoulders rise and fall with shallow breaths. She turns and grabs our hands. Her eyes are glossy, with what looks like tears. I almost fall to the floor in shock.

"You're right. I have been keeping a secret from you both," she says, "I should have told you much, much sooner, but I was afraid of how it would affect our relationship."

Aislinn and I exchange glances. "What is it?" My sister, the braver of us, asks.

"On the night you were born, Aislinn, I didn't just give birth to you," she grips our hands tightly, breathing rapidly. "The first baby I had was small and sickly. The healer, Clarisse, took her away quickly. She was so pale and cold, I never thought I would see her again. I didn't even get to hold her before she was whisked away. Clarisse thought it would be best in case she didn't survive. I was so exhausted by the time I brought you into the world, Aislinn. You came into this world a fighter. Large, pink, and healthy. You were so strong."

She takes a few shuddering breaths, closing her eyes. "They refused to let me see my firstborn, saying she was frail and it wouldn't do me any good to get attached. I wept for her, even as I held you, Aislinn. When the King arrived to meet his firstborn, I didn't know what else to do, so I introduced you as his heir. He was overjoyed. I didn't want to ruin his joy, so I never mentioned the baby I thought I lost. It was a few days later when Clarisse brought my firstborn child to me, to allow me to say my goodbyes. She was still so frail, no one thought she'd make it."

Tears, actual tears run down our mother's face. She doesn't wipe them away, only grasps our hands harder.

"My firstborn was raised in the shadows, kept alive in secret by Clarisse. It would have been the worst kind of offense for a king to lose his firstborn due to weakness, so the healers kept her a secret, to spare him that insult. She hardly grew her first year of life, and we thought there was no way she would survive. But she did."

Mother hiccups a sob and continues. I feel numb. I know what she's about to say. I think a part of me has always known it.

"About a year after giving birth, I experienced a stillbirth. My maids and I decided it was the perfect cover to introduce my tiny firstborn as a second child. She was small enough to pass as an infant," her tearful eyes lock onto mine, and warm tears roll down my own cheeks. "Once I brought you into the light, you started to shine, Elana. You grew and developed like a healthy child. No one suspected that you were actually older than your sister."

Aislinn drops our mother's hand and turns towards me. "You are the rightful heir. You're the firstborn." There are tears in her blue eyes, but a proud smile plays on her lips.

Aislinn is my twin. A smile stretches across my lips. I've always known, deep down, that our bond was more than most sisters. She's always been my other half.

"Why keep up the ruse?" I ask, "Why think you could fool the Gods?"

"I wanted to protect you. You were older, yes, but you were never as strong or healthy as Aislinn. Plus, it would have been the ultimate shame for your father if the ruse was discovered. At least when the phoenix chose you, it seemed like their divine intervention rather than our deception."

Her words sting me. Thinking that I've always been that much weaker than Aislinn hurts, even when I know it's true.

Aislinn laughs suddenly. It's not a joyous sound, but a harsh one. "Elana isn't the weak one. She's stronger than I could ever be, mother. And I'm sorry you never saw that. She's the bravest person I've ever known. She rose to the challenge of being heir, even when she had no training. She went through with the trials, even when offered a way to get out of them. She's the best of us all."

My eyes sting as I look at her. Aislinn possesses physical strength I can never compare to. But perhaps we were blessed with different kinds of strength.

My sister, no, my twin looks at me with pride.

I shake my head at her, tears pooling in my eyes as I attempt to blink them away. I pull her into a tight hug, squeezing hard. She hugs back with as much intensity. "Love you, twin."

Evening hours start to fall when preparations are complete. The wounded are loaded into carts, and those who can't fight are packed and ready to depart. Rayna and Nami are well-rested, and will begin their task of extending the fortifications once Aislinn, Mesfin, Amira, and the majority of the remaining army begin their distraction.

Twilight bleeds into the world. The darkness comes alive around me, as if it anticipates the fight to come.

Mere hours after our family has been reunited, Aislinn says an emotional goodbye to our mother, then bids farewell to Rian and Queen Nami.

Ash walks with one of the wagons, and I see a girl with bright orange hair resting on a pile of hay. That must be Igraine, the companion she filled me in on briefly. When Ash asked if I had my powers back, it almost broke my heart to see her face fall when she realized I'd be unable to help the girl. The healers of Melinor are capable, and when she makes it to Clarisse, there will be no one more skilled, but it'll be a long journey until then.

Amira will send us a signal via one of her fire messages when it's time for us to move.

Rayna and Aislinn break away from the crowd, sharing a hug that lasts several moments too long to be considered friendly. I understand their hesitancy to make their relationship known, since Aidan and I haven't even announced our courtship formally yet.

A pang of longing for a boring, war-free life hits me, and I hope Aidan and I will have that chance someday. I imagine a world where we rule our kingdoms together, splitting our time between them, or maybe even building a new home right on the border. The biggest battle we'd face is what family name we give our children. We could take trips to Aaranor to visit Ceridwen at the Archives, and travel to Melinor, where Aislinn would live with Rayna.

A peaceful existence is all I want.

"Elana, are you ready?" Aidan asks, slipping his warm hand into mine. I turn to him, drinking in his half smile and his golden eyes. What I wouldn't give to take Rayna's tunnel and disappear with him somewhere away from this nightmare.

Instead, I give him a nod and follow him to a small gate in the rear. Parisa, Novan, and a small force of Ocarin guards wait there while Matteo and half the Adrithian guards went with Aislinn to the main gate to help provide the distraction. Once the ships safely make it down river, we'll join our main fighting force.

"Everyone knows their assigned task?" Rayna asks, shaking her hands in front of her.

I give a nod. I'm on defense, keeping the enemies away from our most vulnerable. Aidan and Rian are on offense, incinerating those who get in the way of the walls expanding. Rayna and Nami are, of course, on fortifications. Once we load up the ships, I'll cloak them in shadows until they're out of catapult and crossbow range. Then Rayna, Aidan, and I will rejoin the main battle and drive the enemies out of the city.

The plan is simple. I try not to think of the million ways it could all go to complete an utter shit.

# CHAPTER FORTY-FOUR

## AISLINN



**M**y power takes hold of the gate. It's encased in ice, which shatters with half a thought.

*"Remember, Aislinn, you have a limited supply of energy which your power feeds off of. And that takes time to replenish, so try to pace yourself,"* Hale cautions.

*"You must know me well enough by now to know that I don't pace anything,"* I respond.

The gate flies outward, shattering the ice to little shards which rains down upon the unsuspecting enemy army. I hold my hands out wide, grabbing hold of all the metal that I can feel on the other side of the wall, lifting them up high above the heads of the wielders. Most of the metal feels wrong, like it's been tainted, but it responds to me regardless. Screams erupt and are abruptly cut off as the blades and other weapons are turned upon their wielders.

Hale heaves a heavy sigh. *"Why do I even bother?"*

*"An excellent question."*

I move outside the gate, flanked by Amira and Mesfin. Fire erupts from Amira's hand, clearing a path for us, and Mesfin whips up a wicked wind, blowing the fire into a violent cyclone. Those that are in the way  turn to ash almost instantly.

The lines start to break. I see Hotharians, with their elaborate golden armor, among the ranks that drop their weapons and run, pushing through the hordes of the Empress' unfeeling soldiers.

I try not to attack them when I can help it. I remember what Igraine said about most Hotharians wanting peace, and only going to war because their king commanded it. So when I steal blades and toss them back into the enemy, I aim for the soldiers in black armor.

I'm practically drunk on this power. If there's a limit to what I can do with this ability, I'm not finding it here. I rip through their soldiers, stealing weapons and using shields like battering rams. With a single thought, I shred through line after line of soldiers. Gods, this power feels amazing. Unstoppable, even.

Fire bursts again to my left, and a gust of wind intensifies the flames, sending the inferno into the enemy's flank. Mesfin shouts an order, and our forces explode out of the gates with a battle-cry. They crash into the shattering lines of enemies, pushing them back. Matteo and the Adrithian guards who didn't leave to protect Mother flank my sides. Their presence is comforting.

*"Incoming!"* Hale shouts, and I feel it again. Another metal ball heading for our forces. Took them long enough to get the trajectory right. This time I'm ready. I catch it midair, only taking one step back this time, and reverse its course, sending the deadly ball straight into the catapult that launched it.

A group of enemy soldiers in front make a push forward, driving their spears into our charging line. I rip the spears from their hands and bring them down a few rows back. Their line buckles, and our warriors break through.

"I think we have their attention now!" I shout to Amira, from where she's fighting on my left, as I send another metal chunk back into the catapult it was fired from.

She gives me a mirthless grin. "I think you might be right." She raises one of her hands, and a single flame breathes to life, flapping its wings and taking off to the opposite side of the castle.

"*Go*," I think. "*Get the people to safety, sister.*"

We continue to fight in a deadly dance, and time passes in a blur. I fall into the rhythm of the battle, cutting down those who stand before me, and reinforcing the soldiers who fight alongside me when needed.

When I feel a small portion of my power drain, I switch to my sword, wielding it with speed and precision. Blood splatters my face and my borrowed Melinorian armor, but there's no time to stop and wipe it off.

The sun dips below the horizon, casting the scene around me in shadows. There's no moon, so the sky will soon be as dark as pitch. I use my power to rip an axe free from an attacker's hand and send it into a deadly spin, using it to cut down another dozen or so enemies. Again, I'm hit with that feeling of wrongness. It doesn't hurt to wield their weapons, but it churns my stomach and makes me want to gag.

"Hale, why do their weapons feel wrong?" I ask my ancestor as I swing my sword in a wide arc, taking out two enemies who try to get in close with shortswords.

"*It's unlike anything I've encountered before. Somehow the metal has been infused with a kind of poison. It feels dangerous, Aislinn. Be careful.*"

Taking his advice to heart, I swiftly dispatch the next line heading in my direction. I take a moment to evaluate my surroundings. Our force has successfully reclaimed...the road in front of the gates. That's it. Their army is dense, making our progress slower than I'd hoped.

Someone with a pure metal sword swings at me from my right and I turn, catching the blade with my power as they start to arc down. I meet the startled gaze of a Melinorian warrior, who, when he sees my face, drops the sword and stumbles back a step.

"A-apologies, Your Highness. I didn't realize it was you," he bows low, and I stop an arrow that races for his back. He may be an idiot, but he doesn't deserve to die for it.

I let out an aggravated sigh. "It's fine, soldier, but for now, go help any wounded. You clearly need to rest your eyes before you go attacking any more of our allies."

He nods his head and rushes away, going to the side of an injured woman nearby.

"*It's getting a little difficult to see friend from foe,*" Hale grumbles.

"You don't say."

I hold out my hand and halt the approaching men in their full suits of armor while I scan the battlefield for Amira. She should be covering the left flank, which I note with surprise, has already made it across the road and is beating the enemy back behind the first row of buildings. I can't abandon the center column, but it's getting too difficult to see.

Hale clears his throat. "*Remember, Aislinn, you can manipulate all the properties of metal. If you need to tell her something, send a message.*"

"I don't exactly have a piece of parchment or quill with me," I snap back, picking up a group of charging soldiers by their metal armor and tossing them back into their own allies.

"*Did I tell you to use a quill and ink? Come on, Sable, you must think quicker than this if you want to survive this battle. Carve your request onto a piece of metal.*" Hale has the utter nerve to sound annoyed. He's literally a voice with no body, and he has the audacity to be annoyed.

I suppress my retort and pick up a shield from a deceased enemy, then use the tip of the arrow I forged for Rayna to carve my request into the metal. Searching the darkness for the blasts of fire, I send it soaring in Amira's direction.

Moments later, the streets around the palace are aglow in flickering light. Flames hover above our heads, illuminating our forces and the enemy's in orange, yellow, and red light.

When I see how far the Empress' army still extends, I almost wish we'd been kept in the dark.

# CHAPTER FORTY-FIVE

## ELANA

A blazing orange wyvern streaks across the sky above us, leaving behind a trail of embers, which fall to the ground like snowflakes, burning bright in the setting sunlight. It's a beautiful sight that churns my stomach and sets my heart into a frantic rhythm. It's time.

"Are you two ready?" Nami asks Aidan and Rian who nod from the head of our group, ready to launch the assault.

"Elana, are you ready?" She asks me next.

"Yes," I reply, gripping my twin daggers and feeling the shadows coiling at my feet.

"You don't even need to ask. Let's do this," Rayna says before Nami gets the chance to ask her.

Rayna raises her hands, and the ground starts to shake violently. I have to bend at the knees to keep my balance. I can't see what's happening, but I can hear it. As we discussed earlier, two rock walls are rising from the ground, providing us with a clear path forward to the river once her and Nami drop the wall in front of us.

The rumbling stops, and the temperature around us plummets as Nami fortifies the walls with a thick layer of ice. Meanwhile, the section of battlements in front of us collapses down into the sandy soil beneath our feet.

Dozens of startled enemy forces panic. The smart ones, clad in gold, take in the heirs and monarch in front of them and try to run away, while the stone-faced soldiers, likely from Tyne, start to rush us.

Aidan and Rian decimate the first lines with an intense wave of fire, fueled by Rian's wind. They don't stand a chance. It's an effective strategy, one that was suggested by Mesfin and Amira. I have no doubt they're deploying the same tactic on the other side of the palace.

The stench of burning bodies hits me for a brief moment, and I gag and nearly vomit before a breeze mercifully blows the scent away.

Aidan charges forward, burning everything in his path. One catapult ended up inside our fortifications, and he races to take it out before it can fire upon us.

The enemy struggles to load the bucket quickly, and by the time they manage it, Aidan's upon them, and it's already over.

Rian draws his naginata from his back, swinging in terrifying arcs, taking out handfuls of the Empress' soldiers at a time. I know he's trying to conserve most of his power for the trip through the Dread Bay. Both he and his mother will need to be well-rested in order to safely see the ships through the bay.

"Elana, heads up!" Rayna warns me as she fortifies the wall against a hit from an outside catapult.

Four soldiers broke through past Aidan and Rian, and sprint for me, weapons drawn. My shadows lunge, capturing three of the men with tendrils like snakes, holding them fast.

The fourth man leaps to evade my coiled darkness. I stumble back to try and put more distance between us. My daggers pulse in my hands reassuringly, urging me to hold my ground. The man swings, and I grip tight as the daggers move of their own accord, parrying the man's sword and slicing deep into his thigh. He pushes forward, unaffected by the pain that would cause most people to pause. His black eyes reflect nothing as he stabs forward. My daggers pull me to the side to evade the strike, then slash past his guard, and open up his side. The man finally staggers, reeling from the loss of blood. The dagger in my left hand presses the advantage, stabbing forward, ending the man's life with a slash to the throat.

Blood pours from him and I make a startled noise as some of it splashes on me. I stare at my dripping daggers and swallow back the bile. I tell myself that he had to die. In order to protect the people at my back, I had to end his life.

Blowing out a cleansing breath, I open my eyes and find the three men I'd trapped in my shadows struggling, trying to pull the tendrils of darkness away. A lump catches in my throat. Once again I think of the palace staff and injured soldiers, and my mother. I will end three more lives to ensure they're safe. The darkness wraps around their heads and twists sharply, snapping their necks.

Shadows fall away from their limp bodies, and I carefully step around them, forcing myself to look away. I don't want their faces haunting me.

Rayna clears the rubble and the bodies, most of them nothing more than piles of ash, so the wagons and carriages can move unhindered to the docks. Our progress is steady, if not slow at times. Twice more I have to defend the injured from attackers. My mother and the Adrithian guards are near the rear alongside Parisa, Novan, and the rest of the Ocarin guards.

We're nearly to the docks when a piercing whine has me whipping around. A spiked metal ball soars over the wall. I instantly raise a barrier of solidified shadow, but the metal's impact shatters it. The ball slams into a wagon full of injured Melinorian soldiers. I cover my mouth from the gasp and run to try and help any survivors.

The wagon lies in pieces. The horses pulling it are uninjured, but spooked. It looks like their tethers snapped upon impact. The ball hit the center of the wagon and rolled over it, stopping when it hit the ice-coated wall.

I already know there are no survivors. Smears of blood and scraps of clothing litter the ground. I refuse to look closer, because I know if I do, I'll see the remains of people who were on their way to safety, people who couldn't defend themselves. If only I could have stopped it, if only my shadows were strong enough. Dizziness threatens to overwhelm me, but I grit my teeth. I'm a healer, Gods damn it. I can handle a little gore.

"Keep moving," I shout, waving the next wagon forward, around the carnage. "We have to keep going."

As much as I want to inspect every bit of the carriage to make sure no one survived, we can't waste the time getting to the ships. There are more lives to think about than the half dozen that were on this wagon.

I task a few guards with moving the debris out of the way and keep the line moving, then sprint back to the front of the procession of the injured. Rayna checks in with me as I approach. "What happened?"

"Catapult, over the wall," I say between catching my breath, "hit a wagon."

"Any survivors?"

I shake my head, and her face crumples. My heart breaks for her, for this loss of her people.

Aidan suddenly appears. His tawny skin is damp with sweat and flecked with splatters of blood. His eyes find mine, and roams over me from head to toe, inspecting me for any injury. He pauses on the sight of my bloody daggers, but his shoulders relax when he finds no wounds on me.

"The way is clear," he declares.

Nami, Rian, and several experienced sailors get to the ships first, preparing them for the journey. Aidan, Rayna, and I focus on helping the injured off the wagons and onboard. Healers scatter around with supplies, checking wounds and replacing bandages as needed. I spot a curly halo of bright orange hair and move to help Igraine onto the ship.

"You must be Elana," Igraine says, and I nod as I put one arm around her to steady her as she walks. "Princess Aislinn talked about you a lot. She worried about you."

I give her a sad smile. "I heard what you did for my sister, and how you helped her. Thank you for that. You kept her alive, at great risk to yourself. I owe you everything."

She huffs a humorless, pain-filled laugh. "I did what anyone would do, seeing a princess of the continent in such conditions. Please know, Your Highness, that the common folk of Hotharia only want peace. So many sons, brothers, husbands have been conscripted against their will into this war. The king's loyalists stole our men from their fields, their homes, their shops and academies for this senseless fight."

I grip her harder, disturbed by this news. What could I say to her, though? We're at war, and we can't just stop fighting them. "I am sorry for the tyranny of your king, and once we defeat him I'll do my best to ensure the innocents who were forced into battle are freed."

She lets out a contented sigh as I help her sit on a bench onboard the larger of the two ships. Here, she will be safest alongside my mother and Rian. I stare down at her angry, welting burns. Gods, she must be in so much pain. I desperately wish I could heal her. Reaching inside, I feel for the light, a hidden shard, a kernel, anywhere, but it feels as empty as ever.

Instead, I take her hand in mine, and provide as much comfort as I can in those few moments. "Safe travels to Aaranor, Igraine."

Another cart arrives at the edge of the docks, and I release her hand to help the newest wave of injured onboard.

We work as quickly as possible, loading people and supplies onto the two ships. After what feels like hours later, the last wagon is before us. Novan helps an elderly man onto the ship, while Aidan assists a wounded soldier. Then it's time to say our goodbyes.

Mother embraces for several long moments. When she pulls away, her eyes are glassy. "Stay safe, Elana."

I give her a wobbly smile of my own. "I will, Mother. Love you."

"And I love you." Her gaze catches on someone at my back. "Protect my daughter, Prince."

"I swear she will be safe," Aidan says, then surprises me by bowing low to my mother.

I must be dead, because she does something equally surprising; she places her fist over her heart and dips her head. Then she spins on her heels and climbs aboard the ship, leaving me staring after her, mouth agape like a fish.

Long arms wrap around my side, tugging me to a tall, lean form. "Elana, you promise you'll give them Hells for me, won't you?"

I smack his arms until he releases me. "Of course I will, Rian."

Aidan grumbles from my side. "You know we're in the middle of a battle, right?"

Rian gives me a meaningful look. "I am available, in case you get tired of grump here."

When I give him a rude gesture involving a single finger, his grin widens and he ruffles my hair like I'm a toddler. "Save that energy for the enemy."

Sighing heavily to cover up my answering smile, I put my hands on my hips. "I hope you have a safe trip. Get everyone to Aaranor safely."

"You can count on us. And don't worry, I'll say hello to Ceridwen for you."

"Thank you," I say, smiling as I think of my scaly friend.

Rian boards the ship and takes his place next to his mother. Her and I exchange nods, and then with no further delay, the planks are raised and Rian fills the sails with wind.

My mother and I watch each other as the ship starts down the river.

I suck in a deep breath and summon shadows around the ships, cloaking them in darkness as they sail silently towards the sea. Our little group stays on the docks until the ships are well out of firing range of catapults.

"Safe travels, Mother," I whisper.

A hand grips my own, and I relax for one moment into Aidan's side, breathing in his cedar scent now mixed with tangy blood and sweat.

"We need to rejoin the fighting," Rayna says, though her voice is gentle.

I turn around, facing her, Parisa, and Novan. The dozen or so Ocarin guards are scattered behind them. I'm startled to find everyone staring at me. Even Aidan, whose hand is intertwined with mine, looks down at me, as if waiting for my approval.

Unsure what else to do, I square my shoulders and withdraw one of my daggers. "Okay, let's go."

# CHAPTER FORTY-SIX

## AISLINN

"*T*o your right," Hale warns, "*remember to conserve your power.*"

I don't respond, focusing on meeting the man to my right's poisoned axe. He's tall, so tall I only come up to his shoulders, but his height gives him a greater reach with his axe. As he swings, he positions his shield to protect himself. A decent fighter, then. This will be fun. Pure black eyes reflect no malice, no determination as he attacks. He's simply going through the motions, driven by whatever that goddess has done to his mind.

I take a quick step back to avoid the swing, then slash up as his hand pulls back. The hand gripping the axe drops to the ground. The man doesn't falter for one moment, he merely lashes out with his shield, trying to use brute strength to overwhelm me. I dance out of the way, and go low, cutting under his guard and severing one leg. He topples and one last swing of my sword removes his head.

Blowing out a sharp breath, I scan the area. We've made it fully across the road, and are working our way to Oraphia's city square. Piles of deceased enemies lie in our wake.

Flashes of fire still burst to my left, although they aren't as regular as they were at first. Gusts of wind batter the forces on my right, but weaker than before. The army with us is still fighting. We haven't lost many, but their slower movements and sloppy footwork suggests they're tiring. Even Matteo and the rest of the Adrithian guards who fight near me are moving sluggishly. If this keeps up much longer, we're bound to start losing warriors.

"We need to end this quickly. Our army is tiring," I say to Hale. "Any ideas?"

*"Entice that bastard Skade out of hiding. If we can end their leader, it could shake the lines enough for us to get an edge,"* Hale suggests.

"Okay, and how do we get his attention?" I wonder aloud.

*"Hmmm,"* his voice is contemplative. *"You see that catapult straight ahead?"*

I narrow my eyes, focusing through the flickering light of Amira's fire. I see the dark outline of a trebuchet a few blocks ahead. They're bringing it into position to fire.

"Oh yes, I see it. And I think I know where you're going with this," I say with a feline smile.

*"You're going to need backup."*

Scanning the soldiers around me, I meet Matteo's confused eyes.

"Captain!" I shout at him, and he rushes over. I point straight ahead. "Gather the Adrithians. We're going to make a push for that catapult. Once there, we'll secure it and fire on the enemy. I'm going to try to lure Skade out of hiding so we can end this."

Matteo nods, but I don't miss the way his eyes bulge slightly. "We're with you, Aislinn."

We take a few precious moments to rally everyone. More than a dozen in total. Our small force hasn't lost anyone, I'm relieved to see. All these faces are familiar to me.

"I'll lead the charge," I tell them. "Once we're there, I'll need you to watch my back."

Nodding, weapons thumping, and fists over hearts is the only reply I get. It's the only one I need.

I inform the leader of the Melinorian forces fighting alongside us of my plan, letting her know to continue the push forward but stay out of the way of Skade, if he appears.

I turn and sprint for the lines, throwing back the enemies by their armor, pinning them to the buildings to open a path forward for us. I rip their weapons from their hands, sending them scattering.

We make it to the catapult, and work together to turn it around. I rely on my fellow Adrithians to keep the enemies off my back while I load up the bucket.

"*Scraps of metal will spread out and damage a wider range,*" Hale advises as I start to load one of the large metal boulders.

"Good idea," I respond, abandoning my plan and instead summon the enemy's discarded weapons and shields.

"What idea?" Matteo's face appears on the other side of the bucket, where he's securing the rope at the base of the catapult.

Since there's not enough time to tell him that I'm speaking to my long-dead ancestor's soul that resides in my sword, I just say, "nothing, ignore me."

Matteo gives me a look like he's about to argue, then shrugs and continues his task.

*"Maybe you should speak to me in your head from now on."*

I roll my eyes. *"Maybe you should stop speaking to me when people are around."*

*"Ah, but where's the fun in that?"* Hale's disembodied voice chuckles.

Once the metal is set, I waste no time in pulling the release lever. The metal shoots from the bucket, scattering and turning into dozens of deadly projectiles. I can't tell the extent of the damage, but I do see bodies fall as their lines buckle. Matteo helps me reset the arm and we turn it slightly. I reload it as quickly as possible, once again jamming it full of any piece of scrap in the vicinity. The pieces crack through the air and descend on enemy soldiers.

We fire it twice more before a shudder goes through the enemy ranks. "Get out of here!" I shout at the Adrithian guards behind me. They know I'm the only one who's a match for Skade.

He steps out of the retreating line of enemies. His eyes widen when he sees me. I flash a toothy grin and give him a little wave with my fingers. His face scrunches and reddens in anger.

I guess Calder didn't tell his daddy that I escaped? Pity.

*"Can you feel it? He's gathering his power,"* Hale says, and I focus my senses to the area around me. Under the din of the battle, and the clashing of weapons, the shouts, the moving of feet, there's a current of energy. It flows between me and the objects of the element. Now, there's another wave of energy there, vibrating slower than mine. Skade's power.

*"You feel it. Now disrupt it."*

I rip through his energy, severing his tenuous hold on the metal nearby.

Across the way, Skade physically stumbles, as if his balance was tied to his power. His dark eyes meet mine, filled with confusion. He seems to shake himself, but then he raises his arms over his head and the wave of his power picks up again on his side. Dozens of weapons rise over the enemy ranks, slowly spinning until they're aimed in my direction.

"Surrender, Princess, or I'll unleash Tolliver's full might upon you and your people," Skade shouts across the empty expanse between us. His booming voice echoes against the nearby homes and shops.

"I'll never surrender to you, Skade. And this time, I'll have your screams."

He throws his arms out in my direction, and the swords, spears, axes, and arrows fly at me.

*"Do you feel his hold over them? It'll weaken once it gets closer. That'll be your chance to take them."*

Hale is right. I feel the moment his power loosens its grip, and I strike, snapping his tenuous hold over the weapons and bringing them under my control. They halt in midair, then whip around and race back to him.

He puts his hand out and the weapons scatter right before they make contact, hitting his line of soldiers instead. His eyes widen and his mouth gapes like a fish. I hear him stammer, "that's not possible."

"Tolliver sends his regards," I yell, just to rile him.

Skade takes the bait and stalks closer, bringing with him a handful of the poisoned weapons. They hover in the air around him, like deadly wings. "It doesn't matter if Tolliver blessed you, too. I've got years of experience wielding this power. I've done things with it that you can't even imagine."

I narrow my eyes at the weapons. It doesn't take much imagination to realize he created those abominations. It makes me wonder how he did it, though, and what kind of poison he used.

*"Focus, Aislinn. He's pooling his energy. Get ready to deflect,"* Hale warns, and my pulsing sword brings my attention back to the fight.

Skade sends his weapons at me, not all at once, but staggered so I have to exert my power in multiple bursts. I catch them all and send them back in his direction. He stops them, and we trade the weapons back and forth several times, until he realizes that method isn't going to work.

"*On your left*," Hale calls a fraction of a moment before I feel it. I spin, bringing my sword up to deflect an arrow aimed at my neck.

"*Front!*" He yells and I face forward once more to see Skade rushing me.

His greatsword dwarfs mine, but my skill has always been my speed. I move twice as fast as he does, opening up superficial cuts along his side, his legs and his shoulder. He hasn't landed a single hit on me. His eyes narrow on my sword, as if he can't figure out why he's unable to manipulate it.

We break apart, and he catches his breath while he summons more weapons to throw at me. I block most of them, but there's one spear that flies so fast that I barely have time to slow its trajectory. My tenuous hold on it slips for a moment, and I duck out of the way in time for it to sail harmlessly over my head. I wait for it to hit the ground behind me, but there's a dull *thunk* instead as the spear finds purchase.

I whirl, my stomach sinking as I see a man slump to the ground, the shaft of the spear protruding from the center of his chest.

"No, Matteo!" I shriek, closing the distance between us. I slide to my knees in front of him, bruising them on the cobblestone road.

His breaths come in shallow pants as he slowly grips the spear, as if he intends to yank it out. His face is locked in a grimace.

"Leave it in" I grab his hand, squeezing it. "It'll keep you from bleeding out. I'll go find a healer, or, or my sister," I mutter, glancing around for someone, anyone, who can help him.

There's no one. Not even Skade. The coward must have turned tail and ran.

"Let me die honorably," Matteo groans, releasing my hand to once again pull on the shaft of the spear. I can't imagine how painful it must be. The tip of the spear comes free from his chest with a squelch, and he drops it to the sand.

"Matteo, I'm so sorry."

He wheezes, and the wet sound in his throat tells me he has moments. "Princess," he rasps, "it's been a pleasure to serve your family."

Tears prick my eyes as I try to smile at him, then fail and settle for a shaky laugh instead. "I told you to call me Aislinn, remember?"

His lip quirks up as he opens his mouth, but no more words escape. His chest stills, and his eyes stare unfocused past me.

I suck in a shaking breath. "Thank you, Captain Matteo, for protecting my family and for being my friend."

# Chapter Forty-Seven

## Elana

We make it to the front of the palace, where our combined forces have made startlingly little progress. There appears to be three flanks. Flames burst from the left flank, and a vicious wind blows on the right. The center flank is furthest along, and I can't see who's leading the charge, but by elimination I would guess it's Aislinn.

"I'm going to help my parents," Rayna says.

"Be careful!" I shout after her as she runs down the road to the right.

Flames dance down the path to the left. I turn to Aidan. "You should go find your mother,"

He shakes his head. "I'm not leaving you. I promised your mother I'd keep you safe. I can't do that when I'm not with you."

I let out a quick sigh. "Fine, I'm heading straight to find Aislinn. Come with me if you want."

"Parisa, take the Ocarins to reinforce the left flank," Aidan orders.

"Stay safe, nephew. If you need us, send a signal," Parisa says, leading Novan and the rest of the Ocarins to back up his mother and the forces she leads.

Aidan and I take off running, pushing through the disorganized chaos of Melinorian soldiers. We pass several Adrithian guards who fall into line behind us. The silhouette of a catapult lies ahead, but we don't get far when I recognize the long blonde hair of a woman kneeling on the ground over a prone body.

"Ash!" I scream, sprinting the rest of the way to her. Breathing heavily, my shock hardly registers Matteo with a vicious wound punched through his chest. I fall to my knees beside my sister, tears welling up in my eyes.

I'm too late to help, although I doubt I could have done anything to save him, even if I had my powers. My chest aches. I don't even know if he has a family back home. Does he have a wife who will now be a widow? Children who will grow up without a father?

"It was Skade," Aislinn whispers, and I'm taken aback by the simmering rage in her eyes.

"I'm so sorry," I say, placing my hand on her shoulder, trying not to let the tears fall that build in my eyes. "Where's he now?"

"He's gone. That bastard fled the first chance he got. But I won't let him get far. Can you two hold the line here?" She stands, gripping her sword tight in her hand, wiping her eyes with the back of her unbloodied hand.

"Ash, no, we should stick together," I say, worried she'll find herself in trouble behind enemy lines and no one will know.

She turns to me, giving me a stare that shows every bit of her unbridled fury. "Elana, he has to answer for everything he's done."

I stand up straighter, not backing down from this fight. "Is your vengeance worth your life?"

She gives me an appraising look. "I'm going."

Just like that, she sprints down a side street, disappearing into the inky blackness beyond Amira's fire.

I stare after her, equally concerned and pissed. "Fuck," I mutter under my breath, then startle when one of the Adrithian guards appears in front of me, bowing low. She's a tall woman wearing a leather helm.

"Your Highness, would you like us to follow her?"

I blink, taken aback at the request. My gaze goes to Matteo, and I don't want any more of my people to die here. If Ash wants to pursue vengeance on her own, then that's on her. I won't send more Adrithians to their deaths. "No. I'm sure she's going to be fine."

Aidan lets loose a stream of fire at the approaching enemies, providing us cover while a few Adrithian guards help me move Matteo's body to one of the nearby buildings. I close his eyes and offer him a quick goodbye. He deserves so much more, but it's the best I can do right now.

We rejoin the fight at Aidan's side. I find I don't have much appetite for striking killing blows, but I'm more than happy to immobilize enemies with my shadows while either Aidan or the Adrithians strike them down.

I understand now why their progress has been so slow. The vastness of the army before us is daunting. For every soldier we dispatch, two more pop up in their place. I'm exhausted by the time we've made it past a handful of homes.

Suddenly, there's a fiery wyvern in the sky. A barrier of fire erupts in front of our small force, giving Aidan time to reach a hand up towards the wyvern. A piece of parchment falls into his hand. The wyvern continues its flight to our right, likely heading towards Rayna and her parents.

Aidan reads the words on it and spins back to the palace, dread painted on his features.

"What does it say?" I ask, already there's a sinking feeling in my gut.

"We've been betrayed," he says, narrowing his eyes at the palace gates, cloaked in the darkness of midnight. "The enemies found Rayna's tunnel and used it to get inside the palace's fortifications."

I let out a gasp and turn to stare through the dark at the palace. As we watch, flames lick through the windows of the palace, spreading through the interior.

"Oh Gods," I whisper, turning back to Aidan. "What do we do?"

He shakes his head, brows pulled together in uncertainty. "I don't know." It's the first time I've ever heard him utter these words, and that unsettles me more than the fire that's rapidly lighting up the sky around the palace. "If we abandon this flank, the enemy could overwhelm us, but if we don't stop the attack at the palace we'll have nowhere safe to retreat to."

"This is Rayna's home," I argue, my feet already moving several steps in my desire to save it.

"Elana, if we leave this fight, they could launch a surprise attack on our other forces. We'd be dooming them," Aidan says, his expression full of conflict as he looks between the palace and the army in front of us, held back by his flames.

"Then what do we do?" I ask again with more urgency as panic sets my nerves on edge.

Aidan opens his mouth to speak, but snaps it closed as a familiar figure with shoulder-length blonde hair marches through the palace gates towards us, leading several dozen men.

"Calder," I snarl his name like a curse. "That bastard will pay for what he did to my sister."

Aidan glances between the approaching army and the one he's holding off with fire. "He has the worst fucking timing. I'll take him. You hold off the enemies on this side."

I glare at him, insulted he thinks I can't beat Calder. "Absolutely not. Water is your weakness, and he looks fully rested. I'll take my guards and decimate him."

Instead of giving him a chance to argue, I turn to the guard who addressed me before, assuming she's the highest ranked. "Adrithians, you're with me."

She nods and gives orders while I charge ahead. "Fuck. Elana, wait!" Aidan shouts at my back.

All around me, shadows stir, gathering strength. It's the darkest hour, the time of night when they're at their strongest.

I release a burst of darkness, knocking the Hotharians down and holding them there while my guards strike. Calder shields himself with ice, but his companions falter. Calder ignores the death of his people, stepping forward to send a wave of frothy water my way. My shadows solidify in a wedge shape before me, harmlessly parting the wave before it hits me.

Tendrils of darkness creep up Calder's legs while his eyes are on me. They tighten and hold fast while I charge, but in my haste I didn't realize he turned the ground to ice. I slip, my feet scrambling for purchase as my arms flail to catch my balance. Tendrils of shadow reach out to steady me, but it takes my focus off Calder and the fight for one moment too long.

He may not be able to move, but water can. A wave surrounds me, swirling around me in a circle, splashing high above my head.

"Elana, just so you know, this isn't how I wish to end things, but the Empress demands your death," Calder says, managing to sound smug and regretful simultaneously.

The torrent of water spins closer and closer to me, cutting off any chance to escape. I suck in a deep breath as it splashes over my head. Ice seals around me, closing me in a bubble of water. I thrash, kicking out at it with my legs to no avail. Oh Gods, not again.

This feeling is one I had hoped to never experience again. As I did during the trials, I panic as the water churns around me. My mind goes blank as I flail, getting sucked into the vortex at the center. Bubbles rip from my mouth as I'm spun, disorientating me further.

I need to calm down. I need to breathe. But I can't do that here. My lungs burn and beg for me to open my mouth and suck in needed air. An orange glow erupts outside the ice bubble. Fire. Aidan.

"Elana!" His roar is muffled by the ice and the water, but still his voice grounds me, brings me back from the edge of panic. I kick towards the glow, reaching my hand out to the unyielding ice.

His fist pounds relentlessly as fire melts the ice. It's not going to be fast enough. I need to breathe. Something pulses at my hips and I remember my daggers. So sharp they can cut anything.

I unsheathe one, moving quickly because my vision starts to blur. With all the determination I possess I grip the hilt with both hands, raise it over my head, and bring it down into the ice. There's a cracking sound and then the world explodes.

I'm propelled forward, crashing into something warm and solid. There's a grunt, and then arms wrap around me as the weight of the water at my back pushes us down.

I suck in air and water splashes into my mouth, causing a fit of coughing.

"I've got you, Magpie," Aidan whispers to my hair.

"Where's Calder?" I wheeze, gasping for breath in between hacking up water from my lungs.

"Bastard ran," Aidan says, sighing.

Like father, like son.

My mind struggles to catch up with what's happening around me. How come we aren't being attacked?

Heat licks my skin, and I finally notice we're surrounded by fire. The group of Adrithians gather around us, weapons pointed outwards in case any stragglers get through Aidan's fire. The flames rage as high as the buildings. I look up, about to say something snarky about his stamina, but my words die in my throat. His eyes are bloodshot and the muscles in his neck are strained.

"Aidan, stop. You're using too much energy," I say, turning my whole body to face him, gripping his forearms. Aidan's muscles quiver beneath my touch. Shit, his energy is almost gone. He used so much more than me getting to the docks. How much does he have left? "Let me use my shadows."

Slowly, too slowly, the fire shrinks. I throw up a solid shield of darkness.

He lets out a shaky breath, leaning down and planting a soft kiss to my hair. "It was worth it. I did promise your mother, after all."

"Are you afraid of my mother?" A smirk pulls one corner of my lips up.

"Yes," he says, catching his breath. "Have you met her? She's terrifying."

I smack him playfully. "I'm going to tell her you said that."

The fire shrinks down and extinguishes. Enemy forces batter my shield, testing it for weak points. I give them none.

"Please don't. I'll never hear the end of it," Aidan teases, his low voice huskier than usual.

I draw back and inspect him. There are dark bags under his eyes. I grab his wrist and press several fingers to the inside of it. His pulse is quick, but beating steadily. "How are you feeling?"

He takes one long breath. "Like shit, but I'll be fine. You're the one who almost drowned...again."

"Yeah, I had too much fun the first time, I wanted to try it again," I reply dryly.

"Your Highness," the same guard from before approaches. "What should we do now?"

I glance between Aidan and the Adrithian guards. Some lean on their weapons, several kneel down with shaking limbs, catching their breath. All are exhausted. I should rally them, say some grand words to give them hope and make them fight for the continent, or die trying. That's what Aislinn would do, what Father would do. But I'm too damn tired for pretty words.

So instead, I open my mouth, and say, "rest. We recover as much strength as we can, and then we get back to the war."

# CHAPTER FORTY-EIGHT

## AISLINN

I feel Skade running for his pathetic life, shoving through his allies as he retreats. His blonde head reflects Amira's firelight. I watch his retreat from the rooftops. He pushes his way to our right flank, where Mesfin and Desta lead their forces. The ground shakes, and I realize Rayna's down there, too, fighting alongside her parents.

Jumping between the roofs, I keep even with him, tracking his progress through the street. When he's moments away from launching an assault on the monarchs of Melinor, I leap from the rooftop, landing on a balcony over the first story, then jumping to the ground, where I roll to break the impact.

I land in the middle of the bulk of Melinorian forces. They startle and turn their weapons on me. I don't have time for this. I force them back a few steps using my power. "I'm Aislinn Sable. Let me through now, or else your royal family will face Skade alone."

The soldiers exchange wary glances, but step aside, giving me a straight shot to where Mesfin fights next to his wife. I take off at a sprint.

"*On your left, he's about to attack,*" Hale shouts.

My head whips to the side as I run, seeing several dozen weapons rise up from the enemy army and fly towards Mesfin and Desta. Wind won't be able to stop them. My hand flies up out of instinct, catching the blades before they cross the line of enemies. I send them straight down into the attacking forces.

"Aislinn!" Rayna shouts as she runs to me. An immense sense of relief washes over me as I take in her relatively unscathed appearance. She's breathing heavily, and her skin is drenched with sweat and blood that I don't think is hers, but she's alive. "What happened to your forces?"

"Elana and Aidan showed up and are leading the center," I respond, opening my mouth to tell her I chased Skade here, when a massive fire erupts behind us.

We spin around and Rayna gasps, putting her hand to her mouth, eyes full of horror. The palace is burning.

"No!" Desta shrieks, and it's an anguished sound that can only come from watching your home be destroyed.

A fiery bird -no, a wyvern- streaks across the sky towards Mesfin, circling over his head several times before he reaches up and snatches a single piece of parchment from the air.

"They've taken the castle. Someone showed them where Rayna's tunnel was," Mesfin says, anger shaking his fist.

"We have to save our home," Desta says, wiping her eyes and moving in the direction of the palace.

"We cannot abandon the flank, Desta," Mesfin says. "Our army will be overrun."

"*Skade approaches,*" Hale says, and I feel the pull of nearby metal, bending to his will.

"Leave this street to me," I say, facing the Hotharian king once more. "Go save your home."

Rayna grips my arm tightly. "You can't face him alone. I'll stay, too."

Panic seizes me as Matteo's death flashes before me. He died because he stayed behind when I ordered him to go. I don't want the same fate for Rayna. "No. Go with your parents and take back the palace. We'll need a place to retreat to."

"I'm not leaving you, Aislinn, and that's not up for negotiation," Rayna says, facing her parents. "We can hold the flank."

Mesfin and Desta embrace their daughter quickly, then rush off towards the burning palace.

Reaching out with my power, I feel the metal around me come to life. I roll my shoulders and tell Rayna, "watch out for attacks from behind. I'll keep Skade's focus on me. I'll leave the soldiers to you."

She nods, then takes a few steps back, raising herself up on a platform of rock. She withdraws her bow, then her quiver of arrows, setting it next to her.

The enemy ranks part for Skade. "You're like a Gods-damned armored cockroach," he mutters.

I picture the insects, with their rock-like shells, long antennae, and spiked legs. Surprisingly, I've been called worse. "Why don't you try finishing the fight this time instead of running away?"

He flashes me a look of disdain, and the metal under my control shakes, wavering under the pull of his power. I grit my teeth and clench my fist, breaking his hold. I don't give him time to recuperate, instead letting the weapons fly at him, and rushing forward, drawing my ancestral blade. He bats the weapons away with a flick of his wrist, and draws his hulking greatsword in time to parry my blow.

Wooden arrows soar over my head, striking enemies that surge around me. Rayna does her job well, keeping them out of my way. Skade and I exchange blows, and I keep a firm grasp on the metal surrounding us, in case he decides to wield it against me.

He tires quickly, while I gain momentum, having stepped into the one thing I'm the most comfortable with. I drive him back in the dance of blades, forcing him to yield several paces while I hit him with swing after swing, opening up several shallow cuts on his arms in the process.

Sweat pours down his face, and it's like fuel for me. I push myself harder, swinging mercilessly as I think of my father, who taught me these moves, and Matteo, who was always up for getting his ass beat in the training yard. I think of the guards who traveled with me to the border of Hotharia. Tallisa and Gregory, who didn't deserve to die like they did, and even that bastard Donne. I think of my mother and sister. The two I will keep fighting for until my dying breath. I think of Adrithia's future, bright under Elana's compassionate rule. I think of Rayna, who protects me even when her home burns. We have a shot at being together, and I won't let anyone take it from us. Lastly, I think of my ancestor, Hale, who gave his life so we could have a chance. He guides my hands with his, encouraging me with his determination.

My sword crashes into Skade's, sending sparks flying. There's a sharp noise, and then Skade's sword shatters. He stumbles back, staring at the sheared end of the blade in shock. I catch one breath, and pull my sword back with both hands. The world seems to slow as I feel Hale's power alongside my own, driving the blade forward and across, severing Skade's neck in one vicious swing.

His body crashes to the ground with a clang, weighed down by the precious metal he loved to drape himself in. His head falls next to his body, landing face-up in the blood-soaked sand. I allow the immense relief to drive me to my knees as I catch my breath.

I expect the enemies to falter, to see their fallen ruler and run the other direction, but they push closer. The ground rumbles as Rayna knocks a row of attackers down, picking them off with her bow. Her accuracy is unmatched, and so is the speed at which she fires arrows. I allow myself a moment to admire her, the warrior, before I pick up my sword once again.

"Father!" A bellowing cry has me spinning on my heels. Calder stands at the corner of a nearby building. He's breathing hard, and his gaze is locked on his father's head.

"Shit," I murmur under my breath, picking up my sword and standing, not taking my eyes off him.

The air around him crystalizes, turning into hundreds of tiny shards of ice. "You bitch. I'll kill you for this."

His hands push forward, and the shards fly for Rayna and I. They smash into a wall of stone. Rayna's back on the ground next to me, bow in hand.

"We can't fight him and the Empress' army," I say, pushing the wave of enemies back by their armor.

She peers around me at the horde, then with a flick of her wrist, the multi-story stone buildings on either side of the street collapse into it, crushing the enemies who dared to approach us and creating a pile of rubble, effectively cutting off their approach.

A wave crashes around us, churning and splashing over our heads. Ice starts to grow from the bottom, sealing us in a bowl of water.

"Hells no," Rayna says, and suddenly we're standing on a pillar, high above it.

I feel for my power, but it's weak. I grip my sword hilt tighter.

*"Your energy is almost depleted. Be careful not to draw from it while fighting him."*

"*Not a problem,*" I think back. I've beaten Calder once already without weapons, and I look forward to doing so again.

"I'm going in close," I tell Rayna.

She gives me a nod and lowers us back to the ground. "I've got your back."

We rush him together, and he fires ice shard after ice shard at us, which we deflect as easily as swatting away an insect. Rayna hangs back, firing arrows at him, which he uses an ice shield to block.

I move in, swinging as I go, aiming to incapacitate, but not kill. He summons an ice sword, which immediately shatters upon contact with mine.

"Give it up, Calder. Your father is dead. Your soldiers are being decimated. Ally with us against the exiled goddess. We won't blame you for the choices of your father," I say as I drive him back against the building.

He sneers at me, dark eyes narrowing. "Never. Father pledged our lives to the service of the Empress. I will uphold that promise."

I shake my head. "Have it your way, then, but I can't promise we'll be lenient against you."

"I don't want your leniency. Your kingdoms will fall, and your people will be the Empress' slaves," he says, laughing without humor. From this close I see how red the whites are, as if he hasn't slept well in months.

He sends a wave of water my way, and I spin out of the way, keeping my sword trained on him.

"Look out!" Rayna shouts, colliding with my shoulder and sending me sprawling to the cobblestone.

I roll upon impact, spinning to see the massive ice shards embedded in the ground where I'd been standing. Gods, Rayna saved my life. She stands facing away from me, catching her breath. Calder slides down the wall of the building, face paling, eyebrows high.

"No, I didn't mean to, Rayna, I'm so sorry," he says, tears welling in his eyes.

I look between them, confused, until Rayna turns around, and all words, all joy leaves my body in an instant. A shard of ice, as long and wide as my forearm protrudes from her right shoulder. She looks down at it in shock, then looks up at me. "Aislinn, I-."

Her eyelids flutter and she falls forward. "Rayna!" I shriek, lunging to catch her.

Calder sits on the ground not too far away, his head in his hands, whimpering. "Calder, if you want to help, then make sure this stays frozen. It's the only thing keeping her from bleeding out." He stares at Rayna through matted blonde hair, nodding.

I lower her limp body to the ground, cradling her head and shoulders in my lap. "Rayna, please hold on."

Her breath is labored and raspy, and her eyelids squeeze as she groans in pain. "Don't you die on me. Don't you dare," I say through gritted teeth. "I just got back to you."

This can't be happening, not to Rayna.

Where's my sister? She can fix this. She has to.

"Elana!" I scream. I have no idea where she is, or if she can hear me, but right now she's Rayna's only hope. I scream her name over and over again.

I cling to Rayna's shoulders, whispering to her not to leave me. Demanding she keep breathing. I press my forehead to hers. Her skin is damp, and breaths shallow.

"*Gods, please save her,*" I silently pray to all the Gods. Tolliver, Avani, anyone.

"*Help is here,*" Hale whispers to me.

Then there's a hand on my shoulder, and I look up with blurry vision into my sister's horrified face. Her clothes and hair are drenched and clinging to her, like she just stepped out of the bath.

"We got a message from Amira. What happened?" She yells, moving around me to inspect Rayna's wound. Behind her, Aidan stares down at Calder, looking like he's about to strangle him.

"She pushed me out of the way," I say with a trembling voice.

Elana crouches down next to me, inspecting the wound. She sucks in a breath at the sight of the ice slowly turning red with blood.

"Gods, Aislinn, I…," she trails off, and I reach out, grabbing her stone-strengthened shoulder plate.

"Heal her, Elana." I demand.

Tears fill her eyes as she glances down at Rayna. "I don't know if I-I can."

The urge to grab her and shake some sense back into her fills me, but pure panic stomps it down. "You can. You must."

"I haven't been able to heal since the coast," she says, and her shoulders shake as tears well up in her eyes.

"Damn it, El. Just try," I snarl, glaring at her stricken expression. "Rayna needs you to try. Didn't you say she helped you during your trials? You owe her this. Try."

Tears trace down Elana's cheeks as she sucks in a few breaths and nods. She leans over Rayna, putting her hands near the ice shard as she closes her eyes.

Moments pass by and nothing happens.

El's hands start to shake with the force of her sobbing. "It's not working. I-I can't feel the light anymore. Nura has abandoned me."

Frustration has me clenching my fists over Rayna's chest. My sister is one of the smartest people I know, so why doesn't she see what's happening? "The goddess didn't abandon you, Elana. Gods cannot take away what they've granted. Otherwise Tolliver would have stripped Skade's gift from him before all this started. Her power is within you. Your guilt over Father's decision is holding you back. You have to forgive yourself."

"I don't know how to do that," she cries, wiping away tears with an arm.

With Rayna's life slipping away by the second, I have to do something. Opening my mouth, I say the words I'm sure I will regret. "I need to tell you something, El. I'm sorry I didn't tell you earlier. Father's alive."

Her breath hitches as her mouth pops open. "What? What do you mean, he's alive?"

"I was hoping to tell you later, when all this was over, but there's been no time," I swallow the bitter taste of the half-truth. "He's alive. When he fell off the cliff, he survived."

"*You gamble with your sister's emotions, Aislinn. She may never forgive you for this,*" Hale chastises and I grit my teeth.

"That should have been the first thing you said," El says through heaving breaths. "Where is he, why isn't he here with you?"

Rayna's normal bronze skin is pallid, and I know we only have moments before she's too far gone. I speak quickly, the lie slipping off my tongue far too easily.

"He, too, was held hostage in Calder's army, but he got free before me. He was injured and wasn't able to break me free so I told him to go without me. To get help from the Gods. But that's why you need to overcome this, so you can heal as well."

"He's alive." Elana's tears turn to happy ones as she catches her breath. Aidan kneels on the ground next to her, putting his hand on her shoulder. Over her head, he stares at me, suspicion apparent in his narrowed gaze.

Calder, too, stares at me through his messy hair. I shoot him a murderous glare that I hope is enough of a threat to keep his mouth shut.

I return my focus to Rayna, whose breathing has become so slow that my heart gutters, thinking we're too late.

Elana sucks in a deep breath and closes her eyes. Her shoulders relax and moments later her eyes snap open.

"Calder," she demands. "Melt the ice when I tell you."

He gives a shallow nod from his spot on the ground. Aidan keeps him in his sights in case he tries anything while Elana positions her hands around the ice. Warm light illuminates from her palms.

She lets out a breathy laugh, and tears run down her cheeks freely. "Now."

The ice melts, water pulling away from the wound and disappearing into the air. Elana covers the wound with her hand. The light glows brighter, until it gets so bright I have to avert my eyes.

Long, agonizing moments go by and nothing happens, until slowly, Rayna's skin regains its rich color, and her breathing evens out. The pained lines on her face smooth out.

The glow from Elana's hand fades away and she sits back, smiling down at Rayna. "She's going to be alright."

I let out a sharp breath that's choked with a sob, bending down to press my forehead to hers, whispering silent thanks to Nura for blessing my sister with her power.

Hands come up and gently grip the back of my head. "Hey, there." Rayna's voice whispers to me.

Joy spears through me at the sound of her voice. I give her a watery smile, even though the urge to scream at her for putting herself in danger like that is strong. "You took that ice shard for me."

"Yeah, well, you'd do the same for me," she replies, and before she can say anything further, I bring my lips to hers, kissing her fiercely. Her hands grip my hair tighter and she angles her head, deepening the kiss.

I've never kissed anyone upside down before, and when our teeth accidentally knock together, we both chuckle and pull away.

"Gods, if I had known that all it would take to get a kiss would be almost dying, I'd have done that years ago," Rayna teases, and I help her into a sitting position.

I groan, wiping my hands over my eyes. "Don't joke like that, please."

"Glad to see you're okay," Elana says with a tired smile, standing up.

"Likewise," Rayna offers her a wide grin, moving her shoulder and staring at the hole in her armor and tunic in disbelief. "Thank you for healing me."

Elana glares down at Calder. Shadows appear around his wrists and ankles, binding them together. He doesn't protest, merely stares at the manacles. I can't help but smirk at the irony.

There's a brilliant flash of orange light, then another wyvern appears in the sky. It swoops low, dropping a parchment into Aidan's waiting hands.

He reads, then spins around, staring at the palace.

"What does it say?" I ask, my patience fraying.

"We're regrouping at the stables," he replies.

"Regrouping?" I ask with narrowed eyes, loathe to abandon our flank after the progress we've made so far. And why at the stables, of all places? Horses are great in battle, but not in enclosed areas like a city.

"My mother doesn't say why. Maybe she *saw* something."

I blow out an aggravated breath, pushing down the feeling of failure as I help Rayna to her feet.

We rush to the stables, moving as quickly as we can, though we're all clearly exhausted. Both Aidan and Rayna are moving slowly, and there's only so fast Calder can shuffle along in his shadow manacles.

The stables lie just outside of the palace gates in the direction of the docks. There's little strategic advantage to grouping there, unless, like Aidan said, Amira saw something useful.

Outside the stables, and protected by a towering wall of flames, I see Amira, Edward, and her small force of Ocarins, alongside Rayna's parents and their remaining soldiers. The group of Adrithian guards I left Elana with also hovers nearby.

Amira approaches, her sharp gaze trained on all of us. "We need to abandon the city."

# CHAPTER FORTY-NINE

## ELANA

I stare at Amira like she just sprouted wings and screeched at us. "What?" I ask.

She addresses all of us in turn. "We cannot retake the city. I've seen what happens if we stay and try. Their army is too vast, and we all perish. We need to leave before it's too late."

Rayna sucks in a harsh breath, giving Amira an accusatory stare. "After everything, you want us to give up and run away? Aislinn killed Skade, and we took Calder hostage. Doesn't that count for something?"

I whip my head around to my sister who casually forgot to mention that she killed the king of Hotharia? What the Hells?

She shrugs. "There wasn't time to tell you, what with Rayna almost dying and everything."

I roll my eyes at her, and focus on the conversation at hand.

"While that's enough to ensure Hotharia's cooperation, the fact of the matter is that most of this army doesn't care about Skade or Calder. Their allegiance is to the Empress alone, and they won't surrender until we kill them all, which as I said we cannot do," Amira says, urgency sharpening her words. "How much power do each of you have left?"

My pool of darkness is dwindling. The pool of light feels as bright as the sun, and is brimming full, but I glance between Aislinn, Rayna, and Aidan, noting their shifting feet and downturned eyes. They're clearly exhausted, and not in any position to continue this fight.

"How do we get out of here?" I question. "There are no ships left at the docks, and we can't take the tunnel, because the enemy knows about it and are likely waiting to ambush us there. So, what do we do?"

Amira turns to Rayna, raising her brows at her.

Rayna lets out a low sigh. "I can get us out." I turn my surprised look upon her, and we wait for her to continue. "I built a second tunnel. After what happened with your guard, Elana, I was worried we might be betrayed, so I created a second one in secret. It follows the river, taking us west out of Oraphia."

"That was good planning, Rayna," Mesfin gives his daughter an approving nod. "Is the tunnel far?"

Rayna stares at the ground, then looks up at Amira. "We're standing on it."

Amira smiles. She knew. Of course she knew.

We waste no time in moving aside so Rayna can open the entrance to the tunnel. It's not as wide as the other one, but it's wide enough for a single horse. This tunnel was made in a hurry, not crafted for wagons and sick and elderly refugees. This is a last-resort.

I let a ball of light burst to life in front of me, then send it into the tunnel. It multiplies as it travels, illuminating the length of the cavern.

There are few supplies in the stables, but we pack up what we can. I toss a few blankets over Misty's back. We work quickly to saddle up every horse in the stable. There aren't enough for everyone, so some ride double, and even more opt to walk. I let an injured Melinorian soldier ride Misty, while I agree to ride with Aidan on his massive warhorse.

Rayna and her parents are the first to enter with Calder tied to the saddle of a horse between them. They're followed by their soldiers. Only several dozen remain out of the hundreds that stormed through the gates hours ago. Amira and Edward make the descent next, Parisa and Novan right behind them, followed by the dozen or so Ocarin guards.

I wave through the Adrithian guards next. Aidan, Aislinn, and I will be the last to enter. Aislinn promised she had enough power to seal the tunnel behind us, and I'm staying to make sure she can manage it. Aidan stands nearby in case we need him.

Amira's fire wall grows dim the further away she moves, and through the shrinking flames I spot a head of dark hair. My heart skips a beat. I gasp, and grip my sister's arm as she prepares to step into the tunnel leading a borrowed horse.

"Wait, Aislinn, look! It's Father!" I point at the man, dressed in a simple black uniform amid the sea of enemies on the other side of the flames. He looks older, and he's grown his facial hair out more than I've ever seen, but it's unmistakably him. He must have infiltrated the Goddess' ranks to get close to us. "Ash, we have to get him!"

I unsheathe my twin daggers and ready my shadows for a fight. I expect Aislinn to do the same thing next to me, but she's staring through the flames at him in horror. I turn back around, expecting to see him go down amid the sea of soldiers, but he's untouched. We need to get to him. He's surrounded by enemies that could turn on him at any moment.

Turning back to my sister, who has gone as pale as me, I give her a little shove to break her out of her stupor. "Ash, we have to save him." I raise my blades, showing her I'm ready.

"I'll use my shadows as a shield. Aidan, can you clear us a path to him?" I ignore my sister's shocked state and turn to the other person I know I can count on. His brows furrow as he glances between Aislinn and my father, but he gives me a nod.

"Yes, I can get us there," his voice is stiff, and lacks his usual eagerness for a challenge. It's a lot to ask of him, to risk his life when we're so close to safety, but now that I've got access to my light powers again, their cursed weapons can't poison us.

I give him a confident nod, and turn back to Father. He raises a blackened sword, and the Goddess' forces turn to him. My heart nearly stops. No, no, no. Please don't let them realize he doesn't belong there.

We can't afford to wait any longer. I grip the hilts of my daggers. "We have to go, now!" I shout, bringing my shadows up in a protective circle around us.

"Elana, wait!" Aislinn shrieks, lunging forward to grab my bicep before I start to run. "It's not him."

I give her an incredulous look. "What do you mean it's not him? Look at him, Aislinn! That's our father, and we have to help him!"

Wrenching my arm free, I glance at Aidan. If she's not going to help, then we'll do it ourselves.

"What do you mean it's not him?" Aidan asks Aislinn, warily.

Ash swallows and gives me a pleading look. "It's not him...anymore. Elana, I'm so sorry. I felt the same way when I saw him the first time. But he's gone. There's nothing left of him."

My mind whirls, and I can't comprehend what she's saying. I shake my head. He's right in front of us. I can see him through the fire. "He's there, Ash, and we need to help him."

"No!" She shouts, and her tone startles me. I don't remember the last time she's yelled at me. "You're not listening. Our father is dead. That thing over there is a husk, an empty shell that the goddess is somehow controlling. There's nothing to help, nothing to save!"

"You told me he was alive," I practically whisper, staring at her.

Ash breathes heavily. "I lied. Rayna was dying, and we had no time, so I told you what you needed to hear so you could heal her."

I reel back, sucking in a breath. She lied. Something we promised we would never do to each other. The betrayal hurts more than if she had physically hit me.

"Fucking Hells, Aislinn," Aidan mutters from next to me, running his hand through his dark hair.

"No, no, that can't be. He's not gone," I say, staring back at Father. His sword is raised and he shouts something to the army around him. They raise their weapons in response and begin crossing the flames, setting themselves on fire. The first few rows of enemies go down, burnt to a crisp in a moment, but the fire weakens, and each enemy makes it further and further. Father stares ahead, unaffected by the carnage around him. The flickering flames reflect on his face, revealing solid black eyes.

"He needs help. I can help him. With the light, I can heal him," I practically whisper, moving ahead. If I can just get to him...

A hand like iron yanks me back by my shoulder. "Elana, he's gone. I'm so sorry I didn't tell you the truth sooner, but he's gone. And now we need to leave Oraphia. Right now."

I pull away from her viciously, my anger at her flaring. "Don't touch me."

She flinches at the venom in my tone, but I don't regret it. She steels her expression. "If you stay here, Elana, they will kill you. We're leaving. You can hate me for this later, but I'm getting you out."

"We can't leave him again, Aislinn. We already let him down once. I won't do that again."

"I'm sorry, but we don't have a choice."

Aislinn raises her hand and the metal bars from the palace fortifications rip from its hinges and fly towards us, along with every scrap of metal, shield and sword nearby.

No. Not again. I won't let her do this. I take several steps forward, intent on getting through the flames to Father, but she turns and shoves me down into the tunnel. My feet leave solid ground, then I'm falling backwards. Aidan shouts my name, reaching for me. His hand misses mine, and I tumble, hitting my head on something solid.

Blackness consumes me as I watch the tunnel being sealed up, and any chance of saving my father disappears...again.

# CHAPTER FIFTY

## AIDAN

I've never wanted to kill Aislinn Sable more than when she carelessly shoves her sister into the tunnel. Elana's face is a mask of horror as she falls. I desperately reach for her, but she drops out of my reach, plummeting into the cavern below.

There's a sickening crack as she hits the ground. Nothing could have prepared me for the heart-wrenching feeling that sound invokes. The tunnel around us plunges into inky darkness. I slide down the rocky slope and fall to my knees at her side, pulling her body against me. She's so still. It fucking terrifies me. Dark liquid soaks my hand where it cradles her head. Sheer fucking panic rips through me as I realize it's blood.

"Gods-damn it, Aislinn. She hit her head," I fling the accusation at her like a weapon.

Her face is set in determination as she leads my horse and hers past the entrance and seals it behind her using every piece of metal in the vicinity. The tunnel slowly darkens as the pre-dawn light is blocked.

"I did it to save her," Aislinn replies with a tone revealing no remorse. "Can you do anything about this darkness?"

The irony of her injuring her sister to save her isn't lost on me. I squeeze my hand into a fist as I glare in Aislinn's direction, but don't get a chance to respond before hundreds of flames light the way. Thanks, Mother.

I lift Elana into my arms as I stand, then start walking away without another word.

"We have the horses. We'll move much quicker if we use them," Aislinn says, trailing me.

I clench my jaw and bite out, "she has a head wound. I'm not tossing her over a horse."

To that, Aislinn has no response, and we walk in silence.

"You understand why I did it, right?" Aislinn asks after some time.

I'm in no mood to talk to her, but we've got a long hike, and my family is far ahead. "I'm sure you're about to justify it to make yourself feel better."

Aislinn lets out a scoff. "She would have gotten herself killed."

"So your solution was to toss her into a pit and hope she lands on her feet?" I snarl, feeling my skin heat with my anger. Not wanting to cause Elana any more harm, I force myself to take a deep breath, letting go of the fire like Mother taught me.

"Come on, you know I didn't mean to do that," Aislinn hisses.

"I know what I saw, which was you shoving her without a care for her safety."

Aislinn stares at Elana as we walk. "Is she going to be okay?"

Gods, I am so close to snapping. But for Elana's sake, I hold back the worst of my anger. "I don't know. Her head is bleeding pretty bad."

"Shit," she says, casting worried glances in her sister's direction every few steps.

The journey through the tunnel is painstakingly slow, and I stop several times to rest and readjust Elana in my arms. Her heartbeat is faint, but at least it's there. Every step I take sends a pang of anxiety through me as I worry if each breath is her last. I constantly reassure myself that she's okay. Her skin is still flush with life.

Elana has been my light these last few months. I was the one drawn to her, like a helpless moth to a flame. I call her Magpie because she's been fluttering through my thoughts every waking moment since we first met in the forest of the Gods' Territory. I have to believe she's going to be all right.

When I lost my closest friend, Nadia, a heavy sadness weighed on me for months. It was only with the support of those near me that I endured. If anything were to happen to the woman in my arms, I fear I would set the world ablaze in my grief.

Aislinn and I don't speak more. She appears lost in her thoughts as she leads the horses along. Something feels different about her. From the little I heard from Elana, she had an incredibly rough journey getting here. It wouldn't surprise me if it changed her.

Eventually we make it to the incline and fresh air.

Rayna sees us first, and her relief when she locks eyes with Aislinn turns to concern when she sees Elana in my arms. Parisa is by my side in a moment, helping me lower Elana down to the soft sand, kneeling next to her. Aislinn explains what happened while Parisa takes a look at Elana's scalp, using some clean water from a canteen to wash away some of the dried blood. Her face pinches at the sight of the wound, and she flashes Aislinn a quick glare. My aunt rips a strip of fabric from the cleanest part of her shirt and hands it to me to tie around her head.

Someone starts clapping. The noise is so jarring that I glance up to see who has lost their mind. Edward, the useless, sorry excuse for a father, claps loudly and starts laughing.

Amira shoots her husband a glare. "Edward, show some decency."

His head swings around to give her a look that reminds me of the giant winged snakes that infest the rainforests near Luxoria.

"I'm surprised. I can't believe you all managed to survive. I thought showing Calder's forces the tunnel into the palace would be your death sentence."

My hands fumble the knot as I stare at him. Parisa's sure fingers finish it off for me.

"The Empress all but assured me your deaths. No matter, though. I'll just have to do it myself," the bastard shrugs, and quicker than I've ever seen him move he withdraws his sword, spins and plunges it into my mother's chest.

I leap to my feet. Mother stares at the blade. She doesn't appear surprised, only resigned. She knew. She fucking knew this would happen.

Her pained eyes find mine, and she opens her mouth to speak, but Edward yanks the blade, pulling her close to him as he does so. He puts one hand on her shoulder, placing a mockery of a kiss on the side of her head. She turns to him, whispering something to his ear. His face twists in outrage. He grips the elaborate hilt of his sword and twists it violently, cracking bones, before yanking it free from her.

Parisa screams a gutteral, almost animalistic sound that's cut off as a sob racks her body. I run to my mother, catching her as she falls. Out of my peripherals, I see Aislinn using her power to rip the sword from Edward's hand and holding her own to his throat.

"My son," Mother whispers and I lower my ear to hear her better, waiting for instruction, advice, a goodbye, anything. But no more words leave her lips.

When I pull back, her face is slack, and her eyes are unfocused, staring past me. Her blood stains the sand red. I glance over at the only person who could save her, silently willing her to awaken.

Rayna gently shakes Elana, pleading with her. "Wake up. Please, we need you, Elana. Please, wake up."

She doesn't stir.

My vision blurs as I hold my mother. My aunt collapses next to me, shaking slightly as her tears flow freely. Novan sinks to the sand on her other side.

I lose track of how long we sit there, lost in our grief, but her body slowly loses its warmth. The queen of fire, who always burned so bright, snuffed out.

I press my forehead to her temple and whisper, "may the Gods watch over you, mom."

When I pull away, I notice the shadow of her third eye, which marks her as a seer, is closed. The seer trait will now likely disappear from our family line. It's incredibly rare for the ability to be passed onto another living relative once the current seer dies.

I gently lay my mother's head on the sand and get to my feet. Parisa takes my place, whispering her goodbyes to her sister. Tears fall down her cheeks, cutting paths through the dirt and blood caked on her skin. Novan, as if sensing my intent, is by my side in an instant.

My father is held between two Ocarin guards. There's a lazy smile on his face. I have every intention of burning him alive and leaving his corpse here in the sands to be picked over by scavengers, but as I raise a flaming fist, he waggles his index finger in my direction.

"Ah, ah, ah, if you ever want to see your little brother again, Aidan, you'll let me leave," the bastard says.

My heart freezes. Alek should be safe in Luxoria, surrounded by our household guards and staff. Surely mom would have *seen* if he were in danger, right? "What the fuck did you do to my brother?"

"Oh, he's alive, for now. But if I don't make it back to Oraphia to send a message, he won't be for much longer. The Empress' assassins are everywhere. Believe me when I say they're a lot closer to Aleksander than you are."

His cocky grin makes me want to wring his neck, but his threat stills my hand. "I hope you realize what you're doing. That so-called Empress won't let you keep any of the power you're so desperate to kill for. The only thing she wants from you is servitude."

Edward's cocky grin remains in place. "We shall see."

My brother is the only reason I don't turn him to ash. It's for him I blow out a calming breath before I reply, "I'll allow you to go crawling back to her for now. But know this, traitor, my face will be the last thing you see in this life. And when your end comes, I'll make it slow."

My hand heats, burning with my hatred for him, fueling the white hot rage. Edward blanches when she sees the hand, tugging against the guards holding him.

"Hold him," I demand the Ocarin guards. Edward thrashes in their grip.

"Queen Amira Ashfall's blood is on your hands. The entire continent will know your shame." I grab the collar of his armor with one hand and place my burning palm against his cheek.

Flesh sizzles and he screams as the heat scorches, then blackens his skin. I grip his face until his screams turn to half-conscious whimpers. He's alive when the guards toss him into the tunnel, and Rayna seals it with a fresh layer of rock.

I summon the last of my power, pushing past the point I know is safe, to summon a bird made of fire. Just like my mother taught me, I pour my will into it, picturing the destination I want it to fly to, and the person it must seek out. I pull a piece of parchment and a small stick of charcoal from an inner pocket of my armor and scratch a hasty message.

The magpie takes the message in its little claws and flies off, its long tail feathers trailing behind it and leaving nothing but wisps of embers behind. I watch it go, feeding it my will, my hope and desperation that it will be enough to save my brother.

# EPILOGUE

## The Empress

On the bridge of a ship, The Empress digs her razor sharp nails into her palms. For the first time in centuries, she can feel her family's presence. It lingers like an ash cloud above the continent. The power of her sisters mingles with the power of her children. Each unique, each possessing strengths and weaknesses. None of them compare to her own power.

Now, nearly at the shores of Astrellia once more, she sucks in the energy of the land.

"Mommy's home," she smirks, keeping her eyes trained on the coast ahead. Her fleet of ships cuts through the tides, mightier than any force Astrellia has ever seen.

The war comes back to her in a rush. The argument, the misunderstanding, that led to her being expelled from her homeland, a land she helped create. Left to rot on some forsaken island, where her power was but a trickle.

"Sisters, I'm coming for your precious chosen one. I'll destroy her, and all of the so-called heirs, then the continent will be mine to conquer. There's nothing any of you can do to stop me. This land will turn red with blood before I forge it anew. All will worship me."

# ACKNOWLEDGEMENTS

I can't believe this is already the end of book two! This trilogy is officially more than halfway done, and the best is yet to come.

Writing this book has been such a journey, and it simply would not have been finished without Andy's help. The master of motivation and hiding my phone so I wouldn't get distracted while writing and editing. Thank you for pushing me to meet my goals and making sure this gets published on time.

Did you know my dad made me cry at the release party for book one? He rode his Harley all the way from Nova Scotia to Wisconsin to surprise me! How cool is that?! Thank you to my parents, brother, and sister-in-law for always cheering me on when I send too many book-related messages in our group chat. Love you!

To my friends in and out of the bookish community for supporting, sharing posts, and recommending my book to readers, you all rock. To Ashley, Katie, and Mackenna for showing up at my events and hyping me up!

Laura, thank you once again for the absolutely stunning cover art! You continue to amaze me with your talent.

To my arc readers and my street team, you're all so wonderful, and I'm so grateful for you every day.

Finally, to you, dear reader, for continuing to read Elana and Aislinn's story. I'm so honored to share it with you.

A dreamer born into a world without dragons, monsters, and magic, Morgan has spent her life daydreaming in the clouds.

From practicing sword fighting with sticks in the backyard, to mixing her own potions in the mud with various wildflowers, she's always kept a little spark of her own magic alive.

With her debut novel, The Awakening of Gods, she hopes to introduce you to one of the many fantasy worlds she regularly dreams about. Morgan lives in Wisconsin with her partner-in-crime and two rescue dogs, Cleo and Piper.

You can follow along with her author journey on Instagram or Threads @authormorgankielisch. Or sign up for the newsletter on her website: www.morgankielischbooks.com